Verity's captor delivered a stinging slap to her jaw, bringing her painfully back to full consciousness. Her head throbbed, ringing with his words. "The key, goddammit. Where's the fucking key?"

He was frantic, Verity realized, focusing with a jerk. And possibly even more scared than she was. The knife he held was not entirely steady, and his breath came in irregular pants. He wanted the key Khalid had given her in the worst way—and he wasn't going to kill her until he'd got it, or at least found out where it was.

There was power in the knowledge that her attacker couldn't afford to kill her. That she had a small bargaining chip to keep herself alive. Confidence surged back, enough for Verity to register another important fact about her attacker. He was wearing a mask. Not a knitted ski mask like a bank robber, or even a coarse plastic one like little kids wore at Halloween. His mask was an expensive latex creation of the sort used by actors and professional entertainers. The sort that would be undetectable at a distance, and would leave his victims unable to provide a description of their attacker.

Just like the mask Khalid's assassin had worn yesterday afternoon.

"Ms. Cresswell masterfully creates a full, rich story...unwinding the tale piece by piece in such a way as to capture readers from the very first."
—*Romantic Times* on *The Refuge*

Also available from MIRA Books and
JASMINE CRESSWELL

THE REFUGE
THE INHERITANCE
THE DISAPPEARANCE
THE DAUGHTER
SECRET SINS
NO SIN TOO GREAT
DESIRES & DECEPTIONS

Watch for the newest novel from
JASMINE CRESSWELL
Coming September 2002

THE CONSPIRACY

JASMINE CRESSWELL

ISBN 1-55166-838-6

THE CONSPIRACY

Visit us at www.mirabooks.com

Printed in U.S.A.

For Molly Elizabeth Candlish, who arrived in time
to make Thanksgiving a true celebration.
And for William Christian Candlish, whose safe
arrival in the world made Christmas extra special.

Prologue

Kashmir, December 25, 1999

Freezing your ass off on a mountain pass in the Himalayas sure was a hell of a way to spend Christmas, even if it had been a good few years since you last believed in Santa Claus. Michael Strait buried his chin deeper into the zippered collar of his down jacket and trudged doggedly along the snow-covered path, heading toward the abandoned military checkpoint that loomed directly in front of them.

He couldn't see any lights or other sign of life in the ramshackle barracks, but that wasn't surprising. Yousaf was a cautious man, and in this empty territory, even the beam of a flashlight could be seen from far away.

Less than a hundred yards to go now, thank God.

A small truck stood in a lean-to next to the barracks, the sort of beaten-up vehicle that could be seen everywhere on Kashmir's roads. Michael knew that, despite the appearance of the body work, the engine inside the decrepit-looking truck was brand-spanking-new, the transmission expertly refurbished and the brakes in perfect condition.

He knew because he and Farooq had driven here from Srinagar in a truck just like it. Driven 120 miles on what had laughably been shown on the map as a road, although

Michael had used several other less flattering epithets to describe it. Unfortunately, the suspension on the truck hadn't been modified to the same high standards as the engine, and they'd traveled with bone-jarring, teeth-jolting discomfort over the last fifty torturous miles. His brain still felt as if it were rattling inside his skull.

The path leading to the barracks was liberally strewn with barbed wire, which had forced Michael and Farooq to complete the final three hundred yards of their journey on foot. The barbed wire looked new, so it certainly hadn't been left behind by the Indian military. It had probably been put there by Yousaf, who used this barracks regularly as a place for his transportation teams to rest up for the night.

Michael frowned, contemplating the barbed wire with a hint of unease. If Yousaf was looking to provide a little extra cushion of safety for his teams, then barbed wire was serious overkill. This territory was effectively abandoned by everyone except the occasional group of nomadic shepherds. But if an Indian military patrol did chance to travel past here, the barbed wire would act like a red flag. The soldiers' attention would be drawn straight to the barracks.

Farooq caught his jacket on some wire and swore profusely, the first time he'd spoken since getting out of the truck. He unsnagged the wire and resumed his dispirited march in Michael's wake, the specially insulated knapsack that held the software for the weapons guidance system bobbing on his back. Farooq wasn't fond of any form of physical exercise that didn't involve beds and women, and his expression revealed exactly what he thought of this nightmarish trek. He would undoubtedly have been complaining mightily if he hadn't been too cold—and probably way too scared—to speak. Michael suppressed a grin. He supposed that was at least one reason to be grateful for the subzero temperatures.

Farooq had picked up the software at the airport in Ladekh only two days ago. The missiles themselves had crossed the border from China three weeks ago, and had already been delivered into Afghanistan, transported across three hundred miles of rugged terrain by loyal foot soldiers of the Kashmir Freedom Party. Yousaf, commander in chief, had done his job well.

Tomorrow the missiles would be flown from Afghanistan to Iraq. Saddam Hussein was desperate to rebuild his stockpile of tactical nuclear weapons and had paid generously for this useful addition to his arsenal. The children of his country might lack milk and medicine, but Saddam had made sure that his generals would have some fancy new weapons to play with when they welcomed the birth of the twenty-first century.

Thanks to Saddam's obsession with nuclear toys, Michael and Farooq were about to complete the final stage of a deal that would make everyone involved lots of money. Starting with the miserably underpaid army officers in Kazakhstan who'd sold the missiles to the Chinese and earned themselves and their troops the equivalent of ten years' pay in the process.

The missiles now winging their way to Baghdad had once been the pride of the Soviet military, but last year a "clerical error" had taken the weapons off the inventory lists of Kazakhstan's government and onto the inventory of the world's illegal arms supply. In a country governed by bureaucrats too poor and too corrupt to provide even the basics of civilized living, nobody wasted energy keeping control over weapons that were universally seen as a burdensome inheritance from the old Soviet Union.

The moneymaking on the sale didn't end in Kazakhstan. The Chinese, aided by one of their most helpful American brokers, made a handy little profit when they resold the missiles to Iraq. Even better than the profit from their point of view, they also had the enjoyment of knowing they were stirring up a potent brew of international mischief. By paying the Kashmir Freedom Party to transport the weapons into Afghanistan, the Chinese managed to cause trouble for the Indian government, one of their favorite enemies. And by helping to broker a final sale to Iraq, they had the supreme pleasure of knowing that they were seriously undermining the policies and security of the United States.

From the Chinese point of view, there was nothing like a deal that made you money *and* pissed off Uncle Sam, Michael reflected. They would be laughing all the way to the bank over this one.

The sale to Iraq had provided profits that trickled all the way down the food chain. The Kashmir Freedom Party had already been paid two hundred thousand dollars for its services. It would receive another two hundred thousand tonight, when the deal was completed with the delivery of the guidance system software, and the key that was required to arm the launch system.

To American ears, a grand total of four hundred thousand dollars might not seem like a lot of money for transporting two hundred missiles over hostile terrain, at night, by mule and yak and the backs of men. In a region where the average annual income amounted to less than five hundred dollars a year and half the children went to bed hungry each night, it was a fortune.

The missiles, of course, were useless without the guidance software, and this was what Michael and Farooq had been charged with delivering tonight to the Iraqi buyer. For all that Yousaf was undisputed commander in chief of the Kashmir Freedom Party, Farooq was its brains, as well as its chief financial officer. Nobody had questioned Farooq's right to retain custody of the most valuable part of the arms shipment and it was considered fitting that he should be present when the final payment was made.

Farooq was the man who'd first set the Freedom Party on the road to prosperity by brokering arms deals among the loose confederation of freedom fighters operating throughout the Muslim world. The freedom fighters tended to be poor and not well organized, so at first it had been a struggle to make significant profits, or even much profit at all.

But Farooq came from a family with a history of business success, and he'd been trained since childhood to go out and make deals. He persevered, becoming more and more successful, until he finally made contact with the American official who handled quite a few of China's illegal arms deals. Together, Farooq and The American found ways to utilize the resources of the Freedom Party—men and intimate knowledge of the terrain—so that fewer shipments got intercepted. Soon, a succession of deals kept a steady flow of arms traveling out of China, into Afghanistan, and thence to the world.

Michael Strait's role in the Party was to invest the money wisely, so that Yousaf and his other fire-breathing lieutenants would have adequate funds available to carry on their struggle for the liberation of Kashmir from the yoke of Indian oppression. Of course, nobody in the Freedom Party knew that his name was Michael Strait. As far as they were concerned, he was Abdullah Ghulam Nabi, brother-in-law of one of Farooq's cousins, and a hotshot financier who'd actually attended college in America and worked at the New York Stock Exchange. Most of the members of the Freedom Party had never traveled outside

Kashmir, but even they knew that the New York Stock Exchange was a mysterious place where rich Americans made even more money. They were astonished and grateful when Abdullah showed them how they, too, could invest their money and double its worth in just a few short months.

If only they knew, Michael thought. He shivered, chilled by a sudden gust of bitter wind. Jesus! It was cold enough to freeze the balls off a Siberian tiger.

They had finally reached the barracks. No guards were posted outside the door, a recognition of the fact that, in this cold, they would be nonfunctional within minutes. Now that he was this close, he could see that cloth had been hung over the windows to prevent any light escaping, but the siding was old and full of cracks, allowing a faint glow of light to emerge, along with the enticing smell of burning charcoal. Michael realized just how much he was looking forward to getting out of the wind and drinking a mug of hot tea, brewed over the charcoal brazier. A really elegant cup of Christmas cheer, he thought ironically.

There was no special reason to suspect a trap, no hint that anything was amiss, but Michael had been trained in a hard school, and he had learned never to make assumptions that might cost him his life. Farooq, for all that he yearned for the soft life, had been playing with terrorists since he was seventeen and he knew better than to assume that just because he and Michael were expecting to meet Yousaf and the Iraqi, that was who they would find inside the barracks.

Michael drew out his Glock automatic, taking off his padded gloves and shoving them into his pockets, but leaving on his insulated glove liners. Even so, his index finger lost sensation so fast that he could barely curl it around the trigger. He nodded silently to Farooq, who was going through the same motions, indicating that Farooq—who was left-handed—should stand to the right of the door, while Michael took the left.

From sheer force of habit, Michael positioned himself so that his body was protected by the barracks wall—albeit a pretty thin and shaky wall. He knocked on the door with the butt of his gun, a quick sharp tattoo. Then Farooq called out their names and gave the password. *Victory.*

Michael barely refrained from rolling his eyes. The Kashmir Freedom Party might make its money transporting high tech weapons, but at times its organization reminded him of a bunch of Boy Scouts playing games at summer camp.

The door was opened, faster than Michael had expected. Aziz, one of Yousaf's most loyal lieutenants, greeted him. "Welcome," Aziz said in Kashmiri. "You've made good time. Yousaf told us not to expect you before ten."

A flicker of movement caught Michael's eye, right on the far flank of his field of vision. He didn't stop to think. Didn't stop to analyze why the movement alarmed him. He simply hurled himself down into the snow, his survival instinct honed by eight years of intensive training and six months of living on the edge, constantly expecting to be unmasked. His gun held firmly in both hands, he rolled away from the door, hearing the burst of gunfire from inside the barracks.

The shots, he realized, were being aimed as much at Farooq as at him.

Farooq had managed to take cover behind the truck, and was aiming fire into the doorway. Aziz went down, and there was a lull for a couple of seconds, enabling

Michael to spring into a crouching position and then to run like hell for the back of the barracks.

There was no door at the rear, but there were two very small windows, both of them positioned about four feet from the ground, both of them glass-paned, the shutters hanging on half-rotted hinges. The cold was getting to him now, the rush of adrenaline no longer enough to counteract the effects of having lain full-length in the snow. His body shaking, Michael pushed a new clip into his Glock and blew out the glass from the right-hand window.

He got lucky. The cloth fastened over the window collapsed. For a split second, he had won a double advantage over the three men shooting from inside the barracks. He could see them in the light. They couldn't see him in the dark. Plus they were facing front, toward Farooq.

Michael managed to take out the man at the right-hand window before he even swung around. A shot from Farooq felled the man in the door. The third man swung back and forth between the rear window and Farooq at the car, firing wildly from his Belgian FN rifle. Michael ducked, counting shots. There were thirty bullets in the FN's clip. He reckoned most of those were long gone.

He waited for silence, and then the telltale sounds of the rifle being reloaded. The instant the sounds came, he stood up, aimed through the window, and took down the third gunman.

Michael drew in a slightly unsteady breath. He was alive, and so was Farooq. They still had the guidance system for the missiles.

What the hell. Maybe this wasn't going to be such a bad Christmas after all.

One

Verity Marlowe spent the first hour of the twenty-first century arguing with her dead husband. She had not previously been in the habit of seeing ghosts or communing with visitors from the other side of the veil, but then, until Sam's death six months previously, she had not been in the habit of consuming large quantities of vodka either.

At the time of Sam's appearance in her living room, the glittering Millennium Ball had just descended safely in Times Square, none of the world's major computer systems appeared to have been eaten by the Y2K bug, and Verity was contemplating the unwelcome truth that the world was still spinning safely on its axis. Since Washington, D.C. hadn't been blown up either by terrorists, religious fanatics or computers, her life seemed unlikely to come to a conveniently swift end.

Verity considered this a major bummer.

Not quite drunk, she squinted at the TV and wondered what she was supposed to do with herself for the fifty or so years that she could statistically expect to continue living. The prospect of filling so many more years was utterly daunting. Heck, she couldn't even decide what she was supposed to do with herself for the rest of the night.

It was at this desolate moment that her former husband materialized right in front of her TV screen. He was scowling, missing sections of his torso, and fuzzy around the edges, but it was unmistakably Sam Marlowe. In life, her husband had been the gentlest of men. In death, he had apparently become a great deal more aggressive. He interposed himself between Verity, slumped on the sofa, and Dick Clark babbling cheerfully from the TV set, and gestured toward her with a combination of contempt and anger.

You look like shit, he said by way of greeting. His body parts kept coming and going, but his voice sounded remarkably steady. Firm and deep, just as it had been in the good old days, before he was diagnosed with a cancerous tumor growing on his brain, wrapping around the cortex and strangling all that made him wonderful.

Verity was hurt by Sam's rudeness until she realized he was merely a figment of her own grief-stricken imagination. She might be drunk, but she wasn't quite drunk enough to accept that Sam's ghost was really in her living room, wafting like a celestial Ping-Pong ball between the pseudoantique floorboards and the molded plaster ceiling.

She couldn't think why her subconscious had come up with such a peculiar creation until she remembered that the ghost who appeared to Scrooge was called Sam Marlowe, and she'd watched a rerun of *A Christmas Carol* only a few nights ago. She was relieved to have found a reason—other than weeks of steadily increasing alcohol intake—to explain why her mind was playing such weird tricks.

"Go away," she said, averting her gaze from the fuzzy outline of Sam's face. "You're not here."

If I'm not here, then I can't go away, can I?

"Oh, please." She slumped deeper in her chair. "You sound like a character from *Alice in Wonderland.*"

Sam chuckled, but without mirth. *Do I? That always was one of my favorite books, you know. It's a pity people read it when they're kids and rarely go back to it later on, when they could really appreciate it.*

In life, Sam had been an English lit professor at George Washington University. In death, he apparently retained his interest in the Victorian writers. Verity watched him, reluctantly fascinated, as he continued to float up and down in front of her TV.

Sam stared back at her, then sighed. *I guess you're not in the mood to talk about Lewis Carroll. What's up with you, Veri? You're too smart to throw your life away just because I'm dead.*

Anger knotted her stomach, powerful enough to make her shout. "You shouldn't have died. You were too young to die! There's no possible reason for what happened to you. You were such a good, kind person. Oh God, Sam, I can't bear it that you're gone." Tears poured out of her eyes, ran down her nose and dripped into her mouth. It had been months since she'd cried, but the choking sobs didn't feel healing. On the contrary, they induced a strong urge to puke.

Sam's features faded, then coalesced into a giant frown. *And I can't bear it that you've become such a self-pitying slob. For goodness sake, Veri, snap out of it. Can't you find some more useful way to honor our marriage than to drink yourself into oblivion every night?*

"No, I can't. I like the way I'm mourning you just fine. And if you're a manfesh—manifesh— Oh shit! If you're popping out of my subconscious, I wish you'd bury yourself back under whatever mental rock you just crawled out from. Go away! You're not the sweet Sam I remember."

But your memory isn't very good right now, is it? How many brain cells do you think you pickled in alcohol over the last week?

"Oh shut up! You know what? You're a real pain in

the ass now that you're dead.'' Verity reached for her glass and realized it was empty. She staggered to her feet and made her way into the adjoining kitchen. Clearly she hadn't drunk enough to numb the pain of Sam's loss and this uncharming creation of her subconscious was the result.

She'd wanted to be semisober for the end of the world, if it happened, but it had obviously been a mistake to sit down in front of the TV without her emergency supply of vodka right on the coffee table. A big mistake. She should have learned by now that life was always better when you had a generous supply of chilled martinis nice and handy.

The vodka bottle stood in its appointed spot in the center of the fridge. A no-name brand, bought in the convenient 1.75 liter size. Usually by this stage of the night Verity dispensed with the unnecessary hassle of pouring the vodka into a glass, but in honor of the new century she decided to go formal. And, truth to tell, the knowledge that Sam's ghost was right there in the kitchen watching her was somewhat inhibiting. Even though she knew he wasn't real—wasn't even there—chugging vodka straight from a bottle so large that she needed two hands to hold it seemed…demeaning. And this Sam, unlike the real Sam, would be more than likely to tell her in no uncertain terms what he thought about people who tried to solve their problems by slithering into the bottom of a bottle.

For some reason there didn't seem to be any glasses in the cupboard, so she helped herself to a coffee mug instead. She scooped ice cubes into the mug and added vodka. As a concession to the fact that it was now morning, she checked in the fridge for orange juice to make a screwdriver. What could be healthier than orange juice? Except that there wasn't any orange juice. Not much of anything else, either, unless you counted a few unpleasant-looking objects, none readily identifiable, that she was reluctant to touch for fear of what she might then discover adhering to her fingers.

Giving up on her momentary health kick, Verity raised the coffee mug to her mouth. A wave of nausea swept over her as the ice cubes chinked against her teeth, so intense that she barely made it to the bathroom in time to throw up. When she finally finished retching, she sat back on her heels, too weak to get up.

Sam floated into the bathroom, materializing out of a large pink shell on the wallpaper above the sink. *You're a real mess, aren't you?* His words were harsh, but his voice sounded gentle, kinder than it had done earlier.

She started to yell at him to go away, then gave up. She slumped against the wall, too tired to stand. "Yep, I guess I'm pretty much of a mess. But I'm hurting, Sam." She drew in a shaky breath. "I loved you. I miss you so much."

I loved you, too.

"I want to stop hurting. What can I do to stop the pain, Sam?"

Stop chugging vodka and take back your life. Return to work. I can't believe you've been on leave of absence for six months already. You should be worrying about your boss. Good old Dick-the-Prick. You know he's so insecure he'll be doing anything he can to undermine your position.

"I can't worry about Dick Pedro and what he might be doing," Verity protested. "I'm in no shape to go back to work. I have a demanding job, in case you've forgotten. If I screw up analyzing the incoming intelligence from India and Pakistan, there could be a real disaster."

Stop drinking and you'll be in fine shape for working.

Her teeth were chattering. "I can't go back to work. Don't suggest that again."

Okay, but at least get some sort of a social life going. Call a friend and arrange to have lunch. Go out on a date. And—one last time—quit with the drinking.

The idea of dating a man who wasn't Sam almost made her throw up again. Either that, or the prospect of stopping drinking scared her to the point of nausea even if the suggestion did come from a dead man.

"You always did have obnoxiously simple solutions to difficult problems," Verity said, closing her eyes so that she could listen to Sam's voice without having to watch his chest fade in and out of existence.

That's one of the reasons you loved me. You were the one who could make an international incident out of choosing between french fries and baked potato. Remember?

Her breath caught in the middle of a sigh. "I remember everything about our marriage."

Far from being impressed, Sam made an annoyed clicking sound. *It's time to move on, Veri. Our marriage is over. Finished. Dead.*

"No!" Her eyes flew open. "Our marriage isn't dead as long as I'm alive."

Sure it is. You're trying to breathe life into a corpse, and it isn't going to work. Tell me, when was the last time you actually picked up the phone and spoke to a friend?

"I...don't remember."

Of course you don't. It was too long ago. You haven't checked your answering machine for weeks. You haven't spoken to your mother since Christmas Eve—

"She's gone on a cruise with her church ladies," Verity protested.

Okay, but have you spoken to anyone at all for the past week?

"No," she admitted. "You're the first."

And you can't exactly count this as a normal conversation. Seeing as how I'm dead.

Verity pounded her fist against the bathroom wall. "Stop it! Don't use that word. Don't keep reminding me that you're dead."

But I am dead. And you need to accept that fact.

Sam was right, of course. The knowledge settled like a leaden weight in the pit of her stomach. For six months, she'd been trying to avoid facing reality and it wasn't working. Her heart pounding, Verity confronted the bitter truth that Sam would never again sit across the dinner table, laughing at his own bad jokes. He would never again try to convince her that she loved baseball, or steal all the buttery pieces of popcorn when they went to the movies. He would never again make love to her. And unless she wanted to waste the rest of her life having drunken dialogues with a phantom, she would never hear his voice again.

Using the wall as a support, she slowly dragged herself to her feet. "I need to stop drinking, don't I, Sam?"

Yes, of course you do. That's why I came back.

She turned away. "I'm scared, Sam. I don't think I can face life without you when I'm sober."

Sure you can. You never had a problem with alcohol before. You can do it, Veri. Make me proud. His face blurred, blending with the fishes on the bathroom wallpaper until there was nothing to be seen.

Verity gave a frantic cry. "No, don't leave me, Sam! Please don't go!"

Silence was her only answer. She tugged open the bathroom door, but there was no sign of her husband in the hall. She looked for him throughout the entire house, in every closet and in all the drawers, since ghosts could presumably fit into very small spaces. But like most other things in her life these days, her search was a failure. Sam was gone.

Two

Next morning, the pale winter sun was already high in the sky when Verity woke after a night that had been surprisingly restful. Yawning, ignoring the inevitable hangover headache, she swung her feet out of bed and dragged on Sam's old terry cloth bathrobe before shuffling into the kitchen to make coffee. She wasn't sure of the precise time because she'd lost her watch, her battery-operated travel alarm had ceased functioning before Christmas, and the clocks on her microwave, oven and VCR all displayed different times. Since she had no plans, however, the exact time wasn't significant.

Except that this morning—or afternoon—Verity found herself irritated by the fact that she didn't know something as basic as the hour of day. She made herself a mug of black instant coffee because there didn't seem to be any milk, and switched on her radio, relieved to discover it still functioned after weeks of disuse. She listened, head throbbing, to a Mozart symphony playing on NPR until the announcer informed everyone that it was one o'clock and time for a news update.

Mildly pleased to have identified a problem and solved it, all within the space of twenty minutes, Verity quickly reset her clocks, grinning at her own efficiency when she walked from clock to clock and saw the same digital display on each.

Her moment of satisfaction soon dissipated. She had

at least twelve hours to fill before she could hope to fall
asleep again. What was she going to do for twelve long,
empty hours? She could look through her wedding pictures, but she'd done that yesterday. And the day before,
and the day before that. She could listen to her favorite
tape of Sam playing the guitar, but she'd done that yesterday, too. Or she could find something to eat for breakfast, which was really lunch, since it was past noon. And
since it was lunchtime, she could drink a nice glass of
white wine and get rid of her damned headache...

Or not. A niggle of an idea inched its way, crablike,
into her mind. Supposing she decided that today she
wouldn't drink any alcohol? No wine at lunchtime, no
pick-me-up brandy in the middle of the afternoon, no
vodka while she zonked out in front of the TV at night.

Verity's stomach swooped in terror and she ran to the
fridge, tugging open the door and reaching for the bottle
of Chablis chilling in readiness for just this moment. Except that when she held the bottle cradled against her
chest, it didn't feel comforting. It felt cold and hard, and
a damned inadequate substitute for Sam.

She put the wine back in the fridge, slammed the door,
and leaned against it, panting as if she'd just completed
some death-defying physical challenge. Maybe she had,
Verity thought shakily. Maybe she had.

She wouldn't attempt to make plans for the whole day,
she decided; that was too intimidating. She'd just plan
the next couple of hours. What could she do that didn't
involve drinking? She needed to shower. She'd slept in
the nude, and her skin felt gritty and unwashed beneath
Sam's bathrobe. Her teeth had a furry coating, and her
hair was matted.

Okay, she would shower and get dressed. This was
progress. At least she had a plan that would take care of
the next half hour. Verity tried to remember when she'd

last bothered to get dressed in anything more than Sam's old robe and realized it must have been right before Christmas when she'd made her most recent run to the liquor store. At least nine days, possibly eleven or twelve.

Her knees wobbled but she walked as swiftly as she could into the bathroom. It felt strange to be a woman with a purpose, even if most of her former friends would have laughed themselves silly to hear that Verity Marlowe—previously known as Ms. Anal Retentive—nowadays considered washing and getting dressed to be a major project.

Dropping Sam's robe over the edge of the bathtub, Verity caught a glimpse of herself in the mirror. She quickly turned away. Then, with an effort that seriously tested her willpower, she swung around again and looked into the mirror, something that she'd avoided doing for weeks. Her reflection stared back and her stomach lurched in shame.

She honest-to-God looked like a bag lady. Her long, light-brown hair wasn't just matted, it was visibly filthy. Her face was puffy, her skin muddy and mottled. Her father, a Baptist missionary minister not much given to idle compliments, had once told her that her eyes were as blue and clear as the mountain lakes of Kashmir. If he was looking down from heaven, she wondered how he would describe her eyes now. Red and blotched as spilled strawberry jam? No, the Reverend Jeremiah Hullman wouldn't waste his celestial breath on finding metaphors for something so distasteful. He'd simply tell her the truth: that she looked like a drunk. A self-indulgent, dirty drunk.

Hurriedly turning away from the mirror, Verity paused on the brink of stepping into the shower to confront another disaster. Now that she actually looked at the inside of the shower stall, she saw that the corners were slimy with fungus and the glass door panels coated with a thick gray crust of soap scum. She felt herself gagging and quickly searched under the sink for cleaning products. Fortunately, she found a plentiful supply. Why wouldn't she, when she obviously hadn't used any for weeks?

Verity scrubbed and mopped for an hour before she was willing to step into the shower and wash herself. Once she was clean, she spent another hour filing her nails, combing the snarls out of her hair, and slathering lotion over every inch of her body. At the end of her marathon session, she looked in the mirror again.

This time she looked less like a bag lady and more like a cleaned-up refugee from a prison camp run by guards with special training in brutality. Quite apart from the generous scattering of bruises where she'd banged into various objects, her collarbones jutted out and her rib cage was clearly visible. Before Sam got sick last spring, she'd been trying without success to lose ten pounds. Well, she'd sure lost 'em now. In fact, she'd moved way beyond athletically trim and was pushing hard on the boundaries of clinically emaciated.

Staring at her protruding ribs, Verity was consumed by the sudden realization that she was hungry. No, more than hungry. She felt literally starving. Ravenous. She rushed to the kitchen, salivating at the thought of a muffin, or a bowl of cereal with fresh milk.

After her experience with the shower, Verity was almost prepared for the sight that greeted her when she opened the fridge. Almost. She quickly slammed the door on various piles of mold and organic remains. At least cleaning the fridge would fill in a few more hours, she thought wryly. But before she tackled yet another revolting cleanup job, she needed food, and she obviously wasn't going to find anything safe to eat inside her own house.

Fortunately, she wouldn't have to walk far to find something tasty. She lived at the intersection of R Street and 31st, in the heart of Georgetown. The house was a narrow three-storey built right before the Depression, a home she and Sam would never have been able to afford except that he'd inherited it from his grandmother the year before he died. Verity loved the house, despite the fact that it hadn't been updated since Formica was big in the 1950s. Before Sam got sick, the two of them had spent many a weekend discussing ideas for renovation. They'd even designed a dream nursery and tossed around dates for starting the family they'd always planned to have but never quite gotten around to procreating.

Verity quickly shut down a spurt of maudlin regret for the child she and Sam would never have. Some sorrows were simply too painful to pursue. Pulling her coat out of the closet, she added a hat and woollen gloves and stepped outside with more enthusiasm than she'd experienced in months.

Sam had died on the Fourth of July, and when she'd last noticed the weather, the pavements had been steamy with summer rain. Now there was a dusting of snow on the bare branches of the trees and on the ledges of the buildings, although it would most likely vanish before the afternoon was over. Sam had grown up in California, and she'd often teased him for being a wimp about winter. Having been born and raised in Kashmir, she was made of sterner stuff. In the mountains surrounding Srinagar, the passes were impenetrable from November to March, and every breath you exhaled at this time of year turned into a cloud of tiny ice crystals. Since the house the church had rented for her missionary parents contained no fixed form of heating, let alone central heating, Verity had been only a toddler when she learned to keep herself warm by carrying around a little handheld charcoal brazier—a fire-and-burn hazard that would have had child welfare advocates in the States screeching for a legislative ban.

Verity was surprised to feel a sudden pang of nostalgia for the distinctive sights and sounds of her childhood home. Surprised because it had been so long since she'd felt any emotion that wasn't directly related to Sam and their time together. Even more surprised because her feelings about Kashmir had for years been ambivalent, shading toward hostile as her frustration over the on-again, off-again civil war mounted.

Good smells wafted out from The Croissant Cottage, and she forgot about Kashmir's problems as she turned eagerly into the doorway of the little café, stomach gurgling in anticipation. Just as she pulled the door open to go in, one of her neighbors came out.

"Hi, Jeannie." Verity's voice felt croaky from disuse, but there was no way to pretend she hadn't seen the neighbor, so she resisted the temptation to slink past in silence.

"Oh, Verity, it's you. Hello." Jeannie sounded distant, and she looked at Verity with what appeared to be barely concealed distaste.

Strange, Verity thought. Jeannie had always been perfectly friendly in the past and had offered both sympathy and practical help during the last horrendous week of Sam's illness. Verity decided she must be imagining Jeannie's antagonism.

"It's a pretty morning, isn't it?" she said. "Do you have the day off work?" Her neighbor was a hotshot lobbyist and a workaholic, so the question seemed appropriate.

"It's New Year's Day," Jeannie said shortly. "And it's Saturday. Of course I have the day off work."

Damn! How had she managed to forget that it was

New Year's Day? Verity flushed. "Oh, yes, of course. Sorry, I had an...exhausting...night and I'm still not functioning too well." It didn't seem a lie to claim that meeting the ghost of your dead husband was exhausting.

"I can imagine." Jeannie's voice was now several degrees beyond cool. "Anyway, Gerry's waiting for me at home, so I'd better get going. I just stopped by to pick up some coffee." She held up a black-and-gold bag of gourmet beans to validate her statement.

The shiny label on the bag of coffee triggered a sudden humiliating flash of memory. The last time she and Jeannie met had been on this same street, around Thanksgiving, when the ache of Sam's loss had seemed particularly heavy. Verity hadn't exactly been drunk, at least not by the standards of the past two weeks, but she'd been a good part of the way there. She remembered bumping into Jeannie and dropping the wine she'd been carrying. Of course, the bottle had broken when it hit the pavement, splashing red wine all over Jeannie's expensive gabardine slacks and soaking her shoes. Verity had made a few incoherent excuses, but she'd been more concerned about buying another jug of wine than she had been about the accident, and she certainly hadn't offered to pay the dry cleaning bill for Jeannie's slacks. No wonder Jeannie's attitude was frosty. She wasn't the sort of woman to have any sympathy for a drunk, even a drunk who was mourning the loss of her husband.

Inwardly flinching, Verity nevertheless forced herself to smile politely. "If Gerry's waiting at home, don't let me keep you. Wish him a happy new year from me, will you?"

Jeannie merely nodded, giving Verity a wide berth as she strode briskly toward R Street. Verity watched her departure, aware that she was trembling. God, she needed a drink to take the edge off that nasty little encounter.

She really, really needed a drink, but The Croissant Cottage didn't have a liquor license. Maybe she should go someplace else. The liquor store was just a few hundred yards away at the intersection with Thirtieth…

Verity turned and bolted inside the café.

An hour later, fueled by a bowl of hearty minestrone and a wheat roll, which was all her squeamish stomach could accommodate, she walked home with renewed energy, stopping off at the corner deli to buy a precooked chicken and a few basic food supplies. Once home, despite the nutritious lunch, she was so weak from the culmination of six months of increasing self-neglect that she couldn't clean for more than a few minutes without stopping to rest. But she persevered and by dinnertime the kitchen was tidy, the dirty dishes had been washed and she'd done two loads of laundry.

Appallingly, two machine loads was all it took to wash every single piece of soiled clothing she could find lying around the house, apart from some sweaters that needed to be dry-cleaned. Changing clothes didn't seem to have been a preoccupation of hers over the past several weeks, Verity concluded. As for her sheets, they were past redemption. She threw them in the trash, and made up her bed with clean linen, trying not to dwell on the question of precisely how long she must have been sleeping on the same set of sheets.

With the most important chores done, and the winter afternoon fading into night, the shadows of Sam's absence pressed in on her. Verity badly wanted a drink to reward herself for having worked so hard. Heck, she'd gone all day without a drink, so she deserved something to celebrate her success, didn't she? And herbal tea sure wasn't going do it for her. She took the bottle of vodka out of her newly-clean fridge and stood at the counter looking at it for a long time. She could imagine just how the cool liquid would taste as it trickled down her throat, numbing the pain in her weary muscles, along with the hollow ache in her heart.

She deserved at least a small drink after the kind of day she'd put in, Verity decided. Why not? Who was to stop her? Who would even know? A little fearful, she looked over her shoulder, half expecting to see Sam waving an admonishing finger, but the kitchen was reassuringly empty of ghosts.

Relieved to be alone and able to indulge, Verity took one of her sparkling-clean glasses from the cupboard and carefully poured out a serving of vodka. Reassuring herself that the clean glass proved she was back in control of her life, she added ice a cube at a time, relishing the sound of ice clinking against crystal. When the glass was full to the brim, she looked at the resulting drink with a longing so intense her stomach cramped with desire.

The ring of the doorbell interrupted her just as she was about to raise the glass to her lips.

Visitors. Verity's hand clenched around her drink. Who could be coming to see her at this time of the evening? Nobody she wanted to see, that was for sure.

The bell rang again, insistently. If she answered, she wouldn't be able to drink her vodka. Verity's head jerked from the glass toward the front door and then back again.

Go away, stupid person. Let me drink this in peace.

She lifted the glass, then slammed it back down again, sloshing vodka onto the counter. Damn, now she'd messed up the clean counter! She stared fixedly at the spilled liquor, trying to push away the unwelcome truth: it didn't matter who was at the door. The interruption had been a gift from the benevolent God she no longer quite believed in. If she had a grain of sense left, she would answer the summons.

Verity closed her eyes, summoning every last dreg of

her willpower. Then, hand shaking, she upended the glass into the sink and ran to open the door.

Michael Strait stood on the doorstep, holding a package roughly wrapped in brown paper. His too long hair brushed the collar of his ankle-length black trench coat, and a day's growth of beard shadowed his already sallow skin. His coat was made of leather, she noticed, a subtle rejection of his mother's Hindu heritage. Not that Michael discriminated: he rejected his father's Methodism, too.

Verity supposed there must be somebody, somewhere in the world, that she wanted to see less than Michael Strait. Right now, though, she couldn't imagine who that would be.

"Hello, Verity." His gaze flicked over her, performing its usual swift and comprehensive assessment. Surprisingly, Verity caught a fleeting impression of sympathy before his features rearranged themselves into his standard expression of impenetrable detachment.

"Hello, Michael. It's been a while." She didn't even attempt to smile. She wished with all her soul that she hadn't poured away her vodka, hadn't opened the door. In the best of circumstances, she had memories of Michael that made her cringe. Tonight, his presence seemed a calculated insult to Sam's memory.

"I've been in Kashmir for eight months," Michael said. "I was setting up a cloth-weaving factory near Srinagar, and going out into the countryside to establish sources of supply for the raw cashmere. I was out of touch sometimes for a couple of weeks at a stretch, and by the time I heard about Sam's death, the funeral was already over."

"I did get your letter."

Michael dismissed the letter with a chopping gesture. "Sam was my best friend. If I'd known in time, I would have flown home for the funeral. As it was, I only returned to Washington a few days ago.'' His voice deepened slightly. ''I never even knew he'd been sick until it was all over.''

''No, it was unbelievably quick. Less than nine weeks from the first diagnosis to the...end.''

''Your letter that got forwarded to me said he had cancer....''

''Yes. A malignant brain tumor, a glioma. He died on the operating table.'' Verity drew in a shaky breath. ''The surgeon said his death saved us a very unpleasant couple of months.''

Michael's gaze became opaque and he glanced away. Much as she disliked him, Verity didn't misunderstand his silence. Michael was a man who handled painful emotions somewhere deep inside himself, and they weren't for sharing.

''I'm sorry for your loss,'' he said finally, bringing his gaze back to hers. ''Really sorry. Sam was a good man and a great friend.''

''Thank you.'' Verity knew she sounded stiff and withdrawn, which was precisely how she felt. She and Michael had rubbed each other the wrong way ever since their first meeting at an official reception for the Indian ambassador over three years ago. If it hadn't been for Sam, their mutual dislike wouldn't have mattered, since Michael's interest in Kashmir was strictly commercial and there was no reason for their paths to cross with any frequency. Unfortunately, Sam had accompanied her to that particular reception, and he and Michael had struck up an immediate and lasting friendship.

Why extroverted, easygoing Sam had enjoyed Michael's company was a mystery Verity had never been able to solve, especially since Michael spent months at a time out of the country. Maybe their mutual desire to beat each other to a pulp on the racquetball court had been all it took to keep the link of friendship forged between the two of them.

When she'd asked Sam why he liked Michael so much, he'd just grinned and told her that the ways of male friendship were destined to be forever unfathomable to the female mind. She'd erupted with predictable fury at such blatant chauvinism, attacking Sam with a cushion. He'd merely wrestled away the cushion, and kissed her into silence. They'd ended up making love on the living room sofa, laughing almost until the moment of climax.

Her marriage had been extraordinarily full of laughter, Verity reflected. Perhaps that's why she felt so unbearably sad and empty now that she was alone.

"I brought you this photograph of Sam," Michael said, holding out the package he was carrying. "I shot it one day last spring after we'd been playing racquetball. I'd just bought a new camera and I wanted to try it out. The picture turned out well and it occurred to me that you might like to have a copy."

She was going to have to invite him in, Verity realized, accepting the package with a murmur of thanks. But unless she got real unlucky, Michael would have the good sense to refuse. He must know they had nothing to say to each other now that Sam was dead.

It turned out not to be her day for getting lucky. No surprise there. She'd just spent eight months filled with days when she hadn't gotten lucky, starting with the day when Sam complained of a tremor in his right hand and a headache that wouldn't quit.

Michael followed her into the living room and stood, silent but watchful, while she unwrapped the photograph. Despite her resentment of his intrusion, her breath caught in her throat when she saw the picture he'd brought. Sam, tanned and healthy, smiled out at her from an elegantly simple silver frame, the laughter lines at the corner of his eyes crinkled, a towel slung around his neck, his reddish-blond hair damp with sweat. He looked so vibrantly alive that she could almost feel the warmth and good humor radiating from him, and the pain of his loss was suddenly so sharp that for a moment she thought she was going to black out.

It was a while before she could lift her eyes to Michael's. "Thank you for bringing—" She got no further. The lump in her throat swelled, closing off speech. She felt tears well up but she fought them with bleak determination. Be damned if she was going to cry in front of Michael Strait, a man who had all the natural empathy of a lump of concrete.

When she was sure she had herself under control, she set the photo down on the coffee table. "Thank you for bringing me this," she said. "I appreciate your... thoughtfulness. I didn't know you were such a talented photographer."

In typical infuriating Michael fashion, he didn't follow her conversational lead and talk about Sam or the photo or his new camera. Instead he closed the small gap between them and crooked his finger under her chin, tilting her face toward the window, to catch the waning light. "What the hell have you been doing to yourself?" he asked, anger threading his voice. "There are bruises on both your cheeks and you look as if you're trying to starve yourself to death. Have you eaten today?"

The note of anger was almost as surprising as his earlier flash of sympathy, jolting Verity into an unguarded reply. "As it happens, I had minestrone for lunch, and I'm going to have baked chicken tonight." She jerked her head away from his grasp, annoyed with herself for having answered him, furious with him for having touched her. "Not that it's any business of yours."

"It's my business if you're starving yourself. Look how this sweater hangs on you." Michael grabbed a handful of sweater to illustrate his point and her pants immediately slid several inches down her hips.

"Jesus!" he said, dropping his hands, his dark eyes fixed on her rib cage. "The beggars in Calcutta are fatter than you."

Verity badly wanted to deliver some verbal blow that would crush him. Unfortunately, it was difficult to be scathing when your pants were in imminent danger of falling down. She tugged her sweater away from Michael and clamped her elbows to her sides, anchoring the offending pants in place.

"So what?" she retorted, with all the sophistication of a high school freshman. "It's fashionable to be thin. Most models are a lot skinnier than I am!" She was all too aware that, far from sounding witty, she merely sounded defensive.

"You're wrong," Michael said without heat, just infuriating certainty. "Even those pathetic kids who are doing heroin for lunch with a cocaine chaser for dessert aren't as thin as you."

Having made his point, he changed the subject again. Typical, infuriating Michael. Never give your sparring partner time to regroup. "I called your office at the State Department before I came here. They told me you've been on leave of absence since two weeks before Sam died."

She tilted her chin to an aggressive angle. "That sounds remarkably like an accusation, Michael. I wasn't aware that it was a crime to take time off work to mourn the death of one's husband."

"Sam was a good man, one of the best. Mourning him is appropriate—"

"Thank you so much." Verity's smile was sugar

sweet. "I feel a *lot* better now that I have your permission to grieve."

"You're not grieving," he said tersely. "You're wallowing in self-pity because you're still alive and Sam is dead. Why didn't you just fling yourself onto his funeral pyre like a good Hindu widow and be done with it?"

A haze of anger filmed her vision. It was the first time in her life that she'd literally seen red. "Have you quite finished insulting me, Michael? No, don't answer that." Verity drew in a shaky breath. "I think it's time for you to leave. Thank you for bringing me the photograph of Sam. I appreciate the gesture—"

"Your boss is worried about you," Michael said abruptly. "He claims that you're drinking too much. Way too much. Are you?"

"It's none of your damn business whether I'm drinking too m—"

"On the contrary. Sam was my friend. He doesn't have a future anymore, but I sure as hell don't intend to stand back and watch you throw away yours. I owe him that much—"

"To save me from myself?" Verity's anger boiled over. She was shaking, palms damp with suppressed tension. She swung away, unable to tolerate his gaze. "Get out of here, Michael, before I say or do something we both regret."

"Like the last time we met?" he said. "Is that why you're hell-bent on starving yourself, Verity? Are you punishing yourself for the sin of having once desired a man who wasn't your husband?"

His arrogance was intolerable. Verity felt as if she might fly into a thousand separate pieces if she had to look at him again. She gripped the back of the sofa so that she wouldn't grab the nearest solid object and hurl it at him.

"Leave, Michael." She spoke through teeth clenched so hard her jaw ached. "Go now. Go *now*."

He went without saying another word. He didn't need to. He'd already inflicted a mortal blow to the shrine Verity had spent the past six months erecting in memory of her perfect marriage. He'd reminded her that however much she'd loved Sam, there had been one brilliant, star-splashed night in Kashmir when she'd come terrifyingly close to betraying him.

With Michael Strait, of all people.

Three

Far from sending her back down the slippery slope to drink and despair, Michael's visit infused Verity with a perverse flood of energy. In the wake of his visit, she not only refrained from drinking, she even forced herself to pop a vitamin pill and consume three nourishing meals each day, not because she cared about eating healthy food, but because she was determined not to validate his accusations. Next time they had the misfortune to meet, she vowed she would be so damn fat she had to waddle.

For several days, Verity's rage continued to build an invigorating head of steam. By Monday, having stewed over Michael's various insults for more hours than she cared to count, she reached the conclusion that the best way to prove him wrong was to go back to work. Refusing to feel scared at the prospect of picking up the threads of her old life so conclusively, she tried to call her boss, Dick Pedro, and arrange a date for her return. Only to discover that her phone service had been cut off, presumably for nonpayment of the bill.

After two hours spent arguing with the phone company, Verity returned home triumphant, with the reinstatement of her phone service promised for the next day. Her new, take-no-prisoners attitude had barely been dented by the time spent shuttling between her bank and the phone company offices, getting certified checks, and dealing with a counter clerk at the phone company who

had all the customer service skills of a homicidal socio-
path on work release. She'd even remembered to buy a
replacement battery for her wristwatch, so now she could
join the rat race, obsessing about the rapid passage of
time along with all the other virtuous citizens, who didn't
stay home grieving but went to work and did their bit to
boost the national economy.

Riding on an organizational high, she hauled a plastic
laundry basket full of unopened mail into her living room
and hunted through the reams of paper in search of utility
bills and other vital pieces of correspondence. If she
didn't take care of this soon, she realized, she'd wake up
one morning and find herself without light or heat. She
was in the midst of a merciless assault on her unpaid
bills—with magazines, flyers and junk mail scattered all
over the floor—when her front doorbell rang.

She sprang to her feet. *Michael Strait,* she thought,
seized by instant, sizzling fury. Fortunately, there was no
law that required her to answer the door. She quickly sat
down again, ignoring the repeated ringing and knocking
until she heard the muted sounds of a man's voice calling
her name.

"Verity! Verity, are you in there? It's Dick Pedro."

Dick Pedro! Her boss. Oh, jeez. Why in the world had
she assumed it was Michael Strait?

"I'm coming, Dick! Hold on." Her boss had last
called to see her right before Christmas, bringing a huge
poinsettia as a gift from her colleagues at the State Department. Verity remembered just enough of that meeting
to be quite sure she'd embarrassed herself, particularly
with a man as uptight and humorless as Dick.

Determined to correct the degrading impression that
must be lingering in her boss's mind, she rushed toward
the front door. Her too loose pants slithered downward
and she caught her toe in the hem, then tripped over an

uneven floor plank. She fell flat, narrowly avoiding smashing her nose into the floorboards.

Winded, sprawled on all fours as she caught her breath, she was humiliatingly aware that Dick Pedro must have seen her pratfall. The front door had three narrow glass inserts, each less than two inches wide, but Dick had been peering inside, with his nose pressed up against the center pane, and he must have enjoyed a clear view of her stumble. Not to mention an equally splendid view of his Christmas poinsettia, which was shedding brown leaves over the hall table. Visibly dead from lack of water.

Striving for lost dignity, Verity scrambled to her feet, pushed her hair out of her eyes and opened the door with what aplomb she could muster. "Hello, Dick. This is an unexpected pleasure." Her gaze moved past him to the street, where a black Lincoln Town Car waited at the curb, with a uniformed driver behind the wheel. Dick was Deputy Assistant Secretary of State for Asian Affairs, but he didn't merit chauffeur-driven limos for paying routine calls on junior employees. What in the world was going on?

"Hello, Verity." Dick spoke abruptly. "Your phone isn't working, so I couldn't reach you. Hence the in-person visit."

"Sorry. I had a bit of a problem with my phones, but I got it fixed already. The phone company promised me I'll have service again before midnight tonight."

"Good." Dick barely let her finish speaking. He was never a particularly friendly or cheerful man, having been promoted to one level above his competency, where he now lingered, a living embodiment of the Peter Principle, crabby in the knowledge that he would never be promoted again. This afternoon, however, he looked significantly more dour than usual, even for Dick.

"Is there the slightest chance that you're sober?" he

asked, his thin nose twitching as if scenting the wind for alcohol fumes. "Please tell me that there is."

"I'm stone-cold sober," she said, flushing slightly.

"Are you?" Dick's sarcasm was undisguised. "In that case, the reason you fell flat on your face was...?"

"Because I was running to open the door and I tripped on a loose floorboard." Verity could feel herself getting rattled and drew in a calming breath. "Okay, Dick, what's this all about? Since I'm officially on leave of absence, I assume there's a point to this interrogation?"

"Yes." He gestured to the car. "We need you at the office."

"*Now?* As in right this minute?"

"Now," he confirmed. "There's a chance that there's going to be a serious...incident...involving Kashmir."

"What sort of an incident? How serious is serious?"

"Very serious. Get your coat, Verity. Time is of the essence. It's really inconvenient that I couldn't reach you by phone." His tone of voice suggested that she'd screwed up her phone service with the express purpose of causing him problems.

Since India and Pakistan disagreed about who owned Kashmir, and since each country had recently tested nuclear weapons in a display of macho posturing that had chiefly served to ignite hotheads in both countries while infuriating the rest of the world, Verity knew that a *very serious* incident involving Kashmir had the potential to become a major international nightmare. The CIA had identified Kashmir's disputed border as the area of the world where nuclear warfare was most likely to break out. Few countries would be happy to find themselves prizewinner in the contest for becoming ground zero for nuclear winter. India and Pakistan, however, seemed to delight in rattling their atomic bombs at each other in a game of chicken that was unlikely to have any winners.

After so long away from the daily pressures of keeping the US government informed about one of the most volatile areas on the planet, Verity was curious as to what specifically had provoked this latest crisis. But it was also instinctive to protest the prospect of renewed involvement in world affairs. In the wake of Sam's death, her own misery occupied a hundred percent of her attention and she had lost her capacity to worry about global problems. Who had time to worry about the chance of nuclear war, when there was Sam to mourn?

"Look, Dick, any information I have on Kashmir is almost eight months out of date," she said. "There's nothing I can tell you that Andrew Breitman doesn't know, with the added advantage that he's up-to-date—"

"I agree, but Andrew's excellent qualifications are irrelevant in the current situation." Dick's sucked-lemons expression became even more sour. "I don't want you back at the office because of the exaggerated notion some of my colleagues have about your abilities, Verity. A notion I don't share, to be perfectly frank with you. I need you to come with me because Khalid Muhammad is in town and he's insisting on talking to you. Your presence is Mr. Muhammad's choice, not mine. Believe me, I don't feel happy about entrusting sensitive negotiations to a woman who may or may not be sober enough to avoid tripping over her own feet if she walks too fast."

She'd known that Dick hadn't believed her explanation about why she'd fallen. In view of the way she'd behaved during his last visit, Verity couldn't entirely blame him, much as she disliked him. She wrapped her shame in a protective coating of anger. "You know what, Dick? I don't have to listen to you insult me. The fact is, I'm not interested in returning to work at this point in my life and I don't care that Khalid Muhammad specifically asked for me. As far as I'm concerned, you can take yourself back to whatever secret hidey-hole you have Khalid stashed in—''

''If you refuse to come with me, I'll call in the Secret Service and force you to live up to your responsibilities.'' Dick Pedro's voice was cold with anger. ''You can't blow off this one, Verity. You're a State Department officer, and you have a sworn duty to uphold. We're facing a serious situation, and I'm ordering you to come with me.''

''I resign.''

''Your resignation isn't accepted. Get your coat.''

Should she force Dick to make good on his threat to compel her cooperation? What was he going to do—drag her bodily down the front steps? A volatile mixture of dread and excitement set Verity's stomach churning. There were a dozen good reasons why she shouldn't agree to do this, most of them fear related. What if she screwed up—big time? What if she'd forgotten how to concentrate and allowed some crucial tidbit of information to slide into oblivion? Before Sam died, she'd always prided herself on her ability to focus on the big picture while simultaneously spotting telling details that other desk officers had overlooked.

Could she still do that? The past week of sobriety and proper food had packed on a couple of pounds, and improved her superficial sense of well-being, but a few days of healthy living couldn't have made a real dent in the ravages she'd worked on her body over the past six months. She wasn't ready to tackle a major crisis, and if Dick didn't recognize that, then she had a responsibility to take herself out of the picture. Incompetence, a looming crisis and Kashmir made for truly lousy companions. Verity recognized that even if her boss didn't.

''It's almost noon. I don't have any more time to waste,'' Dick Pedro said. ''You're coming with me one way or another, Verity. Make it easy on both of us and come willingly.''

''All right, I'll come with you,'' she heard herself say, stumbling over the words just a little. Having made the commitment, the beat of her excitement grew stronger, and her fear a little weaker. ''But you have to give me a couple of minutes. I ripped the hem on these pants when I tripped. I need to change them.''

''You have five minutes.'' Dick stepped into the hall and signaled to the driver to wait. He didn't merely glance down at his watch, he actually clicked on the timer. ''Your five minutes start now. Then I'm coming up to get you.''

Verity took the stairs to her bedroom at a run. Dick could fume and fuss all he pleased. If nuclear war was about to break out over Kashmir, she was at least going to find a belt so that her damn pants wouldn't fall down while she did her bit to prevent the annihilation of humankind.

How odd it was to remember that only a few days ago she'd been hoping the Y2K bug would bring the world crashing to a halt. Now she felt a real urgency to prevent disaster. Her grief over Sam's death still lodged like a leaden weight in the pit of her stomach, but along with the grief was a touch of embarrassment at the incredible self-absorption she had wallowed in for the past few months. She even felt a spark of professional pride because her skills were needed to avert yet another crisis over Kashmir—a battleground where more than twenty-five thousand people had been killed during the past fifty years of civil war. In truth, Verity acknowledged, it felt good to be needed.

As long as she could avoid screwing up.

Right now, she needed to dress the part of a competent career woman, even if she felt a total fraud. She rummaged through her closet and selected a pair of gray tailored slacks that were the tightest she owned. They still sagged at the waistband, so she cinched them in with an old leather belt, poking an extra hole with a nail file. Then she tugged on a lamb's-wool sweater that was long enough to cover the belt and had gray flecks in the pattern that more or less coordinated with the color of her slacks. Dick's allotted five minutes must be almost up, but she took an extra few seconds to drag a brush through her hair and wind it into something that approximated a French twist.

She gave a quick glance toward the mirror, relieved at the clear-eyed person who stared back. Hey, she thought, slamming the brush back into the drawer. If the lights in the meeting room weren't too bright, she could darn near pass for a woman who had her act together.

The tension surrounding Dick when she returned downstairs was almost tangible, making Verity feel calm by comparison. He opened the front door while she was still putting on her coat. "Ready?" he asked.

"Ready." Verity grabbed her purse from the hall table, where it was sitting after her morning's excursion to the phone company offices.

The feeble sunshine of early morning had given way to a freezing drizzle, typical of Virginia in winter. She hurried to the waiting car and the driver opened the door. Dick stood behind her as she stepped into the car. Verity had the impression that it wasn't so much courtesy on his part, as determination to make sure that she didn't change her mind and bolt back into the house.

"The Creighton Hotel," he instructed the driver, before closing the sliding panel that gave them soundproof privacy.

"Why are we meeting in a hotel?" Verity asked. "If

there's a crisis brewing, shouldn't we be meeting somewhere that has access to secure phone and data lines?''

"Of course we should," Dick snapped. "But Khalid Muhammad won't stir from his hotel suite. He has his wife and two children with him, although I haven't actually been introduced to them." Dick sounded peeved by the omission. "Khalid whisked his family into one of the bedrooms as soon as Andrew and I arrived."

"In some ways he's a very traditional Muslim, despite all his western education," Verity said. "He believes in keeping an impenetrable barrier between his political activities and his family life."

"I'm aware of that," Dick said. "But his desire to sequester his family isn't just routine Islamic reticence on his part. Not this time. Khalid is obviously worried sick about his family's safety. He has a retinue of four armed bodyguards protecting his hotel suite."

"*Four* bodyguards? Right there in the hotel?"

"Yep. One for each family member."

"And they're all armed?" Verity asked. "How in the world did Khalid get four armed Kashmiri bodyguards through Customs and Immigration?"

"They aren't from Kashmir. They're Americans, hired from Capital Security. Must be costing Khalid a fortune, because those Capital boys don't come cheap."

Verity had heard of Capital Security. Owned and operated by two ex-Secret Service officers, its employees were all highly trained, many of them also ex-Secret Service. "You're right," she said. "Khalid must be very worried about his family's safety to have gone to such lengths. He's not the sort of man to hire professional bodyguards just for the sake of it."

Dick grunted. "Here's the rest of the bad news. He arrived in Washington last night and got in touch with the emergency duty officer at the State Department almost the moment he landed. He claims to have come expressly to warn us that there's going to be a series of terrorist attacks against the United States. According to Khalid, a lot of folks in the Vale of Kashmir are more pissed than usual with the Indian Government.''

''And they're blaming us, of course.''

''What else?'' Dick said wearily. ''Isn't it always the Americans' fault?''

Verity's heart slammed against her ribs. ''That's really bad news,'' she said. ''Khalid isn't a scaremonger, far from it. He's also very well-informed, with contacts in almost every Kashmir political group, even among the minority Hindus and the Buddhist leaders in Ladekh. We need to treat his warning seriously.''

''We are, of course. He says the terrorists got a message to him in Frankfurt two days ago. Told him to take the next flight out of Germany to Washington and to deliver their message to the Secretary of State in person.''

''What's the message?''

''He's waiting for you before he tells us everything, but here's the short version of what we know so far. Unless the U.S. intervenes to force the Indian Government to release two dozen Kashmiri freedom fighters who are due to face a firing squad next week then—quote— there will be immediate and unfortunate consequences. For the U.S.''

Verity grimaced. ''Definitely not good news. Has the Secretary of State been informed?''

''I left an urgent message with her assistant, so I assume she's been informed by now. I'll request a face-to-face meeting as soon as I'm absolutely sure Khalid isn't blowing hot air.''

''Why are the Kashmiri men in jail?'' Verity asked. ''What has the Indian government accused them of doing?''

"Setting up an ambush and wiping out a platoon of Indian soldiers who were on patrol along the cease-fire line in Kashmir."

"How many Indian troops killed?"

"Twenty," Dick said. "With several more injured."

She shook her head. "The Indian government isn't going to release freedom fighters who slaughtered their troops. Not a chance. Especially not this government, which draws most of its support from Hindu nationalists. The Indian government has more than a quarter of a million troops tied up one way and another in their efforts to keep the peace in Kashmir. They're not going to look the other way if a group of insurrectionists—probably supported by Pakistan—has slaughtered their soldiers."

Dick frowned. "I know. But Khalid insists the Indian government has arrested the wrong men. He claims they haven't been given a public trial because the Indian government can't produce a shred of evidence that these are the specific men who are guilty. He also predicts there will be riots in Kashmir if India goes ahead with the military-style executions. That's quite apart from the specific terrorist retaliation he's warning us about."

"Unfortunately, as you know, there are riots and demonstrations in Kashmir on a regular basis. The Indian government will simply crack down harder, that's all." Verity sighed. The situation sounded depressingly like the sort of intractable muddle that had been typical of Kashmiri politics ever since the collapse of British Imperial rule in 1947. The hasty partition of the Indian subcontinent had caused a million deaths as Muslims and Hindus scurried frantically to move to the side of the border friendly to their religion, and Kashmir—led by a dithering playboy maharajah—had been left as a festering internal sore, its borders contested by India, Pakistan and China.

Verity tucked a loose strand of hair back behind her ear, trying to feel more put together. "What is it that you need from me, Dick? My opinion about the likely guilt or innocence of those Kashmiri men is basically irrelevant. Whether or not to bring pressure to bear on the Indian government is a decision that has to be taken at the highest levels. If there's an active, believable threat of imminent terrorist action that threatens U.S. lives and property, we're not even talking the Secretary of State here. We're talking the President."

"Yes, but the President's decision has to be based in part on our assessment of how serious the threat of terrorist attacks might be. Also, the potential volatility of the situation, and the extent to which this incident is likely to provoke a strong enough reaction inside Kashmir to destabilize the entire region."

"Andrew Breitman is far better informed than I am concerning the general political situation in that area. He's an expert on Pakistan, plus he spent five years in China, so he has a broad perspective—"

"I know. But Andrew isn't better informed about the political players in Kashmir, and he never met Khalid until today. What I need from you right now is your take on Khalid. How far can we trust him to be giving us a straight story?"

Verity shrugged. "That's a deceptively hard question to answer. In Kashmir, there usually isn't any straight story."

"Jesus, don't start going cryptic on me, Verity. I've had enough of that this morning from Khalid."

"Sorry. What I meant is that facts are even more slippery commodities in Kashmir than they are in other places. Even when Kashmiris try to tell the strict, simple truth, what you actually get is the facts as perceived through the prism of somebody's rigid set of prejudices."

"That happens anywhere and everywhere," Dick pointed out.

"Yes, but prejudices are deeper and more bitter in Kashmir than in most other places," Verity said. "On the other hand, Khalid counts as a moderate by Kashmiri standards, so his version of the facts is probably quite reliable."

Dick tugged at his mustache. "How likely is he to be honest but delusional? You know him personally. What's your take on his mental stability? He already reminded me that he attended the school in Kashmir where your mother was principal, so you've known him since he was a kid."

"I met him eighteen months ago, too, when I escorted that congressional delegation to India and Kashmir." Verity looked out of the car window, where a few snowflakes were making a desultory effort to reach the ground. Surprisingly, even though that trip to Kashmir brought back memories she normally tried to keep buried, she was becoming more confident the more questions Dick threw at her.

She scarcely hesitated as she delivered her verdict. "Khalid has always struck me as eminently sane. I saw nothing to contradict that judgment during our last meeting."

"I agree he gives a darn good imitation of a rational man. But if we scratch beneath the surface, are we going to find a Muslim fanatic? Could he have been using his reputation as a moderate to conceal more radical views? There's also the possibility that he's a regular, run-of-the-mill fruitcake who's prepared to invent whatever lies it takes to get some one-on-one face time with the President of the United States."

"He's no fruitcake, that's for sure." Verity frowned, summoning childhood memories of the mischievous, good-natured boy Khalid had been, meshing them with more recent images of the battle-scarred and sophisticated political negotiator he'd become. "Everyone in Kashmir tends to see wicked plots where actually there's nothing going on except gross incompetence, or maybe sheer bad luck. Khalid can't totally escape from his heritage, any more than the rest of us, but I'd say his vision is a lot clearer than that of most of his countrymen."

Dick gave a contemptuous snort. "Yeah, well, that's not saying much."

Verity lifted her shoulders, feeling unexpectedly defensive of the land of her birth. "You know how high the frustration level is in Kashmir. The ordinary people there have been made pawns of Pakistani and Indian politics. They see our government actively trying to bring peace to Northern Ireland and the Middle East, not to mention places like Bosnia and Kosovo. Not surprisingly, they wonder why nobody in the international community cares about what's happening to them. After all, they were promised a plebiscite where they could vote on their future. That was half a century ago and they're still waiting."

Dick's fingers drummed on his briefcase. "At least America has never been the Great Satan as far as Kashmiris are concerned. The Muslims there are too busy hating the Indian government, and the Hindus are furious with Pakistan for encouraging troop incursions across the border. Stir in worries about China's and Afghanistan's territorial ambitions, and lingering resentment at British colonialism. America actually comes quite low down on the Kashmiri hate list."

"True," Verity agreed. "But I wouldn't be shocked if some fanatical Islamic splinter group has finally figured out that threatening a major act of international terrorism is a great way to attract the attention of the U.S. government. Not to mention the world's media. If you recall, the Al Farran group kidnapped a group of foreign tourists back in 1996. Then they tried to bring pressure on the Indian government, using the tourists as hostages...."

"I remember," Dick said. "But the tourists were all different nationalities, a couple of them escaped, and the whole endeavor fizzled for lack of organization. Right?"

"Right. Of course, tourists immediately stopped going to Kashmir, so the insurrectionists couldn't try that tactic again. Since then, the only really surprising thing is that nobody in Kashmir has tried taking their cause overseas. A spot of international terror would work wonders in raising world awareness of the situation."

Dick made an impatient clicking noise. "Well, you said it yourself. Terrorism requires organization and discipline if it's going to be successful. Which is hardly a strong suit for most of the so-called freedom fighters in Kashmir."

Verity pulled a face. "It only takes one small group of dedicated fanatics, though, and the whole picture in Kashmir could change."

"Dedication doesn't equal efficiency. Thank God."

"True. But I'm sure Osama bin Laden would be delighted to train a cadre of violent, fanatical Kashmiri freedom fighters to be both deadly and efficient. Discipline and long-term planning are his strong suits. There aren't many multimillionaires willing to live in a desert cave for the sake of their cause, even if they do have a few good-looking wives to keep them company."

"Oh, Christ." Dick Pedro winced at the mention of bin Laden's name. "There's no evidence that bin Laden is dabbling in Kashmiri politics, is there?"

Verity shrugged. "No more than anywhere else. But he has terrorist training camps in Afghanistan that he operates under the protection of the Taliban government.

And Afghanistan shares a border with the part of Kashmir controlled by Pakistan—''

"The Taliban," Dick interrupted, his voice acid. "Now there's a bunch of religious loonies who are rabid enough to make you nostalgic for the good old days when the Communists were in charge."

Verity gave a rueful grin. "Yep, I'm with you there. And the shared border means that it's easy to infiltrate trained terrorists into Kashmir via Pakistan. In my opinion, we'd be foolish to ignore a possible connection to bin Laden."

"You're confirming everything Andrew Breitman already said." Dick sighed gustily. "Damn! I hoped you'd tell me Khalid Muhammad was nuts, and that we could all go home and forget about him."

Verity shook her head. "No, he's not nuts. Anything but."

"Then provided Khalid doesn't do or say anything to change your opinion about his mental stability, I guess you've convinced me that we have to treat this threat as real, imminent and serious." Dick's voice was morose. "As soon as you elicit a few specifics about the pending threat from Khalid, I'll notify the Counter Terrorism Center."

Verity was surprised that the Center hadn't already been notified, until she remembered that Dick Pedro was a typical bureaucrat, determined to protect his turf at all costs. The Counter Terrorism Center was theoretically an interagency government unit. In practice, it operated as a department of the CIA. Housed at CIA headquarters in Langley, with additional staff seconded from the FBI and the State Department, specialist personnel were added as needed to cope with specific threats.

Since the CIA was the agency Dick most loved to hate, he would resist notifying the Counter Terrorism Center for as long as possible, even though they dealt with terrorist threats on a daily basis, and would have resources far beyond anything available to Dick through regular State Department channels. God forbid that someone from CTC should actually be the person who extracted precise details of the threatened plot from Khalid. Dick would want to claim that glory for himself.

Verity knew better than to challenge Dick's decisions. He was much too insecure to tolerate second-guessing from his subordinates. However, she wasn't prepared to sit back and allow colleagues overseas to be put at risk because of Dick's professional hang-ups. "Has a warning already been sent to all our embassies and overseas missions?" she asked. "Our people in India and Pakistan especially need to know what's going on. Presumably they must be the ones most at risk."

"What are we supposed to notify them about when we don't know ourselves what's going on?" Dick asked tartly. "But to set your mind at rest. Yes, we sent out a standard general warning two hours ago, before I came to fetch you. Unfortunately, we couldn't be very specific because Khalid refuses to give us any details we can be specific about. He insisted on waiting for you."

And if the warning was merely general, the chances were high it would be given scant attention by embassy personnel, who received far too many vague threats of terrorist activity. "An attack on the U.S. Embassy in New Delhi would be the most logical target," Verity suggested.

"Andrew already suggested that, so we did specifically warn the embassy to go to a heightened state of alert. Jesus, what a nightmare." Dick grabbed a handkerchief from his pocket and mopped his forehead. "Every time we pressed Khalid for details, he clammed up and insisted he needed to talk with you. He keeps repeating that his life is at risk, and also his family's safety, although why that means he can only speak to you, God knows. He claims he barely made it out of Kashmir alive because his enemies are planning to assassinate him."

Verity liked what she was hearing less and less. Everything she knew about Khalid suggested that if he was frightened, then he had cause for his fear. Which wasn't good news for those people and governments who hoped to prevent India and Pakistan from going to war yet again over possession of Kashmir. Moderate conciliators like Khalid were already far too thin on the ground. They didn't need to lose yet another.

The car drew to a halt outside the hotel in the heart of Washington, D.C.'s fashionable Embassy Row. "Okay, this is it," Dick said. "Crunch time. Get the information out of Khalid as soon as you can, Verity. If this guy is giving us the straight skinny, there's a hell of a lot at stake here."

Khalid and his family had taken over the presidential suite on the top floor of the hotel. Guarded by two burly men, one black, one white, both polite but implacable, Verity and Dick were subjected to a quick but efficient search for concealed weapons before they were allowed to enter.

Khalid came from a rich merchant family and the suite was larger than many homes, with two bedrooms, two bathrooms, a kitchen, and a palatial, high-ceilinged central sitting room, complete with grand piano. The sitting room was so large that the two remaining bodyguards, posted at the door to the master bedroom, didn't even make the sitting room appear cluttered.

Andrew Breitman was seated at a lacquer-surfaced conference table, making notes on a laptop computer when Verity and Dick came into the suite. He stood up to greet Verity with a hug and a smile that seemed all the more friendly in comparison to Dick's surly behavior.

"You look wonderful, Veri, much better than the last time I saw you. It's sure great to have you back onboard. We've missed you."

She returned his hug, then unwound her scarf and slipped out of her coat, laying it on a nearby chair. "It's good to see you Andrew. It's good to be here, in fact." Surprisingly, it was. "Although, obviously, I wish the circumstances were less threatening." She looked around. "Where's Khalid?"

Andrew grimaced. "Shut in the bedroom with his family. Said he needed to spend some quality time with his kids. In other words, he had no intention of answering any more of my questions. It's been damned frustrating waiting for you to get here, Veri. I keep thinking of all those poor bastards in our embassies overseas who don't know that a bunch of whacked-out freedom fighters are quite likely planning to blow them into eternity. All in the name of Allah and justice, of course."

Dick coughed, indicating that he considered Andrew's comments indiscreet. Dick was one of those government officials who slapped a Cosmic Top Secret stamp on the departmental lunch order from the local Chinese takeout restaurant. Huffing with self-importance, he walked up to one of the guards. "Please let Mr. Muhammad know that Ms. Marlowe has arrived and is waiting to speak with him."

"No need. I heard your arrival." The door to the master bedroom opened, and Khalid Muhammad came out. Of average height and slender build, his presence was nevertheless commanding. Even in grade school, Khalid had been imbued with a subtle dynamism. Holding on to power in a part of the world that usually rewarded mod-

eration with assassination had merely enhanced his cha-
risma and his aura of carefully controlled calm.

He turned to Verity, greeting her by touching his right
hand to his forehead and then his heart. "*Salaam alekum.*
My pleasure in the day has improved immeasurably with
your presence. I am honored that you came when your
sorrow at the loss of your husband is still heavy."

Verity returned his greeting, the gesture fluid and natural, despite years of disuse. "*Valekum as salaam.* I am
honored that you requested my presence. And the ache
of my husband's loss is less painful because I am able
to be of service to you and to my country."

Khalid gave a small, weary smile. "Now that you are
here, there is perhaps some slight hope that tragedy can
be averted. Alas, I am not optimistic. I know that the
chances of persuading the government of your country to
intervene in the internal affairs of India are slim. And
unless those twenty-four Kashmiri prisoners are released
from custody, I see no way to prevent the hotheads of
the Kashmir Freedom Party from acting."

Dick Pedro interrupted, clearly annoyed that he
couldn't understand what was being said. "You need to
speak in English, Mr. Muhammad, if these discussions
are going to take us where we all want to go."

"Of course. Forgive me for forgetting that you and
Mr. Breitman cannot speak my language." Khalid delivered the apology with perfect smoothness, but Andrew
shot a wry, covert glance in Verity's direction. Unlike
Dick, he was quite observant enough to pick up on the
subtle condescension in Khalid's apology.

Andrew cleared his throat. "Er...Dick...before we
proceed, we need to come to some arrangement with Mr.
Muhammad about his guards. They're civilians, not
bound by the Official Secrets Act, and we can't have
them in the room."

"Of course, of course. I hadn't forgotten." Dick looked furious that his subordinate had managed to get in a dig about security, trampling on Dick's preserve. He loosened his tie, a subtle indicator that he was approaching meltdown. "Mr. Muhammad, for your own safety, you understand that we can't conduct these conversations with extraneous personnel in the room. If you reveal sensitive information, we might be required to lock up the gentlemen in question to contain the spread of that information. They would then be unavailable to act as your bodyguards, something I'm sure you wish to avoid as much as we do."

"Of course. I understand." Khalid spoke quietly to one of the guards. "Shawn, how do you wish to handle this? I would suggest that you and Larry take a short break. There is a TV in the second bedroom if you would like to wait there...."

Shawn considered the safety ramifications of this plan for a few seconds before shaking his head. "Better if Larry and I take your sons into the second bedroom with us," he said. "That way your wife gets some privacy and your sons will have a double line of protection. Patrick and George outside in the hallway, Larry and me inside. In an hour from now, we'll switch off with Patrick and George."

"Good thinking. Then you will all remain more fresh and alert."

Shawn gave a taut smile. "Don't worry, Mr. Muhammad. The four of us have worked together before and we've stayed alert in situations a lot more pressured than this."

"I am glad to hear it. But please don't be deceived by the apparent tranquility of this setting. The men who have threatened to kill my family are ruthless and they will not hesitate to act if their interests are threatened."

"We understand, sir."

Khalid went to the master bedroom and emerged moments later with his two small sons in tow. He waited for the bodyguards to escort the boys into the second bedroom before gesturing for Dick and Verity to sit down. "This could be a long and tiring session. We may as well get comfortable."

Dick took a seat at the table and leaned forward, clasping his hands. "Well, Mr. Muhammad, it's time for us to get down to brass tacks. No more delaying tactics from you, if you please. I've brought Verity Marlowe to this meeting as you requested. Now you need to give us some specific details concerning this terrorist act you believe will be committed against the United States. As you yourself have said, time is undoubtedly of the essence if we're going to avert a tragedy."

Khalid replied without hesitation. "I cannot give you specifics, Mr. Pedro. Not because I am unwilling, but because I am unable. I find myself in the invidious position of being a mere messenger—a prophet of doom not in full possession of the facts."

"*What?*" Dick Pedro leapt to his feet. "You have to be joking! You've kept us here since eight-thirty this morning and then sent me out on a wild-goose chase to pick up Verity Marlowe, just so that you could tell us you have *no information?*"

"I said that I am unable to give you specific details of the attack that is threatened," Khalid replied coolly. "I have information, plenty of it. Unfortunately, much of it reflects badly upon me, and is therefore easy to disbelieve. That is why I requested Verity's presence. She has known me long enough to give credit to my sincerity, even if what I have to say is frustratingly vague. She also knows that I have a large family, including no less than twenty-six first cousins. Therefore, when I admit to you that one of the Kashmiri men imprisoned by the Indian government happens to be my cousin, she will understand that my opinion concerning his innocence is little influenced by the fact that we are blood relatives. She will also know that I am not likely to be so crazed with the need to rescue this cousin that I have abandoned the moderate principles of a lifetime and thrown in my lot with some fanatical splinter group of terrorists."

"Your *cousin* is one of the Kashmiri men awaiting execution?" Dick spluttered.

"Yes." Khalid inclined his head. "As I just explained."

"Your reputation for personal integrity is well-known," Verity intervened quickly, since Dick looked ready to pop off with a terminal stroke at any moment. "As was your father's before you. Indeed, your entire family is known for its moderate views."

"Your courtesy and praise are both appreciated." Khalid's smile was tinged with bitterness. "Sadly, integrity is not enough these days to protect the innocent in Kashmir, especially those of us who dare to believe in peaceful negotiations. I am not accustomed to seeing myself as a victim of circumstances beyond my control, but in this case, I feel helpless before the workings of fate. Here are the facts. Three weeks ago I was kidnapped and taken to a mountain rebel camp—"

"Kidnapped?" Dick interrupted. "Did you report this to the police in Kashmir, Mr. Muhammad?"

"Of course not," Khalid said, obviously struggling to keep his patience. "The Kashmiri police are notorious for their corruption, and I had not the smallest desire to embroil myself in their clutches, or impart sensitive information to provincial officials who were quite likely to misuse it. Unfortunately, I can tell you nothing useful about the rebel camp, either in terms of its location, or its leaders, since I was blindfolded the whole time and never spoke to the man in charge. The leader, whoever he was, always conveyed his orders silently, through the medium of the guards assigned to watch me.''

"Do you think the rebel leader was afraid that you would recognize his voice?'' Andrew asked.

A question she should have thought to ask, Verity rebuked herself. After months without practice, concentrating on both the details and the big picture was proving every bit as difficult as she'd feared.

Khalid turned toward Andrew, a slight glow of approval in his eyes. "A good question, Mr. Breitman. I have wondered that myself. It seems a reasonable supposition, but I have a wide acquaintance, and the list of suspects is hardly narrowed by the fact that I might have recognized the voice of my chief captor. For what it's worth, I was not badly treated by my kidnappers, except that it was bone-chillingly cold and I was threatened with exposure if I failed to cooperate. A threat I took very seriously.''

"As you should,'' Verity commented. "If you'd been left naked outside on a mountain ledge in December, you would have been dead within the hour.'' For Dick's benefit, she added a reminder about the conditions in Kashmir. "Kashmir is in the Himalayas, and Srinagar is almost six thousand feet above sea level, even though it's always described as being in a valley and having a moderate climate. Several of the nearby mountains reach heights in excess of fifteen thousand feet so at this time of year the cold can be literally life threatening within minutes, fatal within the hour.''

"Believe me, I had no desire whatever to test the sincerity of my captors' threats,'' Khalid said. "Once they were convinced they had secured my complete attention, I was informed that my help was needed to effect the rescue of twenty-four Kashmiri freedom fighters held in federal prison in India. I already believed the men in question to be innocent of murder, so I had no hesitation in offering to use my best efforts to attempt a negotiated settlement with the Indian government.''

"And this journey to the States is your attempt at mediation?'' Andrew Breitman asked, looking up from his laptop.

"No.'' Khalid took a sip of iced fruit juice, gesturing to indicate the others should also help themselves. "My captors rejected my offer of mediation. Rejected it with guffaws of disbelieving laughter, in fact.''

"Unfortunately, they were probably right to be scornful,'' Verity said, pouring a glass of juice in the hope that liquid might work some magic on her increasingly fierce tension headache. Dick had hustled her off so fast, she didn't even have an aspirin in her purse.

"Indeed.'' Khalid nodded in acknowledgment of her comment. "The Indian government has already rejected pleas for clemency from the leaders of many Muslim states. There is no reason to suppose I would have succeeded where others have failed. I have no official status within Kashmir, except as the leader of a moderate political party that the Indian government refuses to acknowledge.''

"So how did you escape from your kidnappers?'' Dick asked. "Or did they choose to set you free so that you could deliver a message to us?''

"If you knew the mountains of Kashmir, you would realize that escape was impossible.'' For the first time, Khalid sounded openly impatient with Dick's lack of understanding. "No, I didn't escape, Mr. Pedro. I was set free less than twenty-four hours after I was first captured. My kidnappers escorted me to the outskirts of Srinagar, where they left me bound and gagged in the courtyard of a mosque, having informed me they would be in touch within days. They also informed me that if I failed to cooperate with their demands, my sons, Abdul and Saiyad, would be killed.''

Verity gasped, knowing how he adored his two young sons. "Khalid, I'm so sorry. Thank God you managed to get out of Kashmir before they could carry out their threats."

Khalid looked at her with a sadness so profound it tore at her heart. "You are too optimistic, Verity. I haven't escaped danger just because I am in Washington, D.C. instead of Srinagar. The kidnappers' threats to murder my children could be carried out here with very little difficulty. There are enough immigrants in this city—in this country—that it's all too easy to infiltrate spies and assassins among the genuine refugees."

"But your chances of safety here are much greater than in Kashmir," Dick Pedro said. "After all, the United States is a country where the rule of law reigns supreme, and our law enforcement officials are noted for their honesty."

Did her boss practice being a pompous ass, or did it come naturally, Verity wondered. She managed—just—to resist the urge to remind Dick about the appalling murder statistics of the nation's capital and the corruption scandals that periodically convulsed big-city police departments. She felt Andrew Breitman's gaze seeking hers, and they exchanged covert glances of mutual incredulity at Dick's fatuous remark.

"I hope very much that you are right, Mr. Pedro." Not surprisingly, Khalid sounded less than optimistic. "However, my experience in Germany does not give me much confidence."

"Will you tell us precisely what happened in Germany?" Verity asked.

"My kidnappers found me," Khalid said simply. "By leaving Kashmir under cover of darkness, and by keeping my destination secret even from my servants, I naively hoped to escape from the clutches of my kidnappers and their allies. With great difficulty—and I thought considerable ingenuity—I was able to smuggle my wife and children out of Kashmir and into Pakistan. From Pakistan we flew to Egypt. We did a little detour via Saudi Arabia, and flew from there to Frankfurt, a large enough city to provide concealment. Or so I imagined. Unfortunately, my kidnappers appear to be better financed and better organized than I would ever have expected, and their reach clearly extends beyond the narrow boundaries of Kashmir. They found me again in Germany. So much for my dream of safety for my sons." Khalid's voice broke, and he quickly cleared his throat.

"Did you travel to Germany under an assumed name?" Andrew asked. "Did you use false documents?"

"Of course I used false documents," Khalid said. "The object of the exercise, Mr. Breitman, was to escape the notice of my kidnappers. We changed papers and names twice during the course of our journey—"

"But you failed anyway," Dick said. "Despite the assumed identities. Is that why you're staying here under your own name?"

"Yes." Khalid's eyes became opaque with grief and anger. "What is the point of a deception that doesn't work? We had been in Frankfurt for only five days when I paid a visit to a trusted business partner, seeking his help in accessing funds without revealing my identity to the bank. I was gone for two hours. My wife and I had registered at the hotel as Mr. and Mrs. Ali Mahmud, but when I returned I found my family bound and captive, with three masked gunmen standing over them. The gunmen, it was clear, knew exactly who we really were."

"When did this new attack on your family take place?" Dick asked.

"That was on Saturday." Khalid reached for his glass of juice, and then pushed it away untouched, as if too tense to swallow. "We flew out of Frankfurt the next morning and arrived here in Washington late yesterday evening. I am in the States today for one reason only. I have come because I am commanded by my kidnappers to act as their messenger. The delivery of a message to your Secretary of State is the payment I was forced to give in exchange for the lives of my wife and children. I can only pray that once my message is delivered, my kidnappers will not decide to kill their messenger and renege on their deal. It occurs to me that this is a very fragile hope, but I must cling to it as best I can."

Verity searched for words of consolation that didn't seem insultingly trite. Dick Pedro, not burdened with any excess of sympathy, cut straight to the chase. "Precisely what is the message you've been asked to deliver to us, Mr. Muhammad?"

Khalid replied in a monotone, as if by rote. "That the United States government is to make it clear to the government of India that the twenty-four Kashmiri heroes are to be released. The Kashmir Freedom Party holds the Secretary of State personally responsible for the lives and safety of its innocent members, who are currently being tortured in an Indian prison in Bombay."

"I'm certainly willing to pass on your message to the Secretary of State," Dick said. "However, I must point out to you, Mr. Muhammad, that the United States government has no power to coerce India to release its prisoners. Quite apart from the fact that the United States is not in the habit of intervening in the internal affairs of sovereign nations—"

"Mr. Pedro, we don't have time to exchange the standard diplomatic nonsense,'' Khalid's expression was as impatient as his tone of voice. "You know, I know and the Kashmir Freedom Party knows that the American government has the muscle to get those prisoners released if it has sufficient incentive to act."

Verity's stomach cramped at the word *incentive.* She glanced at Andrew and Dick, who had both clearly understood the implicit threat. She was the one who gave voice to their joint fears. "*Incentive* is a troublesome word, Khalid. What *incentive* does the Kashmir Freedom Party intend to employ to coerce the cooperation of the United States government?"

Khalid glanced at his watch. "It is already past one o'clock," he said, refusing to meet Verity's eyes. "In order to underline the importance which the Kashmir Freedom Party places on the involvement of the United States government in the release of the innocent prisoners, I must ask you to telephone the press officer at the State Department, in order to receive a message direct from the Kashmir Freedom Party."

Verity's heart pounded hard and fast. Messages from groups of subversive fanatics, delivered via the press officer at the State Department, were likely to be seriously bad news.

Andrew obviously shared her worries. "If your people want help from the United States, Mr. Muhammad, I hope they know better than to try to blackmail us into cooperating." He sounded severe, but he was already dialing the number for the State Department press room, as if he knew his warning was irrelevant.

"They are not *my people* and I don't know what their plans are," Khalid said wearily. "Those who kidnapped me are not the sort to reveal their intentions to a mere messenger."

"If that is what you are, Mr. Muhammad. A mere messenger.'' Dick Pedro was no longer bothering to conceal his distrust.

"I need to speak to the duty officer," Andrew said into the phone. "I have Deputy Assistant Secretary of State Pedro on the line. This is an emergency. No, the line isn't secure. We're calling from the Creighton Hotel.''

After a few seconds, he handed the phone to Dick, who took it with a frown. "Who am I talking to? Oh, Dennis, yes, hello. This is Dick Pedro. I've been told that you have a message waiting for me from the Kashmir Freedom Party.''

The response that came from the other end of the phone was inaudible, but it was evidently bad news. The blood drained from Dick's face and he had to clear his voice twice before he could speak.

"Was anyone else killed?" he asked. Again the pause. "I see. And CNN is already running the story? What have we said to the press so far? Good. Whatever you do, Dennis, don't make any statements until I've spoken with the Secretary of State. I'm coming back to the office right now." He glanced at his watch. "I'm at the Creighton Hotel but I have a limo. I should be there within fifteen minutes. By two at the latest, if traffic's really bad. Yes, goodbye.''

He hung up the phone and looked at Khalid, not attempting to conceal his loathing. "Are you expecting me to believe that you had no idea what these so-called kidnappers of yours planned to do, Mr. Muhammad?''

"No," Khalid said. "I don't expect you to believe me, Mr. Pedro. Nevertheless, the fact is that I have no idea what message they planned to send.''

"I'm sure you could make a good guess," Dick Pedro said angrily. "And yet you refused to give me any details until it was too late for us to take effective precautions—''

''Dick...'' Verity put her hand on her boss's arm, drawing his angry gaze away from Khalid. ''What's happened? What have you just learned from the press officer?''

''The American Consul General in Bombay has been assassinated,'' Dick said, his voice hoarse. ''An hour ago, the Kashmir Freedom Party claimed responsibility for the murder.''

Four

Khalid didn't move, didn't even blink, but he looked as if he might vomit.

"Oh, my God!" Andrew half rose from his chair before slumping back down. "You mean George Douglass? George has been killed? My God, I dated his sister a couple of years ago!"

"Yes," Dick confirmed. "George Douglass. We've known each other for fifteen years. He was a good man."

"Does he have a wife and children?" Verity asked.

"He sure does," Dick said, white-faced with shock and outrage. "He's got two kids still in grade school, and now he's dead because of a bunch of lunatics from Kashmir." He spit out the last word as if it were profane. "Fucking lunatics," he muttered under his breath, abandoning all pretense of diplomatic discretion.

No, not lunatics, Verity thought. On the contrary. The consul had been killed by a group of extremely smart fanatics who'd finally figured out how to focus the attention of the U.S. government on their cause. The Kashmir Freedom Party had stopped killing locals and started slaughtering Americans. An excellent way to get the attention of the most powerful nation in the world.

Still stunned by the violent death of a man he knew quite well, and obviously liked, Dick Pedro left to meet with the Secretary of State, while Andrew was assigned the task of notifying the Counter Terrorism Center that the State Department had reason to believe the assassination of the Consul General in Bombay was only the first step in a program of organized terror designed to thrust the United States into the middle of the Kashmiri struggle for independence. He warned the Center that more anti-American terrorist activity could be anticipated, probably in the near future.

Since they were in a hotel room and had no access to a secure phone or data connections, Andrew's conversation was brief, and as noncommittal as possible. "They're sending over two of their antiterrorist experts," he said, hanging up the phone. "Mr. Green and Mr. Brown. Green is from the FBI. They didn't say what agency Brown works for."

Verity rolled her eyes. "Obviously, he's CIA. Why do they refuse to identify their employees by their real names, I wonder? It's such a meaningless habit."

Andrew grinned. "I didn't know the CIA cared about being meaningful. Much less about working in real partnership with other government agencies." Quietly, only for Verity's ears, he added, "What do you think the chances are that either one of these so-called experts will be able to locate Kashmir on the map?"

"Slim to none," Verity said, just as quietly. "Still, right now, I'm grateful for any help we can get. And, for all its obsession with secrecy, the CTC has an impressive record of preventing terrorist attacks."

Andrew grunted. "Yep, I guess we have to grant 'em that."

She hoped to God Agents Brown and Green would be able to provide some insights into the current mess. Bad as it was to know that George Douglass was dead, it was even worse to worry about when and where the terrorists might strike next. Another embassy? A military base? Vulnerable tourists on an overseas vacation?

Verity's stomach had started churning at the news of George Douglass's murder and hadn't stopped since. Her head was pounding, and she desperately needed a drink. Not the too sweet mango juice Khalid had provided for them, but vodka. Neat, on the rocks. Her craving for alcohol disgusted her, but that didn't change her need.

The knowledge that George Douglass had already died terrified her. She was supposed to be The Expert on Kashmir, and people were looking to her for help, but the truth was she hadn't the faintest idea what to warn everyone to watch out for. God, she wasn't fit to deal with a crisis. She felt shaky, inadequate, and hopelessly rusty.

"Let's hear if CNN is carrying any report on the situation." Andrew got up from the conference table, shutting down his laptop. "That's better than sitting around waiting for the men in black to get here and take over. Mr. Green and Mr. Brown." He sent Verity a wry smile. "Jesus! Do you think they're trying to make a joke?"

"I doubt it. When did you ever meet an FBI agent with a sense of humor?"

"Never," Andrew admitted. "And the folks over at Langley are worse. They make FBI headquarters look like a hotbed of comic relief."

Andrew was efficient, well-informed and took his job with a cheerful dose of irreverence, so he didn't have much in common with Dick Pedro. However, he shared his boss's disdainful attitude toward the CIA. Both he and Dick were men who appreciated the art of diplomacy, and they often had a hard time concealing their dislike of the CIA's generous budget and close-to-the-chest tactics.

Andrew glanced over at Khalid, who was lost in thought and paying no attention to them whatsoever. "What do you make of his reaction?" he murmured.

"Seems genuinely upset," she replied softly. "Don't you think?"

"Hmm...I wonder. Anyway, let's find the TV and see what CNN has to say."

Watching TV news reports seemed like a better deal than watching Khalid pace, and a lot better option than staring into space while she gnawed on the bone of her own inadequacy, Verity decided. She and Andrew roamed the giant room in search of a TV set, and she eventually found it hidden in an alcove behind the doors of a cherry wood cabinet. She flipped through the channels until she had the set tuned to CNN.

There were chairs in front of the TV, but neither she nor Andrew thought to sit down. After waiting through the inevitable raft of advertisements, they had to listen to an update on a blizzard paralyzing air traffic at O'Hare before the topic finally turned to the assassination.

The newscaster stared into the camera, his expression bizarrely cheerful, as if he'd forgotten to tone down his professional, all-purpose smile. "Returning to our earlier breaking news, CNN can now confirm that the American Consul General in Bombay, George Douglass, was killed at 7:30 p.m. today, local time in Bombay, which is eleven in the morning, eastern standard time. Early reports indicate that a grenade or other explosive device was lobbed under the consul's car when it was stopped at a red light.

"Mr. Douglass, who is descended from a cousin of the famous American abolitionist, Frederick Douglass, was en route to an official dinner given by local government leaders. His wife, Maya Hardcastle Douglass, had been expected to accompany him, but she is suffering from a mild case of the flu, and decided at the last minute to stay at home, thus saving her life.

"The car in which Mr. Douglass was being transported

was driven by V. J. Shantilal, a local chauffeur employed full-time by the consulate. Mr. Shantilal was also killed in the blast, along with at least half a dozen pedestrians who were crossing the crowded road at the time of the explosion. Exact numbers of the dead and wounded have not been released by local Indian authorities.

"An organization known as the Kashmir Freedom Party has claimed responsibility for the blast. Kashmir, in the far northwest of India, has long been considered a flashpoint for violence, since religious differences, political ambitions and geographical disputes are on a collision course in this region, which was once famous as a tourist destination because of its high mountains and scenic lakes.

"The terrorists gave no indication as to why the American Consul General in Bombay was targeted as their victim. Bombay, a city of ten million people on the west coast of India, is more than a thousand miles from Kashmir. It's also a major commercial center. American government buildings and offices throughout the Indian subcontinent have been put on a state of heightened alert in the anticipation of further terrorist attacks. Stay tuned to CNN for regular updates on this tragic story."

Verity muted the sound as the announcer switched to another news item. She realized that Khalid had finally stopped pacing and come to stand beside her. She turned to look at him and saw that his features were twisted with pain.

"I should have guessed that they would not stop at mere threats," he said, rubbing his hand across his eyes. "And yet I confess that I expected them to kidnap an American official and make demands, not resort immediately to murder. It's so pointless! How do they blackmail the U.S. government to bring pressure on India if Mr. Douglass is already dead? It makes no sense."

"The actions of terrorists rarely make sense," Andrew said coldly. "You should have realized that from the first, Mr. Muhammad."

"Yes, I should." Khalid's shoulders slumped. "And yet, I confess, that I didn't want to believe the Freedom Party had escalated its fanaticism to such a level that it would kill for no real purpose other than to wreak violence against an innocent man."

"You were in a difficult position," Verity said, wanting to offer some comfort, but not willing to grant him absolution. A lot of people had already died, and she dreaded to think how many more were still at risk.

"The situation was more than difficult," Khalid said harshly. "It was impossible. Have you any idea what it's like to see your children cowering in their mother's arms, guns pointed at their heads? When I saw my two young sons at the mercy of black-hooded terrorists, eyes gleaming through the slits in their masks like a personification of every child's worst nightmare, I didn't allow myself to inquire too deeply into the plans or motives of the men who held the guns."

"Few of us would," Verity murmured.

"But some men, wiser than I, might have found a way out of the dilemma." Khalid appeared tormented by his own thoughts. "How am I to live with the knowledge that I saved my sons by sacrificing the life of Mr. George Douglass? That his children are now orphans, and his wife a widow…"

"Most of the blame belongs to those arrogant members of the Kashmir Freedom Party who believe that their political desires are more important than the life of the American Consul General," Verity said. "But this isn't the moment to worry about who's to blame for the past. What we need to concentrate on right now is preventing another tragedy. We need any information you have—

anything at all—which might enable us to forestall another terrorist act.''

"This is only the beginning," Andrew said, looking at Khalid with slightly less approval than he'd have directed toward a cockroach. "Killing George Douglass is just the Freedom Party's way of warning to us to pay attention." He had a thick head of wavy brown hair that he kept cut in a short, conservative style, but he'd combed his fingers through it so many times in the past hour that it was standing up in a spiky halo.

He ran his fingers through the spikes yet again. "They're going to need hostages," he said. "Somebody innocent they can use as a bargaining chip to get those prisoners released from jail."

Andrew turned to Khalid, barely polite. "Any idea what the Freedom Party's next move might be, Mr. Muhammad?"

Khalid pressed his hands to his head, his expression one of despair. "None. I keep telling you that I am not party to their plans. I am their victim, not their supporter. However, if I can help in any way, I will. I ask again that you arrange an interview for me with the Secretary of State. I'm willing to offer myself as a negotiator, or even as a hostage. Any information about the Freedom League that I have, I will share—''

Khalid broke off almost in midword. He looked past Andrew, his eyes wide and staring. He suddenly elbowed past them so that he was standing right in front of the silent TV screen, his gaze fixed on the image of a young man, clad in the traditional embroidered cap and robe of a Kashmiri Muslim. "Turn up the sound!" he commanded, his voice cracking with urgency. "For God's sake, do it now!"

Verity found the remote and clicked the sound back on. The voice of the CNN announcer returned to the room. "...seen in this rare 1997 photograph. Farooq Muhammad has been identified as the leader of the Kashmir Freedom Party, and a warrant for his arrest has been issued by the Indian Government. Farooq is considered fanatical in his beliefs, and highly dangerous. His current whereabouts are unknown, but according to a spokesman for the Indian government, he is responsible for the precision, speed and tight discipline demonstrated during the attack on American Consul George Douglass. In view of his family's extensive overseas contacts, there is a considerable risk that he has already escaped from Bombay and may be plotting further terrorist acts from the safety of a hideout in Pakistan, Afghanistan, or some European city with a large Muslim population. We have to take a short break now, but stay tuned to CNN for all the latest details concerning today's tragic attack on the American Consul General in Bombay, India...."

Khalid continued to stare blank-eyed at the TV screen, even when an advertisement for chicken noodle soup replaced the image of Farooq Muhammad.

Frustration about to boil over, Andrew Breitman interposed himself between the television and Khalid. "Okay, Mr. Muhammad, what gives now?" he demanded. "You obviously know this Farooq person. Who is he? Is he by any chance another one of your twenty-six first cousins?"

Khalid didn't answer. Verity wasn't sure that he'd heard the question.

"Mr. Muhammad, who is this Farooq Muhammad person?" Andrew persisted. "Why are you looking so—angry?"

Khalid remained silent. Feeling oddly as though she were betraying a friend, Verity answered Andrew's question. "Farooq Muhammad is Khalid's younger brother," she said.

Five

Andrew looked first at Khalid and then at Verity, astonishment and dismay mingled in his expression. His previous bluster had apparently been caused more by general frustration than any genuine suspicion that Khalid was actively involved in the terrorist projects of the Kashmir Freedom Party. Now his doubts were visibly mounting.

Perhaps because he had no idea what to say to Khalid, he turned to Verity. "Do you know Farooq personally?" he asked. "Did you have any idea that he was the *leader* of the Kashmir Freedom Party?

"Of course I didn't know Farooq was their leader," Verity said. "I didn't even know he was a member. I would have said something at once, if I'd known."

"But you do know him?" Andrew persisted.

"Sort of. I know both of Khalid's brothers. Ali is the youngest child in the family, and he's only seventeen or eighteen. Farooq is the middle brother, four years younger than Khalid and me. I only met him on one occasion after I left school, so we're not close in any way. My impression has always been that Farooq is bored by religion and much more interested in commerce than he is in politics. He was young the last time I met him, no more than twenty-two or three, but he'd been trained by his uncles since early childhood to take on the burden of running the family's business, and he obviously had a real flair for trade. So he stuck to negotiating international business deals, while Khalid was the one who took on the task of dealing with politics and diplomacy and making friends with foreigners in high places. Ali is supposedly the scholar, the one who's destined to go to MIT and make a name for himself as a research scientist.''

Andrew's brow furrowed into a frown. ''Well, either little brother Farooq has changed a lot since you knew him, or he was deliberately hiding his true beliefs.''

''Farooq was hiding nothing,'' Khalid said, sounding utterly drained. ''Verity's impression of my brother is accurate. He enjoys running the family business because it gives him an excuse to travel internationally, and he much prefers the comfort of life overseas to the hardship of life in Kashmir. As for being connected to a fanatical nationalist organization, it's laughable. He is so far removed from a fanatic belief in Islam that my uncle has been unable to arrange a suitable marriage for him. The families we approached were not willing to have their daughters married to a man who is totally indifferent to tradition and would like to make his permanent home in America.''

''So why has the Indian government accused him of being the leader of the Freedom Party?'' Andrew demanded.

''Who can say why the government of India chooses to persecute my family?'' Khalid sounded weary to the bone. ''Farooq has never expressed the slightest interest in politics, and he has never been the leader of the Kashmir Freedom Party. I have no idea why he has been accused of murdering Mr. Douglass, but I can assure you those accusations are false. All of them. The enemies of my family are drawing a noose around us, attempting to ensure that the voice of moderation in Kashmir is silenced forever.''

''Your brother's marital state doesn't seem to me to

be proof of anything except that he's chosen to remain single." Andrew didn't attempt to conceal his scepticism. "How can you be sure that Farooq isn't the leader of the Kashmir Freedom Party, Mr. Muhammad? Isn't it a secret organization, with the members' identities closely guarded?"

"Well, yes, but Farooq is my brother. I know him well—"

"You said that the commander of the men who kidnapped you never spoke. Could he have remained silent because he knew you would recognize his voice? That you couldn't fail to recognize his voice?"

"My brother was not responsible for my kidnapping," Khalid said flatly. "Nor did he threaten my family in Germany, I will swear that on my life. On the lives of my two sons. Family loyalty is everything in Kashmir."

"Indeed," Andrew said, with heavy emphasis. "Family loyalty is everything in Kashmir. Is that what you're demonstrating right now, Mr. Muhammad—family loyalty?"

Khalid rubbed his eyes. "As you must know, Mr. Breitman, I meant that my brother would never threaten me. I did not mean that I would conceal Farooq's complicity in a plot to murder my sons."

"Since you're so convinced of Farooq's innocence, perhaps you could encourage him to come forward and speak to the authorities?" Andrew suggested. "Do you know where your brother is at this moment, Mr. Muhammad?"

Khalid's hesitation was so slight, Verity wondered if she'd imagined it. "No," he said. "I have no idea where Farooq is. He is unmarried, and normally resides in the house that was once my father's, along with my great-uncle, my mother and my one remaining unmarried sister. If the report from CNN is accurate, however, I have to assume he is not currently residing with my great-uncle. I can only pray that no harm has come to him at the hands of our enemies."

Andrew frowned. "Frankly, Mr. Muhammad, your brother's suspected involvement with the Kashmir Freedom Party sheds a harsh light on everything you've told us so far. The more adamant you become in defense of him, the more difficult it becomes to avoid wondering if your own sympathies have changed over the years. Or even to wonder if you might yourself be a member of the Freedom Party."

"I am quite sure, Mr. Breitman, that you have just expressed exactly the view that the true leaders of the Kashmir Freedom Party wish you to hold." Khalid's voice was bitter. "But you would be wise not to be deceived by the tricks of my enemies. However powerful the circumstantial evidence against me, your government should believe me when I say that I am not now, and have never been, a member of any organization that advocates a violent solution to Kashmir's troubles. I want with all my heart to prevent bloodshed in my native land. I pray, even as we speak, that the death of George Douglass will not be a prelude to more violence. Peace and freedom are the goals for which I have worked my entire adult life."

"Right. I hear you and I'll take your statements under advisement, Mr. Muhammad." Andrew was barely keeping up the pretense of neutrality, and Verity couldn't blame him. She'd known Khalid for twenty-five years, and even she felt twinges of doubt. In the crucible of Kashmiri politics, how could she be sure that Khalid hadn't cracked, and reformed himself in an entirely different mold from the one she thought she knew?

Andrew pointed to the table. "If you'd come and sit down, Mr. Muhammad, I'd like to go over your story once again. Maybe you'll find yourself remembering a few important details that you'd previously overlooked."

"Perhaps," Khalid said tiredly. He followed Andrew to the table, and as he passed by Verity, he stumbled. "I'm sorry," he murmured, hastily distancing himself and offering her an apologetic bow. All forms of physical contact between unrelated men and women were considered shocking in Kashmir. "I must be even more fatigued than I realized."

"It's been a hard day for all of us," Verity said. And it was barely afternoon. She waited for Andrew to turn his back, then quickly tucked the scrap of paper Khalid had passed to her in the sleeve of her sweater. Heart thumping, she walked over to the table and poured herself another glass of juice, her mind whirling as Andrew led Khalid through his story again, this time drawing out dozens of details that had previously been skipped over. Where and how he'd obtained his fake travel documents. The names of the hotels where he'd stayed in Cairo and in Frankfurt. The clothing worn by the gunmen who'd held his wife and sons hostage. The way the gunmen smelled, the accent they'd spoken with, what they'd used to mask their faces. Khalid provided the details willingly. Unfortunately, all three of them knew that his apparent willingness to cooperate proved nothing at all about his sincerity, much less the accuracy of his information.

Somehow Verity managed to wait for a full fifteen minutes of a mind-numbing question-and-answer session before quietly getting up from the table and murmuring an excuse about finding the bathroom. Andrew was keenly observant, and she wanted to avoid even the remote chance that he would put together Khalid's stumble and her retreat to the bathroom.

Once behind the locked door, she opened Khalid's note. Written in Kashmiri, and presumably prepared in advance of her arrival, the message was brief and to the point.

"I must speak to you alone. As soon as you can find an opportunity, ask to see my wife. Pretend that you and she are old acquaintances. My wife's name is Miryam. My sons are Abdul, the elder, and Saiyad, the younger. Destroy this note."

What could Khalid possibly need to say to her that was so secret he wanted to be sure nobody else could hear? Anyway, given that Andrew and Dick didn't speak Kashmiri, he could say anything he pleased, secure in the knowledge that nobody else would understand. So why had he gone to such lengths to arrange a method whereby he could speak with her alone? What could be so sensitive that he was afraid to reveal it in the presence of others, even in a language they didn't comprehend?

Verity read the note three times, although its content was simple enough to be understood at a glance. Finally, fingers shaking, she tore the slip of paper into a dozen pieces and flushed them down the toilet. Simply by virtue of destroying the note instead of showing it to her superiors, she had already contravened regulations and compromised her own position. Her intuition told her to trust Khalid, but her intuition might not be worth much these days. As an ex-drunk—a very recently ex-drunk— how reliable was her judgment? Sound enough to risk her career over? To put people's lives at risk?

When she returned to the sitting room, Khalid sent her a questioning look and she answered with what she hoped was an almost invisible nod of her head. Khalid immediately pushed his chair back from the table, and stood up. Verity worried that Andrew would wonder why Khalid seemed suddenly refreshed and purposeful, when seconds before he'd been visibly weary.

It didn't help that Khalid used the excuse of being tired

to break off the interrogation, despite his newly energized appearance. "Mr. Breitman, I'm exhausted even if you are not. It's long past lunchtime and I am also hungry. I believe you and Verity must be, too, not to mention my wife and sons. It would be my pleasure to call room service and order us all some refreshments. The gentlemen from your Counter Terrorism Center will be here soon, and then the onslaught of questions will start again in earnest. Let us eat while we have the chance."

"I'd welcome a break," Verity said, trying to sound casual and failing hopelessly, at least to her own ears. "To be honest, Andrew, I'm starving."

"Then in that case, it's settled. I will call at once." Khalid walked over to one of the room's many phones.

"Let me make the call," Andrew said quickly.

"Of course." Khalid had already started to dial, but he hung up and stood aside, gesturing for Andrew to take his place. Then they all three exchanged strained smiles as they glossed over the uncomfortable truth that Andrew was making the call to room service because he didn't trust Khalid not to pass on some secret, coded message under the guise of ordering lunch.

"Would a fresh fruit platter and an assortment of cheese, muffins and crackers be acceptable?" Andrew asked, aware that Khalid would have religious dietary restrictions to observe.

Verity and Khalid nodded, and Andrew placed the order. "Since everything is cold, they think they can have the food up here in twenty minutes," Andrew said.

"Excellent," Khalid said. "If you will excuse me for a moment, I will let my wife know that lunch is finally on its way."

Verity spoke quickly, in English. "Khalid, it would be a great pleasure for me if I could chat with your wife for a few minutes. Miryam and I enjoyed such a pleasant afternoon together the last time I was in Kashmir. With your permission, I would like to renew our acquaintance. And some time I'd also like to say hello to Abdul and Saiyad, although I don't suppose they remember me.''

Khalid pretended to hesitate, then bowed graciously. ''But of course, Verity. I'm sure my wife will be delighted to speak with you. One minute, if you please, while I just let her know that she should prepare herself to receive a visitor.'' He walked quickly toward the bedroom and let himself inside, closing the door behind him.

''Good thinking, Verity.'' Andrew murmured approvingly. ''I didn't realize you'd been let into the privileged circle of people who've been introduced to Khalid's wife.''

''I'm a woman, which makes a big difference,'' Verity said, not exactly answering Andrew's question, and so not exactly lying.

''True. Anyway, I don't suppose Khalid's wife knows anything useful, even if he's neck-deep in terrorist activities. But since he's willing to allow you access to her, you can at least ask her a few questions and see if her story is the same as his.''

''Yes, that's exactly what I plan to do,'' Verity said, thinking how fortunate it was that Andrew couldn't see inside her mind. ''Although I'm sure Miryam won't speak in much more than monosyllables if Khalid stays in the room with us. I'll try to get rid of him, but I probably won't be able to.''

''Do your best, but don't sweat it.'' Andrew lowered his voice. ''There's no point in ruffling Khalid's feathers too much. We need to keep you in your role as friend, so that he feels as if there's someone in the U.S. government who's on his side.''

''Right.'' In the circumstances, Andrew's advice was ironic.

"As soon as the guys from CTC get here, they're going to take Khalid and his family into custody. CTC operatives don't work under the same diplomatic restraints that we do, so they'll just keep hammering Khalid with questions until they get the answers they need. As for his wife, she'll have to answer any and all questions, however much Khalid wants to keep her and his boys out of it."

Andrew had barely finished speaking when Khalid opened the bedroom door, permitting a brief glimpse of his wife, a plump woman wearing a colorful embroidered veil, seated on a chair next to the king-size bed. Her hands were clasped, and her gaze downcast, the picture of dutiful Islamic submission. Khalid's manner gave no clue as to whether he'd heard Andrew's final remark but it didn't much matter either way. He was smart enough to have figured out for himself that the power of the United States Government would soon descend upon him full force, and the illusion that he was at liberty to control who could speak to his wife would be shattered.

Khalid inclined his head toward Verity. "Miryam is very much looking forward to renewing her acquaintance with you. She sorely misses the companionship of her women friends. Do, please, come inside."

Verity entered the bedroom, delivering a deep bow of greeting to Miryam. Khalid's wife rose gracefully to her feet and returned the bow, clicking her wrists rapidly together three times so that the gold bangles she wore chimed prettily—a standard form of greeting among women in the eastern sections of Kashmir. Verity responded with an elaborately polite greeting in Kashmiri. Khalid left the door open just long enough to allow Andrew to observe this piece of pantomime, then he shut the bedroom door.

Once the door was closed he didn't waste any more

time in the pretense that Verity was there to converse with his wife. "I believe there is a micro recording device attached to Mr. Breitman's computer," he said, speaking in Kashmiri. "That is why I needed to go to such lengths to speak with you alone. I was afraid that if we spoke in his hearing, even in Kashmiri, he might later have our conversation translated, thus putting you at risk for not having reported what I tell you."

What in the world could Khalid need to say to her that was so sensitive, Verity wondered. And was he being neurotic to assume Andrew's laptop contained a recording device? Possibly not. It would make sense to have a word-for-word record of what had been discussed available for later analysis, and Dick Pedro was a stickler for covering his bureaucratic ass in any and every way possible.

She scanned the room, suddenly nervous. She was breaking so many rules in speaking to Khalid like this that she couldn't afford to be recorded any more than he could. "How can you be sure this bedroom isn't bugged?" she asked.

"Because I had the men from Capital Security sweep it thoroughly as soon as we arrived," Khalid said dryly. "Once they pronounced it clean, I've kept it permanently guarded. Why else do you suppose that my wife has never left this room and we have denied access to both Mr. Pedro and Mr. Breitman?"

"I assumed it was because you prefer to keep politics and family life separate."

"Which is what you were supposed to assume," he said grimly. "In fact, my seemingly stubborn adherence to the traditions of Islam also provides me with one small space where I can talk freely, secure in the knowledge that my words are not being recorded."

Verity was sad to think what life in Kashmir must be

like these days that Khalid would go to such apparently paranoid lengths to preserve his ability to hold a private conversation. "What do you need to tell me, Khalid? If room service is as prompt as they promise, we have only a few minutes."

"You're right, and I'll try to be brief. First, let me reassure you that everything you have heard me tell Mr. Pedro and Mr. Breitman is true. I am the same man you have always known, a passionate believer in the need for a negotiated settlement to the problems of Kashmir. Nothing has changed, and I am not suddenly the enemy of peace and reason. I was kidnapped and taken to the mountains, exactly as I described. In Germany, my sons were threatened, exactly as I described. However, I have not told your Mr. Pedro and Mr. Breitman the entire truth, and for an excellent reason. I cannot trust them."

Verity was puzzled. "I don't quite understand what you mean, Khalid. You don't trust them to be objective? You don't trust them to understand the complexities of the current situation? I can assure you that Dick Pedro has twenty years of solid diplomatic experience, and although Andrew Breitman doesn't have much firsthand experience of Kashmir, he's an expert on the politics of the region. He's had diplomatic postings to both Pakistan and Afghanistan, as well as a temporary assignment to Kazakhstan—"

"I have nothing specific against Mr. Pedro and Mr. Breitman on a personal or professional level," Khalid said. "They are probably the excellent, well-informed government servants that they appear."

"Then what's the problem? What do you mean by saying that you can't trust them?"

"I fear devastating betrayal if I give certain information to the wrong people. And almost anyone employed by your government might be the wrong person, including Mr. Pedro and Mr. Breitman.''

"Betrayal? I'm sorry, Khalid, I'm really having a hard time understanding what you're getting at.''

"Because I am avoiding coming to the point,'' Khalid admitted. He drew in a breath that was audibly shaky. "I have to inform you, Verity, that there is a traitor burrowed deep into the structure of your government and he is manipulating the turmoil in my native land for his own selfish purposes. An American has infiltrated the Kashmir Freedom Party and taken over the planning of their terrorist activities.''

"What?" Verity was not so much shocked as she was incensed. "Are you suggesting—you can't be suggesting—that an American government official knew the Freedom Party was going to assassinate George Douglass and that he did nothing?''

"No, I'm not *suggesting* that,'' Khalid said. "I'm asserting it. With conviction. A traitor buried within the bureaucracy of your government planned the assassination of George Douglass. I suspect that other and even more terrible plans are in the works.''

Verity shook her head. "Your claim is absurd. For one thing, you and I both know that fanatic Kashmiri Muslims wouldn't listen to an American—''

"I agree we would have every reason to think that, but we would have been wrong. It is a fact beyond dispute that an American is working hand-in-glove with the terrorists who are currently in control of the Kashmir Freedom Party.''

"On what precise grounds are you claiming that an American government official was involved in planning the murder of George Douglass?'' Verity asked, her voice cold with the effort of restraining her anger. "You'll need to produce some very convincing evidence if you expect me or anyone else to believe something so outrageous."

"I have convincing evidence, but I cannot produce it. Not here. Not now. The consequences of an incautious revelation could be devastating for my family." Khalid paced the room, followed by the worried gaze of his wife. She remained dutifully silent, but her silence was filled with a tension that matched her husband's.

"You have evidence that you can't produce?" Verity shook her head, her anger escalating. "You're an intelligent man, Khalid. You must understand a statement like that does nothing to persuade me to take your accusations seriously."

"I realize my story is not convincing...." Khalid sounded helpless, a state of being so uncharacteristic for him that Verity felt her first twinge of alarm. If he really believed what he was telling her, the implications were dire.

"I know that what I'm asking you to believe stretches the borders of credibility," Khalid spread his hands, palm upward. "I appeal to the bonds of our childhood friendship, and the fact that you have always known me to be an honest man. Therefore, I repeat the truth. The slaughter of Mr. Douglass was organized by an American. It's possible the traitor in question is with the CIA, but based on everything I know, I believe he's more likely to be with the State Department."

Verity pressed one hand to her forehead and the other to her stomach, not quite sure whether her queasiness was worse than her headache or vice versa. "Look, Khalid, I'm not naive enough to pretend that no State Department employee has ever turned traitor. Ditto for the CIA. But most of the traitors in our history have acted out of burning conviction that U.S. policy was misguided, or because they had strong family ties to another country. Why would any American risk his whole life—his career, his freedom, his friends, his family—for the sake of Kashmiri independence? Face it, we're not exactly talking a hot button issue here. I'm the only State Department officer who lived in Kashmir for any length of time as a child. Maybe there are a couple of CIA types floating around Langley with strong personal links to Kashmir, but if so, I've sure never met them. To be brutally frank, apart from me, nobody in the State Department has much of an emotional investment in the future of your country."

"I know." Khalid shot her a wry glance. "Believe me, Verity, were it not for the fact that I know this traitor to be a man, you would be the most obvious suspect and we would not be having this conversation. I would be too afraid to trust you."

"You would suspect *me* of betraying my country? Of masterminding the murder of George Douglass—my colleague?" Verity wondered if her eyes were truly flashing flames, or if it only felt that way. "Wait, let me make sure I've got this right. You're expecting me to risk my entire career because I'm supposed to have blind faith in your integrity. Presumably on the sentimental grounds that we stole almonds from the same tree in the school playground and both disliked mean old Miss Hickey when she was our third grade teacher. You, on the other hand, can suspect me of whatever you please. Childhood friendship be damned."

Khalid shrugged uneasily. "The stakes in offering each other our trust are hardly equal. For you, trusting my word might, at worst, prove to be a bad career move. For me, trusting you—and being betrayed—would put the lives of my entire family at risk."

"Okay, point taken. But that doesn't change the fact that you're making it awfully hard for me to help you."

Her voice deepened with frustration. "Give me some reason to believe you, Khalid. Some factual reason. Something beyond the fact that we liked each other when we were kids."

Khalid made a swift, chopping movement with his hand, as if dismissing her doubts. "You are well-informed about political factions in Kashmir, and your knowledge isn't merely theoretical. You've seen the reality on the ground. The Kashmiri prisoners are being held in Bombay precisely because it's so far away from Srinagar. Ask yourself if the Kashmir Freedom Party that you knew two years ago would have had either the financial resources or the organizational ability to threaten me and my family in Frankfurt, Germany. Much less bring off a successful terrorist attack in Bombay, almost fifteen hundred miles from their home base."

"It seems unlikely, given what we knew about the Freedom Party in the past," Verity conceded, deciding not to point out that she had only Khalid's word that the incident in Germany had occurred. "However, my opinion about their capabilities isn't a fact, merely a surmise, based on outdated information. Organizations change. New leaders arrive on the scene—"

"Indeed, you are correct. New leaders arrive on the scene. And the new leader who has taken over the Kashmir Freedom Party is an American. Until four or five years ago, the Kashmir Freedom Party was made up of hotheaded young idealists with little money and scarcely sufficient discipline to arrange for the explosion of firecrackers outside a police station in Srinagar. There is zero possibility that, by themselves, they could have organized the assassination of the American Consul General in Bombay. However, in the past two or three years, the Freedom Party has received generous infusions of cash that have, in turn, bought weapons, warm clothing, better food and legions of new recruits. The money that made today's tragedies possible came from an American source.''

"Or perhaps we should look to Osama bin Laden or some other Muslim fanatic with too much money and too few scruples," Verity suggested. "The fact that the Kashmir Freedom Party suddenly has more money and can afford to be more efficient proves nothing at all about American involvement in its activities. It proves only that someone has provided strong leadership and financial backing. Try to look at this from my point of view, Khalid. Is it more likely that the leader of a group of Kashmiri insurgents is an American—or that the leader is your brother? Who is, forgive me, a member of virtually the only family left in Kashmir with the wealth to provide significant financial support to a rebel movement.''

Miryam smothered a gasp and Khalid visibly bit back an angry retort. "I requested your presence here today because we are old friends. And I believed good friends—''

"But I'm not here right now solely as your friend, and you know it." Verity steeled herself not to give ground. "I'm a diplomat, albeit a junior one, and I'm here as a representative of the United States government. And here's something else you already know. It's my duty to report everything you've just told me to my superiors.''

"I beg you not to do so, Verity.''

She was irritated by his repeated attempts to milk old loyalties. "Don't beg, Khalid. That's appealing to our friendship again. We're two professionals, and I need concrete facts. Give me something to work with, not a personal plea.''

"I cannot. Not here. Not now.''

"You're an old hand at international negotiations,

Khalid, and you understand the rules. Why did you pass me that note if you're not willing to give me any hard information? We're not in school anymore, trying to escape the beady eye of our teacher. We're grown-ups, facing adult problems.''

He didn't reply, just turned to look at his wife. Verity followed his gaze and saw that tears ran silently down Miryam's cheeks. With a sudden flash of unwelcome enlightenment, Verity wondered why it had taken her so long to grasp the simple fact that Khalid expected to die in the near future and was desperately trying to find out if she was willing to bend the rules on his behalf.

Verity turned away from the sight of Miryam's distress, wondering if she was being gullible to fall into the trap of believing that because Khalid expected to die, then he must be telling the truth. Fear of death didn't preclude the possibility of lying. On the contrary. There were innumerable instances of murderers and other criminals who lied right up to the moment of their execution. Not to mention the deathbed attempts to enhance their reputations pursued by every stripe and variety of ordinary human beings.

Verity felt panic claw at her insides. Dammit, this was exactly why she'd warned Dick Pedro that she wasn't ready to come back to work. Wading through this type of ethical and intellectual quagmire was too much of a responsibility. Especially since Khalid seemed determined to tug at her heartstrings instead of appealing to her intellect. Her heartstrings were frayed, and it was all too easy to tweak them.

She didn't want to be here. She wanted to go home and look at her photos of Sam. She wanted to curl up in Sam's big old chair and watch TV, letting Regis Philbin soothe her into sleep with his promise to make her into a vicarious millionaire. Most of all, she wanted a drink.

A long, cold vodka on the rocks that would blunt the
hard edge of her fear of screwing up.

In what must have been a very bold act for her, Miryam broke the silence, addressing Verity for the first
time. "You have shared friendship with my husband for
many years, so you must know in your heart that he is a
good and honest man," she said. "Please help us, Miss
Marlowe. You are our only hope."

"I will do my very best, Mrs. Muhammad." Verity
knew her courteous but noncommittal response was a
cop-out, but there was nothing more she could promise,
however sorry she felt for Miryam. Then, with an effort
that left her head throbbing, she dragged her attention
away from her own feelings of inadequacy and focused
it back on the discussion.

"Khalid, we're getting nowhere. So far, all you've
done is spin a cobweb of suspicion that's too fragile to
bear any weight. You've flung out a startling accusation,
but you've told me nothing—*nothing*—that would be
genuinely helpful in bringing a possible American traitor
to justice."

Khalid didn't respond at once. Instead he took a corner
of his wife's veil and gently wiped the tears away from
her cheeks. He finally turned back and looked straight at
Verity. "If I tell you that my brother was not in India
when the attack on Mr. Douglass occurred, would you be
more inclined to believe that I have access to some very
important information?"

"Yes, I would. But it wouldn't convince me of Farooq's innocence. This is the age of computers and cell
phones and satellite links. He didn't need to be in India
to have masterminded the attack on George Douglass."

Khalid's wife made a low murmur of protest and he
abruptly walked over to the drape-covered windows, his
back turned to Verity's searching gaze. "What if I told

you that I know where Farooq is hiding, and that he has information that will lead you to the traitor operating within your government.''

''Then I would say that you need to give me the information so that we can notify the FBI. We can then make arrangements for Farooq to be interviewed, and his innocence established.''

Khalid gave an angry laugh. ''Do you hear yourself, Verity? Do you realize the nonsense you're spouting? Within minutes of the FBI being informed of my brother's whereabouts, the orders for his assassination will go out.''

The muffled sounds of one of the guards entering the main living room to announce the arrival of their lunch couldn't have come at a less opportune moment.

Verity spoke quickly. ''Dammit, Khalid, we're out of time and you need to quit beating around the bush. You must have some sort of a plan or you wouldn't have insisted on having me brought here. Tell me what your plan is.''

Khalid looked at her with a fierceness that was searing in its intensity. ''If you reveal nothing—*nothing*—of what we have just discussed, then I will arrange a private meeting with you later on tonight. I will come to your house.''

''Khalid, you know that might not be possible. Once the FBI takes you into custody, you won't be free to move around at your whim—''

''Then I'll insist on having you brought to me. First, though, I have to know if I can trust you not to reveal what we've just discussed. This is a test, Verity. For the sake of my brother…no, for the sake of preventing tragedies far worse than the murder of Mr. Douglass—don't fail the test.''

A brisk knock on their bedroom door was followed by

the sound of Andrew's voice letting them know that lunch had arrived. Khalid threw open the door, not allowing Verity the chance to say another word. With a strength of will she would have found admirable in other circumstances, he somehow managed to greet Andrew with a cheerful smile and a casual remark about being hungry as a mountain lion in midwinter.

Obviously anxious to hide her distress from prying eyes, Miryam slipped away into the bathroom. Khalid avoided continuing the discussion with Verity by dint of crossing to the other bedroom and urging his sons and the two bodyguards to help themselves to some food. Forced to leave the privacy of the master bedroom, Verity didn't dare to risk speaking to Khalid, not even in Kashmiri, for fear that he was right and the State Department had equipped Andrew's laptop with a built-in recording device.

Khalid, she realized, had placed her in an effective and constraining box. Suppose she told Andrew that Khalid knew where his brother was hiding, what would happen? She was quite sure Khalid would deny every word. He would pretend that she'd misunderstood, and flat-out refuse to tell them anything more, thus blowing the one good lead they might have to find the people who'd killed George Douglass.

On the other hand, if she didn't reveal what they'd talked about, she was not only risking her career, she was taking a huge chance that Khalid was playing her for a sucker, and deliberately exploiting their past friendship in order to misdirect the efforts of the American government. It wouldn't be surprising if he'd lost patience with the thankless task of negotiating a settlement to Kashmir's half century of civil war.

Maybe Khalid had finally grown sick of having his country's future kicked around between India and Pakistan like some sort of nuclear football. Verity found it hard to imagine him throwing in his lot with the Kashmiri freedom fighters, but not impossible. Years and years of frustrated hopes could change the character of even a moderate, peaceful man. And if Khalid had joined up with a bunch of terrorists, everything he'd just told her could be a ploy to distract her attention from...

From what? If Khalid was lying, what could his purpose be? To protect his brother? The cycle of question and answer, doubt and trust, spun faster and faster until Verity felt light-headed from stress and worry. For the first time in a couple of days, her longing for a drink wasn't going away. It was sitting front and center of her consciousness, a craving that seemed to become more powerful by the moment.

Everyone except her was busy eating, but the thought of sitting down at the table made her stomach roil. She escaped to the bathroom and splashed her face with cold water, wondering what excuse she could make to slip downstairs and grab a quick drink at the bar. God, she wanted a drink! She could pretend she needed to purchase some unspecified feminine product from the hotel gift shop, and the vaguer she was about what she needed, the less likely it would be for a roomful of men to pry. She was just about to leave the bathroom to execute this plan, when Sam's voice spoke with perfect clarity into her left ear.

Come on, Veri love, get with the program. You don't really want to start that whole stupid drinking cycle all over again. Why are you stressing? You're plenty smart enough to figure out whether or not Khalid is lying and what you should tell old Dick the Prick. Stop obsessing and trust your instincts. You have great instincts, you know.

Verity clutched the edge of the sink and glanced

quickly into the gilded mirror, immeasurably relieved to discover that pieces of Sam's torso weren't hovering behind her. Just in case, since ghosts might be like vampires and not have a reflection, she sneaked a peak over her shoulder. Still no sign of Sam, thank goodness. But the auditory hallucination was bad enough. Good grief! As if there wasn't enough to worry about, now she had to cope with her whacky subconscious conjuring up another ghostly visitation from her dead husband.

Verity walked back into the living room, rubbing her forehead.

"Sam, I love you a lot but go away," she muttered, sure no one could hear her over the water running in the sink.

You were calling out to me.

"Of course I wasn't. And if I was, my subconscious clearly needs to get a life—"

Use some tact, Veri love. Life could be considered a touchy subject for a ghost.

"Don't make bad jokes, Sam. I can't deal with you and Khalid at the same time as it is."

Then shape up and I'll go away. There's a lot at stake here.

"You think I don't know that already?" she whispered in a parting shot as she returned to the living room.

Verity's queasiness was getting worse, and the smell of sliced apples and oranges on the tray of refreshments didn't help. She wanted a drink. Dammit, she wanted a drink!

Eat something, sugar babe. Sam's voice was gentle. *You'll feel better if you do.*

Afraid that if she continued arguing with the disembodied voice inside her own head, a full-blown vision of Sam might materialize on top of the grand piano, Verity took a muffin and forced herself to eat the whole thing, washing it down with weak tea when she started to gag. Surprisingly, the hot drink and the food seemed to take the edge off her craving for alcohol, even if it didn't bring any miraculous resolution to the dilemma of what she should do about Khalid.

Score one for ghostly advice, she thought wryly.

Saved your cute ass this time, honey.

Verity refused to dignify that remark by continuing the dialogue, and she was feeling almost in control of herself again when the sound of masculine voices penetrated the suite from the outside hallway. Sipping a second cup of tea, she listened with half an ear to the bodyguards checking out the newcomers. The agents from the Counter Terrorism Center had apparently arrived.

Patrick opened the door to the suite and announced that the latest visitors were free of weapons. "These two gentlemen are Mr. Green from the FBI and Mr. Brown, who is on temporary loan to the Counter Terrorism Center. They've shown me their IDs." He didn't bother to hide the irony in his voice. Patrick was ex-Secret Service, and he could recognize a pair of spooks using false names when he saw them. "They say that you're expecting them, Mr. Muhammad."

"Yes, we are," Khalid said. "Please ask the gentlemen to enter, Patrick."

Patrick returned to his post and Mr. Green and Mr. Brown entered the suite in single file.

"We're real glad to have you onboard," Andrew said, walking toward the door, hand outstretched. "We sure could use some of your expertise in coming up with ways to prevent another tragedy."

As the men came farther into the room, Verity half rose from her chair and then sank back down again, staring at the newcomers in silent, openmouthed astonishment.

The two agents wore conservative gray suits, white starched shirts, and neatly striped ties. One of them was gray-haired, blue-eyed and totally unknown to her. The other one was black-haired, brown-eyed and she knew him well. Far too well.

He was Michael Strait.

Six

She couldn't tell if Michael had been warned to expect her presence, or if he was as astonished as she was. His expression, set into its usual mode of maximum inscrutability, betrayed no hint of what he might be thinking or feeling. If anything. As for what she was feeling, Verity could only manage to disentangle anger and surprise from the knotted skein of her emotions.

The gray-haired man stepped forward, holding out an FBI badge. He looked disconcertingly like a taller version of Tommy Lee Jones playing a U.S. Marshal in *The Fugitive*.

"I'm Norman Green," he said, shaking Andrew's hand. "I work on permanent assignment to the Counter Terrorism Center. This is my colleague, Michael Brown, who is on temporary loan to the center." He flashed a bland smile, not identifying Michael's permanent job or government department. "Michael is very familiar with Kashmir and its problems."

Andrew smiled a greeting at both men. "Good to meet you, Norman. Michael. I'm Andrew Breitman, desk officer in charge of southeast Asia at the State Department. And this is Verity Marlowe, our in-house expert on Kashmir." He waved her forward.

Heart thumping, Verity shook hands with the FBI agent and nodded in curt acknowledgment to Michael. She then withdrew to the far side of the room, watching in silence as Andrew introduced the two CTC agents to Khalid.

Her head thrummed, struggling to assimilate the unbelievable. *Michael Strait worked for the Counter Terrorism Center. He was almost certainly with the CIA.* It was going to take a while to wrap her mind around those astonishing pieces of information. From the moment they met, he'd deceived her and Sam about his profession, pretending to be a business entrepreneur with no interest in politics.

His deception gave her a sense of betrayal that she recognized as unjustified, since she knew he couldn't have told them the truth however much he might have wanted to. Deep cover agents wouldn't survive for long if they rushed around announcing their true occupation to all their friends. Still, she felt an odd mixture of hurt and righteous indignation as she watched him talk to Khalid. In English, she noted. Probably because he didn't want anyone to realize that he spoke perfectly good Kashmiri.

Michael looked different today, she thought, and not just because he was clean-shaven and wearing a conservative suit with a sober striped tie. There was a subtle aura of power about him that she'd never noticed before. Or perhaps she *had* noticed it at some fundamental, gut level. Maybe that was one of the many reasons why she'd always felt uneasy in Michael's company. She'd sensed that he wasn't being honest either with her or with Sam and she'd resented a masquerade that her conscious mind hadn't even recognized.

Michael's claim to have been out of touch for months in the back country of Kashmir during the period of Sam's illness became easier to understand now that she knew his true occupation. If she'd been using even half her brain the evening he came to her house, Verity reflected, she'd have realized that no business entrepreneur could afford to take six whole months to organize a supply source for raw cashmere, even if he had just built a new factory. Presumably he'd been attempting to infiltrate some radical Kashmiri political group on behalf of the Agency and hadn't been able to break his cover....

Verity's thoughts skittered to a halt, then started up again more slowly. What if Michael's assignment in Kashmir had been to infiltrate the Freedom Party on behalf of the Agency? And what if he'd become so caught up in the group's activities that he'd decided to take over the leadership and subvert the group to his own ends? Agents working under deep cover were always at risk for going rogue, so she wasn't entirely out of line to wonder if Michael could be Khalid's American traitor. As a CIA operative whose mother was a member of one of the most prominent families in Kashmir, Michael fit Khalid's profile to perfection.

Verity had barely reached that conclusion before she doubted it. It was true that Michael had strong personal links to Kashmir, but his mother's family was Hindu, and all the members of the Kashmir Freedom Party were devout Muslims. Unlike America, where the public school system and a fluid workplace brought people of diverse faiths together, different religious groups in Kashmir led totally separate lives. They wore different clothes, attended different schools, pursued different trades according to their ethnic group, and sometimes spoke different languages. Justice was often administered in separate religious courts.

Given all that, Michael would have an impossible time convincing a group of devout Muslim fanatics to trust him, unless he pretended to be a Muslim himself. Would he be able to pull off such a trick? Debatable, Verity decided. His hair was already black, and he could stain his skin a darker shade to wipe out visible signs of his father's Scandinavian ancestry, but physical appearance would be the least of his problems. Before admitting Michael to any of their secret conclaves, Freedom Party members would demand to know who his parents were. Whatever answer he gave, Michael would be in trouble. Family genealogies were maintained in compulsive detail, and he would be running a huge risk that somebody's cousin or nephew or brother-in-law would step forward and announce that Michael didn't belong to the family he claimed. And the punishment for being declared an imposter wouldn't be polite rejection of his application for membership. His punishment would be certain, painful death.

If all this wasn't argument enough against Michael's infiltration of the Freedom Party, why would he even *want* to join a struggle that was essentially against the interests of everything his mother's people stood for?

Then Verity remembered. Michael's mother had been disowned by her high-caste Brahmin family when she married an American. Since his maternal grandparents refused to acknowledge his existence, Michael had never even met them. On the one occasion that he and Verity had spent time together in Kashmir, he'd mentioned how much his mother regretted the estrangement and how deeply she missed her extended family. It was one of the sorrows of her life that her children were denied access to half their heritage.

Given those circumstances, was it too much of a stretch to wonder if Michael had joined forces with a group of Muslim insurgents as punishment to the powerful Hindu family that had rejected him and his mother?

It was her peripheral awareness of Michael placing a phone call that nudged Verity back into full consciousness of her surroundings. He was calling someone at the

State Department, using a portable scrambling device to secure the hotel phone line. He was saying that, in his opinion, it was vital for Khalid Muhammad to be granted an interview with the Secretary of State as soon as possible. The director of the CIA and senior military personnel should be present at the meeting. He requested a response within the next thirty minutes. Apparently he was senior enough that he had a realistic expectation of getting an answer within such a short time frame.

Michael ended the phone call with a brief word of thanks. He glanced up, catching Verity off guard, and she wasn't able to look away quite swiftly enough. Their eyes met and she thought she saw a hint of apology in his gaze. Was he letting her know he regretted the past three years of lies? He'd always had an infuriating ability to read her deepest emotions, so he probably understood that she felt irrationally betrayed by his deception.

Verity didn't know how to respond—wasn't even sure if she was imagining Michael's apology—so she turned away, focusing on Norman Green, who was replying to some question Andrew must have asked.

"Yes, that's all under control. We'd already made arrangements to take Mr. Muhammad into protective custody before we left the Center," Norman was saying. "A comfortable house has been set up for him and his family, and transportation is on its way. We think it's important to get Mr. Muhammad to safety as soon as possible—"

"I thank you for your generous offer of government protection," Khalid said coolly, as if the FBI agent's remarks had been addressed to him rather than Andrew. "As it happens, I prefer to remain here in this hotel."

Norman shook his head. "I'm sorry, Mr. Muhammad, but the security risks at this hotel are unacceptable—"

"It is good to know that we share the same goal of keeping me alive," Khalid said dryly. "But incarceration in a government safe house doesn't seem the best way to achieve our mutual goal of my survival. My family's safety at this moment is assured by bodyguards who come from the most respected security firm in the United States. Unfortunately, I have no great faith in the ability of your government to protect me and my family. We have all seen what happened to Mr. George Douglass, and that tragedy occurred when American personnel in India were on high-security alert. I have no desire to meet the same end as Mr. Douglass.''

Michael crossed to the center of the room. He spoke quietly, but with absolute finality. ''I regret that we can't offer you a choice in this matter, Mr. Muhammad. You'll be safe in our hands, I personally guarantee it.''

''But I do not know you, Mr. Brown.'' Khalid put deliberate emphasis on the patently fake name. ''Therefore your personal guarantee means little to me. By contrast, I have selected my bodyguards with great care and have absolute trust in their professional abilities.''

Michael shook his head. ''Your bodyguards may provide you with the illusion of safety, Mr. Muhammad. But it *is* merely an illusion.''

''Why do you say that?'' Khalid frowned. ''They have protected me very well so far.''

''Not really.'' Michael reached into an interior pocket of his jacket and drew out a 9mm Sig, tossing it from one hand to the other, before aiming it at Khalid's heart. ''When the guards outside your hotel room checked us for concealed weapons, Agent Green and I performed a simple trick and passed this off between us. Very little sleight of hand was required, despite the fact that your guards carried out a full body search. Fortunately for you, Agent Green and I don't plan to use this gun to harm you or your family. But if we can get past your guards with a weapon this deadly, think how much easier it would be for trained assassins to do so. Especially since they're likely to arrive with submachine guns and simply blow away anybody who happens to stand in their path.''

The color drained from Khalid's cheeks and it was a moment before he replied. ''A vivid demonstration, Mr. Brown. Nevertheless, despite the risks you have just exposed, I choose to remain here. And that is surely my right.''

Michael returned the gun to his jacket pocket. ''Regrettably, Mr. Muhammad, it isn't your right. We have the authority to arrest you if we must. Either way, you, your wife, and your sons will be taken into protective custody.''

''You would most likely prefer to pack your suitcases yourself,'' Norman Green said, as if the matter of the family's removal were already settled to everyone's complete satisfaction. ''We'll have them brought to the safe house before the end of the day. Maybe you'd like to inform your wife that you're all being moved to Virginia? It would be most helpful if she would get started on the packing. As you can imagine, time is of the essence here.''

Khalid was at least four inches shorter than any other man in the room. Verity admired the dignity of his bearing as he drew himself to his full height. ''I suppose it would be useless to demand that you tell me by what authority you override my wishes? This is supposedly a free country, a bastion of individual human rights held up as a shining example to countries like mine. What crime am I accused of committing that allows you to imprison me against my will?''

Michael's gaze remained steady. ''At this moment, Mr. Muhammad, you are accused of no crime, nor are you going to prison. The United States government is merely acting to protect the safety of you and your family.''

"Of course," Khalid said with rich irony. "How could I possibly have misinterpreted your actions?" He turned away, catching Verity's eye, and she saw the desperate plea he was sending her.

She'd already broken half the rules in the book, so she might as well add the other half, Verity decided resignedly.

"Mr. Green," she said, careful to address her request to the FBI agent and not to Michael. Unless you counted one ambiguous exchange of glances, both she and Michael seemed to be avoiding direct communication of any sort. "You probably haven't been informed that Khalid Muhammad and I are old friends from way back. Perhaps I could help his wife with their packing? I'd like to offer Mrs. Muhammad some reassurance, since I speak her language and she doesn't speak English."

Norman Green glanced at Michael, who nodded almost imperceptibly.

"Yes, that might be a good idea," Norman Green said. "Go ahead, Ms. Marlowe."

The FBI agent's glance had been very revealing, Verity thought. He'd been asking permission from Michael, confirming her conclusion that Michael was the senior-ranking official, even though Agent Green had appeared to take the lead when they first entered the room.

She followed Khalid into the master bedroom and waited while he explained to his wife that the Americans thought they would be more easily guarded if they moved to a special government safe house. Miryam was distraught at the prospect of moving out of the hotel and burst into tears. Khalid calmed her by lying. This move was his idea, he said, and he had total faith in the highly trained agents who would be guarding them. Nothing could keep their sons more secure than a government safe house, guarded by Secret Service officers.

Khalid's lies did the trick, since Miryam didn't seem to consider the possibility that her husband might deliberately mislead her. Drying her tears, she put a suitcase on the bed, then walked across to the dresser and started to pile brilliantly colored silk head shawls neatly inside it. The only question she asked was how long she had to complete the task of packing.

"If you have everything under control here, I will take Verity to the other bedroom so that she can help with the boys' packing," Khalid informed his wife. "Don't forget to pack my shirts separately in the small, brown suitcase. Please use care so that they do not become creased."

Miryam bowed, humbly acquiescent. Teeth clenched, Verity followed Khalid out of the master bedroom, reminding herself that she shouldn't impose Western ideals of marriage on a relationship that clearly worked well for both Khalid and Miryam.

Verity had assumed that Khalid was anxious to finish their earlier conversation, and that he'd suggested going to the other bedroom to pack the children's cases so that even his wife wouldn't hear what he had to say. But when they went into the second bedroom, he didn't attempt to give them privacy by closing the door. Instead, he chatted casually to his sons in Kashmiri, then switched back to English as he showed Verity the various drawers and closets that contained Abdul and Saiyad's clothes.

Like their mother, Khalid's sons seemed nervous at the prospect of moving yet again, but they didn't query their father's decision. Far from asking a lot of questions, or running around and getting underfoot like typical small boys, they silently tidied their Lego into its storage case and returned their crayons to a plastic container. Then they sat cross-legged on the floor, waiting for further instructions.

Their obedience struck Verity as unnatural. Little girls

in Kashmir tended to be passive and dutiful, trained from their earliest years to be servants to their much more important brothers. Boys, by contrast, grew up as lords of their universe, and it was unusual for the sons of a man as wealthy and important as Khalid to be so submissive.

Verity smiled encouragingly at the boys, and they returned her smile with tentative half grins, but they didn't budge from their cross-legged seat on the floor. "Your sons are very well behaved," she commented to Khalid, adding tiny shirts to a suitcase already half-full of underwear, pajamas and sweaters. She spoke in Kashmiri, so that the boys would hear her praise.

"Not usually." Khalid answered her in English, his voice and his expression equally grim. "This quietness is new for them."

"Perhaps they're feeling homesick. That wouldn't be surprising."

"No, that is not the problem, at least not the major one." Khalid sighed. "They disobeyed their mother and opened the door to our hotel room in Germany without requesting permission. They blame themselves for what happened next, and nothing I've said serves to convince them they are in no way responsible for the actions of the brutal criminals who attacked them. Sadly, they seem to believe that if they now follow my instructions to the letter, no more harm will befall us."

Since Khalid was speaking English, any of the men in the living room could probably overhear what he said. Nevertheless, Verity felt a rush of conviction that Khalid hadn't told the story for effect, but because it was the simple truth about what had happened to his family in Frankfurt. Abdul and Saiyad were definitely behaving like children who'd been traumatized, something she should have noticed a lot earlier. The way they clutched each other's hands and constantly looked around for reassurance that one of their parents was near suggested children who were suffering from something more than simple homesickness.

"Poor little guys," she said, sending them another smile and telling them in Kashmiri how good and helpful they were being. "I wish I could help you find a family counselor who speaks Kashmiri, but that might be too much to hope for, even in Washington, D.C."

"We'll just have to muddle through as best we can," Khalid said. He took half a dozen picture books from a bedside table and handed three to each of his sons. "Take these to your mother, please," he said, finally dropping back into Kashmiri. "Ask her to pack them with your other books."

"Yes, Daddy." The boys left and Khalid bent down to pick up a piece of Lego that had wedged itself under the door, closing it in the process.

The instant the door closed, Khalid was transformed from concerned parent to man of action. In a breach of Kashmiri custom and etiquette that left Verity immobilized with shock, he unbuttoned his shirt and pulled up his traditional silk undergarment, exposing an expanse of smooth, dark-brown skin, with a giant Band-Aid stuck on his right side.

"You have to help me," he said, ripping off the Band-Aid. An oddly shaped stainless steel key that had been taped against his body fell out. He caught it, and pressed it into Verity's hand.

The key was warm from contact with his skin. "Khalid, I can't accept this." Verity backed away, leaving her palm flat, denying possession. "What do you expect me to do with it?"

"I'll tell you later." He closed her fingers around the key with feverish urgency, fumbling to rebutton his shirt. "Keep the key safe, Verity."

"You know I have to turn this over to my superiors. I can't keep making private deals behind their backs." She turned away so that she wouldn't have to cope with the sight of Khalid stuffing his shirt back into his pants. With an American, she would scarcely have noticed the action. With Khalid, the intimacy was disturbing.

"If you tell anyone you have this, there will be an even worse tragedy than the assassination of George Douglass." Khalid's voice was harsh with desperation. "That key opens a safety deposit box that contains something of vital importance to the American traitor—"

"*What?* I thought you didn't know who he was?"

"I don't. I know only that he is in desperate need of the contents of that box."

"What are the contents?"

"I don't know—"

"Then why do you have the key?"

"Verity, there is no time for this discussion. Tell anyone that you possess it, and your life span will be measured in minutes. You must remain silent until I am able to make contact with my brother. You promised that you would help me. Keep your promise, I beg."

"You're asking too much, Khalid, and telling way too little. If you want my cooperation, at the very least you have to tell me where your brother is."

"I can't, not now." He tugged at his tie, adjusting the knot, then reached out, grasping Verity's upper arms. "Many lives are in your hands," he said. "Help me, Verity—"

He broke off as a cursory knock sounded on the door, followed almost immediately by Michael's entrance. Verity slipped her hand into the pocket of her pants and let the key drop through her fingers into the pocket. Khalid was a smart enough conspirator to keep his gaze fixed on her face, giving Michael no reason to pay attention to the tiny movement.

Michael's eyes flicked over the pair of them, the blandness of his expression in itself an accusation. "Did I interrupt something? I'm sorry."

"I was requesting Verity's assistance in contacting my family back in Kashmir." Khalid stepped away from Verity, dropping his hands. It was a good thing he answered Michael, since Verity was speechless. He gestured toward the bed. "As you see, we have almost finished packing my sons' suitcases."

"Good, although I'm afraid we'll have to leave the rest of the packing to your wife. My request has been granted, Mr. Muhammad. Dick Pedro has just called to say that the Secretary of State wants to meet with you right away. The director of the CIA will also be there, along with some senior personnel from the Joint Chiefs' office. We've promised to have you in the Secretary's office within forty minutes. We'll make arrangements to have you driven back here after the meeting so that you and your family can travel together to the safe house."

"Praised be Allah that the Secretary has agreed to meet with me," Khalid said, his face suffused with visible relief.

"Yes, but her schedule is really tight. We need to leave as soon as possible, Mr. Muhammad. Your Secret Service escort has already arrived."

"I must inform my wife that a meeting with the Secretary of State has finally been arranged," Khalid said. "I must also let my sons know that I'm leaving. You understand that the incident in Germany has left them anxious whenever I am gone."

He walked out into the main room and found his sons sitting quietly on the sofa, along with two newcomers, who were introduced as Glenn Zephyr and Charlie Berkower, the Secret Service agents sent to escort him to the State Department. Glenn and Charlie both looked gloomy enough to be chief mourners at a funeral, but since Verity had never met a cheerful Secret Service agent, she didn't make the mistake of assuming that there was anything specifically wrong.

Khalid greeted the agents politely, then bent to scoop up Abdul and Saiyad, holding one in each arm and hoisting them almost shoulder high. "I have to go and talk with an important lady in the American government," he said in Kashmiri. "I will be home soon, but you must be very good boys while I'm gone."

"I don't want you to leave us," Saiyad said.

"We want to come with you," his older brother agreed. "We want to see skyscrapers."

"Soon you shall, although there aren't too many skyscrapers in Washington. You'll have to wait until we can go to New York for that."

"Is Mickey Mouse in New York?" Saiyad asked.

Khalid smiled and hugged both boys before letting them slide to the ground. "No, he's in Florida, but we'll see Mickey Mouse, too, don't worry. I haven't forgotten that I promised you a trip to Disney World if you were good. And you have both been very good indeed." He held out his hands. "Come, let us go and tell your mother that I will be leaving you all for just a little while."

The boys each took one of his hands and Khalid went into the master bedroom, leaving the door slightly ajar. "I will be no more than two or three minutes," he said. "Trust me, I do not intend to keep Madam Secretary waiting."

Seven

Michael and Norman immediately began a low-voiced conference with the Secret Service agents about security arrangements for the safe house. Andrew shrugged into his overcoat, then zipped up the briefcase where he'd just stowed his laptop. It was a rare occurrence for a midlevel State Department employee to be summoned to a meeting with the Secretary of State, especially one where the director of the CIA and senior officers from the Joint Chiefs would also be present. Not surprisingly, Andrew looked eager to be on his way.

He helped Verity into her coat. "Dick wasn't sure if you and I would be needed at this meeting, but he's asked for us to go along so that we're available if necessary. I have my car parked downstairs in the hotel garage. Do you want to ride with me? The limo they've sent for Khalid is going to be pretty crowded, what with the CTC contingent, and the Secret Service guys as well as Khalid."

Verity smiled. "Thanks, that would be great."

"My pleasure." He gave her shoulder a quick squeeze. "It's good to have you back, Verity. I didn't realize how much I missed working with you until you were actually here on the spot. Your personal acquaintance with Khalid is invaluable in steering us through this mess."

Verity mumbled a disclaimer, feeling guilty. Andrew

was a friend as well as a colleague, and she disliked conspiring with Khalid to deceive him.

Fortunately, Andrew was too anxious to get to the meeting to notice her discomfort. He gave her a brief smile, already walking toward the door of the suite. "I'll go and hustle up the car. Sometimes that can take a while and we can't afford to keep the Secretary waiting."

Verity hooked her scarf around her neck, but paused in the act of pulling on her gloves. "Wait, Andrew. I'd better say goodbye to Mrs. Muhammad. It might look rude otherwise and we don't want to cause offense at this point."

"You're right, but we're already running late." Andrew frowned, glancing at his watch. "Why don't I go on ahead and get my car? You can meet me out front. I have to drive right past the main entrance, so that would probably be quicker than me hanging around here while you say your goodbyes to Mrs. Muhammad."

"That should work," Verity said. "I'll be out front in six or seven minutes. Two or three minutes to say goodbye, three or four minutes to catch the elevator down and walk out front."

"Should be perfect timing. Hopefully the parking valets won't all be on midafternoon break." Andrew nodded to Michael and Norman Green, and the two Secret Service agents. "Gentlemen, I'll see you at the State Department." He gave a mock salute to the bodyguards. "Shawn, Larry, take care. Nice to have met you guys."

Verity said a swift, formal goodbye to Miryam, who seemed torn between relief that her husband was about to meet with the Secretary of State and reluctance to be left alone in the hotel room with their two boys. With unexpected gentleness, Khalid reminded his wife that all four bodyguards would remain to guard the suite, so that she and the boys wouldn't be unprotected as they had been in Frankfurt.

Verity slipped away so that Khalid could offer Miryam a final few private words of reassurance. She knew that no Kashmiri husband and wife would embrace while a third party was in the room, whatever the circumstances.

Khalid reentered the living room hard on her heels, shrugging into his overcoat. He carried a slender, soft-sided leather briefcase, which he handed to the Secret Service agents without even being asked. "This contains documents I need for my meeting with the Secretary of State. You'll want to search it, I presume."

Verity glanced at her watch. "If you'll excuse me, Khalid, I need to get going. Most likely Andrew is already waiting for me downstairs."

"We can come with you," Khalid said, glancing toward Michael and Norman. "We're ready to leave, aren't we, gentlemen?"

"Not quite," Michael said. "We need to take another minute here, Mr. Muhammad. We still need to outline the precise security arrangements for getting you out of the hotel, and also the procedure once we get to the State Department. We don't want any surprises, however minor."

"We certainly don't," Khalid said.

Verity turned and bowed to Khalid, anxious not to keep Andrew waiting. "Andrew Breitman has offered to drive me in his car, so I'll see you at the State Department, Khalid. I'm really pleased you've been granted a meeting with the Secretary. I know it's what you wanted."

He returned her bow. "Yes, it is an almost immeasurable relief." He sent her a meaningful glance. "And thank you for your help today, Verity. It meant…it means…a great deal to me."

"It's been a pleasure." She would give Khalid back his all-important key after he had his meeting with the Secretary of State. At that point he would presumably agree there was no further need for subterfuge, since he would have told all his suspicions to the Secretary. Hopefully even Khalid wasn't neurotic enough to suspect Mrs. Albright of treacherously infiltrating the Kashmir Freedom Party and planning the assassination of George Douglass. Thank God the Secretary of State happened to be a woman, or Khalid might have harbored residual doubts and remained silent about the supposed American traitor.

Verity said a quick, general goodbye to the other men, avoiding eye contact with Michael. She waved to the bodyguards and left the suite, hurrying to catch the elevator. The lobby was crowded but she was energized by relief that Khalid was getting the chance to present his case in person to the Secretary of State. Her mood lightening, she dodged her way through the throng to the revolving glass entrance doors, emerging slightly breathless onto the red-carpeted sidewalk.

The outside air felt frigid after the pleasant warmth of the lobby. The wind had picked up with the approach of dusk, and the freezing drizzle of midmorning had returned. Verity shivered, tucking her hands under her arms. The only car waiting at the curb was a black limo with State Department license plates, obviously Khalid's transportation. The chauffeur—another Secret Service agent, complete with earpiece and the regulation gloomy expression—stood ramrod straight, muttering into his lapel mike and waiting for his passengers to arrive. Didn't those Secret Service guys ever unbend and crack a smile, Verity wondered. Maybe looking as if they had active hemorrhoids was a requirement for employment. Or maybe the bulletproof body armor they wore under their suits was as uncomfortable as it looked.

The hotel doorman darted out into the rain, blowing his whistle, and a cab screeched to a halt. The doorman opened the rear passenger door, smiling as he pocketed a tip from the woman getting in. The cab zoomed away, cutting off the driver of a sleek BMW. The BMW driver risked getting his arm wet in order to lean out and give the cabbie the finger.

There was still no sign of Andrew's car. Somewhat belatedly, Verity realized she should have asked him what he was driving these days. Did he own the same blue Chrysler Concorde that he'd been driving eight months ago, or had he traded it in for a new model? She'd taken a couple of minutes longer to arrive downstairs than she'd promised, which meant that either the parking valets were working slowly today, or some overzealous traffic cop had forced Andrew to drive on. In this rush-hour traffic, a circuit of the block could take ten minutes or more. Andrew was not going to be a happy camper if he'd been forced to circle the block. For all his easygoing outlook on life, he took his career seriously. He would want to be ready and waiting if Mrs. Albright happened to request his presence for any portion of the meeting with Khalid Muhammad.

Verity stepped off the curb to scan the passing traffic more closely, then hurriedly retreated beneath the shelter of the canopy when a van drove by, spraying her with freezing mud.

She was dabbing at the hem of her coat with a soggy tissue when Norman Green came out of the hotel, holding the heavy glass door open so that Khalid could walk straight through, surrounded by his escort. One Secret Service agent walked in front of Khalid, the other walked on his right side, and Michael brought up the rear. A smartly dressed woman followed Khalid out of the hotel, then elbowed her way in front of the group when Khalid paused to give Verity a friendly wave as he strode past. Somebody needed to give the woman a lesson in basic good manners, Verity reflected.

"Still waiting for Andrew?" Khalid called out to Verity, over the roar of traffic. He started to say something more, but the simultaneous honk of a car horn and a drumroll of what sounded exactly like the firing of an automatic rifle drowned out whatever he was trying to tell her.

Verity had no time to ask him to repeat the words she hadn't heard. She felt a foot hook around her ankles— Michael's foot, she realized—and then almost simultaneously she was shoved hard in the back. Caught off balance and too surprised to resist, she pitched forward, landing on the pavement with a force that jerked the breath from her lungs. The explosive noise of gunfire stopped, punctuated by a single, ominous shot.

For a moment the roar of traffic obliterated all other sounds. Then she heard Michael's voice. "Stay down," he ordered her, his hand resting heavily on the small of her back to emphasize his instruction. "Don't move. Christ, Verity, do you understand what I'm saying? I have to check out how much damage has been done, but you need to stay right where you are. Do—not—move, okay?"

Verity heard Michael's words, but her head was spinning and she couldn't make any sense out of them. Why had he tripped her? Two pratfalls on the same day was at least one too many, she thought dazedly. And this one had been a real humdinger. The sidewalk felt as if it had risen up and smacked into her body, squashing her lungs into her spine. Her hands were splayed out in front of her and she hurt just about everywhere. Hurt enough that it was hard to breathe and impossible to contemplate getting up. She lay on the damp sidewalk, eyes closed, mind fading to a blank.

She must have passed out for a few seconds. She didn't hear any footsteps, but she sensed Michael's return and felt him kneel down beside her. A splatter of red dropped from his arm onto her glove, but she ignored it, not ready to deal with its significance.

He spoke urgently, although his hand smoothed her hair from her face with unexpected tenderness. "Jesus, Verity, don't you dare die on me. Say something, for God's sake."

He sounded so frantic she wanted to answer him, but her throat was closed tight and she seemed to have forgotten how to form words. She felt his hands move swiftly over her body, pressing and stroking. Then his fingers brushed lightly across her face again before reaching inside the collar of her coat and coming to rest on the throbbing pulse of her carotid artery. The sensation of her blood beating against the tips of his fingers was oddly reassuring and she lay quiescent as a welcome warmth spread out from that tiny point of contact.

She felt strangely bereft when Michael removed his hand, tucking her scarf back around her throat. "Hang in there, Verity. You don't have any gunshot wounds that I can see. Your pulse is strong and you're doing great. Charlie's taking care of Khalid, so I have to go and check out Norman—"

"Don't leave me." In normal circumstances, she would never have let the plea escape her lips, but banging her head on the pavement seemed to have jolted her free of inhibitions that she'd held rigidly in place for more than a year. Ever since Kashmir.

Michael rested his hand very briefly against her cheek. "I must go and tend to Norman, but I'll be close by.

Don't move until we're sure there isn't another gunman in the area and that you didn't break any bones when you hit the ground, okay? Keep your head down, honey, and I'll be right back.''

Michael Strait telling her to stay down and not move should have been sufficient incentive to jerk her instantly upright. Calling her *honey* was cause for a full-scale frontal attack. Verity tried flexing her arms to see if getting up was a possibility, but her muscles remained stubbornly nonfunctional, so she had no choice but to obey. Anyway, right at this moment, pretending she didn't care about him seemed a really stupid waste of energy.

She lay with her cheek resting on the dirty carpeting for another thirty seconds or so, struggling to shape the scene in front of her eyes into something more meaningful than random patterns of light and shadow. That surprisingly difficult task accomplished, she lifted her head just enough to roll onto her side and suck in a few reviving gulps of fresh air.

As soon as she turned her head from left to right, she realized that Khalid was lying next to her, so close they were almost touching. His face was angled toward hers but his eyes were closed. On the far side of Khalid's body, Verity could make out the crumpled figure of a woman, also lying on the ground. One of the Secret Service agents—she'd forgotten his name—was winding a woolen scarf around the woman's upper arm, tying it into a sort of tourniquet.

Fear swept over her, but she fought against it, refusing to make a rational assessment of what she was seeing. Instead, she let the mists drift back into her mind, clouding reality. She watched with no more than abstract interest as an overweight general in full dress uniform ran back toward the hotel lobby. No, it wasn't a general, she corrected herself. The fancy cap and the uniform with all that gold braid belonged to the hotel doorman. And the doorman wasn't just running, he was also screaming at the top of his lungs. He was yelling for somebody to please sweet Jesus call an ambulance. Call the cops. Call the fucking cops. They're all dead, by God. Holy Mother of God, they're all dead.

Understanding finally washed over her, sending an icy chill deep into her bones. The scene around her sharpened into shocking clarity, like the blurred images of a horror movie where the camera angle suddenly tilts to reveal the truth.

Khalid's fears of assassination had been proven well-grounded. Horribly well-grounded. Khalid and his entire escort had obviously been shot at as they came out of the hotel. All of them had been wounded, several of them critically. She had survived relatively unscathed because she happened to be standing farthest away from Khalid when the shooting started. And also because Michael had thrown her to the ground at the very first shot, before the Secret Service agents even had a chance to pull their weapons and return fire.

With considerable effort, Verity pulled herself into a sitting position. Head swimming, rockets of fire exploding behind her eyeballs, she stretched out her arms, patting down her body. Her nose was bleeding, but there were no other sticky patches of blood. No limp, broken bones. No bullet holes. For a woman who'd been hoping for the end of the world only ten days earlier, she was amazingly relieved to find that her body was free of bullet holes. In fact, apart from gashes and scrapes, she seemed to be pretty much okay, provided she ignored what felt like someone using a hammer and chisel to excavate a tunnel inside her brain.

Fighting an acute desire to throw up, she leaned toward Khalid. "Are you all right?" she croaked. "Tell me where you're hurt, Khalid. Please speak to me. Let me help you."

Khalid didn't reply.

Verity's senses all began to work at once, adding smell, taste and touch where before there had been only sight and sound. She wiped grit from her mouth, and clenched her teeth against a wave of pain that swept over her body. What could she do to help the others?

One of the Secret Service agents—wasn't his name Charlie?—had already attempted some basic first aid on Khalid before turning his attention to the woman. The woman who'd pushed in front of Khalid and thereby earned herself an assassin's bullet as a reward for her bad manners. The punishment seemed excessive, Verity thought, fighting a wild desire to laugh. A case of cosmic justice operating at its most incomprehensible level.

There was a scarf tied around Khalid's thigh, and the expensive gray cashmere was already soaked with blood. In addition, there was an ominous patch of blood seeping out from the general region of his abdomen. Unfortunately, it looked as if it were going to take a hell of a lot more than a makeshift tourniquet to save Khalid's life.

She had barely formed the thought when she registered that Michael was speaking from somewhere behind her.

"We came under attack from an assassin armed with an M-16 semiautomatic. There was no warning and no time to return fire before Khalid Muhammad was hit. We need two ambulances and a fully equipped emergency medical team. We have five people down, all seriously injured, one of them probably a civilian bystander who happened to be in the wrong place at the wrong time. Plus one confirmed death, in addition to the shooter."

Michael paused for a moment. "No, the shooter turned the gun on himself before anyone could take out his weapon.'' He paused again. "Yes, I'm absolutely sure he's dead. He has no face left.''

No face left? Verity felt her grip on consciousness start to fade and she grabbed for it, focusing with ruthless determination. Her bruised flesh yelling in protest, she swiveled around so that she could see Michael as well as hear him.

He was squatting next to Norman Green who, in turn, was propped up against a giant concrete flowerpot. The flowerpot contained a small fir tree decorated with fairy lights. The lights sparkled in the gloom, casting a halo of light around Norman's blond hair. Norman's arms were crossed over his stomach, his face distorted by pain. He moaned softly, as if even that slight sound required more effort than he could give.

Michael had an arm around Norman's shoulders and, as Verity had surmised, he was talking into a cell phone. While she watched, Michael wedged the phone between his cheek and his shoulder, then stripped off his overcoat and put it over Norman. Michael's movements were stiff—clumsy—as if it hurt him to perform the simple task of removing his coat.

Michael had been shot, too, Verity realized, at least if the blood seeping through his jacket was anything to go by.

A low groan from behind caused her to twist back into her original position, bringing her once again face-to-face with Khalid. It was the unfortunate woman passerby who had groaned, though, not Khalid, or even the Secret Service agent who was spread-eagled on the ground at right angles to Khalid, his arms splayed in a position that was gruesomely reminiscent of the chalk outlines of murder victims drawn by law enforcement officials. The agent on the ground was called Glenn Something, Verity remembered. Glenn's body gave no twitches and no blood gushed from the wound in his head, an ominous sign that his heart had stopped functioning. Her stomach cramped painfully at the realization that the Secret Service agent— a young man who couldn't be much out of his twenties— was almost certainly dead.

As for Khalid, he still hadn't stirred. Not a promising sign, she thought, heart beating fast with fear. "Khalid," she said again, kneeling beside him. "Khalid, speak to me. Please answer me. I need to hear your voice."

Of course he didn't respond. How could he, when he was obviously wounded almost to the point of death. She lay down alongside him, feeling tears clogged at the back of her throat but unable to release them.

Andrew came running up and threw himself down beside her, pushing her hair out of her eyes to inspect her face. "My God, seeing you huddled on the ground there, I thought you were dead. You have a huge lump on your forehead and your nose is bleeding. Jesus Christ, Verity, what happened? My God...Khalid...Glenn...Charlie. Jesus, the blood. My God, what happened here?"

"I don't know. Somebody tried to kill Khalid."

"It looks like they succeeded," he said grimly. "And not just Khalid. My God." He looked dazed, as if he might pass out at any moment.

"Khalid's still breathing," Verity said. "And Charlie and Michael are okay."

Andrew glanced down at her coat, pushing the lapels aside to search for wounds. "Jesus, Verity, you're covered in blood—"

She looked down. "It's not mine. Maybe Khalid's... Maybe from my nose." She rubbed her forehead and found that she did, indeed, have a huge lump to go along with her bloody nose.

"Well, thank God you're okay at least." Andrew pulled out a cell phone from his pocket. "I'll call for an ambulance." He glanced around, mouth turning down. "Maybe two or three of them."

"Michael called already. The doorman, too." It was really hard to translate her muddled thoughts into words. "You were late, and I didn't know what car you were driving...."

"Same old Chrysler Concorde. The parking valet couldn't find the damn car and he wouldn't let me go look for myself. Damned idiot."

"That damned idiot probably saved your life," Verity said dryly.

Andrew paled as he realized the truth of her words. Then he drew in a deep breath, calming himself. He looked around, shuddering as he absorbed more details of the bloody scene. His gaze rested on Khalid and his Adam's apple bobbed as he swallowed, then swallowed again.

"Are you sure Khalid isn't dead?" he said finally.

"He's still breathing. I don't know how long he's going to last."

"Jesus, I can't believe what I'm seeing." Andrew turned to Charlie. "Shall I fetch some blankets? Some water? I feel so goddamn useless."

"Blankets might help some, I guess." Charlie's voice was thready, and he swayed as if fighting to retain consciousness. "Khalid and this woman must be going into shock."

"At least they're both still breathing." Verity clung to hope, even if it was fragile. "If emergency services get here soon, maybe we can save them."

Andrew nodded. "There's a good chance. We have fine hospitals in the area and they work miracles nowadays."

His gloomy tone of voice completely belied his optimistic words. The final protective veil that had been stretched between reality and Verity's emotions ripped wide-open. For the first time she realized—fully realized—what had just happened.

Khalid was almost certainly going to die. Very possibly within the next few minutes.

The imminent threat of Khalid's death transformed her previous lethargy into a burning need for action. "Oh, my God, Miryam!" She shook Andrew's arm when he didn't immediately respond. "Please go and get Khalid's wife, Andrew. Bring her here, and for God's sake, hurry!"

"I don't know if I should." Andrew gnawed his lower lip, infuriatingly indecisive. "It might not be safe for her to come down. Maybe the killers are still around." He scanned the passing traffic and the crowd gathering at the hotel doors, as if expecting a gunman to pop out and start shooting at any moment.

"The gunman killed himself. There's no danger anymore. Andrew, please go! Miryam needs to say goodbye to her husband—"

"There could be other gunman waiting in the wings, and she'd be a prime target—"

"If the assassin had accomplices, they'd have come to finish off the survivors by now." Charlie's voice was getting shakier by the second, but his powers of reason seemed to be working better than Andrew's.

"Miryam would want to be with her husband, whatever the risks," Verity said. "Andrew, go and fetch her, please. I'm sure it's what they both would want."

"Well, okay. You know them better than anyone else, so if that's what you think is best…"

"I do. It's definitely what they would want."

As soon as Andrew had left, Verity lay down beside Khalid again, her mouth pressed almost to his ear, so that the din of street noise wouldn't drown out her voice.

"Khalid, you have been hurt, but help is on the way." This time she spoke in Kashmiri, hoping that the soft rhythms of his native language might reach him and console him in a way that English could not. She ripped off her right glove and touched her fingers to his lips. Even though Charlie had said he was still breathing, she was relieved beyond measure when she felt a hint of warm breath against her icy fingertips.

"Hold on Khalid," she said gently. "Hold on, my friend. Help is coming."

"Verity." He spoke so feebly that she saw the movement of his mouth almost before she realized he had said her name.

"I'm here. The doctors will soon be here, too." She cursed the rush-hour traffic that would delay their arrival. Cursed the violence of Kashmiri politics that had led to this. She took his hand. "Only a few minutes more, Khalid. Be strong, my friend."

"Tell Abdul and Saiyad…love them. Love…my sons."

"Yes, I'll tell them. And you can tell them, too—"

"…wife is…good…woman."

"I'll tell her of your praise, Khalid. Of course I will. But you have to display strength, so that you can tell them yourself. Miryam will be here in just a minute. I sent Andrew to fetch her."

"Dying." His breath rattled in his throat and Verity bit back a scream of protest. Not again. She'd done this with Sam, just a few months ago. Held him in her arms and watched the life drain out of him. Oh, God, please no. She wasn't ready to do it again.

Allah, Jahweh, whatever your name is, don't let this happen. Please, please, let him live.

"Sorry…for…what I did to you."

"You didn't do anything. What do you mean, Khalid?"

Silence answered her question. Khalid's stillness was terrifying and she had to fight the urge to shake him into alertness. She leaned over him, her tears dripping onto his face. She wiped the tears away, leaving a streak of blood and dirt on his cheek.

"The people of Kashmir need you, Khalid." He was the only respected voice for moderation in the whole country. And he was about to die for his belief in peace, diplomacy and nonviolent negotiation, Verity thought bitterly.

His eyelids flickered. "My brother…"

"You have a message for him?" Verity asked, weak with relief that Khalid was still hanging on to life.

"Find him…." Khalid's eyes closed.

"Oh, my God, yes. Where can I find Farooq?" Belatedly, Verity remembered that there was a lot more at stake here than the loss of her childhood friend. Kashmir's fate might be hanging in the balance. Finding the people who had murdered George Douglass might not be possible if Khalid died. She dreaded to contemplate the violence that was likely to convulse Kashmir unless the dogs of war were hauled back and locked tightly in their pens.

"Tell me where I can find your brother, Khalid. Please, tell me before it's too late."

"The gardens…" Khalid finally opened his eyes wide, but they were hazy and out of focus. He gave a gurgling cough that sounded ominous. Was blood already filling his lungs? Verity wondered. She felt panic come clawing back. He was going to die, and then they would never find Farooq. And until Farooq was in custody, who knew what further terrorist activities might be unleashed against the United States?

"Don't let more people die, Khalid," she begged. "Tell me where to find your brother."

"Your mother's gardens…the…azaleas…national…"

"Yes, my mother has always loved to garden. Those azaleas that bloomed in our garden in Srinagar each spring were her pride and joy." Dear God, his mind was wandering but she was afraid to change the subject in case he faded back into unconsciousness. Still, she had to try. "But what about your brother? Tell me where I can find Farooq, Khalid."

Khalid's gaze focused for just a moment and he looked straight into her eyes. He spoke with unnerving clarity. He even smiled. "I always loved you, Verity. You never realized that, did you?"

Oh, God, she wasn't prepared to deal with this. Not here. Not now. Where was Andrew? Where was Miryam? What the hell was she supposed to say in answer to such a statement from a dying man?

She reached out and touched him gently on the cheek. "We were good friends, weren't we, Khalid? We shared some wonderful times together."

For a split second she had the illusion that Khalid smiled, but he gave her no answer.

Verity slipped her fingers down his cheek and once more held them to his lips. No breath moistened her fingertips. She felt tears on her cheeks, but inside she seemed to have returned to the state, so familiar after Sam's death, of feeling nothing at all.

She sat up, brushing away the tears. "I think he's dead," she said to nobody in particular.

Gray-faced himself, Charlie searched for a pulse, first in Khalid's wrist and then in his wounded and bloody neck. "You're right, he's dead." He used the thumb of his left hand to close Khalid's eyelids. "I'm real sorry. You two had known each other a long time, hadn't you?"

It was a moment before Verity could speak. "Yes," she said. "We'd known each other for a long time. We were good friends."

Eight

The paramedics drove Verity to the emergency room, where harried doctors examined her, then dispatched her to various technicians who drew blood and took pictures of her innards before delivering her back to the over-worked resident on duty in the ER. According to him, the tests showed that there were no significant injuries to any important body parts. Her internal organs were fully functional and her heart pumped blood with pleasing regularity. Her skull was intact, and her brain basically undamaged.

Verity considered the latter part of this diagnosis debatable. Her cranium felt as if it had been scooped hollow and the resulting space refilled with jagged rocks that were banging around, pounding against the inside of her skull. She communicated as much to the resident, who was busy scrawling his initials on the pages of her medical chart.

The resident assured her she'd feel much better after a night's sleep, cited her mild concussion as grounds to refuse her request for a major infusion of narcotic pain-killers, and suggested she could take a couple of ibuprofen instead. Far from offering sympathy, he pointed out how lucky it was that she'd been wearing a long winter coat with woolen slacks and had fallen onto carpet, albeit over concrete, so her legs and arms had been protected and she had no cuts deep enough to require stitches. Verity tried to feel suitably grateful and failed.

With a final infuriatingly cheerful smile, the resident hung her chart on the privacy curtain and told her the nurse would soon come in to give her a list of warning symptoms to watch for over the next twenty-four hours. He then dashed out of the cramped examining cubicle to take care of a teenager whose younger brother had settled a dispute over the TV remote by splitting open her stomach with a hunting knife. He couldn't have made it more plain that on the scale of big-city emergency room violence, Verity's narrow escape from an assassin's bullet sailed well below the interest threshold of overstressed, underrested medical professionals.

For a few minutes after the doctor left, Verity lay on the examining table and drowned in self-pity while the jagged rocks continued to bump and rattle their way around the inside of her skull. She listened to the other patients groan and to the clang of stretchers being wheeled into the elevators. For light relief, she stared at the IV stand and blood pressure machine and tried to ignore the smell of disinfectant mingled with fried chicken that seemed embedded in the walls of the ER.

She quickly decided that she needed to do something more productive than lie and suffer while her mind unreeled a nightmarish collage of recent memories. Now that the shock was wearing off, the scene outside the hotel kept playing on her mental screen with grisly repetition. From the moment Khalid walked through the swinging glass doors until the moment his hysterical widow had been carried back into the hotel by Andrew and a paramedic, Verity found each successive image more disturbing than the last.

Unfortunately, the harder she tried to push the memories aside, the faster and more vividly they crowded in, outtakes from the theater of the absurd combined into a horrific, real-life drama of brutal, senseless death. She felt again the death sigh of Khalid's breath against her ice-cold fingers. She saw the crumpled body of Glenn Zephyr, the Secret Service agent who'd taken a bullet to the throat in a vain attempt to shield Khalid. Twisting on the narrow examining table, she was consumed with sadness for the waste of it all.

In a mingling of traumatic memories she could have done without, she once again lived the dreadful moments when she'd watched Sam's surgeon walk down the long hospital corridor toward her, knowing from the doctor's expression that he was going to tell her Sam had died on the operating table, hoping—God, how she'd hoped!— that the surgeon wouldn't speak the words she knew he was going to speak.

Verity scrubbed her fingers across her eyes, swallowing tears. *Enough already.* Crying would only make her headache worse without doing a damn thing to help the victims. She refused to lie here mixing and matching maudlin images of Sam's and Khalid's deaths. Nor was she going to wait passively for the nurse to arrive with a take-home sheet of instructions. The doctor himself had declared her healthy, so there was no reason why she shouldn't go in search of the nurse and get the heck out of here.

She sat up, waited a moment for the world to stop spinning, and was just getting ready to slide her legs off the examining table when she heard Michael's voice on the other side of the privacy curtain. "Verity? Is that you in there?"

She gripped the edge of the seat. She absolutely was not in a fit state to deal with Michael Strait. "No."

"Hmm. The nurse said you were in this cubicle, and

there's a chart clipped to the curtain with your name on it. May I come in?''

"No."

"Okay. Do you have clothes on?"

"No."

The rattle of the curtains being pushed aside was followed by Michael's appearance in the opening. "Pity," he said, his dark gaze running over her fully clothed body. "I was optimistic that you might be telling me the truth for once."

"I never tell lies," she said hotly. "Not even to you." Since this was patently false, she finished her slide off the examining table and reached for her damp, muddy coat that was draped over the cubicle's only chair. She moved too fast and swayed groggily. Michael was at her side in an instant, his arm around her waist, supporting her.

"Don't touch me!" She jerked away, heart racing, and scowled at him for good measure.

"Sure." He stepped back with an ironic gesture of surrender. "Next time I'll let you fall. Your body could probably use a few more bruises right about now."

Verity intensified her scowl. Which was a really smooth move—glaring at Michael because she herself was behaving badly. She moderated her expression, drew in a shaky breath, and decided to start over. "Was there something specific you wanted, Michael?"

"Only to find out how you are."

A little late, she remembered that she would be dead if it weren't for Michael having pushed her to the ground at the first burst of gunfire, when the assassin's M-16 was still aimed directly at Khalid. He'd saved her life and she was snapping his head off for no more valid reason than the fact that her own feelings scared her. It was, perhaps, time to stop behaving like a sullen adolescent and demonstrate some appropriate gratitude.

"Thanks for asking," she said quietly. "I guess I'm pretty much fine. Except for my head, which aches like crazy where I banged it on the sidewalk—"

"I'm sorry. There was no time to warn you. I just reacted."

"Good grief, Michael, I wasn't complaining! Far from it. I'm deeply grateful you had the presence of mind to shove me down, out of harm's way."

He glanced at the bump on her forehead. "Giving you a concussion in the process, it seems."

"Only a very mild one." Ashamed of her earlier rudeness, she gave him a smile that turned out to be a little more fragile than she'd have liked.

He saw the wobble in her smile, of course. His gaze rested on her mouth, then flicked away. "You fell pretty hard, and I was right on top of you. I was afraid you might have broken a bone or two."

"No, not a one. Not even a sprain. The doctors claim I'll be ready to climb a mountain by tomorrow morning. Or at the very least be ready to go back to work."

He grimaced. "Right now, returning to work might be more demanding than climbing a mountain."

"Yes, given the situation in Kashmir, it might." She was grateful for his low-key response and for his intuitive understanding that she wasn't ready to be sympathized with. That she would fall apart if he was too kind.

"How about you, Michael? Didn't I see the paramedics put your arm in a sling back at the hotel?"

"That was just a precaution. Turns out there was a lot of blood, but not much real damage. The bullet went straight in and out, so it was only a flesh wound." He touched his left shoulder. "The doctors gave me a shot, stitched me up and told me to go home. Right now, I'm floating on Percoset, so I'm entirely pain free. Tomorrow, I'll probably be sore as hell. In fact, I might be forced to resort to the sling again in an effort to squeeze out some sympathy.''

''Go for the sling. You've earned it.'' She raised her eyes to meet his, finally enough in control of herself to acknowledge how closely death had brushed past her. ''You saved my life, Michael. Thank you. I'm sincerely grateful, despite what you might conclude from the way I snapped at you just now. Chalk up my bitchy behavior to a mixture of delayed shock and a truly nasty headache.''

He smiled, which had a transforming effect on his austere features. ''You're entirely welcome, Verity.''

His rare smiles were infinitely more disturbing than his frequent frowns, and Verity dropped her gaze, battling yet another set of troublesome memories. This time of a star-bright night in Kashmir when Michael had smiled at her with exactly this same sort of devastating tenderness. She'd been captivated then, just as she was now. On that magical night, she'd responded to his presence with a rush of sexual attraction so intense that even she—Crown Princess of Denial—hadn't been able to ignore its existence.

Even now, with all the advantage of hindsight, Verity didn't understand how she could have experienced such powerful sexual need every time Michael came near, all the while remaining happily married to another man. How had she managed to feel warmth, respect and affection for Sam at the very same moment her insides were knotted tight with desire for Michael? She supposed it was proof positive, if she'd ever been in doubt, that sexual attraction and true love had remarkably little to do with each other.

Until her encounter with Michael in Kashmir she'd

never been disloyal to her husband, never betrayed her marriage vows, not even in her most intimate thoughts. But that night on the shores of Dal Lake had changed everything. She would never forgive herself for having gone so willingly into Michael's arms, never forget the longing she'd felt—a yearning for sexual adventure that made a mockery of all the solid and worthwhile qualities her marriage stood for. The barrier she and Michael had maintained with obsessive care almost since their first meeting had been swept away, and the abyss that loomed in front of them had been revealed in all its terrifying depth.

When Verity got back to the States, she discovered that her relationship with Sam remained as warm and loving as ever, but her opinion of her own integrity had been radically altered. Her relationship with Michael, already tense and problematic, gave way to ice-cold hostility.

The evening that caused all the trouble had happened entirely by chance, a prime example of the malevolent intervention of the goddess Kali in the affairs of her human subjects. When Verity discovered that she and Michael were both going to be in Kashmir during the same two-week period, she'd realized for reasons she elected not to spell out that it wouldn't be smart for them to meet.

She had been assigned to escort a small fact-finding congressional delegation around Kashmir, and Michael had supposedly been on a buying trip for his import-export business. He had accepted her excuses about a heavy travel schedule without protest and agreed there would be no time for them to get together. In fact, he'd deliberately avoided comparing his itinerary to hers, as if he shared her reluctance to meet thousands of miles away from the protection of Sam's company.

Unfortunately, their attempts to avoid each other hadn't succeeded. They'd been so damned honorable—

so reluctant to discover the details of each other's schedules—that they had no way of knowing in advance that they'd both been invited to dinner at Hawa Mahal, the Palace of the Wind. This was the summer home of a descendant of Kashmir's last maharajah, a middle-aged profligate who maintained the slightly ramshackle but still magnificent two-storey palace on the shores of Dal Lake in Srinagar.

Verity was caught off guard when she entered the former throne room of the palace and saw Michael standing at the right hand of her host, deep in a conversation that had the royal descendant breaking into repeated roars of laughter. Michael had chosen to wear formal Hindu-style dress, the first time she'd ever seen him in anything other than standard American casual clothing. Resplendent in royal-blue silk embroidered with glittering silver thread, he bowed in greeting as Verity approached. He also addressed her in perfect Kashmiri, another thing he'd never done before.

Verity returned his bow, feeling as if she'd walked into a fairy tale. This handsome stranger was instantly recognizable as Michael Strait, and yet he was also a make-believe prince from a land of myth and legend. In retrospect, she realized her protective armor had been fatally breached the moment Michael first touched the tips of his clasped fingers to his chin and offered her the traditional *namaste* greeting.

To add to the general aura of fantasy, the night had been one of rare perfection, the heat of high summer having passed and the damp chill of winter not yet having arrived. The air caressed the senses, rich with the scent of night-blooming jasmine in its final flower, more potent because the killing frosts of winter would soon arrive. The thousand candles lining the halls of the palace added to the dangerous illusion of a night taken out of time, with no consequences in the everyday world back home in America.

Verity found herself repeatedly gravitating toward Michael during the two hours before the formal dinner started. When the maharajah offered to entertain the congressional delegation with tours of his gardens and his impressive collection of eighteenth century Sikh art—not to mention his equally impressive collection of pornography—Verity opted not to accompany the delegation, choosing to stay and talk with Michael instead.

During that final hour before the banquet, they conversed with greater intimacy than in the entire two years of their previous acquaintance, filling in the details of their personal lives, their hopes and dreams, fears and hang-ups. Michael talked about his Nordic grandparents, a couple who'd been missionaries in India during the fifties, a decade before Verity's parents had arrived in Srinagar. He also talked about his maternal grandparents whom he'd never met, and the regret he felt at not knowing anyone from his mother's extended family.

For her part, Verity revealed some of the difficulties she'd experienced on transferring to college in the States, having spent the first eighteen years of her life in Kashmir, raised by parents who'd been in their forties when she was born. Studying since she was five years old in the small, private school run by her parents, she had been academically well prepared for college. Socially, she had been a disaster. Her rigidly formal manners struck her fellow students as somewhere between naive and infantile, or worse, offensively standoffish. As for dating, she might just as well have grown up in a nineteenth-century convent for all the understanding she had of American mating and dating rituals. Not to mention such normal, everyday functions as calling out for pizza, or washing her own clothes. Her parents had been strict disciplinarians, living modestly as was fitting for missionaries, but they had nevertheless employed three indoor servants and two men to help in the garden. Hiring servants was considered the duty of anyone who could afford it, since in the ravaged economy of Kashmir, whole families often depended on the meager wages earned by a household cook or washerwoman.

If doing her own laundry and preparing her own meals had been revelations to Verity, they were nothing in comparison to the astonishment she felt at the complete absence of rules governing relations between the sexes. Verity laughed as she told Michael of her amazement when she learned that she could have men—more than one, not related, not even attending the college—sleeping in her dorm room all night long and nobody was going to protest.

"Or even notice," Michael said. He gave her a look that was full of sympathy. "You can laugh now, but it must have been tough at the time."

"Yes, it was," she admitted. "For the longest time so much personal freedom wasn't liberating for me, it was simply scary. And to add to my problems, I didn't look foreign, or speak English with a weird accent, so the other students didn't cut me any slack. They expected me to be a regular American, you know?"

Michael asked her if she still sometimes felt torn between her childhood in Kashmir, and her family heritage rooted so securely in five generations of solid American citizenship.

"I used to feel much more conflicted before I met Sam," Verity said, aware of a sudden need to inject her husband's name into their conversation. Perhaps to remind both of them that she was a married woman before their conversation became even more intimate.

"Sam is so good-humored and uncomplicated, and although he's really smart he never seems to get hung up on the sort of moral and personal dilemmas that used to obsess me before I met him," she explained. "The world is an easy place for Sam to navigate, and when I'm with him, it seems fairly simple to me, too. *God's in his heaven and all's right with the world.* Do you know that line from the Browning poem? I've always thought it might have been written to describe Sam's attitude to life."

Michael smiled. "You're right. Sam is one of those incredibly fortunate people who's born happy and manages to stay that way. You give him depth, and he gives you balance. You're lucky to have found each other."

"We sure are," Verity said, feeling a rush of affection for her absent husband. Sam was such a sweetie-pie, she thought fondly. Such a dear, kind person. Without his love and wisdom she would never have overcome the twin dragons of isolation and dislocation that had been her daily companions during her freshman and sophomore years in college. She could never regret her decision to get engaged to him on the day she finished her undergraduate degree, or her decision to marry him at the end of her first year in graduate school. How could you regret a life filled with easygoing companionship, stimulating discussions and friendly laughter?

Her conversation with Michael switched back to more general topics. When the formal dinner finally began, she found herself seated between two members of the congressional delegation, a seventy-year-old congressman who kept squeezing her thigh, and a slightly drunken Southern senator who seemed to feel it was his duty to harangue their host about how inefficient the Indian infrastructure was.

"You need to buy American," he boomed down the length of the long banquet table, "and then you won't keep getting all these aggravatin' breakdowns of your public facilities. There are too many soldiers here in Kashmir, way too many bureaucrats and not near enough businessmen. You're never goin' to lift your economic production until you have decent roads and clean water. Not to mention you need to find workers who won't steal you blind the minute you turn your back."

Michael had been seated directly opposite Verity, between the two congressional aides accompanying the senator. The aides, both young, ambitious and on their first overseas assignment, were trying—with increasing desperation and zero success—to get their boss to shut up before he said something unforgivably tactless.

Verity caught Michael's eye with greater and greater frequency and, as one exotic dish followed another, their shared embarrassment at the senator's bad manners gradually changed into amusement. Before too long, they were struggling to control their laughter.

When the senator emphasized yet another of his crass points by making a sweeping gesture that sent a glass of iced mango juice cascading into her lap, Verity could see that Michael was losing the battle to control his laughter. She made a hasty escape from the table, fighting an attack of hysterical giggles as a swarm of servants immediately surrounded her and started patting at her sopping wet skirt with towels and napkins, spreading juice over a wider and wider area of her skirt, to embarrassing effect.

Escaping from the well-meaning servants before her cream silk dress could be totally ruined, Verity decided she needed some fresh air before she returned to her assigned task of listening to the senator make an idiot of himself. Even a diplomat as junior as she was deserved a break, she decided. She'd snatch a few blissful minutes with no groping hands reaching for her thigh and nothing more irritating drumming against her eardrums than the squawk of their host's peacocks, or maybe a raucous greeting from one of his pet mynah birds kept in a gilded cage on the veranda.

She made her way back through the reception area, originally the maharajah's throne room, and walked out onto a balcony that afforded a splendid view across Dal Lake to the famous gardens of Shalimar, which had been laid out by the Mughal emperors in the sixteenth century. A fountain in the courtyard beneath the balcony cascaded foaming water into four white marble basins that gleamed in the moonlight, the splash of the water louder here than the distant murmur of voices from the banquet hall.

The night briefly held the sort of unearthly beauty that Verity associated with her fondest memories of childhood. The Vale of Kashmir, she mused, was truly one of the most naturally beautiful places on the planet, and looking at this garden she could almost forget the devastation human beings had wreaked elsewhere in the valley.

Had she known that Michael would make an excuse to follow her? Verity wasn't sure, could never be sure how innocent her intentions had been. But she felt no surprise when she heard the sound of his footsteps echoing on the tiled floor of the empty throne room. She turned, elbows resting on the balustrade as she waited for him to join her.

He smiled as he approached, an unguarded smile that sent a warm shiver of sensation pulsing through her. "If I murder the senator will you be a witness for the defense?"

"You plan to claim justifiable homicide?" she asked, returning his smile.

"Mmm." He propped himself against a pillar carved in intricate honeycomb latticework, his skin an enticing shade of café au lait against the gray stone. "Do you think it would fly?"

"I think it would be an open-and-shut case. Go for it. You'd earn the gratitude of thousands. Especially me."

He laughed softly, then reached out, tucking a strand of hair back behind her ear. "You look even more beautiful than usual tonight. Kashmir agrees with you, I think."

"Yes, I think it does, too." Her breath came a little faster, but she chose not to notice the warning sign. "It's wonderful to be back, even in the company of the Right Honorable Senator Asshole. It's five years since I was last here."

"That's too long," he said, following her lead and leaning on the balustrade to stare out into the velvet darkness. "For all the problems of the insurrection, the miserable economy and the soldiers turning Srinagar into an armed camp, the beauty of Kashmir is a passion that gets into your blood."

Verity nodded her agreement. "Yes, it is. Although there are days when I think my feelings for Kashmir are closer to a virus giving me a fever than anything more pleasant."

It was a moment before Michael turned to look at her, and when he did, his eyes were hooded. "Does that surprise you? It shouldn't. I've discovered to my cost that passion is almost always like a fever in the blood. One that won't be tamed however many drugs you feed it."

The air around them vibrated with sudden tension. Their mood had shifted with lightning speed but somehow Verity never doubted that they'd stopped talking about her passion for Kashmir and moved on to a discussion of other, far more dangerous passions.

She had to swallow before she could speak. "Maybe that's your mistake," she said. "Feeding your fever."

"How so?"

"In folk medicine, the wise women advise you to starve a fever. You should try that perhaps."

He spoke into the night, not looking at her. "I've tried starvation, too. Believe me, Verity, I've tried it. Nothing works. The passion is still there, burning me up, consuming me."

She closed her eyes, afraid to look at him, even in profile. Her voice shook a little when she replied. "Honor and loyalty and friendship are more enduring emotions than passion. Certainly more important ones."

"Are they?"

"Yes." She spoke with all the firmness she didn't feel.

"I'm sure you're right, but sometimes I wonder. Don't you ever wonder what it would be like to indulge your passion?"

"No, never."

His smile was tinged with irony. "You don't lie well, Verity. It's one of your more endearing qualities."

"I'm not lying." She tried to make the denial sound calm, measured. And honest, of course. An essential quality when lying through your teeth.

"Shall I test that?" he asked quietly.

"No!" The instant panic in her voice would have been laughable in other circumstances.

Michael leaned his back against the pillar and looked down at her. The silence between them became heavy with truths neither of them dared to speak. He wasn't smiling anymore and his expression was unreadable, but she had no trouble divining what he was thinking, or what he wanted.

His desire was easy to read because she wanted the same thing, and the knowledge that they couldn't have what they wanted—that it would be disastrous to act on sexual feelings that had no roots in other, more noble emotions—didn't seem as clear and strong as it should have been.

"You need to go back to the banquet," he said, but even as he spoke, he reached out to cup her face with his hands.

Of course she should go. She should have left the minute he came out onto the veranda. She was a married woman. A happily married woman, for heaven's sake. Given what they had both tacitly acknowledged, and what had lain unacknowledged between them for months, it was crazy to be alone out here with him.

Crazy, dangerous and oh so enticing. Guilt shivered down Verity's spine and she wrapped her arms around her waist, feeling goose bumps erupt beneath her skin. From somewhere, she dredged up the strength to say what had to be said, trying to make light of it, as if they were discussing her professional obligations. Anything but their mutual desire to break her marriage vows.

"You're right, I should go. If I stay out here much longer, our friend the senator will report me for being delinquent in my duties." But she didn't do the smart thing and leave. She didn't even move. Her feet were weighted, Super Glued to the ancient tiled mosaic of the veranda, although the rest of her body felt airy and floating, and her face burned with awareness of Michael's brief caress, as if tiny sparks of electricity danced across her skin in the wake of his touch.

When she didn't retreat, Michael's breath exhaled in an unsteady sigh. He took her arms and unfolded them from around her waist. He looked at her in a silence weighted with the words they wouldn't speak.

Now would be a good time to get out of here, Verity told herself. Now would be a really good time.

But she still didn't move.

Michael leaned slightly toward her, moonlight striking

sparks from the glittering jewels on the collar of his jacket. Mesmerized, she watched the flash and shimmer of colored light as she felt him trace a delicate line across her cheekbones with the tips of his fingers. She realized that his hands were trembling and thought how strange it was that sexual passion produced physical symptoms that could make a strong man so vulnerable.

"Verity..." he murmured. "Jesus, Verity...I want..."

His voice faded into silence and Verity had just enough willpower left not to ask him what, exactly, it was that he wanted. At some level she must have hoped that if they didn't actually put anything into words, maybe they could still salvage the situation from total disaster.

In the distance, she heard the mischievous call of a mynah bird, trained to imitate a human voice. *Pay attention!* he cawed in Kashmiri. The bird was answered by a harsh shout from one of the strutting peacocks. The sounds filled her mind, crowding out worries about right and wrong, loyalty and betrayal. No saving image of Sam flashed onto her mental screen. Instead, every cell of her being felt filled to overflowing with lush, sensuous impressions of the garden, the flowers, the stars—and Michael.

She whispered his name, feeling the final protective mental barrier crash into oblivion as she did so. The blood flowed hot and heavy in her veins, and the yearning to be held surged in her heart. Before she could have second thoughts, she took a fatal step toward him. She was instantly wrapped in his arms. She laid her head on his chest, soft and yielding against the muscled hardness of his body.

He slowly tightened his hold, kissing her with tenderness, then with hunger and finally with searing passion. She kissed him back, not with tenderness but with an instant, explosive craving that must have been as evident to him as it was to her. Until that moment, she had never realized that a kiss could pack an erotic punch more dramatic, more heartrending than the actual moment of sexual climax. For a few earth-shattering moments, held within the circle of his embrace, she felt that the secrets of the universe were hers to reach out and grasp.

But she'd only kissed him for a minute or two, Verity always consoled herself. Maybe three or four minutes. Well, maximum five or six. Then she'd broken away and run back through the deserted throne room, never stopping and never looking back. She'd hidden in a bathroom until she could pull herself together, frantically shoving awareness of how avidly she'd responded deep down into the lockbox of memories too dangerous to allow free.

Fifteen minutes later, she'd returned to the banquet hall and resumed her seat between the brash senator and the congressman with straying hands. Nobody seemed to notice anything wrong with her demeanor, although she doubted if she'd actually made any intelligent comment—or even a vaguely relevant one—for the remainder of the dinner.

She hadn't seen Michael again that night, or for the rest of her stay in Kashmir. Later she learned that he'd left the palace, making the excuse of a family emergency. She ought to have been grateful for his tact, although gratitude was the last emotion she felt toward him at the time. Or at any moment since. From that night on, she'd devoted a great deal of energy to pretending that she'd never responded to his kiss, that she'd never felt a shiver of primeval, cataclysmic longing when his lips touched hers.

The pretense had always been problematic, more so after Sam's death. Today's hail of bullets seemed to have left it in ruins.

Verity took a sip of tepid water from the plastic cup

on the medical tray, reasserting control over memories that held far too much in the way of regret, shame—and longing. With grim determination, she replaced images of the maharajah's palace with images of the carnage outside the hotel in Washington, D.C. It was past time to get this conversation back on track.

"Do we have any leads on Khalid's killer?" she asked. "Has any group claimed credit for the attack?"

"Not so far," Michael said. "It seems likely that the Kashmir Freedom Party is involved, but we're taking care not to jump to conclusions. The FBI has file photos of a few known Kashmiri radicals currently believed to be in the States, but I don't know how far they've come in the interrogation process. I'm only semi in the loop while I'm here at the hospital. I did hear that they ran a preliminary fingerprint match and came up empty."

Verity grimaced. "And since he put the gun to his head and pulled the trigger, we obviously don't have an accurate physical description, either."

"No, we don't. You came downstairs this afternoon a few minutes before we did, so you're the only person who got a good look at the assassin before he blew his face away. Could you identify a mug shot, do you think?"

Regretfully, she shook her head. "I don't believe so. The collar of his coat was turned up and he was pretending to talk into his mike, standing sort of hunched up against the hood of the Lincoln—"

"He wasn't pretending to talk into his mike," Michael said bitterly. "That earpiece was the real thing. What you saw was the gunman talking to Charlie Berkower, up in Khalid's suite."

"Good grief, how did the assassin get his hands on real Secret Service equipment?" Verity asked, startled.

"He killed the agent assigned to drive Khalid," Michael said tersely. "Then he took the dead agent's place. At my suggestion, Charlie called down from the suite to make a final check that the area in front of the hotel was clean. That there were no suspicious vehicles or bystanders. The limo driver assured us that everything was completely safe and to bring Khalid right on down."

Verity winced and Michael gave a harsh laugh. "So we brought Khalid right on down. And all the time the real Secret Service agent was stuffed into the trunk of the limo, already dead! What we'd actually done was check in with the assassin, letting him know his targets were about to put in an appearance. Jesus, what a farce! Why didn't we just hand Khalid over to the Three Stooges? He'd have been equally well protected."

"I didn't realize yet another Secret Service agent had been killed," Verity said. "Khalid's murder is sounding less and less like the work of a single Kashmiri fanatic and more like the work of a well-organized group. The gunman who attacked us must have had helpers, don't you think? He couldn't have hijacked a Secret Service vehicle, and killed the driver, and arrived at the hotel on time without help."

Michael nodded. "You're right, this can't have been a one-man show. The last time I checked in with the FBI team, their working theory was that the real Secret Service driver was ambushed only a few minutes before he arrived at the hotel, but everyone is still trying to figure out precisely where and how. Washington's a crowded city with a lot of traffic, and no bystanders have come forward to report seeing anything suspicious. On the other hand, official limos are a common sight here, and people wouldn't necessarily pay much attention, even to a vehicle stopped in an odd place."

Verity sighed. "It's frustrating that I can't be of more use in identifying the gunman. I wish I could remember something that would help, but I was focused on watching for Andrew's car and my attention was pretty much fixed on the passing traffic. If I thought about the driver waiting for Khalid at all, it was only to reflect that he looked like a typical Secret Service type. Slightly above average height. Wiry build. Clean-shaven. Regulation gloomy expression. Regulation earpiece. No distinguishing features that I noticed.''

"The doorman said the shooter was a white guy with blond hair. Is that what you saw, too?''

"Yes." Verity nodded. "Although I have a vague impression his hair was more light-brown than blond. What little bit of it I could see." She looked up, her attention caught by her own words. "That's odd, isn't it? I would have expected the assassin to be Kashmiri, or at least from the Indian subcontinent. But this guy was definitely light-skinned and fair-haired. How many European-Americans can there be who are willing to blow themselves up for the sake of murdering a Kashmiri politician?''

"None, I would guess. We're working on the assumption that the gunman was from Kashmir, despite what you thought you saw. Actually, his body skin was dark brown, entirely consistent with somebody native to the Indian subcontinent.''

"What?" She shot Michael a startled glance. "That's impossible. I wasn't paying close attention, but I'm certain I saw a white man—''

"I'm sure you did, which was what the gunman intended. But the paramedics reported that there were pieces of fake hair and latex adhering to what was left of the assassin's face, so we can probably assume he wore a mask. A real smart move on his part, because if he'd looked Kashmiri or Indian, you might have given him a second glance, don't you think?''

She thought about that, then nodded. "Yes. It would have struck me as odd, given how few Secret Service agents are of Indian descent."

"Which is precisely why he wore a mask, of course."

Verity sighed. "And the upshot is that however many mug shots I study, I'm not likely to be able to identify the killer."

"No, you're not. You or anybody else." Michael punched his fist into his palm. "Damn! Whoever these conspirators are, they're running rings around us with their planning."

"Khalid's story was so full of holes and contradictions that it's not surprising we weren't entirely focused on his claim that he was in danger of being murdered. We'll get his killers eventually, you know we will."

Michael didn't look reassured. "And how many more people will die while we're running around, chasing our own tails at warp speed?"

Verity didn't like the answers she came up with for that question. "The others who were shot," she said, changing the subject. "Have you seen any of them? Do you know how they're doing?"

"I wasn't allowed to see any of them, but from the skimpy reports I could wring out of various people, they're not doing too well. They all suffered far more serious injuries than either of us. The female bystander has been identified from documents in her purse as Rhoda Rushkewitz, a lawyer. She died in the ambulance on the way here. And Glenn Zephyr is dead, too. His body armor deflected half a dozen bullets that would otherwise have been fatal, but one caught him right in the throat."

Verity flinched. "I guessed he hadn't made it. He was lying next to Khalid in a pool of blood, not moving, and when the paramedics arrived, I saw them cover his face. I'm so sorry."

"He'd only been with the Secret Service six months, and his wife is pregnant. The baby's due in five weeks, apparently."

"Oh, lord." Verity massaged her aching temples. "Maybe being pregnant makes it a little easier for Glenn's wife?" she suggested, wanting to find some ray of comfort amidst all the grief. "She'll have the sadness of realizing her baby will never know its father, but at least she has another person she needs to think about. For the sake of their child, she can't just let herself tumble down into a pit of grief."

Like I did when Sam died, she thought. A pit not just of grief, but also of despair and guilt.

"There is that," Michael said. "Let's hope you're right and the baby's birth helps her get over the worst of it."

"What about the other Secret Service agent?" Verity asked. "Charlie Berkower?"

"Right now, he's in surgery. He managed to get off a couple of shots at the assassin, but he took a bullet in his elbow, plus several more in his torso that didn't do major damage because of his body armor. There's a lot of shattered bone in his elbow, so the doctors aren't sure they'll be able to save the functionality of his arm, but at least his life isn't in any danger."

"Is he married, too?"

"No, he's single."

"And what is going on with Norman Green? Or whatever his real name is."

"Norman Green is his real name, and he's not in very good shape." Michael broke off, then continued without visible emotion. "Norman isn't expected to survive, but they're still working on him. He took bullets in four separate places, including one to the spleen and another to the liver. The doctors don't sound too optimistic about his chances.''

"I'm really sorry, Michael. Has Norman been your partner on other assignments before this one?''

"Yes.'' Still without emphasis, he added, "We've worked together on and off for five years. He's one of the really good guys.''

She laid her hand on his arm without thinking, the first time she'd voluntarily touched him since Kashmir. "Don't give up hope, Michael. This is a great hospital with some fabulous medical professionals on staff. Maybe Norman will make it through.''

"Maybe. At least his wife's with him, and their daughter, and he was conscious for a few minutes.'' He turned away. "Christ, what a waste of a life.''

"He's not dead yet. Besides, you sound as if you're blaming yourself. There was nothing you could have done to prevent what happened. You're with the CTC, so I assume you specialize in counterterrorist activities. That means you, of all people, ought to know that there's virtually no line of defense against a determined assassin who's willing to die in order to kill his target.''

"I personally guaranteed Khalid's safety, and I blew it.''

"Well, your guarantee might have been a tad reckless—''

"Might have been?'' he interrupted savagely. "Try reckless, unfounded and arrogant.''

She gave a tiny smile. "Yeah, well, you're an arrogant sort of a guy, Michael. But that still doesn't make you responsible for Khalid's death. He was killed by a crazy Kashmiri fanatic who was trying to explode his way into paradise. Not by you and not by me, however much we may feel we screwed up.''

"That's easy for you to say, Verity, because you *didn't*

screw up. But I just came back to the States after spending eight months in Kashmir. I should have warned everyone more explicitly what we were up against. I knew that Khalid had offended the leaders of the Freedom Party, and that the organization had grown more sophisticated—to the point that they were capable of mounting a terrorist attack on U.S. soil. But knowing all that, I failed to take adequate precautions to get Khalid to his meeting with the Secretary of State.''

"You can play the martyr and blame yourself if you like. The fact is, you weren't responsible for Khalid's physical safety, or for deciding the most secure exit route from the hotel. Charlie Berkower and Glenn Zephyr were. That's the job of the Secret Service."

"But it was my place to spell out the level of risk. Why the hell didn't it occur to me that the limo driver might be a danger?''

"Because suspecting that the Secret Service limo driver was actually an assassin is beyond the bounds of what could reasonably be planned for or anticipated,'' Verity said.

"Maybe, but this was a CTC operation and I'm the senior agent on this assignment. The buck stopped with me. However you look at it, the bottom line is that I screwed up.''

Michael's admission brought Verity face-to-face with an issue that had been shuffled to the back of her mind as the doctors and med techs poked and prodded her. So far, she hadn't informed anyone of Khalid's accusations about a traitor working within the ranks of the American government. At some point very soon she was going to have to speak up. But to whom? If she told Michael, would she be informing precisely the wrong person? By every possible yardstick, he was the most likely suspect to be involved in a fight for Kashmir's freedom, and the fact that he'd been injured in this afternoon's attack didn't prove his innocence. He was a man of passionate convictions, and she could easily visualize him taking a bullet in his arm for the sake of a cause he supported.

And yet, for all that their personal relationship was so fraught, Verity simply couldn't visualize Michael as a man capable of plotting and carrying out the cold-blooded execution of Khalid Muhammad. At some gut level, deeper than reason and statistical probabilities, she realized that she trusted him.

"What is it?" Michael asked quietly. "Why are you looking at me like that? As if you're not entirely sure that you know me."

She shook her head, then changed her mind about keeping silent. "Do I know you, Michael?"

"In some ways better than anyone else in the world."

"But in other ways?" Verity pleated the paper sheet on the examining table, a good way to avoid his eyes. "Do you realize that despite all the time that we've spent in each other's company, and despite the fact that we share a very unusual background, I've no idea how you feel about the political situation in Kashmir."

"That's easy. I feel sick. I feel angry and frustrated that the international community has basically ignored a festering wound for half a century. I'm mad that India has been so brutal in its efforts to retain control, and equally mad that Pakistan keeps sending in money and professional rabble-rousers. I also believe that any solutions to the problems of Kashmir have to be hammered out at the negotiating table, not on the battlefield. Much less in the back alleys and mountain hideouts of fanatic terrorists."

Verity smoothed out the paper she'd just pleated. "Khalid told me that an American government official had infiltrated the Kashmir Freedom Party and was using it to pursue some unstated goal of his own. Khalid claimed that the reason he couldn't talk freely to Dick and Andrew was because anything he said might travel back to this supposedly treacherous American official—with disastrous consequences for him and his family."

Michael didn't seem as shocked or outraged by Khalid's claim as she had been. He frowned and his gaze became momentarily distant. "Why did Khalid assume that any American who infiltrated the Kashmir Freedom Party must be a traitor?" he asked eventually. "Infiltrating terrorist organizations is what CIA undercover operatives do, and Khalid is a sophisticated enough player on the international scene to know that."

"You sound defensive, Michael. Did *you* infiltrate the Kashmir Freedom Party?"

"I was talking in generalities, not specific cases. Any American who attempted a covert infiltration of the Freedom Party would basically be pursuing a death wish. He'd be dead before he could send home his first report."

Verity smiled tightly. "I'm a diplomat, Michael, trained to notice when people give weasel-word answers. And you just gave me a weasel-word answer. Try again. Yes or no, did you infiltrate the Kashmir Freedom Party?"

"You know I'm not going to answer that. And take that smirk off your face. Refusing to answer is not the same thing as admitting I did."

"Right. Then answer this question for me. If you weren't infiltrating the Freedom Party, what exactly were you doing in Kashmir for the past eight months?"

Michael was silent for a moment. Then he looked straight at her, his eyes dark with emotion, although his voice was laced with self-mockery when he replied. "What was I doing? That's easy. Trying like hell to forget about you. Not having too much success."

A tremor ran down her spine, a shiver of elemental response to what she read in his eyes. She had to glance away for a moment before she could reply. "I assume that forgetting me wasn't your official CIA assignment. Did you have another one?" She was surprised to hear a tiny thread of humor in her question.

He gave a wry smile. "Of course. Officially, I was assessing how fast the various resistance groups in Kashmir are growing, and whether the average citizen hates Pakistani interference more than they loathe Indian military rule, or vice versa."

"What was your conclusion?"

"That they're racing to a dead heat. Unless Pakistan stops supporting terrorist activity against the Indian government, and unless India starts paying attention to the wishes of the people of Kashmir, we probably have less than a year before the region explodes. And since these folks all have nuclear weapons with which to express their mutual aggravation, we'd better start sending up fervent prayers for peace to the divinity of our choice." He sent her an inquiring look. "How close is that to your assessment of the situation?"

"Too close for comfort," she said. The chances of either India or Pakistan accepting the gospel of moderation in regard to Kashmir were virtually nonexistent, and the reminder of how near the world walked to disaster was depressing.

Verity realized she was not only tired and dispirited, she ached in just about every bone and muscle from the top of her head to the soles of her feet. She massaged her forehead, where a headache was building to a throbbing, mind-blowing climax.

"I've reached the point where I'm barely functional, Michael," she said, her voice low and weary even to her own ears. "Right now I'm too tired to know what I think about anything beyond an intense desire to escape from this hospital and go home.''

"You're right," he said, getting up from the stool where he'd been sitting. "This isn't the moment to deal with the political problems on India's northwest frontier. We both need to get some rest. I'll call us a cab and see you home."

"Thanks, but there's no need." Her refusal was automatic, a result of three years of self-conditioning. "I'll be fine, Michael."

"I know you'll be fine. It's me who needs the company." He smiled at her, more with his eyes than with his mouth. "Don't fight me on this, Verity."

His smile warmed her, renewing her flagging spirits. "Well, if you really think you can't make it home without my help..."

"I can't." He took her hands, holding them cradled in his clasp. "I need you a lot more than you're willing to acknowledge, Verity."

Heat unfurled in the pit of her stomach and she left her hands in his clasp, a sure sign that this afternoon's blow to her head was having dangerous consequences. "I have to find a nurse and get her to sign off on my chart before I can leave," she told him, her voice unsteady.

With almost comic immediacy, a nurse stuck her head around the curtain, but she paid no attention to Verity. "Are you Michael Strait?"

"Yes, I am."

"Some government big shot is calling you on one of our unlisted phone lines. I've been sent to find you because you need to take the call right away. The line he's used is supposed to be kept strictly for medical emergencies."

"I'll be right with you," Michael said to the nurse. He

turned to Verity. "Stay here. I'll be back in a minute to take you home."

The nurse would have followed him out of the cubicle if Verity hadn't called to her. "Nurse, don't go! The doctor says I can be discharged as soon as you give me some printed instructions for the next twenty-four hours."

"Oh, are you waiting for discharge? What was your problem?" The nurse grabbed Verity's chart and hurriedly read through the notes. "Oh, yes. No gunshot wounds. Mild concussion. Lacerations. Severe bruising. Hmm...wait a minute."

She left the cubicle and returned a couple of minutes later with a computer printout of instructions. She reeled off a list of warning symptoms to watch for over the next twenty-four hours. She read so fast that only the world champion of speed comprehension would have been able to understand what she was saying. She then slowed down enough to instruct Verity to sign three different forms releasing the hospital from legal liability for any mishaps or medical setbacks once she left the ER. Signatures safely on file, she ushered Verity out of the cubicle.

"If you don't have a ride home, you can call for a cab at the nurses' station," she said. "They have the all-night service number."

Verity arrived at the nurses' station just as Michael hung up the phone. He drew her to one side, out of earshot of the medical staff, even though most of them looked far too busy to waste time paying attention to patients' conversations.

"What's up?" Verity asked. "You look worried."

"More bad news," he said, his voice and expression both bleak. "It's already early morning in Bombay, and a local radio station is announcing that at dawn this morning the Indian government executed the twenty-four

Kashmiri terrorists who'd been accused of murdering Indian soldiers. The very people Khalid was hoping to save
in order to prevent more violence.''

"Oh, no!" Verity fought a wave of nausea. "How
could they have done something so incredibly stupid?''

"According to the radio station, the Indian government
has chosen to—quote—demonstrate firmness in the face
of deliberate violation of their national borders by foreign
powers. Pakistan was once again warned that its continuing support of Islamic terrorists is tantamount to a declaration of war.''

Verity leaned against the wall, too exhausted to stand.
"What was the Indian government thinking of?" she
asked bleakly. "They might as well have poured oil over
Kashmir and thrown in a lighted torch.''

"And that surprises you?" Michael's anger was all the
more powerful for being so tightly controlled. "If Kashmir goes up in flames, the Indian government has a perfect excuse to declare war on Pakistan. And you can't
entirely blame them for feeling belligerent. God knows,
Pakistan goes out of its way to offer provocation on any
and every occasion. Both governments have been itching
to fight for months. It's just a case of who gets to swing
the first punch.''

"Or drop the first bomb," Verity said bitterly. "Between them, they'll devastate what's left of Kashmir's
economy and infrastructure and then one lucky side gets
to declare victory over the ruins. That makes perfect
sense.''

"To India and Pakistan, it does. Far better a subdued
and devastated province than an independent Kashmir
that owes allegiance to neither of them.''

"Has the Freedom Party made any public statement
about their plans for retaliation since the prisoners were
executed?''

"Not yet, at least according to the report I was given."
Michael sounded somber. "But brace yourself for the
worst. The Freedom Party will be preparing its retaliation
as we speak. Scenes of a car bomb exploding at an American embassy are likely to be coming to your living room
TV screen some time real soon."

Nine

Verity jolted awake and lay for a moment in the darkness of her bedroom, trying to decide what had caused her to wake up. The sound of a door creaking in the wind, maybe? The house was old, and full of nighttime squeaks, but the noises were so familiar they usually didn't bother her. Perhaps it was her general level of physical discomfort that had roused her. Her body ached in multiple places, as if she had rolled over too fast, forgetting in the twilight world of dreams that her legs and arms were peppered with bruises.

She glanced at the glowing dial of her travel alarm and saw that it was 2:35 a.m. For whatever reason, she was now wide-awake, painfully aware that her head once again felt as if it were being assaulted by rocks tumbling in a concrete mixer. Water and more painkillers were definitely called for, she decided, even though that meant a trip out of her nice cozy bed and into the cold bathroom. At least she didn't feel that sinking pit of grief in her stomach that had been the usual reason for her to wake up in the months since Sam died. The headache seemed almost a small price to pay in comparison.

She sat up, moving gingerly, wincing as she reached for the switch on her bedside lamp. She flicked it up and down a couple of times, but no light appeared. Great. Verity sighed, frustrated but not surprised. Looking back over the alcohol-hazed weeks since Thanksgiving, she couldn't remember when she'd last changed a lightbulb.

Taking care not to do further damage to her aches and pains, she inched over to the opposite side of the bed and switched on the other lamp. Nothing happened. Verity frowned, a little surprised that two lightbulbs would burn out simultaneously. Maybe the bulbs weren't the problem. Now that she was paying closer attention, she could see that her bedroom was pitch-dark, which meant that the night-light she normally kept burning in the wall outlet near the door to the master bath had also stopped functioning.

Probably a fuse had blown. If so, it would have to wait until morning to be fixed, since the main electric box was down three flights of stairs in the basement, and she had no desire to investigate at this hour of the night. A close encounter with a spider was not high on her list of favorite happenings. At least she could still get painkillers from the bathroom, since those lights operated on a different electrical circuit.

Shivering a little as she swung her legs out of bed, Verity groped with her toes until she found her slippers. Pushing them on, she headed for the bathroom. Once there, she fumbled along the wall in search of the switch for the central light fixture, then jiggled it a couple of times to no avail. When she tried the switch for the ceiling fan, it also refused to function.

Drat and double drat, as her mother would say. This many fuses were unlikely to have blown at the same time, leading to the depressing conclusion that electrical power must be out to the entire house.

Fortunately, she'd left the bottle of painkillers standing on the counter beside her sink, so she could at least do something about her headache without rummaging through the medicine cabinet and trying to read the labels of pill bottles in the dark. She stuck a couple of capsules on her tongue and swallowed them with a gulp of water from the tap before feeling her way into the hall. She flicked hopefully at various switches before giving up and accepting that nothing electrical was going to work.

Returning to her bedroom, she lifted up one of the drapes far enough so that she could see the houses on the opposite side of the street. Carriage lights were burning around several front doors, so this apparently wasn't a neighborhood power outage.

Terrific, Verity thought grumpily, retreating back to bed. She had a very good idea of why she found herself in the middle of the night, huddling under the covers, surrounded by darkness. She pictured the laundry basket in her living room, full of unopened mail that she'd been sorting when Dick Pedro arrived yesterday morning. Undoubtedly there was some vital utility bill stuck in among those piles of neglected correspondence. She had a vague memory of writing a check for her utility bill in a rare moment of sobriety right before Christmas, but she was obviously mistaken. Like her phone service, the electric power must have been cut off for nonpayment of her overdue account.

Getting electricity restored was going to prove a time-consuming pain in the butt, much worse than getting the phone service reinstated. Just what she didn't need right now. Verity pulled her knees up to her chin and scowled into the gloom, furious with herself for all those stupid, wasted weeks of self-pity.

Okay, Sam, are you watching this latest screwup of mine? Have you got any words of ghostly wisdom to take care of this new example of my total domestic incompetence over the past few months?

Her question met with profound silence. Her husband's ghost was apparently not in the mood to communicate with her. Or perhaps he needed a brain pickled in alcohol in order to do his best work.

I may not be drunk, but I've got a concussion, Verity thought morosely. *Isn't my brain scrambled enough right now for you to put in an appearance, Sam?*

It seemed not. She rolled onto her side and lay very still, trying without much success to build a cocoon of heat beneath her down comforter. On the edge of sleep, she heard the stairs creak, almost as if someone were walking up them.

Sam was coming to pay her a visit after all. She suppressed a giggle at the crazy thought, then realized that at some level she truly was waiting for him to appear. Absurd to expect her husband's ghost to materialize at her whim, especially since she didn't really have any desire to talk to him about something as humdrum as her failure to pay the utility bill. What she really wanted to discuss with him were her feelings for Michael Strait.

Verity buried her face in the pillow, chagrined at where her meandering thoughts had taken her. There was nothing like sending out a mental summons to her dead husband in order to ask how he felt about her sexual attraction to the man she'd betrayed him with.

You didn't betray me, sugar babe. You were tempted and you resisted. It's the resistance that's important, not the temptation.

She jerked bolt upright in the bed, ignoring protests from at least a half dozen aching muscles. Peering into the blackness, she was oddly disappointed when she couldn't manage to catch a glimpse of Sam. It was easier to pretend she wasn't talking to herself if she could see him.

Over here, Veri. In front of the French doors.

She stared wistfully at the Victorian slipper chair where her husband had so often sat reading late at night.

All she could see was emptiness. Verity tried not to feel sad. Instead of regretting that her dead husband was invisible, perhaps she should be grateful for that vestigial symptom of sanity.

Concentrate, Veri. You need to focus and then you'll be able to see me.

She blinked, rubbing her eyes, and suddenly he was there, wearing his favorite hunter-green sweater and baggy old khaki pants. Unlike the disconnected vision of New Year's Eve, his torso was all in one piece tonight. Either a sign of deepening paranoia, or else a welcome result of her sobriety. She supposed she could take her pick of explanations, Verity reflected dryly.

You said you needed to talk to me about Michael, Sam said. *That caught my attention.*

"I have a confession to make." Verity knew she had to tell him quickly, before she lost her courage. "I've been wanting to tell you this for months. It's about the time Michael and I were in Kashmir—" Verity felt her cheeks grow hot, but she plunged ahead. "Michael and I met each other by mistake at the Maharajah's party in Srinagar and—I kissed him."

Is that all?

"That's enough, isn't it? I wanted to have sex with him." She didn't say that she'd wanted to make love to him. How could you make love to a man you weren't even sure you liked? Sam didn't seem in a hurry to reply, but at least there was a measure of relief to be gained now that she'd finally made the admission, even if it was eighteen months too late. Even if it was to a figment of her own imagination.

But you didn't make love with him, and that's what matters. As far as she could judge from his slightly blurred features, Sam didn't seem particularly surprised or upset by her news. He gave her a smile that was full of tenderness. *You're human, Veri. So is Michael, and so was I. That means we aren't perfect, any of us.*

"I bet you were never tempted to betray our marriage vows."

No, not that. But I took advantage of your youth and your inexperience, which may be a worse sin. I pressured you to marry me, knowing you weren't in love with me—

"Of course I loved you! And you didn't have to pressure me to marry you. What are you talking about, Sam?"

It's true, you did love me, but you were never in love *with me.* Sam sounded a little sad, although the smile he gave her remained warm. *I knew how you felt about me from the beginning, although you didn't. You were too naive to understand the difference.*

"What's the difference between loving someone and being in love? Share some of your ghostly insights on that knotty subject, Sam."

He glanced toward the window, staring as if he could see the view outside even though the drapes were drawn. He hesitated, just for a moment, before turning back to look at her. *In a nutshell? The difference is sexual desire. Nothing more. Nothing less.*

"Oh, please." She was disappointed that he hadn't come up with a more profound response. He was a ghost, after all. Didn't he have access to sources of wisdom denied to mere mortals? She frowned at him. "Sex is such a stupid, trivial basis for a relationship."

Yes, often it is. But sometimes—too rarely—it's the most profound relationship two human beings can share. As for you and Michael...you could say a lot of things about your feelings for him, but I'm damn sure trivial isn't one of them.

"How do you know what I feel toward Michael?"

Easily. He shook off his slight appearance of melancholy and sent her a typical teasing Sam grin. *As you were saying just now, I'm a ghost and that gives me access to sources of wisdom you don't have.*

"I didn't say that to you. I just thought it."

Thought. Said. It's all one to me now. It's been very enlightening to escape from the constraints of a physical body.

"Good grief, Sam. Can you hear everything I think?" Verity was appalled by the possibility.

Not everything. He didn't elucidate, and her vision of Sam abruptly terminated, leaving the antique Victorian chair empty once again. She could still hear his voice, however, even though it rapidly grew fainter.

You're worrying about the wrong things, Veri. Our marriage was great while it lasted but now it's over. Pay attention to the real world and stop agonizing over the shadows of the past. You were right about paying the electric bill. You sent off a check the week before Christmas. You also woke up more than fifteen minutes ago. Why? Don't ignore your instincts. Listen—

"Listen to what?" she called into the emptiness.

There was no response. Her subconscious had apparently grown tired of playing the Sam game. Verity lay back against the pillows, wondering why she wasn't more scared about experiencing her third visitation from a man who'd been dead and cremated since the previous July. How many more conversations could she have with her dead husband before she needed to take herself to a shrink and request powerful tranquilizing medication? Or maybe she should skip the medication and opt immediately for a snugly fitted straitjacket and a comfortably padded room.

At the very least, if she really believed she was in communion with Sam's ghost, she ought to have asked him to post a note on the celestial bulletin board, requesting an urgent conference with Khalid Muhammad. Right now, she could use a bit of otherworldly help in finding Farooq. Or perhaps a few heavenly hints as to what she was supposed to do with the key Khalid had given her. Which, come to think of it, had either been lost in the melee outside the hotel, or was still sitting in the pocket of her slacks.

She must remember to look for the key before she took the slacks to the cleaners, Verity thought, eyes drifting closed. She didn't have the energy to get up and search for it right now, but Khalid had seemed to believe the key was very important. She shouldn't just toss it away, even if she didn't have any idea how she could discover the secrets Khalid insisted it unlocked.

From the floor below her bedroom, she heard a distinctive squeal as the hinges on the door to her office were either opened or closed. Heart racing, she sat up and listened intently, but however hard she strained, she couldn't hear anything more.

The squeak must have been caused by a draft of wind moving the door, she decided. What else could it be?

The house sank back into silence, but Verity no longer felt even remotely drowsy. Resisting a cowardly impulse to crawl under the bedcovers and hide, she considered the fact that she'd now heard a succession of noises indicating that she wasn't alone in the house. She wasn't about to go downstairs to her study and investigate. She was neither brave enough nor brainless enough for that. But if there was an intruder in the house, he'd most likely been prowling around ever since she first woke up. From the nature of the sounds she'd heard, he seemed to be working his way upstairs. Which meant that any minute now, he could arrive in her bedroom.

Verity reached instinctively for the phone, then

stopped without picking up the receiver. The phone on her study desk had a tendency to click when other phones in the house were dialed, which meant she might not be able to make a call without the intruder realizing what she was doing.

In the circumstances, dialing the police emergency number might not be a real smart move. On balance, however, it seemed a slightly less bad option than any other she could think of. Verity decided to risk placing the call. With great care, she lifted the phone handset and waited for a dial tone. Nothing happened. The line was totally, ominously dead, even though she'd checked when she came home from the hospital and her phone had been working just fine at that point. An unexpected example of the phone company keeping its promise and reinstating service on schedule.

Sweat beaded at the base of her neck, but she forced herself to stay calm. Now would be a really bad time to indulge in a panic attack, she warned herself. She needed to review the situation calmly. She had no phone and no lights. What were her remaining choices?

She could opt to do nothing. There was a chance that the burglar might decide he'd collected enough loot without ever coming upstairs. Unfortunately, she couldn't count on that, so she needed a plan in case he invaded her bedroom.

She knew that thieves usually wanted to avoid a confrontation with the home owner, so even if the burglar came upstairs, it might be smart to stay right where she was. The burglar didn't seem to be crazed with drugs or alcohol or he wouldn't have been so quiet. If he was high, or drunk, he'd have bumped into furniture, dropped things, cursed. Presumably, therefore, this burglar wasn't likely to be overcome by a drug-induced psychosis and turn rabid at the sight of her.

So, assuming he was both sober and as anxious to avoid confrontation as she was, she could lie on her stomach, pull the covers up to her chin and pretend to be asleep. It would take guts to lie still, breathing regularly, while an intruder crept around her bedroom, but she could do it if she had to.

Except...what if her analysis was wrong? It would be taking a huge risk to gamble on the hope that the intruder would leave her alone if she feigned sleep, Verity decided. What if he didn't care about avoiding a confrontation with the home owner? There was always one exception that proved the rule, and he might be it.

More than twenty minutes had passed since she'd first been jolted from sleep, so presumably it was at least that long since whoever had first invaded her home. The burglar should have already grabbed a few easily fenced valuables by now. Grabbed them and left. Why was he still here? Even more sinister was the fact that he'd taken the time and trouble to go down to the basement to cut off her power and phone service. Bad guys often severed power lines in the movies, but in real life most burglars only wanted to get in and out of their victim's homes as quickly as possible. Far from worrying about lights and phones, quite often they didn't even care if they set off alarms, cynically aware that by the time the police or security company arrived, they would be gone.

Verity shivered. It suddenly didn't seem at all unreasonable to wonder if this was a burglar who robbed for income, then tortured and raped his victims for a little extra fun. Maybe Khalid's murder this afternoon had left her prey to wild conspiracy theories, but she had an uneasy feeling that this intruder wasn't just a regular burglar. Surviving an assassination attempt apparently wasn't enough drama for one day. Now she had to defend herself against a possibly psycho burglar who got off on torturing his victims.

Verity's fright hardened into anger. Without phone service, she couldn't stop this intruder from robbing her, but she'd be damned if she was going to lie around waiting to be raped or beaten. Or worse. Maybe he'd come into her bedroom or maybe he wouldn't, but she sure as hell didn't plan to hang around to find out.

She needed to find a hiding place. The attic might work, but pulling down the ladder was such a noisy operation that the intruder would be bound to hear her. Rather than trying to find somewhere to hide, she needed to get out of the house so that she could summon help. Fortunately, there was a fire escape that could be accessed from her bedroom. With luck, the burglar would know that in Georgetown the streets were rarely empty at any hour of the day or night, in which case he wasn't likely to take the risk of pursuing her, even if he was a weirdo who liked to molest his victims. Once out of the house, she would be safe, Verity decided.

Trying to be silent—which was ironic in view of the carefree way she'd cruised around earlier, pushing doors open and clicking light switches on and off—Verity slid out of bed and crept into her closet. Gripped by a sense of urgency that was all the more intense because of the amount of time she'd already wasted, she pulled on her discarded slacks over her pajamas. For once her weight loss was useful, since they glided on easily. She grabbed the nearest turtleneck sweater from the shelf and tugged that on, too.

Sounds were muffled inside the closet so she couldn't tell if the intruder was getting closer, but her instincts—for what little use they seemed to be tonight—had started to shriek that her time was running out. That the intruder was finally on his way upstairs.

Her coat and down ski jacket were both in the downstairs hall closet, along with her hats and gloves. Too bad. Breath coming fast and shallow, she tied an oversize pashmina shawl around her head and neck, simultaneously shoving her feet into a pair of rubber-soled loafers. She was going to freeze her butt off outside, but at least she wasn't going to be lying in bed, an impotent victim, when the burglar arrived in her room.

The stairs of the fire escape were tucked away at the side of the building, but they were connected to the master bedroom by a wrought-iron balcony that ran across the narrow frontal facade of the house. Avoiding the floorboard outside her closet that always creaked, Verity hurried over to the French doors that provided access to the balcony. She pushed aside the Victorian slipper chair and slid behind the drapes, sparing a moment to wonder if her subconscious had created an image of Sam's ghost sitting there in a last-ditch effort to warn her not to fall back to sleep.

It was months since Verity had opened the doors to the balcony, and she broke three nails and scraped skin from both knuckles before she acknowledged that the security bolt had rusted shut. No way was this door going to open without tools. And she couldn't smash the glass because, ironically, it was high-tech and shatterproof, specifically designed to foil intruders. Besides, the noise of smashing glass might bring the burglar running before she could make her getaway.

Even as she formed the thought, Verity realized there was no longer any need to worry about attracting the intruder's attention. He must finally have heard her moving about, and—in turn—he was no longer attempting to conceal his presence. She heard him climbing the stairs toward the bedrooms, his tread fast and noisy.

For a single instant, panic had her pounding on the

balcony door. Then a rush of adrenaline kicked in, sharpening her survival instincts. She ran to the door of her bedroom and slammed it shut, relieved that the heavy, old-fashioned key actually functioned. No time to worry about how long the antique door frame would resist the intruder's efforts to smash through the lock. She just needed to get the hell out of the house and she would be safe.

She dashed to the bathroom and slammed that door, too. This lock was new, but pathetically flimsy, so she shoved the bath mat and her towel along the crack between door and tile floor, hoping the thick fabric might jam the entrance for another vital few minutes.

With the bathroom door wedged tightly shut, she climbed onto the toilet seat and ripped out the window screen. For once she had reason to be thankful for her lousy housekeeping standards over the past several months. She'd neglected to put on the old-fashioned storm windows at the end of summer, and with the screen gone, she could slide open the sash window with relative ease.

Panting, vaguely aware of excruciating pain as she added bruises to her bruises, she hauled herself onto the sill before slithering out onto the narrow balcony and pulling the window shut behind her. She'd made it.

As she started to run down the rusty iron stairs, she glanced to the street below and saw emptiness. Damn! There wasn't a soul in sight, not even a drunken college student, wending his way back to the nightlife on M Street.

Through the open window, she heard the crash of the bathroom door bursting open. Oh God! Her pathetic effort with the towels obviously hadn't slowed down the intruder more than a second or two. How fast could she make it down the stairs and around the block to where she would almost certainly find people?

Not fast enough, judging by the thumping sound of the intruder jumping out of the bathroom window and landing on the metal fire escape. Grabbing the handrail for balance, she sped down the next flight of stairs, resisting the powerful temptation to waste time by looking over her shoulder to get a glimpse of what kind of thug was chasing her.

Even without looking, she could hear that her pursuer was taking the rickety stairs two at a time, gaining on her with every stride. It was a trick she couldn't copy. Her muscles were so stiff from their afternoon drubbing that she simply couldn't summon the coordination to take two stairs at once.

She screamed for help, even though she knew the street was empty. There might be pedestrians around the corner, just out of sight. Unfortunately, she didn't have much breath to spare so it wasn't a very loud scream and no helpful bystanders appeared, much less came running to her aid. No neighbors stuck their heads out of the window to see what was going on.

She was going to get caught, Verity realized sickly, putting all her strength into a last desperate burst of speed. To no avail. Her pursuer caught up with her just as she reached the sidewalk, grabbing her from behind and shoving her against the wall, under the overhang of the fire escape. The light from the streetlamps barely penetrated this side alley, and she knew the chances of a passerby noticing her were slim to none. At least she was out of the house. Not trapped inside like a rat in a laboratory cage, helplessly waiting for the experiment to begin.

The burglar held her immobilized by the sheer weight of his body pressing against hers. She tried to scream, but he threw his left arm across her throat, choking off her breath. He held a knife in his right hand, its blade gleaming in the shaft of light as the moon emerged briefly from behind the clouds.

The knife scared her, but she positively gagged when she felt the hard pulse of his erection pressed against her abdomen. Bad as it was to be menaced by a brute wielding a lethally sharp switchblade, the idea of being violated by him was almost worse.

Even so, Verity wasn't about to beg to be released. She remembered reading that many rapists got off on their victims' frantic pleas for mercy. Anyway, she didn't feel in the least like pleading. On the contrary, she felt like giving the guy a violent kick in the crotch. A dangerous impulse to indulge in, unless she was absolutely sure she could disable him with a single kick.

There was a long nail hammered into the wall right behind her, its purpose long forgotten and its rusty head protruding no more than an eighth of an inch. The cement between the bricks had crumbled and if she could wriggle and twist the nail for long enough, she just might be able to work it loose. At which point, she'd have a semblance of a weapon. The mere prospect was enough to give her hope. Unobtrusively, Verity began to twist the nail head.

"Don't scream again if you're smart," the burglar said. Grotesquely, his voice sounded like that of a woman, high-pitched and with a vaguely New England accent. The feminine voice emerging from the male body created a mind-blowing sense of disorientation, and Verity wondered for a moment if she'd finally scrambled her brains to the point of no return. It was a huge relief when it dawned on her that she must be hearing an example of electronic voice disguise.

"Make it easy on both of us," her attacker said, and even though she knew she wasn't really listening to a woman, the feminine tones, contrasted with the all-too-masculine erection, left Verity feeling giddy. "I want the key Khalid Muhammad gave you this morning. Where is it?"

Khalid's key? The request was so unexpected, so out of left field, that for a moment, Verity blanked. Even if she'd wanted to answer him, she couldn't have done so. She stared up at her attacker, her gaze caught by his ugly, overlarge nose and curly auburn hair. He wriggled his erection against her belly, deliberately taunting her. The effort not to throw up, not to reveal her fear, caused her vision to blur.

Oh, God, she didn't want to pass out but she was fading fast.

Her captor delivered a stinging slap to her jaw, bringing her painfully back to full consciousness. Her head throbbed, ringing with his words. "The key, goddammit. Where's the fucking key?"

He was frantic, Verity realized, focusing with a jerk. And possibly even more scared than she was. The knife he held was not entirely steady, and his breath came in irregular pants. He wanted the key Khalid had given her in the worst way—and he wasn't going to kill her until he'd got it, or at least found out where it was.

There was power in the knowledge that her attacker couldn't afford to kill her. That she had a small bargaining chip to keep herself alive. Confidence surged back, enough for Verity to start twisting the nail with renewed resolve.

Enough for her to register another important fact about her attacker. He was wearing a mask. Not a knitted ski mask like a bank robber, or even a coarse plastic one like little kids wore at Halloween. His mask was an expensive latex creation of the sort used by actors and professional entertainers. The sort that would be undetectable at a distance, and would leave his victims unable to provide a description of their attacker.

Just like the mask Khalid's assassin had worn yesterday afternoon.

Verity's stomach lurched. This was not, perhaps, the best moment to have figured out that her attacker and Khalid's murderer were utilizing similar disguises. It was scarcely a boost to her confidence to conclude that she'd been grabbed by somebody who hung out with assassins. On the other hand, at least she knew there was no point in wasting her time memorizing how her attacker looked. She could safely assume he didn't have a big nose or curly auburn hair.

Her attacker pressed the point of the knife into her neck, just deeply enough to draw blood. "It's not worth dying for a key," he said, and even the electronic woman's voice sounded hoarse with strain. "Don't try to be brave, Verity. Tell me where you put the goddamn fucking key."

Making her voice tremble—which wasn't in the least difficult—Verity mumbled a reply. "If I tell you where the key is, you'll kill me."

"I have no reason to kill you once I have the key." The creepy feminine voice was oily smooth.

"Do you think I'm totally stupid? Or just too frightened to think straight?" Verity had finally managed to liberate the nail. Keeping her hand hanging down at her side, she wedged the rusty nail, point out, between her middle and index fingers. Then she brought her arm up in a single, swift movement, aiming for his eyes.

At the last second, she couldn't bring herself to ram the nail into his eyeball. But she hesitated less than a second before jamming the nail into the attacker's latex-covered cheek and ripping downward, aiming for his throat.

The attacker howled and sprang back, his hands going to his face. She had no idea how severely she'd wounded him—wasn't even sure that she'd penetrated far enough to rip skin as well as rubber—but she'd at least succeeded in distracting him enough that she was able to twist sideways and bring her knee up to his groin. Hard. Indifferent to her cuts and bruises, she rammed upward into his testicles with all the force of her fear and rage.

Her attacker doubled over, keening with pain, but he kept one hand over his face, even though she couldn't see any blood dripping from the rip she'd torn in his mask. She dodged past him, half expecting to be brought down by a hail of bullets, but if her assailant had a gun, he decided not to use it. Or maybe between his ripped cheek and battered testicles, he didn't have the coordination to reach for a weapon.

Sheer instinct carried her out of the alley and onto Thirtieth Street. Once there, she headed toward M Street as fast as her legs would carry her. M always had people on it, and there was an all-night bar right at the intersection where she could call the police for help.

She ran so hard that the rasp of her own breathing drowned out other sounds. The streets seemed unusually devoid of people, perhaps because of the cold weather, and it felt like half a lifetime before she reached the safety of the bar. In reality it couldn't have been more than two or three minutes. She stumbled in through the entrance, shaking with exhaustion and fright. She made sure there were customers in the bar before she finally allowed herself to turn around and scan the street for any sign of her attacker.

There was none. M Street had a few pedestrians going about their business, but it was beautifully empty of anyone chasing her.

Shaking from relief, Verity made her way to the bar.

"Hi, Verity. Haven't seen you in a while." The bartender greeted her with a yawn and a half smile. "You look like you could use a drink. What are you having?"

A vodka. Sweet Jesus, she couldn't imagine anything in the entire universe that would taste more wonderful right now than an ice-cold vodka.

Verity drew in a shaky breath. "I just need to use your phone, Pete. Somebody tried to break into my house, and they cut the phone line."

"Jeez, that's a bummer." Pete sounded sympathetic, but Verity wasn't sure he believed her. Drunks, she supposed, had a tendency to invest their lives with dramas that were fueled more by alcohol than real events. And Pete had seen her drunk more times than she cared to remember.

"Pete, I ran out of the house without any money. I need a quarter for the call. Can you spring for it for me?"

He tossed a glass cloth over his shoulder, scrutinizing her. "Sure, but 911 is a free call."

"I know, but I don't want to call 911. I have a friend in…law enforcement. I want to call him." Flushing, she added, "I'm stone-cold sober, Pete. There was a burglar in my house, and I ran down the fire escape to get away from him. He chased me out of the house, and so I ran here where I knew there would be other people."

Better not to mention that the burglar had assaulted her, and worn a mask, and used an electronic voice transformer, or Pete might conclude she was hallucinating, even though she appeared sober.

He gave her a final assessing look and apparently decided there was at least a good chance she was telling the truth. He reached into his pocket and tossed some loose change onto the counter. "Here. Be my guest."

"Thank you." Verity scooped up the coins. "Thank you very much, Pete. I'll pay you back, I promise."

"Whatever." Pete had long ago quit believing in promises made by drunks.

Verity discovered that her legs had developed a wobble that wouldn't quit, and she barely made it to the pay phone in the corner of the bar. She lifted the phone off the hook with a hand that was visibly shaking, and sank into a nearby chair, dialing the one phone number that seemed, for some reason, to be imprinted on her otherwise blank brain.

The phone rang three times and then the answering machine clicked in. "Michael," she said. "If you're there, please pick up the phone. This is really important. I need you—"

"Verity." Michael's voice held no trace of sleepiness. "What's happened? What's wrong?"

She didn't know where to begin with her explanations. "I need you to come and get me, Michael. I'm at King's Bar on M Street in Georgetown."

"Stay right where you are. I'll be there in twenty minutes."

He hung up the phone before she even had time to say thank you.

Ten

Two days after his thirty-fourth birthday, Michael Strait realized that he was hopelessly in love with Verity Marlowe.

Until that red letter day, his dealings with women had been easy and uncomplicated. So easy, in fact, that he'd never quite understood why most of his friends made such a total screwup of their love lives. It was a mystery to him why the vast majority of the male sex spent their lives in frustrated pursuit of the very woman that they were soon trying desperately to get rid of. He couldn't quite grasp either the urgency of the chase, or the despair of the separation.

Growing up with three sisters, the female sex had never seemed as unfathomable to him as it did to many of his friends. That wasn't to say he completely understood what made women tick. Even as a brash twenty-year-old, he would never have been arrogant or misguided enough to claim that. But he could at least grasp enough of the basics to guarantee that any night he went to his bed alone, it was because he chose to do so.

By the time he was in his thirties, Michael had slept with more women than he remembered and certainly more than he cared to count. He wasn't sure quite what it was he was looking for, or even why he wanted it so badly, but he was damn sure he hadn't found it. As relationship succeeded relationship, and the women in his life began to fade into a single good-looking blur, he acknowledged that he'd become more than a little cynical about love and romance. In his twenties, he'd clung to the romantic illusion. By his thirtieth birthday, he had the routine down pat: find an attractive woman, make no promises, have sex until you're both bored, move on.

Observing the romantic activities of his friends did absolutely nothing to burnish his desire to enter the institution of marriage. He had friends who got married because they claimed to be in love; friends who got married because their girlfriends were pregnant; and friends who claimed to have met the woman who was their perfect lifelong companion.

As far as he could see, no reason for marrying provided acceptable odds of success. Whatever their stated reasons for taking the plunge, his friends' marriages ended in divorce with statistical regularity and depressing frequency.

During his twenties, Michael had fallen more or less in love a few times himself, although his romantic experiences always stopped short of the grand passion that had kept centuries of poets busy penning sonnets, and musicians composing sentimental ballads. Twice he'd even considered getting married. On both occasions, he'd pulled back from commitment at the last minute, although he couldn't have explained exactly why, even to himself.

For sure it wasn't because he was waiting to fall more deeply in love. On the contrary, Michael was quite clear in his own mind that he had no desire to be swept away by passion. Having seen his parents' marriage from the inside, he considered that the joys of passion were significantly overrated.

His parents enjoyed recounting the tale of their first meeting at a concert in New Delhi, and how they'd fallen in love at first sight. They'd overcome great obstacles in order to marry, and they were still devoted to each other after thirty-eight years of marriage. His mother was fifty-nine, his father sixty-five, but there was no doubt that they remained physically attracted to each other. From the occasional intimate glances Michael had observed them exchange, he had a suspicion that, even now, far more genuine sexual excitement was generated in their bedroom than in his.

That didn't mean either one of his parents was happy, at least as far as Michael could tell. His mother missed her home and family in Kashmir with an intensity that had only grown deeper as the years passed. She missed the ritual observance of her religious faith, and the social customs of her native land. She missed the mountains and lakes, the communal living and the constant companionship that were an integral part of Hindu society.

On the surface, his father's sacrifices for the sake of the marriage seemed to have been less. And yet Michael had come to realize that in many subtle ways his father had also paid a heavy price to keep his marriage together. His father's parents hadn't rejected his Hindu bride outright, but they were missionaries with all the fervor of their Christian beliefs, and it was painful for them to enter their only son's home and find phallic shrines to the god Shiva slap bang in the center of the entrance hall.

With so much negative baggage left over from childhood, Michael didn't find it surprising that his life didn't seem destined to include any great love affair. And then, two months before his thirty-fourth birthday, he met Verity Marlowe.

Except for his response to her, their first meeting was unremarkable in almost every way, the sort of encounter with a desirable woman he must already have experienced a hundred times in his life. At the request of his division chief at the Agency, Michael had put in an appearance at a reception hosted by the Indian ambassador. He'd dutifully attended, and having exchanged thirty minutes' worth of mind-numbing diplomatic platitudes with the guest of honor, a visiting dignitary from India's parliament, he decided his obligation was well and truly done. He'd been about to make his excuses and leave when Verity Marlowe walked into the room.

Michael found his attention inexplicably caught. Inexplicably, because he was usually attracted to dark, petite, vivacious women and Verity was tall and slender, her coloring fair without being strikingly blond, and her aura was noticeably serene, even at a distance of twenty paces. She had gray-blue eyes that appeared reflective rather than exuberant, and thick straight hair that she wore twisted into a loop at the nape of her neck. It wasn't even as if she had been stunningly dressed. She wore the standard Washington cocktail party getup: a black silk suit, the style sleekly conservative, the hemline more modest than many.

Despite the touch-me-not outfit, a single glance at her gorgeously long legs and generously curved breasts was all it took for Michael to find himself fantasizing about how she would look if he slowly took the pins out of her hair and allowed the resulting mass to tumble in a rippling, honey-brown cascade over his pillow.

In retrospect, he supposed an objective observer would claim that Verity had looked beautiful that night rather than sexy, but Michael had never managed to be objective. Something about her called to him at the most fundamental, primitive level. As she progressed into the room, he found himself staring at her with a predatory hunger so intense and immediate that it caught her attention.

She met his gaze without pretension or flirtation. Her

expression was friendly, but slightly puzzled, as if she wasn't sure why they were staring at each other. Even at a distance, he could tell that her manner had none of the casual openness of a typical American woman. Rather there was an air of containment about her that reminded him of the bone-deep modesty of a woman raised in one of the Asian cultures.

With an incoherent mumble that fell markedly short of his usual casual sophistication, Michael excused himself to the Indian parliamentarian and strode across the room to Verity's side, his heart beating oddly fast. As soon as he was within range, he checked her left hand for a wedding ring. It was safely naked and he breathed a silent sigh of relief. His moral code was flexible—having been raised by a devout Hindu mother and an equally devout Methodist father, he'd learned to save his sanity by avoiding absolutes. However, he had his own moral code that he stuck to pretty closely, and he'd figured out while still in his teens that since the world was full of desirable single women, having affairs with the married ones was a game only for fools and villains.

Over the past decade he'd accumulated a more than respectable store of one-liners that made for great opening gambits when he wanted to attract a woman's attention. That night, though, he hadn't been able to remember any of them. Instead, he'd been forced to fall back on a straightforward, uninspired introduction.

"I'm Michael Strait," he said, shaking her hand. "I'm on the guest list for this party because I operate an international trading company headquartered here in D.C. We buy cashmere and handwoven carpets in Kashmir for resale in the States, and we export water purifying equipment to towns and villages all over India."

In fact, the Mahal Trading Company existed in name only, with backup documentation and office address provided courtesy of the CIA, but having lived with the same cover for more than three years, he'd grown comfortable with the story and had developed credible answers to almost any question he was likely to get asked.

"I'm Verity Marlowe." She responded to his introduction with a friendly smile and returned his handshake. "By coincidence, I grew up in Kashmir, too, but now I work for the State Department." Her smile changed to a soft laugh and her cheeks suffused with an enchanting pink color. "I've never had the chance to say that to anyone before. I only started working at State a week ago."

The old-fashioned Puritan name suited her, he thought, returning her smile. "Congratulations, Verity. I hope you have a long and rewarding career."

"Thanks. I'm excited about it, as you can see."

"Have they assigned you to a department at State yet, or are you still going through orientation?"

"I'm still going through orientation, and my final assignment hasn't been decided yet. I was hired for a position in the press office, but that's already been changed. Since I spent the first eighteen years of my life in Kashmir, I'm hoping I'll eventually be given a job where I can put my knowledge of India to good use."

He raised an eyebrow, teasing just a little. "Don't count on it. The State Department is notorious for assignments that are bewildering in their lack of logic. You'll probably be transferred to South America before the year is out. Or sent on an intensive language training course to learn Hungarian."

"Shh. Bite your tongue." She pressed her index finger to her lip, but her eyes danced with merriment. "Don't give the goddess Kali any ideas. She comes up with enough bad ones all on her own. Are you originally from Kashmir, Michael?"

He found her enchanting, and amazingly sexy, although he wasn't sure whether that was despite her unusual air of innocence or because of it. God knew, innocence was a commodity rare enough in Washington, D.C. to draw any man's attention.

"My mother is from Kashmir. My father's family is from Minnesota."

"That's an intriguing combination."

"It's had its wilder moments. Could I by any chance persuade you to leave this party and have dinner with me?" he asked. "We could discuss our fascinating life histories at length."

She blinked. "But I only just got here!"

"Trust me. You aren't going to miss a thing." He knew he was rushing ahead too fast, that he ought to have spent a lot longer inventing witty dialogue, persuading her that he was an interesting man to spend the evening with. But he wasn't willing to waste time going through the familiar, boring rituals. He felt a burning need to take her away to someplace quiet and intimate, where the two of them could get down to the serious business of getting to know one another. He already felt an almost physical hunger to know more about her.

"I'm sure the ambassador won't notice if you leave," he said coaxingly.

She laughed. "You're right. I'm quite sure he wouldn't. Or anyone else, either."

"I'm starving, and I'd really enjoy having dinner with you. I know a great Indian restaurant near here—"

"The Taj Mahal?" she asked.

He noticed that her voice was carefully neutral. "Not unless you insist," he said, flashing a grin. "The Taj Mahal is for tourists. All fancy china and elaborate silk cushions, but dreary food. I was thinking about Neelam's. Do you know it?"

"Oh yes, I do. Their *masala dosa* is wonderful." Her expression became animated. "It's one of my favorite places to eat."

"Mine, too." Michael said.

Verity gave a wistful smile. "Neelam's reminds me of the Bhargawanda Dhaba in Srinagar. That used to be such a great restaurant until it got blown up."

"It was the best, wasn't it?"

They looked at each other with dawning wonder, as if they'd discovered some hugely important universal truth as opposed to the unsurprising fact that they both enjoyed the food at two restaurants that were noted for their excellent cuisine.

Michael blinked, pulling himself together. "Well, since you obviously enjoy Neelam's as much as I do, what are we waiting for? Let's go. Do you have a coat to pick up from the cloakroom?"

Verity shook her head, not only to indicate no, but as if dispelling a momentary confusion. "I'd love to come with you, Michael, but I can't. The food at Neelam's is much too authentically Indian for Sam." Her voice was warmly affectionate as she pronounced the name.

Who the hell was Sam? Michael felt a premonition of looming disaster.

Verity smiled as she continued. "Sam is convinced that Polish sausage is sophisticated international cuisine, and I've never been able to persuade him to be more adventurous. He prefers to eat at restaurants where he recognizes every dish on the menu and he can identify all the ingredients on his plate at a single glance."

Michael asked the question that had to be asked, very much afraid he wouldn't like the answer. "Who is Sam?" he queried. "Did you come here with one of your colleagues from the State Department?"

"No, Sam is my husband." Verity announced the relationship lightly, as if totally unaware of having said anything shocking.

"Your husband?"

"Yes. Sam Marlowe. He's a professor of American lit at George Washington University and an all-around great person even if he doesn't like Indian food."

"You aren't wearing a wedding ring," Michael said flatly. He knew he sounded churlish and accusatory, but he didn't care. That was exactly how he felt. How could Verity be married? It was all wrong for her to be married.

She glanced down at her left hand, touching her ring finger as if just now remembering that it was bare. "The stone was loose and we had to take it to the jeweler's to be fixed."

Michael was still trying to work out what the hell he could say next, when he realized she was staring past him, looking over his shoulder. "Here's Sam now," Verity said, her whole face glowing. As she watched her husband approach, her mouth broke into a smile so tender that it immediately put paid to any hope that her marriage might be one of the many teetering its way toward the divorce courts.

A kindly looking man in his early forties hurried up, panting, his tie askew. He had a wiry body, ruddy cheeks, hair tinged with red, and his eyes were crinkled by permanent laughter lines. He wasn't as tall as Verity in her high-heeled evening shoes, but he enveloped her in an enthusiastic bear hug, planting a smacking kiss on her cheek.

"Hi, sugar babe." The two of them exchanged a quick, mischievous glance, as if Sam's endearment was an ongoing joke between them. "Sorry I'm late, but I got held up at a faculty meeting. The vice-chancellor was delivering his standard monthly lecture on the budget shortfall."

"You're forgiven." Verity snagged a glass of champagne from the tray of a passing waiter, and handed it to Sam. "Heaven knows I wouldn't want you to miss out on a single word of the vice-chancellor's speech."

"Right." He rolled his eyes over the champagne glass. "There must have been at least a couple of sentences in there that I hadn't heard before, although at this moment I can't imagine which ones they might have been."

"Anyway, you're here now. I'm glad you made it." She hooked her hand through his outstretched arm, and smiled at him. "Sam, you have to say hello to Michael Strait. He owns an international trading company headquartered here in D.C., and his mother was originally from Kashmir. I was just about to ask him how long it's been since his last visit there."

Sam shook hands with Michael and the conversation flowed smoothly among the three of them for another several minutes, mostly about the nonexistent Mahal Trading Company. Michael had never been a man to waste time yearning for the impossible and he wasn't about to start now. Verity was married, so be it. With a pang of regret that surprised him a little for its intensity, he gave a mental shrug and filed her away under the heading of *Unattainable*.

He and Sam soon discovered that they played racquetball at the same health club, and that they'd both just lost their favorite partners to job transfers. Before they left the reception, Sam suggested that the two of them should book a court and play for an hour or two over the weekend. Michael accepted the offer without so much as a premonitory quiver of foreboding. He liked Sam, he needed another racquetball partner. The fact that he'd been briefly attracted to Verity was of no significance. She was married. End of story. Move on.

Sam proved to be a keen but good-natured competitor

on the racquetball court, and his skill level matched Michael's well, a rare find. He was also an all-around nice guy, with an infectious pleasure in the simple joys of life, and an erudite knowledge of American literature that he shared with endearing enthusiasm.

After their first game, when Michael suggested that they should go out for a beer, Sam insisted that Michael should come back to the house instead. Verity always made a huge brunch on Sunday, he said, and there would be plenty of extra food.

They went back to Sam's house. There was indeed plenty of food, all delicious, since cooking gourmet meals was apparently one of Verity's favorite ways to relax. Michael and Verity greeted each other politely, and then avoided talking to each other for the rest of the afternoon.

After that, he and Sam would get together for a game of racquetball at least twice a week whenever Michael was in town. Occasionally he took Sam out afterward for a beer. More often, Sam invited Michael home to his place. There was always some renovation project underway in the old house, and sometimes he and Sam would spend a couple of satisfying hours banging nails, or sanding down forty years of paintwork. Other times they just drank a beer, or ate a meal, or watched a rented movie. It took Michael quite a while before he figured out that it was Sam who always selected sentimental romances, and Verity who chose the science fiction adventures.

Unless she watched a movie with them, sitting on the sofa next to Sam, her legs tucked under her husband's knees, Verity rarely did more than say hello to Michael and then disappear. If he and Sam worked on a remodeling project, she would shut herself in the study and catch up on paperwork. If he and Sam took a beer into the living room, she'd retreat to the kitchen and bury herself in some complicated recipe that required hours of chopping, grinding and peeling before she even reached the point of firing up the stove.

Michael told himself he didn't care about Verity being so elusive. On the contrary, he was glad she kept a low profile. Sam was rapidly turning into the best friend he'd made since high school, which meant that Verity was now categorized not just as *married and unattainable,* but *married to my friend.* A designation that put her so far off-limits that she should have had no presence on his mental horizon.

When Michael happened to mention that his birthday was coming up the following Thursday, Sam insisted that they should get together to celebrate in style. "I'm teaching a special graduate seminar on your actual birthday," he said. "But come over for dinner on Saturday. You know how much Verity loves to bake and she found a great recipe for chocolate cream torte in *Bon Appetit* magazine she's planning on trying."

No warning bells sounded in Michael's head. No premonition of disaster made his blood run cold. Instead he gave his good friend Sam a genial thump on the shoulder and told him he'd come over to the house about seven. He promised to bring the wine.

At the appointed time on Saturday, Michael presented himself at Sam's front door. Verity opened it. "Hi, Michael." She stepped back to give him room to walk in without any danger of their accidentally touching each other. He recognized what she was doing without allowing himself to acknowledge the significance of their behavior.

"Hi, Verity." He handed her the two bottles of wine. He dodged eye contact, once again failing to notice consciously what he was doing. Avoidance had long since become second nature whenever he was in her company. Even so, if he'd been honest with himself, he would have been forced to admit that he'd gathered and stored a hundred secret images of Verity during the months since he and Sam became friends.

"You look great," Michael said. "That's a good outfit on you."

"Thanks. It's new. I'm glad you like it."

He couldn't have described what she was wearing if his life hung in the balance because, of course, he hadn't actually looked at her. He needed to get his armor better in place before he did that. He followed her into the familiar comfort of the living room, anxious to be out of her presence. Anxious to get the barrier of her husband's presence firmly in place.

The living room was empty. "Where's Sam?" he asked.

"He's in bed. He put his back out playing touch football with a group of his students this morning, and he can't move."

"Oh, I'm sorry." Why the hell hadn't she called to cancel? Why would she think he wanted to come over if Sam was in bed? He turned and gave her a fake smile, still without truly seeing her. "I'll go up and see him, if that's okay."

"Actually, he's sleeping. He took some Valium and he's pretty much down for the count."

"Then I should leave." Michael was already half out of the room.

"There's no reason for you to leave," she said. "I'd already completed most of the preparations for dinner by the time we realized Sam needed to go to bed. You'd be doing me a real favor if you stayed and helped me eat some of the food. There's masses of it."

Michael was shocked enough by the invitation to finally bring his gaze into focus and look at Verity. She was wearing dark-gray silk pants and a thin knit top in a rain-washed shade of blue that exactly matched the color of her eyes. The top clung to the swell of her breasts and just skimmed the waistband of her pants. While he watched, she reached up nervously to twist a stray piece of hair into the loose knot at the nape of her neck and a smidgen of bare skin became visible around her midriff.

His reaction to the sight of a quarter inch of her naked skin was an instant erection. The palms of his hands were suddenly sweating, and his mouth was dry. Instead of taking heed of the warning signs and getting the hell out of the war zone, he heard himself thanking Verity for her invitation and telling her that he'd be delighted to stay.

Hell, why not give himself a birthday present of sheer torture?

Surprisingly, the three hours they lingered over dinner weren't hell at all. They were, in fact, three of the most enjoyable hours Michael had experienced in years. He was reluctant to tell Verity the lies about his job that were usually second nature to him these days, even around his family. Instead he steered the conversation away from anything that might force him to trot out one of the standard, Agency-approved fabrications about the nonexistent Mahal Trading Company and his supposed life as a cloth trader. Personal topics also seemed dangerous territory. Instead, they compared opinions about impersonal topics like books and movies, restaurants and Nautilus equipment, college football and Hindu gods. Then they talked about the latest exhibition at the Smithsonian and the upcoming concert season at the Kennedy Center.

Neither of them mentioned Sam.

At the most fundamental level it didn't matter much what they talked about, because communication between the two of them was taking place on another plane entirely. Michael ate without tasting the food, and drank— perhaps too much—without noticing whether the wine was red or white. All the while, he was aware of sliding farther down the perfumed, slippery slope to damnation. He watched himself slide, but he never reached out and grabbed a handhold to haul himself back. One mention of Sam's name would have done it, but he never spoke the crucial word. Instead, he looked into the gray-blue depths of Verity's eyes—and let himself drown.

For all his stubborn refusal to analyze the situation in which he found himself, he never doubted that Verity had fallen under the same spell that held him in its thrall. If he'd needed proof, he was given it when they went into the kitchen together to brew coffee. She went to the fridge and drew out a tiered cake, a fabulous confection of dark, rich chocolate with his name splashed across the center in white spun sugar. He was startled to see her name right underneath, joined by a looped flourish.

Michael and Verity.

"If I'd known how old you are, I'd have bought candles," she said, smiling up at him.

"I'm glad you didn't. Thirty-four candles almost make a fire hazard."

He took the cake from her and set it down on the counter, then shoved his hands into his pockets. He had a tight sensation in his gut that warned him not to let his hands stray where they wanted to go.

"There are two names on the cake," he said, with all the subtlety of an elephant tramping through a flower garden.

"It's my birthday tomorrow. Only three days after yours. I'll be twenty-nine." She took a cake knife from the drawer. "I thought maybe this would be the year I'd wake up and finally feel like a grown-up, but it hasn't happened yet."

"You still have another whole day until your birthday."

She laughed. "I hadn't thought of that. Maybe there's hope for me yet."

"If you miraculously turn into a real grown-up to-morrow, you'll have to tell me what it feels like."

"Okay, it's a deal."

Watching her slice into his spun sugar name, he felt exactly as if she were slicing through his heart. "Happy birthday, Verity," he said softly.

Color rushed up into her cheeks, and then faded away, leaving her paler than before. "You, too, Michael."

They stared at each in a silence so heavy he could almost feel the pressure of her thoughts. She wanted him, he knew, just as he wanted her. Their desire heated the space between the two of them, a physical entity with a life all its own.

The knife dropped from her hands onto the counter with a resounding clang. Neither of them so much as glanced toward it. Her entire body shimmered with visible sexual tension. He wondered if his did, too.

If he took her into his arms, she would respond to him, Michael was sure of it. He knew how her lips would feel when he kissed her. He knew how she would writhe beneath him when he entered her, and how her skin would look when it was flushed in the aftermath of passion. She was everything he'd ever wanted in a woman, everything he craved in a lifetime partner. He finally understood why his mother had given up her life in Kashmir, and why his father didn't mind phallic shrines in his entrance hall. He knew that making love to Verity Marlowe might well be the most amazing experience of his life.

Except for the minor fact that she was married to the man who'd become his best friend.

With an effort of will that beaded sweat along his spine, Michael turned his back on her. He said nothing, because he didn't trust himself to speak. A few seconds later, he heard Verity walk out of the kitchen. He left the house before she had a chance to come back.

Later, in the safety of his own apartment, he told himself that the feelings aroused that night were the result of a peculiar set of circumstances; that they'd never recur; that they'd taken on exaggerated importance because he wasn't in the habit of seducing married women.

He made a million feeble excuses, told himself anything and everything rather than admit to himself that he'd fallen hopelessly in love with Sam's wife. The pretense was never more than a Band-Aid stuck over a gaping wound. And then, after the evening he and Verity spent together at the Palace of the Winds in Srinagar, the wound swallowed the tattered Band-Aid whole.

He had no idea how he would have handled the situation in the wake of the aborted birthday dinner if he hadn't been scheduled to leave for India the following week. He'd used the trip to build back his protective barriers, and from her icy demeanor next time he saw Verity he knew she'd done the same. Thereafter, events in Kashmir heated up sufficiently to provide a constant distraction. He'd shuttled back and forth between India, Pakistan, Kashmir and the States so frequently that he was often out of touch with Sam for weeks at a stretch.

When he and Sam did meet, he kept his contact with Verity to the barest minimum, consistent with not arousing Sam's suspicions. Finally, when he thought the breaking point might be approaching, his boss threw him the lifeline he needed.

The Counter Terrorism division had become increasingly worried by the activities of the Kashmir Freedom Party. For years, the Party had been little more than an inefficient gang of disaffected young Muslim boys. These youths protested the poverty and indignity of their lives by getting together to proclaim their hatred of the oppressive Indian government. Occasionally they would raise sufficient money to buy dynamite, or outdated land mines, or a few precious hand grenades. Then, with no logic discernible to outside observers, they would set off on one of their self-appointed missions, blowing up sections of road used by the Indian military, or lobbing hand grenades through the window of a police station.

Since most of the roads in Kashmir hadn't been repaired since the British moved out in 1947, the potholes caused by Freedom Party's grenades could barely be distinguished from the potholes caused by wear and tear. As for the attacks on police stations, half the grenades failed to go off, and the other half caused minimal damage. Needless to say, the Kashmir Freedom Party didn't rank high on the Agency's list of terrorist organizations to watch.

By spring of 1999 it was apparent that the Kashmir Freedom Party had changed significantly over the course of the preceding two years, transforming itself from an inefficient youth gang into a paramilitary organization that was well-enough financed and organized to pose a genuine threat to stability. Attacks on Indian government outposts in Kashmir became better organized and more successful. The weaponry used in the attacks became increasingly sophisticated. It was obvious to intelligence analysts that the Kashmir Freedom Party had found a new source of funding and was pouring cash into arming and training a more dedicated and radical group of recruits.

Then George Douglass, just appointed as American Consul General in Bombay, reported a piece of astonishing intelligence, gleaned from an unexpected source. Khalid Muhammad, the head of a family known equally for its successful international trading company and for its moderate political views, claimed that the Kashmir Freedom Party's new funds were being generated by the sale of arms illegally exported from China, and smuggled through Kashmir for distribution to various radical Muslim groups around the world. The really astonishing aspect of George Douglass's report was not that remote, rebellious and mountainous Kashmir was being used as a smuggling route. The astonishing part was that Khalid Muhammad claimed the deals were being brokered with the help of an unnamed American government official. Just sufficient proof was attached to Khalid's tip to make what ought to have been an incredible claim seem credible. Khalid's only request in exchange for this information was that the government should find a way to discover who the American traitor was—and then put him out of business.

Michael was asked by the chief of the Counter Terrorism Center to find the traitor. A monthlong investigation in the United States produced no leads, much less any hard evidence that Khalid had been telling the truth. In the end, Michael decided that the quickest way to unmask the American traitor would be to infiltrate the Kashmir Freedom Party. Along the way, he'd get a useful insider's view of an organization that was starting to make serious ripples on the international terrorist scene.

Michael had known he was embarking on a mission that was fraught with danger. Given his mood of reckless despair, the fact that he would be putting his life on the line every minute of every day hadn't seemed such a terrible thing. In fact, it had struck him as somewhat of an added bonus.

The assignment would require one hundred percent of his expertise, and two hundred percent of his attention. Even then, success wasn't assured. Given the circumstances, Michael thought there ought to be at least a fighting chance that he would manage to forget Verity Marlowe.

He'd been wrong.

Eleven

Michael was fully awake as soon as he heard Verity's voice on the answering machine. He was pulling on street clothes even before he hung up the phone and he was driving his Camry out of the garage three minutes later. At this predawn hour, even the crowded roads around Washington were relatively empty, and he made it to Georgetown in record-beating time.

Dick Pedro had given him an earful about Verity's recent drinking problems, and he walked into the bar more than half expecting to find her slumped comatose across the counter, lost in grief for Sam. Instead, he found her seated stiffly upright on a bar stool, dressed in a pair of blood-and-mud-spattered pants that he recognized as the same ones she'd been wearing when he drove her home from the hospital. She didn't appear even marginally drunk. Instead she looked tired beyond the point of exhaustion, and she held a chocolate-brown pashmina shawl wrapped tightly around her upper body, almost as if she needed it for protection rather than for warmth.

"Michael." She said his name with a combination of welcome and relief that caught him off guard. "Thank God you're here." She rose to her feet, steadying herself against the bar.

He extended his arms and she tumbled into them, leaning her head on his chest. "Am I hurting your arm?" she mumbled.

"You're fine," he said. "No problem." With the shock of holding Verity, he'd almost forgotten that he'd been shot, although now that she mentioned it, his left arm felt pretty much as if someone were grinding into his wound with a red-hot screwdriver. Still, he sure as hell wasn't going to let minor physical discomfort interfere with the incredible fact that for only the second time in his life, Verity had voluntarily moved into his arms. And on this occasion, he didn't even need to feel guilty.

He pushed aside the shawl and stroked the tangled mass of her hair, an ache at the back of his throat. Jesus, he'd wanted this for so long! When his hand grazed the side of her cheek, she started to tremble, as if the reassurance of his touch finally gave her permission to express some sort of fear that she'd been holding under rigid containment.

"What happened, Verity?" he asked. "Why did you call me? Tell me, sweetheart." The endearment slipped out. So natural to his thoughts, but until now so forbidden in his speech.

"There was a burglar in my house," she said. "The sounds of him searching downstairs woke me up, but it took me way too long to realize what I was hearing. I kept pretending to myself that everything was okay." Her words started to tumble out, faster and faster. "Then I finally got my act together and tried to escape, but I had to climb out of the bathroom window because the doors onto the balcony wouldn't open. Then he chased me down the fire escape and held me pinned against the wall of the house. He grabbed me and slammed his whole body against mine, and I could feel that he was sexually aroused—" She broke off, her teeth chattering.

Jesus Christ, had she been raped? "It's okay, honey. I'm here now and you're safe." Somehow, he kept his voice low and soothing. She wasn't quite in a state of clinical shock, Michael thought, but she was pretty damn close to it. No surprise there. A burglar—rapist?—invading her home on top of an assassination attempt was more than any normal person could be expected to handle in a twelve-hour period.

The bartender was watching them both without making any pretense otherwise. Leaving his arm firmly around Verity's waist, Michael reached in his pocket for his wallet, fished out a ten, and pushed the bill across the bar.

"Would you make us some tea?" he asked. "We could both of use something hot to drink right now."

"Sorry, no tea. We don't get much call for it." The bartender shook his head. "I have coffee, if you like."

"Coffee would be fine. Put plenty of cream in one of the cups, will you?" Without waiting for a response, Michael guided Verity to a booth in the far corner of the bar, away from the only two other customers. He slid onto the bench next to her, leaning back against the padded leather seat and taking a moment to let the fire in his arm die down.

If he was feeling this bad, Verity undoubtedly felt worse. She hadn't taken a bullet in the arm, but her body had been severely battered when he shoved her down onto the sidewalk. Climbing out of a window and being physically assaulted could only have made her aching muscles ache more.

Her face showed the strain of the past eighteen hours. It was without color, a white mask of fatigue and pain. Michael discovered within himself a hitherto unknown streak of barbarity. If the man who'd done this to her had been anywhere nearby, he would have taken considerable satisfaction in pounding the son of a bitch to a pulp, leaving him with just enough breath to beg for mercy. He'd have liked to hear the bastard beg, Michael thought savagely.

"Tell me how you managed to get away," he said, cradling Verity's hands and refusing to let go when she gave a tentative tug of resistance. A few moments ago, she'd taken a first tacit step toward acknowledging what was between them and he sure as hell wasn't about to let her retreat. "Have you called the police already?"

She shook her head, then winced at the movement. "No. He cut my phone line, and disconnected the electrical power, so I couldn't call from home. And then, once I was here, I decided it would be smart to wait until you arrived before I brought the local cops into it."

"Any special reason why you waited?"

"Yes." For the first time she sounded sure of herself. "This wasn't a regular burglar, Michael. He was wearing a latex face mask, just like Khalid's assassin." She drew in an unsteady breath. "And his voice must have been electronically altered because when he talked to me, it came out sounding like a woman."

"A woman?" He was startled into echoing her words.

"Yes. It was...creepy...being held by a man but threatened by a woman."

Michael swore under his breath. He heard the horror in her voice, even though she was struggling not to show it. His earlier reaction had been too humane, he decided. If the pervert who'd done this to Verity were here right now, he'd beat him to a pulp and not leave him a single gasp of breath to plead for mercy.

"Did he hurt you?" he asked grimly. He waited a beat, then asked the question that had to be asked. "Rape you?"

"Not that, thank God." She hesitated for a moment. "He was sexually excited by the attack, that was obvious, but he didn't break into my house to rape me, I'm pretty sure. He was searching for something specific—"

"Do you have any idea what?"

"Yes. He held a knife to my throat and told me he wanted to know where the key was that Khalid had given me. At the time, I couldn't fathom what he was talking about. I was so disoriented by the attack, I guess."

She laughed, a tiny sound that quavered right on the edge of hysteria. "Afterward, I realized how funny it was. The key he was so desperate to find was in the pocket of these pants I'm wearing. He could have reached over and taken it any time he wanted. There was no way I'd have been strong enough to stop him."

Holy Jesus, Khalid had given her a key. Was it the key to Farooq's safety deposit box? Michael counted to ten so that he could steady his voice. "Do you still have the key?" he asked. Amazingly, he managed to sound no more than mildly interested.

"I guess so." Verity rummaged in the pocket of her slacks and drew out a small stainless steel key with an unusual design of pronged flanges. "Here it is."

She dropped it onto the table, where it lay nestled among the beer mats, a seemingly inconsequential trifle. "Right before he died, Khalid told me this opens a safety deposit box that has something vital that's needed by this American traitor he was so obsessed about. He wouldn't tell me where the safety deposit box was and he claimed he didn't know precisely what was inside although I find that hard to believe."

She had Farooq's key. His heart was damn near leaping out of his body, but Michael managed to pick up the key without looking like a ravenous wolf falling on its prey. At the very least, this meant that Saddam Hussein wasn't going to get the guidance systems for his nuclear weapons. Maybe, just maybe, he could get word out that he had the key. Set himself up for bait and finally put a name to the American traitor who'd turned the Kashmir

Freedom Party into his own personal moneymaking machine.

Even though the key had put her life at risk, Verity was too tired to care much about it. She closed her eyes, leaning back against the padded leather seat. "Tomorrow I'm probably going to regret handing that over to you. Tonight, you can take the darn thing with my blessing."

The bartender arrived with the coffee, which smelled better than Michael had hoped, as if the brewing machine might actually have been cleaned at some point in the past week. Verity was practically falling asleep where she sat, but she was also shivering, and her hands were ice-cold. Michael handed her the mug and encouraged her to take a few sips as he mentally went over the rest of the information she had given him about the attack.

"He knew my name," Verity said suddenly, putting down her mug. Coffee sloshed over the side and onto the table. "When I didn't tell him where the key was, the burglar said, *Don't try to be brave, Verity. Give me the goddamn fucking key.* And that's a direct quote."

Michael didn't respond immediately and she looked up at him, her eyes shadowed with exhaustion. "The person who attacked me was someone I would recognize, wasn't it? I don't know why I'm even asking you. I was the one who heard him speak. And I know my name slipped out as if it were entirely natural for him to use it."

"If the attacker knows you, it would explain why he wore a mask and disguised his voice," Michael conceded, deciding there was no point in denying facts that were self-evident.

"It also explains why he took the time to go down to the basement and cut off my power and phone," Verity said. "He was so afraid I would identify him that he made sure there was no light to see him by, and no phone for me to call out on if I became aware of his presence before he found the key." Her mouth twisted as if she'd just tasted something bitter. "I must know him pretty well if he was that scared of being recognized."

"Not necessarily. I agree the attacker was more than likely somebody you've seen before, but it might not be anyone you know well. It's even possible you don't know him at all. He could be a canny criminal who likes to take plenty of precautions."

"Maybe."

He could see that he hadn't convinced her, which wasn't surprising since he hadn't convinced himself, either. Whoever this bastard was, Verity knew him well.

"It's almost four in the morning," he said. "We both got beaten up this afternoon, and we both need to get some rest. I don't know about you, but I'll feel better and think a whole lot smarter in the morning."

She cradled her hands around the mug of now tepid coffee. "I don't want to go back to my house, Michael."

"Then come to mine." Somehow, he managed to make his voice sound matter-of-fact. As if the choice were hers to make. As if he would have allowed her out of his sight now that Khalid had dragged her into the heart of the violence swirling around the Kashmir Freedom Party.

Verity sent him a wry glance. She might not realize how much danger Khalid had put her in, but she knew that Michael's invitation signaled a major change in their relationship.

Perhaps she was too tired to protest. Perhaps she was finally willing to acknowledge that Sam's death had demolished the mountain that kept them apart, leaving them free to take their relationship wherever they might want it to go. Whatever the reason, she leaned back against the leather seat and gave a tiny sigh of surrender.

"Thanks, Michael," she said. "I'd like to come home with you. I'd prefer not to be alone tonight."

Twelve

In comparison to the other bizarre events in her life over the past twenty-four hours, Verity knew that sitting down to breakfast across the table from Michael Strait ought to rank low on the shock meter. Still, until a couple of days ago, watching Michael grind coffee beans while she sipped orange juice and ate raisin toast would have seemed less likely than sharing her breakfast Wheaties with Fidel Castro.

Cozily wrapped in Michael's too big cotton bathrobe, she savored the smell of freshly ground coffee and decided that what was most surprising about her situation was how content she felt to be here in his cheerful, yellow-painted kitchen. The death of Khalid and the others yesterday left a subnote of sadness to her mood. Her head ached and her muscles throbbed, but at some deep inner level she felt as if a tight bud of happiness were just waiting for a more auspicious moment to burst forth in bloom.

Coffeemaker set to brew, Michael joined her at the table, bringing a portable phone with him. "I'm sure people at the office would like to hear from you," he said, holding out the phone. "They'd probably like to know you're recovering okay from yesterday's attack. If people have been trying to reach you at home, they'll be worried."

She nodded. "Thanks for reminding me. I'm sure

Dick's been at the office for hours. Andrew, too. I ought to let them know I'll be coming in this afternoon.''

"Have you considered staying home today? After last night, you could sure use the rest.''

"So could you," she pointed out. "I've seen how you keep massaging your left arm when you think I'm not looking, but I don't see any signs that you're planning to spend the day in an armchair, curled up with a good book.''

"I have too much to do to stay home.''

She raised an eyebrow. "And I don't? I need to brief Dick about my conversations with Khalid yesterday. The private ones, that nobody else knows about as yet.''

"You can tell me and I'll brief him on your behalf.''

She rolled her eyes at him, amused. "Nice try, Michael, but I'm with the State Department, remember? I brief my people first, and they can inform you folks over at Langley if that seems advisable.''

He narrowed his gaze, as if assessing how serious she was. "I could pull rank and say this is a CTC operation—''

"But you won't. You and I have more than enough to fight about without adding a bureaucratic turf war to our private battlefield.''

Michael scowled. "You're only getting away with this because I plan to sit in on the briefing.''

"Fine. I'll leave you and Dick to slug that one out.'' She sent him a quick grin. "Given Dick's feelings about the Agency, I feel obliged to warn you it will be a fight to the death.''

"He doesn't have a chance of winning this one, honey.'' Michael got up and checked the coffeemaker, taking a pair of mugs from the cupboard. "How about a compromise? I'll concede that you should make your report direct to Dick Pedro, but that doesn't mean you have to go into the office. Why don't I arrange for Dick to come to you? You had a hell of a day yesterday, followed by a rotten night. Officially, you're still on leave of absence. There's no point in playing the hero when you don't need to. Let Dick and Andrew do the running for a change.''

She looked at him speculatively. Could he really arrange for Dick or Andrew to come to her for the debriefing, as opposed to the other way around? How the heck senior was Michael, anyway, that he always confidently assumed other people would fall in with his wishes?

Laughter glinted in his dark eyes. ''God, Verity, don't ever volunteer to work as a spy. You'd be shot within the first twenty-four hours. Let's just say I'm senior enough to be able to pull rank effectively when I need to.''

She didn't believe her private thoughts were anywhere near as transparent as he claimed, at least to the rest of the world. In fact, she and Michael both had the reputation of being self-contained people whose emotions were difficult to read. Except, apparently, by each other.

She settled the discussion by picking up the phone and tapping in the phone number for Dick's office. ''I'm seriously impressed by your bureaucratic clout, Michael, but I need to go into the office. During our conversations yesterday, Khalid asked me to break a lot of rules, and I bent a few of them. To compensate, I want to make this debrief as official as possible—''

A voice spoke out of the phone. ''Dick Pedro.''

''Oh, hello, Dick, this is Verity.''

''Verity, how nice to hear from you. How are you, my dear?'' For once, Dick sounded genuinely delighted to hear her voice.

''I'm bruised and battered. Also tired and a bit shaken, but basically fine, all things considered.''

"My God, that was a terrible…um…a terrible…thing that happened yesterday." Even Dick apparently experienced some trouble coming up with a soothing diplomatic phrase for *mass murder*. "I'm so glad you weren't seriously wounded, Verity. Andrew told me that you had head injuries, so I was quite worried. But then I called the hospital and they informed me you'd been allowed to go home from the ER, so I was optimistic you hadn't suffered any major trauma."

"No, only a mild concussion. I got off lightly compared to everyone else."

"Except for me and Andrew." Dick's relief sounded tinged with guilt. "I can't believe the two of us escaped without a scratch when everyone else was so badly hurt."

"Your planets must have been in favorable alignment, that's for sure. Anyway, Dick, I'm planning to come into the office for a couple of hours this afternoon—"

"Good heavens, you can't be serious! There's no need for you to come in at all. Not even tomorrow, unless you're feeling up to it."

"I'm responsible for handling any crisis involving Kashmir—"

"Your insider knowledge of Kashmir is certainly valuable, Verity, but we can cope for another day or two without you. Now that Khalid is dead, we don't need your special expertise so mu—"

He broke off abruptly, realizing it wasn't politic to admit he was being generous because he didn't need Verity as badly as he had the day before. "There's a lot of activity in our department right now," he continued quickly. "In fact, it's a bit of a madhouse, as you can imagine. But we're coping, Verity. We're coping."

"How? The department is short-staffed since the budget cuts, and I can just imagine how many messages are flying back and forth between here and the embassy in New Delhi. Not to mention the Secretary of State's office calling down every hour for some urgent piece of background information or another.''

''Well, yes, you're right. We're in the swamp, up to our armpits, and the alligators are circling. But Andrew and I both slept at the office last night, so we aren't drowning. Yet.'' His voice became wry. ''Andrew just commented this morning that it's a crisis like this that explains why he and I never managed to stay married for more than five minutes. Wives like to see their husbands during daylight hours, at least on the weekends, and that doesn't seem likely to happen for quite a while as far as we're concerned.''

Dick and Andrew had accumulated three divorces between them, two for Dick and one for Andrew. At great legal expense, Dick had managed to retain joint custody of his twin sons from his first marriage, and he'd only lost half the equity in his town house the second time around. Andrew hadn't been that fortunate. After mere months of marriage, his wife had hired a legal shark who'd stripped him of everything except the contents of his clothes closet. She'd even walked away with the Siamese cat who'd been Andrew's pampered pet since graduate school.

Andrew always seemed philosophical about his brief marriage and its impoverished aftermath, but from past experience, Verity was smart enough when talking to Dick to avoid any subject even remotely touching on wives, lawyers, divorce and the impossibility of balancing the demands of a marriage and a career at State. All, as Dick never failed to point out, on half the money he could have earned in the private sector.

Verity steered the conversation back into safer waters. ''Actually, Dick, there is some specific information about yesterday's meetings with Khalid that I ought to pass on to you. That's why I need to come in.''

"Don't worry. The investigation of Khalid's assassination isn't our job, thank God, and Andrew's already given me a full debrief of your earlier discussions—"

"Mmm, I don't think so. Did Andrew mention to you that Khalid spoke to me a couple of times in private?''

"Yes, he mentioned it.'' Even over the phone, Verity could hear that Dick's attention had sharpened. "I understood those private sessions were more with Mrs. Muhammad than with Khalid himself. You and Khalid's wife are old friends, aren't you?''

"Not really. My friendship with his wife was simply an excuse Khalid invented to explain why he was inviting me into the master bedroom with his wife, despite the fact that he had excluded everyone else. It's too complicated to explain over the phone, especially since this line isn't secure, but when I come into the office this afternoon, I'll fill you in on the details of what Khalid told me. He said some astonishing things, in fact.''

"These astonishing things—are they in any way relevant to his assassination?''

"Yes, I believe they are. At least peripherally, and possibly in a more central way.''

"Then in that case, I do need to hear what you have to say. If I could get away from the office, Verity, I wouldn't ask you to come in. I'm sure you must be feeling really shaken up. But right now I can't figure out any way to leave my desk. In fact— Damn, there's my other phone ringing right now.''

"Take the call, Dick. I'll see you soon.''

Verity hung up the phone. Michael silently pushed a steaming mug of coffee toward her. It was black, not too strong, the way she always drank it in the mornings, although last night he'd remembered to ask the barman to add milk. He knew from watching dozens of late-night movies with her and Sam that she always added milk to any coffee she drank after dinner. Just as she knew from dozens of shared meals that Michael always drank his coffee black, whatever the hour, that he was addicted to Diet Pepsi, and that he shared her fascination with the varied cuisines of India.

In some ways, she and Michael knew so much about each other, Verity reflected, and yet at another level, there was so much left to discover.

She lifted her gaze, not surprised to find Michael watching her. He didn't say anything, but heat flooded her veins the moment their eyes made contact. Now that she'd dismantled the protective barriers that insulated her from awareness of his physical attraction, it took very little to remind her of the sexual currents that flowed beneath the surface of all their dealings.

His gaze held hers, proving the point that a simple glance across the breakfast table was all it took to arouse her. Despite her aches and pains—and his—she wanted to have sex with him. Here. Now. Wanted it strongly enough that she found herself wondering how much of an impediment bullet wounds, bruised ribs and aching muscles really would be.

"I want us to make love, too," Michael said quietly. "But now isn't the right moment, honey. We've waited so long, we can wait a little while longer."

"Dammit, stop doing that!" she said, scowling at him "Between you and Sam, I can't seem to have a single private thought these days."

"What do you mean, *between me and Sam?*" Michael asked.

Oh, brother, she really needed to think before she spoke. She jerked her hands into her lap to conceal their tremor. "Nothing," she said hastily, her cheeks burning.

"I was just rambling. One of those remarks that don't really mean anything." She glanced over at the clock. "Goodness, ten o'clock already. Time sure is rushing by fast today. Maybe I'd better go upstairs and get dressed. Yuk, I hate to think of putting on those dirty clothes from last night." She pulled a face, exaggerating her genuine reluctance in order to distract his attention.

To her relief, Michael allowed himself to be diverted, although she didn't kid herself that she'd convinced him her remark about Sam had been meaningless.

"I could lend you a T-shirt, sweatpants and the hooded jacket I use sometimes for jogging," he said. "It wouldn't be high fashion, but it would be fairly warm, and nobody's going to see you in the car anyway."

"Thanks. That would be great."

"Okay. As soon as you're dressed, I'll drive you home."

She got up and carried her breakfast dishes over to the sink, still disconcerted at having let drop a reference to Sam's ghostly appearances. Over the past few hours she'd let down her guard with Michael in ways that would have seemed impossible only days earlier. But there were limits to how much of her vulnerability she was willing to expose, and her conversations with Sam's ghost definitely weren't included in the topics she intended to share with Michael. She would like him to continue believing she was sane, even if she had moments when she doubted that herself.

You're entirely sane, sugar babe. And don't worry about Michael. He's got a much more flexible concept of the universe than you do, so he has no problem believing that people who are still alive can sometimes communicate with people who are already dead. Besides, he loves you so much that he wouldn't even consider giving you

*up now that he's finally got you halfway to admitting how
you feel about him.*

By a supreme effort of will, Verity refrained from
looking toward the fridge, where she knew she would see
Sam lounging, arms folded across his chest. Verity was
highly embarrassed to think that Sam might have been
watching her and Michael eat breakfast. She sure hoped
he hadn't misinterpreted the apparent intimacy of the situation. As a ghost, gifted with extra powers of percep-
tion, presumably he knew that she and Michael had slept
in separate bedrooms, and that they hadn't exchanged so
much as a chaste peck on the cheek, much less anything
more passionate.

An appalling thought suddenly struck Verity, freezing
her in her tracks. Good grief, if she and Michael ever did
end up making love, would Sam be hanging out at the
foot of the bed, observing? Possibly even interjecting a
comment or two on their technique?

The prospect was too awful to think about, so she shut
down the image. Keeping her head determinedly angled
forward, away from the fridge, Verity directed a bright
smile at Michael. Painfully aware that Sam was still in
the kitchen, even if he wasn't talking, she couldn't relax.

"I don't want to put you to all the bother of driving
me home, Michael. Shouldn't you be getting into the office yourself? I know how busy you must be, and I could
take a cab back to Georgetown—"

Michael walked over to her and grazed his knuckles
along her cheek, smoothing out her forced smile. "If I've
done or said something that's made you uncomfortable,
tell me what it is. Don't go polite and perky and artificial
on me, Verity. We've moved way past that, don't you
think?"

"Maybe we have." She rubbed the spot above her
eyebrow where she could still feel the lump left by yes-

terday's encounter with the sidewalk. As she rubbed, her awareness of Sam's presence faded, and her shoulders slumped in relief. "I just don't understand how we got to—wherever we are. We moved so fast from being hostile to being…something else…that I don't know how to handle the situation."

Michael gave a resigned shake of his head, but his gaze was sympathetic. "You expend way too much energy trying to handle your life," he said. "Sometimes you just have to sit back and let life happen."

"That's a very Indian philosophy," she said ruefully.

"Maybe. Is that a bad thing as far as you're concerned?"

"No. On the contrary. But you have to remember I was raised by two good Christian Soldiers for the Faith. My parents were determined that their only child wasn't going to be corrupted by the prevailing Kashmiri attitude of weary resignation followed by blind acceptance. I had the good old Yankee take-charge, can-do approach to life drummed into me right along with my baby cereal. I guess it's stuck. More firmly than I would like, sometimes."

He smiled. "I think your parents may have missed some of the subtleties of the society they were trying to convert. Just because people in Kashmir aren't getting up each morning and grabbing life by the throat, it doesn't mean they're waiting with pained and weary resignation. Sometimes they're feeling a quiet but joyful anticipation that when some event finally happens, it's going to be wonderful."

She looked up at him, her gaze steady. "Is it going to be wonderful for us, Michael?"

He framed her face with his hands and kissed her very lightly on the forehead, the gesture all the more intimate because his desire was so tightly restrained. There was just a trace of huskiness in his voice when he answered her. "Damn straight it's going to be wonderful."

Verity felt warmed from the inside out. Another of the protective layers she had built between herself and Michael crumbled into dust, leaving her emotions starkly exposed. Not only was it becoming harder to deny what she felt for Michael, she could no longer remember why it had once seemed so vitally important to pretend that she didn't care about him.

She saw with sudden clarity that acknowledging the truth of her attraction to Michael couldn't destroy a single thing about her marriage to Sam that had been real and solid. And there was so much about their marriage that had been good. She and Sam had forged a union based on mutual affection, deep respect and genuine compatibility. They'd brought each other five years of wonderful companionship. Almost every day of their marriage had been happier because they were together. Nothing that happened now with Michael could change that impressive five-year reality.

Just as nothing that she did now could alter the truth that, for all their mutual respect and love, there had been no passion in her relationship with Sam. Her heart had never raced with desire at the sight of him. She had never trembled with the longing to lie naked in his arms. Making love to Sam had been a pleasant expression of their emotional closeness, not a consuming need for physical union.

By contrast, from the night of her first meeting with Michael, she had known that the moment she went into his bed, all the passion missing from her relationship with Sam would be there. It would surround her, sweep her away and totally drown out the cool voice of reason.

But even now, when she could finally allow herself to acknowledge that Michael possessed many qualities she admired, Verity still wondered what would be left when their mutual passion burned out. Did she and Michael share anything important beyond an overwhelming urge to explore the limits of each other's sexuality?

The phone rang, interrupting her flow of thought. Michael had a quick conversation with somebody from his office, promising that he would be there within a couple of hours.

The call served as a reminder of how much still had to be achieved before the end of the day. Verity refocused her attention on the immediate actions she and Michael needed to take, as opposed to a sexual relationship they might start some time in the future.

"I need to report what happened at my house last night to someone in law enforcement," she said, stacking mugs and plates in the dishwasher. "Or maybe I should check my house over first, so that I can make a more detailed report? Right now, I don't even know if anything's been stolen, or whether the guy who attacked me just wanted Khalid's key and nothing else."

"I'm guessing he just wanted the key," Michael said. "In any event, it probably isn't smart for us to try to search the house. We run the risk of messing up the crime scene. If it's okay with you, I'll call in a favor from a friend of mine at the Bureau and arrange for a forensic team to be sent over to sweep your house."

"Is it worth their time and effort?" she queried. "Since the man who attacked me wore a mask, a wig and gloves, he isn't likely to have left behind any physical evidence that would help to identify him."

"True, but you never know when you might get lucky. A fingerprint is probably too much to hope for. But a good forensic team might find a stray hair that fell off his jacket, or something equally helpful and unexpected, so it's worth giving it a try."

"Yes, I guess it is." Verity nodded. "Go ahead and call your friend, but since this clearly wasn't a routine burglary, I don't see any point in involving the local police, do you?"

"No point at all. I'll call my friend at the Bureau now." Michael picked up the phone and punched in a number. Verity listened as he left a voice mail message for Agent Dreyer, who was in the office, but unavailable to take his call.

"What happens if he doesn't return your call within a reasonable time?" Verity asked.

"I'm confident Becky will call me as soon as she gets the message. She and I go way back. She knows I wouldn't say the situation was urgent unless it was."

It was embarrassing to discover that she actually felt a twinge of jealousy because his friend from way back was a woman. Verity decided it was past time to get her brain out of seduction mode and firmly into the business groove. "I'm not punch-drunk anymore like I was last night," she said. "In retrospect, I realize you snatched that key Khalid had given me with excessive enthusiasm. If it does open a safety deposit box, what do you expect to find in there, Michael?"

"I don't know—"

"But you can make a pretty damn good guess. Tell me your educated guess, Michael."

The phone rang yet again, much to Verity's frustration. "You're not saved from answering my question, even if you take the call," she said. "Don't think I'm going to forget what we're talking about."

"It's probably Becky Dreyer returning my call. I need to get it." Michael pressed the talk button on the handset. "Hello?.. Yes, this is Michael Strait."

He listened, his face wiping clean of expression as the caller continued to talk. "I see," he said finally. "Thank you for letting me know. Will you please convey my deepest sympathy to Norman's wife?''

He waited again, and then replied in a voice that was little more than a monotone. ''Yes, I agree. Norman was an outstanding public servant. He'll be missed.''

Not Norman Green, too, Verity thought, although one look at Michael was enough to confirm that her protest was in vain. He still held the phone in his hand, staring at it with blank eyes, not seeming to hear the canned voice telling him that if he wanted to make a call, he needed to hang up and dial again.

Verity crossed the room to Michael's side and unwound his fingers from the receiver, depressing the talk button to cut off the recorded message. Then she laid her hand lightly over his, not speaking, not attempting to offer condolences, just letting him know she was there.

After a few silent moments, he turned his palm upward and grasped her hand, squeezing so hard that she winced. She was quite sure he had no awareness that he had applied so much pressure, much less that he was hurting her.

''I'm sorry,'' she said softly, leaving her hand in his grip.

''Norm died an hour ago.'' Michael's voice was remote, his expression closed.

''I'm truly sorry, Michael.''

''Yeah, I'll miss him. We'd seen each other through a couple of tight spots.''

''From what little I saw of him yesterday, he seemed like a partner you would be able to count on.''

''He was much more than that. He was a friend. You'd never know it, but when he wasn't on duty, Norm had a really whacky sense of humor.'' Michael spoke in a low voice, avoiding her gaze, and she knew that he didn't trust himself to retain control if he allowed himself to look at her.

He shoved back his chair, the gesture sharp with frustration. "When I called the ICU this morning, they'd upgraded his condition from critical to guarded. Now this. How the hell did he go from guarded to dead in the space of a couple of hours?"

He didn't really expect her to answer, Verity knew. He understood as well as she did that with bullets ripping through his liver and spleen, the miracle was that Norm Green hadn't died yesterday, not that the end had arrived suddenly this morning.

She searched for words of consolation that wouldn't come. Norman was dead and nothing would bring him back. She wished she could find something comforting to say but, ever since Sam's illness, her vocabulary seemed to have been drained of all the meaningless platitudes people normally offered to make sense out of the senseless. Because there was nothing else for her to do, she rested her hands on Michael's shoulders, providing the primitive comfort of physical contact since words had failed her.

For several minutes he remained so deeply buried in his own grief that he gave no sign he realized she was still there. Then, at last, a tremor ran through him as he became aware of her touch. He turned to look at her, his gaze bleak, but no longer quite as desolate as before.

He massaged his arm near the spot where the bullet had hit him, the gesture unconscious. "Sometimes I think I should resign from the Agency and take a job as a chef," he said. "I like to cook, and most days, I'd be preparing meals that made people happy. Even on a bad day, the biggest tragedy I'd have to face in my professional life would be a souffle that went flat, or a wedding buffet that the bride didn't appreciate."

"True. But you'd never have the satisfaction of knowing that you successfully prevented a terrorist attack, either."

"Like I prevented yesterday's attack?" he asked, with unusual bitterness. "Yeah, I sure did a great job of preventing that one."

Once again, the phone rang before she could respond. Michael grimaced, then leaned forward to pick it up. "This is Michael Strait."

He paused while the caller identified herself and his voice softened marginally when he continued. "Hi, Becky. Thanks for calling back so promptly. Look, I need a favor. A big one. I want a forensic team sent out to Georgetown to analyze a crime scene. I want you to handpick the team and I need you to give me your best people."

Verity listened as Michael explained succinctly what had happened at her house the previous night, without going into any details about precisely what the intruder had been searching for, except that it was connected to the terrorist attacks on George Douglass in Bombay and Khalid Muhammad at the Creighton Hotel. He explained there was an outside chance the FBI team might be able to find fingerprints that would match with a set in the FBI database, thus providing an identity for the intruder. Failing that, he hoped the team might manage to find a hair, or another source of DNA left behind by the intruder. Even if the DNA didn't help to attach a name and address to the intruder, it would at least help to secure a conviction in the courts once they had him identified.

Michael requested that the search be given top priority, and he needed to utilize very little persuasive charm to secure Becky's agreement that a forensic team would be at Verity's house by noon. The news about Norman Green's death had obviously flashed around FBI headquarters already, and once Michael indicated that the crime scene search was linked to Norman's death, the resources of the Bureau were his to command.

Verity and Michael arrived in Georgetown a few minutes before noon and found a parking space only half a block from her front door. Verity had anticipated feeling a certain amount of reluctance about returning to her house. Until she got there, she hadn't realized just how strong the feelings of violation and invasion would be. She was really glad to have Michael with her, taking the edge off her memories of the previous night's attack.

The FBI team hadn't yet arrived, so the practical difficulties of getting inside gave Verity a few minutes' respite from the moment when she would have to walk into the house and face whatever had to be faced. Last night she'd run out without a front door key, but a window tucked away beneath the fire escape had been opened by someone cutting through the supposedly burglar-proof glass with professional precision. Michael agreed with her that this had probably been the intruder's point of entry.

"Can you climb in through the window without injuring your arm?" Verity asked him. "I'm so stiff, I don't believe I can."

"We shouldn't even try to climb in through here," he said. "We don't want to contaminate the crime scene. This window isn't all that big, and if the intruder did use it as his route to gain access to the house, it's likely to be the best place for the FBI team to find trace evidence. We don't want to risk wiping any of those traces away."

"I guess the same rules apply to the bathroom window upstairs," Verity said. "Whoever the attacker was, he followed me out of that window onto the fire escape. It was a tight squeeze even for me, so he must have crammed himself through by the skin of his teeth."

"That's good news for us. A tight squeeze means more chance of leaving physical evidence behind."

A gust of wind knifed around the corner and she shivered. Michael pulled her against his body, zipping his down jacket around both of them, protecting her from the wind. "That jogging outfit of mine is useless in weather like this. You're turning blue with cold. Do you want to go back to the car?"

"No, I'm okay. The FBI team should be here any minute, and they'll be able to get us inside the house, won't they?"

"Yeah. They'll have one of their specially trained locksmiths with them. I've watched them at work before, and he'll get your front door unlocked so fast you'll wonder why regular people need keys."

"Speaking of keys," Verity said. "I'm sure you remember that we were talking about Khalid's key a little while ago. And I'm also sure you remember that you never answered my question about it."

Michael pulled a face. "I kept quiet in the hope that you'd take the hint and stop asking."

"You're joking, right?"

He sighed. "Apparently."

"Why is Khalid's key so important, Michael? And where have you put it?"

"If I say *somewhere safe* is there any chance that you're going to back off?"

"No chance at all."

"How about—*That information is classified.*"

"Oh, please." She glared at him. "Not in your wildest, most far-out fantasies."

His eyes momentarily gleamed with laughter. "Trust me, Verity, I don't waste my wildest fantasies on boring subjects like keys."

She flushed, almost willing to be diverted until she

remembered what was at stake. "I believe you owe me an explanation, Michael. You wouldn't even have the key unless I'd given it to you last night, when I was obviously too damned exhausted to realize what I was doing. If you can ever locate the safety deposit box it's supposed to open, what do you expect to find inside? And don't stall anymore because it won't work."

Michael hesitated. "Documents that would prove Khalid Muhammad was correct. That a U.S. government official has been using the Kashmir Freedom Party as a means to pursue his own private agenda."

"A political agenda?" Verity asked, puzzled. "It's so hard for me to believe anyone in the U.S. government cares enough about the fate of Kashmir to attempt something so complicated and difficult."

"This has got almost nothing to do with politics," Michael said. "It's all about money."

"Well that makes it a tad easier to believe," Verity said acerbically. "Although it's tough for me to see how the Kashmir Freedom Party could help anyone to make money."

"It's complicated." Michael looked almost as frustrated as she felt. "I'm sorry, Verity. I can't tell you anything more until I've discussed how to handle this situation with the Director. The information is classified to the hilt."

"I almost got killed last night because of that damn key and now you won't even tell me what's going on!"

"*Because* you almost got killed last night," Michael said, his teeth gritted. "At this point, we have no idea who attacked you, and even less idea how to stop him coming after you again. The fact is, you're going to need round-the-clock protection until this situation is resolved."

Verity had already given considerable thought to the

problem of repeat visits from the intruder. "We can stop
the man who attacked me from coming back," she said.
"All we have to do is let him know that I no longer have
the key."

"Great idea, except that we have no idea who 'he' is.
So how do we know when we've given him the message?"

"Khalid claimed that the traitor was someone working
in the State Department. Maybe we should distribute a
memo to all employees."

She spoke flippantly, but Michael's response was somber. "It's a definite possibility. Answer me this, Verity.
How many people knew that Khalid had given you that
key?"

"Nobody," she said promptly. She paused for a moment and then amended her answer, realizing that it
couldn't be true. "Well, I guess somebody must have
known. I mean, obviously somebody knew Khalid had
given it to me, which is why he was searching my
house—"

"But how did the intruder know?" Michael persisted.
"How did he get that information? You spent most of
last night at the hospital and I drove you home. Did anyone call you after I dropped you off at your house? Did
anyone from work stop into the Emergency Room to see
how you were doing?"

Verity shook her head. "I didn't speak to a soul. Anyway, I would never have mentioned the key because I'd
forgotten I had it."

"Then you see the problem," Michael said. "Two
problems, in fact. Who knew you had the key, and how
do we inform them that you don't have it anymore?"

Verity frowned. How could anyone have known she
had the key? It had been buried deep in the pocket of
her pants from the moment she took it from Khalid, so

nobody had seen it in her possession, leaving the conclusion that somebody must have overheard her conversation with Khalid. But how was that possible?

When Khalid gave her the key, she'd been in his sons' bedroom. She couldn't remember if they'd been speaking in English or Kashmiri. Probably Kashmiri, but even if they'd been speaking English, it would surely have been impossible for anyone outside the room to overhear what the two of them were discussing. Nor would anyone have been able to see the transaction. The window blinds had been closed, ruling out the possibility of spy cameras, and the bedroom door had definitely been shut before Khalid stripped off his shirt.

There had been a pool of potential listeners gathered just outside the bedroom door. The sitting room in the hotel suite had been crowded with Secret Service agents and bodyguards, in addition to Andrew Breitman, Norman Green and Michael himself. But nobody in the room could have pressed his ear to the panels of the door without attracting the attention of the entire group, once again forcing the conclusion that nobody could have known Khalid had given her the key.

Unless there had been a recording device in that second bedroom. The thought exploded into her head and Verity took a moment to consider it. Khalid had informed her right at the start of their first conversation that he suspected his hotel suite had been bugged. If his suspicions were correct, plenty of people could have been listening in to her final conversation with Khalid. In fact, if there had been a bug in that second bedroom, it expanded the pool of suspects exponentially.

Somewhat belatedly, it occurred to Verity how odd it was that Khalid had waited until they were in the boys' bedroom before he transferred the infamous key to her.

Why had he waited? Why hadn't he given it to her earlier, when they were in the master bedroom?

Her pulse started to race the moment she posed the question. In retrospect, she realized that Khalid had deliberately led her out of the safely bug-free master bedroom and into the boys' room, where people had been coming and going unsupervised all day long. A room where a listening device could have been planted with relative ease, either by a genuine hotel employee, or by somebody posing as a hotel employee. A room where Khalid had told her earlier that he actively suspected electronic listening devices were installed.

The son of a gun had set her up, Verity thought, too shocked to be angry. For some reason she couldn't begin to fathom, Khalid had deliberately given her the key in a setting where their conversation was likely to be overheard. She could only conclude he'd actively wanted people to know that possession of the key to the all-important safety deposit box had been transferred from him to her. Had he been trying to tell someone that there was no point in murdering him because the key had been passed on? If so, the message clearly hadn't been delivered in time to save Khalid from the assassin's bullet waiting for him on the hotel sidewalk.

She stared blankly ahead, but instead of seeing the brick exterior of her own home, she saw a vivid image of Khalid lying on the rain-drenched sidewalk of the Creighton Hotel.

Sorry for what I did to you. Betrayed...our friendship.

She was pretty sure those were among the last words Khalid had spoken. On the point of death, he had mustered his failing strength to apologize to her. But what had he been apologizing for? Yesterday, she hadn't paid much attention to the real meaning of his dying words. Distraught herself, she'd assumed at the time that

Khalid's mind was wandering and that he was apologizing for some trifling offence he'd committed when they were in grade school.

That interpretation might still be correct, of course, but now she wondered. Khalid might have been more aware of what he was saying than she'd assumed. If so, with death looming, perhaps he had expressed regret for thrusting her without warning or preparation into what he must have known was a situation fraught with danger.

And if he had been sufficiently aware of his situation to apologize for giving her the key, had he perhaps heard her question about Farooq's whereabouts and tried to answer it? For the first time it occurred to Verity that Khalid might not have been totally out of it when he muttered seemingly random comments about her mother's gardens in Srinagar.

"So much for me supposedly being able to read your thoughts," Michael said. "Right now I haven't a clue what's going on inside your head, although I wish like hell I did."

Verity returned to the present with a jolt. "Sorry," she said, still distracted.

"A while back, I asked you who might have known that Khalid had given you the key, and you wandered off into some dark mental alley."

"It was a very relevant alley. I was just going back over the sequence of events yesterday afternoon when he gave me the key."

Michael drew her face around until her eyes met his. "Verity, we're dealing with some desperate and violent people here. If you've been able to guess who might know that Khalid gave you the key, don't keep quiet about it. By keeping silent, you're quite likely protecting the people who planned Khalid's murder. Even if you only have a faint suspicion, share it. Name names."

There was urgency in Michael's voice. "The more people who have access to this information, the less valuable it becomes. Don't keep a secret that puts you at risk, Verity."

Despite her frustration at his refusal to share more of what she was quite sure he knew, Verity realized Michael was correct. She would simply be putting herself at risk by keeping silent. "I wish I could say that I'd had this brilliant flash of insight and narrowed down the field of suspects to two or three people. Unfortunately, I decided just the opposite. There are almost limitless numbers of people who might know that Khalid had given me the key."

"How so?" Michael asked.

He listened intently as she explained how Khalid had led her into the boys' bedroom before handing over the key, despite the fact that he'd insisted on holding their earlier conversation in the master bedroom, precisely because it was the only place he considered safe from electronic listening equipment.

"So you're saying he took you into the boys' bedroom because he *wanted* your conversation to be overheard?" There was anger as well as incredulity in Michael's voice.

"It seems the only logical explanation for his actions," Verity acknowledged.

"The bastard set you up," Michael said, his voice cold with fury. "He wanted to turn off the heat that was scorching his family, and so he turned it onto you."

Verity would have liked to defend Khalid, but she was very much afraid Michael was right. Khalid had used her as bait in the center of a trap, and last night, one of the rats had come searching.

She could only be grateful that she'd found a way to spring the trap and go free. Next time she wasn't likely to be so lucky.

Thirteen

True to Michael's prediction, the FBI locksmith took less than two minutes to open her front door. As for the so-called security bolt Sam had installed only a couple of weeks before his tumor was diagnosed, the locksmith utilized a special hooked tool and had that open within another minute. So much for keeping her home safe from burglars, Verity thought ruefully.

The FBI agents started their inspection of the house interior in the basement, at the point where the intruder had probably gained entry. They discovered that electrical power had been disconnected by the simple method of throwing the master switch on the circuit board. One of the agents dusted unsuccessfully for fingerprints, getting nothing but greasy blurs, then flipped the switch back on. A roar from the furnace signaled that power had returned, and the dank chill of the air began to warm up within minutes.

The phone cable had been ripped out of the wall, but the locksmith was apparently an all-around handyman, and he spliced the wires, instantly restoring phone service. Verity only wished the problem of the intruder's identity could be solved as easily.

The FBI team split up according to their individual areas of expertise. One of the agents remained downstairs, carefully tagging plastic bags of debris from around the broken window. Verity, Michael and the other two agents came upstairs to the main level where a general state of chaos prevailed.

All the kitchen drawers had been emptied onto the counters. Every package and storage jar in the pantry had been upended, leaving the floor layered with flour, sugar and grains of rice. In the living room, every book had been swept from the shelves of Sam's cherished collection of nineteenth-century novels, and many of the antique leather bindings had been damaged, seemingly beyond repair. Sofa pillows and chair cushions had been tossed onto the floor.

In Verity's study, the search seemed to have been even more intense. The contents of her desk and filing cabinet had been strewn over the rug, with each file shaken open so that nothing remained inside. A box of Christmas cards had been scattered on the top of the mess, leaving twenty-four pictures of Santa Claus smiling from all directions.

"I can't believe you stayed asleep while the intruder was doing all this," Michael said. "Those books of Sam's must have crashed onto the floor, and when the cutlery from the kitchen drawers landed on the counters, it would have made a sound like clashing cymbals. How did you not hear what was going on?"

Verity tried to reconcile the chaos of the scene in front of her with the subtle sounds she'd overheard the previous night. How could she have registered the tiny creak of a footfall on the stairs but somehow slept through the thuds and crashes of books being swept from shelves? It wasn't possible, she decided.

"The burglar must have come back into the house," she said, her eyes widening with shock at the realization. "He was so desperate to find Khalid's key that he climbed back into the house and continued the search after our confrontation."

Michael grimaced. "If he did that, he was taking a huge risk. What if you'd called the police from the nearest pay phone?"

"I would have reported an incident that I believed was already over, which means the cops could easily have taken half an hour to get here."

"But they might have had a squad car in the vicinity and arrived while he was still in the house," Michael pointed out.

She shrugged. "He took a risk and it paid off."

"Except that he didn't get what he'd come for." Michael's voice was grim. "No wonder he vented his frustration on Sam's favorite books."

They exchanged a quick glance, both of them realizing the same thing at the same moment. If the intruder had known enough to destroy Sam's collection of Victorian first editions, then it confirmed the likelihood that he was somebody Verity knew.

On hearing that the intruder was quite likely someone Verity knew, the senior FBI agent informed her that she was a lucky woman to have escaped with her life. She was also lucky that the intruder hadn't scrawled obscene graffiti over her walls, or smashed china and glass, or thrown paint on her treasured Kashmiri rugs. As it was, with a few hours of hard work, and a little help from a cleaning service, her house would soon be as good as new.

The doctor at the hospital had also kept telling her how lucky she was, Verity reflected wryly. She could only hope that her amazing good fortune would soon take a less challenging form.

Confident that the investigation was in capable hands, Michael was about to leave for his office at Langley when the phone rang. Verity picked it up and said hello.

"Thank God you're there," Andrew Breitman said

without preamble. "Verity, if you're in shape to make it into the office today, we really need you. Right now. All hell is breaking loose here."

"What's happening?" As she asked the question, Michael's cell phone rang. He walked out into the hall so that he could answer it without intruding on her conversation. "We have a hostage situation developing in Bombay," Andrew said.

"Oh, my God, this is what we've all been dreading. Has the consulate been attacked?"

"No, not the consulate. Terrorists who claim to be members of the Kashmir Freedom Party have taken over the American School in Bombay. They're holding more than two hundred students and faculty members at gunpoint. We don't know which students got out, or exactly who is still inside, but there are almost seven hundred kids attending the school in total, and more than half of them are American citizens. They're the sons and daughters of American executives working with international corporations in India, so this is going to be a huge deal for the media in this country."

"When did the terrorists invade the school? I'm assuming only a few minutes ago?"

"Worse. Several hours ago, it seems. The Indian authorities were trying to keep the situation under wraps, but the terrorists put paid to that hope. They provided filmed footage to the news media, which is how we first knew something was going on. Our ambassador immediately checked with the Indian Government, and—sure enough—they confirmed that the footage was for real. So we're only now receiving the official version of what happened. Meanwhile, every major news channel has already broadcast pictures of a masked gunman pointing a loaded Kalashnikov at a couple of little girls."

Verity gripped the phone, her stomach knotting. "How

old were the children? What's the age range for the school?''

"Apparently it runs the full spectrum, K through twelve. The kids in the picture were little. They couldn't have been more than seven, and they were cowering in front of a blackboard, huddled in their teacher's arms.'' Andrew's voice dipped. "The photo from hell from our point of view.''

"Those poor kids. Their poor families.'' Verity could barely respond, much less think.

"Not to mention poor us,'' Andrew said dryly. "Can you imagine how the American public is going to react when the State Department spokesperson keeps reciting that it's not in this nation's long term interests to give in to terrorist threats?''

"There'll be almost irresistible pressure to meet the terrorists' demands and get the kids out of there,'' Verity said, her sympathies entirely with the American public.

"Yeah.'' Andrew sighed audibly. "To say that the shit just hit the fan big-time would be a massive understatement.''

"I'll come in, of course I will.'' Verity made a mental short list of what had to be done before she could leave her house. "Give me an hour—''

"Take whatever time you need. I'm just so damn grateful you're coming in eventually. We really need your input, Verity.'' He broke off. "I have to go. Dick and I have been summoned to brief the Secretary of State. But get in here as soon as you can. Please.''

Andrew hung up without waiting for her reply. Still a little dazed, Verity walked out into the hallway in search of Michael. He was just closing his cell phone as she approached.

"Presumably you just got the same message I did,''

he said. "The Kashmir Freedom Party has taken over the American School in Bombay."

"Yes. Andrew Breitman called. Not surprisingly, he sounded frantic." Verity blinked, gathering her wits. "I have to go in, Michael, obviously."

"Of course. Me, too."

"It's an incredibly smart choice of target on the part of the terrorists." Now that it had happened, Verity wondered why no other terrorist group had ever done it before. "Attacking a school is a surefire way to grab the attention of every parent in America, and yet it was probably a really easy building for the terrorists to take over. How security-conscious is a school likely to be? From the point of view of armed terrorists, attacking with all the advantage of surprise, there probably wasn't any meaningful security to be overcome."

"In some ways it was a brilliant choice," Michael said tersely. "It also shows a sophisticated understanding of the American psyche." He broke off. "I have to get going, Verity. Will you call for a cab to take you to Foggy Bottom?"

"Yes. I'll call for one right now. I also have to let the FBI team know why I can't hang around and watch them work. By the time I've changed out of your clothes and into something of my own, the cab should be here."

"I'll come to the State Department as soon as I can get away from Langley. Don't attempt to leave your office without me to escort you." Michael didn't kiss her goodbye. He didn't even take her hand. He simply looked at her, for once not attempting to screen the naked fear from his eyes. "Until we're sure the intruder knows you no longer have Khalid's key, it isn't safe for you to be alone, Verity. Promise me you won't come back here without me."

She had no desire whatever to run the risk of another

solitary encounter with a masked man, speaking in a woman's voice. With some experiences, once was more than enough. Besides, for Michael to allow her to see his fear, he had to be worried. Really worried.

"I promise to wait for you," she said.

"Thank you." Michael didn't waste any more time in prolonged goodbyes. He just walked to the door, his stride barely short of a run.

The emotional turmoil once Verity got to the office was greater than the physical chaos she had left behind at home. She was plunged straight into the heart of the ruckus, on pins and needles as she waited for any communication from the terrorists. There was a strong probability that their demands would be delivered in Kashmiri, or at least in Urdu. There were other Urdu speakers at the State Department, most of them with connections to Pakistan, but if the terrorist spoke in Kashmiri, she was the only person able to make the translation.

Meanwhile, she and everyone else in the world who had a computer modem could watch events unfolding inside the school almost at firsthand. The computer lab at the American School in Bombay had apparently been a source of great pride, with state-of-the-art equipment, including digital movie cameras. The terrorists were taking full advantage of the propaganda possibilities presented by the cameras and were sending out live pictures from inside the school. The audio on the equipment had been turned off, presumably to prevent any of the students shouting out messages to their families, but the resulting silent movies were almost more hypnotically compelling than if they'd carried sound.

The streams of heart-wrenching images were uploaded onto the Internet at thirty-minute intervals, in five-minute segments, enabling everyone to see how well-armed the gunmen were, and how effectively they had the school building they'd taken under their control. Thankfully, there seemed to be no evidence at this point of massive slaughter occurring during the takeover.

Still, the major fear of seasoned State Department officials was that the patience of the Indian military would snap under the constant assault of the deliberately provocative pictures the Freedom Party was beaming to the world. Pentagon officials were calling their Indian counterparts, and senior diplomats were working the phones nonstop in a frantic attempt to ensure that the Indian government continued to exercise control over its generals. They pleaded for the government to hold off on any attempt to send in military commandos to recapture the school, at least until the possibilities of peaceful negotiation had been fully explored.

Word from Pentagon experts indicated that a minimum of fifty students and faculty were likely to die in any commando-style assault, even if accurate plans of the school grounds and buildings could be obtained first. And that figure assumed the terrorists wouldn't simply massacre the students and blow up the school as soon as the first shot was fired by the Indian army.

Presumably in deference to Islamic precepts of modesty, the terrorists had herded the male and female students into two separate rooms, the girls into the cafeteria, and the boys into the gym. Pictures showed the girls sitting on the floor, huddled in each other's arms, occasionally sobbing, but apparently finding what comfort they could in each other's company. Their guards seemed to have forbidden them to talk, since there was no evidence of any conversation among them.

The boys initially tried to demonstrate their machismo, pretending that they weren't intimidated by the masked gunmen, and refusing to comply with the order to sit cross-legged in orderly rows. A few hard blows from the gun butts of the terrorists quickly felled the defiant ring-leaders and reduced the remaining boys to fearful silence. The five- and six-year-olds gave up all pretense of feeling brave and crawled onto the laps of any older boy or teacher close enough to hold them.

In order to prevent herself going insane wondering if the youths lying on the gym floor were dead, uncon-scious, or merely too scared to move, Verity occupied herself by arranging the setup of a hot line to the State Department, so that relatives living in the States could call an 800 number and receive the latest official infor-mation from a member of the State Department's office of public relations. She had no idea how comforting it would be to hear a government employee mouth reas-suring platitudes, but at least she felt that she'd provided something for the families of the hostages to do other than click their mouse buttons and watch horrifying pic-tures stream across their computer screens.

The terrorists refused to answer the school phone, so there was no way to communicate with them until they decided they were ready to speak to the world. They fi-nally made their demands known at four o'clock, already well into the night local Bombay time and almost ten hours since the school had first been taken over.

At the usual thirty-minute mark for uploading fresh pictures from inside the school, a blast of martial music indicated that the terrorists had chosen to add sound to this broadcast.

A slender man, wearing a hooded black mask of the type that seemed to be universally favored by terrorists, entered the school's computer lab. Assault rifle slung across his back, he strode past rows of desks equipped with individual computers and took up his position behind a podium that was presumably used in more normal circumstances by the teacher.

At this moment, however, the podium was flanked on either side by a student, each held under restraint by another terrorist. On the right was an Asian youth of probably seventeen or eighteen. On the left was a girl who looked no more than thirteen or fourteen. It was impossible to tell the ethnic background of the female student since her head and shoulders were draped in a black scarf, tucked low over her forehead to cover all trace of her hair. Staring intently at the screen, Verity thought the girl's eyes might be blue, which would suggest she was one of the American students attending the school. In which case, the veil she wore probably wasn't by her choice, but at the command of the terrorists.

Both the students had their hands bound at their backs, and nooses were draped around their necks, the ends of the ropes held threateningly tight by the masked gunmen who guarded them.

It was a scene straight out of every parent's worst nightmare.

The terrorist behind the podium began his oration. Speaking in Kashmiri, he announced that his name was Yousaf. He then launched into a prayer for Allah's blessing. He hoped to meet with favor under the benevolence of Allah's merciful gaze because he and the other members of the Kashmir Freedom Party were acting not just on behalf of the people of Kashmir, but also on behalf of all the poor and suffering people in the world who had been denied justice at the hands of oppressive nations like India and greedy superpowers like the United States.

He spent the next five minutes delivering a paean of praise to Allah, with a few compliments tossed in for all those men who struggled to live according to the rules of the Prophet and the divine edicts of Islam. Women who struggled to live according to the rules of the Prophet were not mentioned.

To Verity, the terrorist's speech seemed a standard example of the sort of homily delivered with mind-numbing regularity by mullahs in Iran, conservatives in Saudi Arabia, the Taliban in Afghanistan, militants in Pakistan and other fanatic Muslim groups scattered throughout the Middle East, as well as among immigrant populations gathered in large cities in America and Europe. However, she knew State Department and CIA experts who studied Islamic culture and the theology would be able to detect subtle distinctions in Yousaf's rhetoric that would enable them to assign him to a specific subsect of Islamic fundamentalism.

Verity had no training in the special skills of a simultaneous translator, but at least forty people were crowded into the viewing room waiting to hear what demands the terrorists were making, and so she translated Yousaf's speech as accurately as she could, concentrating fiercely so that she wouldn't lose the thread of one sentence as she listened to the beginning of the next.

After his initial five-minute sermon, Yousaf switched to another five-minute rant about the evils of the Indian government's Special Powers Act, and the wicked decision by a corrupt Indian military to execute twenty-four Kashmiri brothers in the faith, wrongly accused of murdering Indian soldiers. These martyrs had never been tried in a civilian court of law, and their only true crime had been to state in public speeches that they wished their homeland of Kashmir to be free. As punishment for their attempt to make democratic protests, false charges had been trumped up against them, and their executions carried out, not just in defiance of international law, but in defiance of India's own laws.

"The Day of Reckoning has now arrived!" the terrorist proclaimed. "Our brothers are already in Paradise, but here on earth, they will be avenged!" He flung his arms upward in an exultant affirmation of his bravery in taking over a school filled with unarmed children and teachers.

He then got down to the basics of his real demands.

"The United States government is the ally of the corrupt Indian government in ignoring the desperate plight of the oppressed people of Kashmir. To compensate for its repeated failure to aid our people, the United States government is required to pay the sum of one hundred million dollars in reparations. The sum is to be paid to the Kashmir Freedom Party, for redistribution to the people of Kashmir, for the purpose of rebuilding prosperity in our devastated homeland.

"To this end, we have opened an account in a bank owned by men of faith, who are loyal to the people of Kashmir."

He held up a placard, inscribed with the name and address of the bank, along with a phone number and even an e-mail address, a modern touch Verity found vaguely surreal in the context of the rest of his speech.

Yousaf put down the placard and started speaking again. "Let it be understood that we are not committing the sin of extorting money. No, we are men of honor, dedicated to justice. We demand only the repayment of the debt that is owed to the people of Kashmir by the corrupt and imperialist American government. In view of the justice of our cause, if the sum of one hundred million dollars has not been received within twenty-four hours from now, we shall be forced to take steps to demonstrate the seriousness of our intent.

"You may ask what steps would adequately demonstrate our determination to receive the money that is our due. The answer is simple. If the debt owed by the Americans is not paid to us, we will consider that refusal an act of war. In retaliation, we will start executing the students we are now holding as hostages. We will begin with the two students you see before you.''

The terrorist leader nodded to his two lieutenants, who immediately grabbed either the hair or the headscarf of their captive. Pulling the students' heads back, the camera zoomed in on their faces.

"Look at these two young people well," Yousaf commanded. "Remember their faces, and know that their lives are in your hands."

Verity's voice shook as she delivered her translation of the terrorist's final sentence. The screen went black as the transmission from the school ended.

For a moment, despite the forty people crowded into the viewing room, silence prevailed. Then a babble of angry, panicked comments broke out as everyone started to register the full significance of the threat that loomed much too close on the horizon.

Surprisingly, it was Dick Pedro whose voice rose above the noise, restoring order and at least a semblance of calm. He reminded everyone that the terrorist's speech had been recorded, along with Verity's translation, and both could be downloaded by anyone in the room, since everyone present had appropriate security clearances. Dick requested an analysis of the terrorists' demands from the perspective of each person's special expertise, an initial one-page summation of each analysis to be on his desk within the hour.

"We're up against the wall here, folks," he concluded. "With George Douglass killed only two days ago, the consulate in Bombay is still in a state of shock and we're probably not going to get the kind of backup from there that we'd like. Albert Bree, who was George's deputy, has taken over until we can get a new person out there, but this is a crisis he absolutely didn't need. I'm counting on you all to fill in the gaps from this end. Those kids at the American School and their families are counting on us. Let's not fail them.''

When Verity started to file out of the room along with the others, Dick stopped her. "You did a good job translating that speech,'' he said, his manner awkward as it always was when he attempted to praise a subordinate. "I admit I was worried yesterday when Khalid Muhammad demanded your presence, but you've kept it all together so far, Verity, and I'm grateful that you decided to come in today.''

"I'm glad, too,'' Verity said. "I'm not sure that any Westerner can understand where these terrorists are coming from, but at least I feel this is a situation where my skills are likely to be useful.''

"They can't hurt, that's for sure.'' Dick was called away by an urgent phone call, and Verity returned to her office, where she went over Yousaf's speech word by word, phrase by phrase, line by line. She found several occasions on which her translation hadn't been quite a perfect interpretation of his words, but no occasion on which she had truly distorted his meaning. But the longer she studied the speech, the more puzzling Verity found the details. Eventually, she got up and walked into Andrew's office, needing to talk to someone.

She tapped on his door. "Do you have a minute?''

He gave her a quick smile as he pushed back from his computer. "Absolutely. I've been preparing different versions of the same briefing paper for two days now. I haven't got a darn thing new to say about this situation that's going to be the slightest use to anyone.''

"I seriously doubt that. You understand the region better than anyone else working in this building.'' She took a pile of books and folders off the room's only other chair and sat down. "That's why I need to talk to you, Andrew.

I've looked at this speech until I'm cross-eyed, and as far as I can see, it doesn't make a lick of sense.''

"You can say that again." Andrew pursed his mouth, his mockery bitter. "We Kashmiris don't like the way the mean old Indian government has treated us, so we're going to kill a few hundred Americans." He shook his head. "Yeah, that's sure going to solve a lot of problems."

"I wasn't talking about that sort of illogic," Verity said. "I meant more that the terrorists' plans don't seem to make any sense even from their own point of view. They're protesting the execution of twenty-four Kashmiri prisoners, so what do they attack? A school. Why not an Indian government building? Or at least the American Consulate. What's a school got to do with Kashmir's independence? Why did it even cross their minds to occupy a school?"

Andrew looked at her with evident puzzlement. "We're talking fanatic Muslim terrorists here. The same kind of people who blew up the World Trade Center and spent most of the seventies hijacking airplanes because this was somehow supposed to make the state of Israel vanish from the map. Are you expecting me to make sense of their choice of target?"

"Well, yes, I guess I am. From their point of view, at least. Explain to me what they're hoping to get out of this."

"Okay, let me try to reason like a crazy Kashmiri fanatic. If you can call the process reasoning." Andrew rocked back in his chair, ticking off on his fingers. "Why would I invade a school to protest the execution of Kashmiri prisoners? Well, I guess I'd choose a school because it's easier to capture than an Indian government building, and one heck of a lot easier to capture than the American Consulate General. Ever since the Iranians took over our embassy in Teheran, we've had pretty amazing security systems in place to prevent another disaster like that. Terrorists have succeeded in hurtling cars packed with explosives at the entrance to various embassies, but they've never managed to take over the building."

"But from the point of view of a terrorist like Yousaf, why is it more effective to take over a building than to blow it up?" Verity asked.

"Taking over a school filled with American students makes for way better propaganda than detonating a fusty old government building, especially an Indian government building. I bet there are several million people in the United States who had never even heard of Kashmir before today. And now, thanks to all those helpful maps on CNN, they know that it's located in a crucial land-locked position between China, Afghanistan, Pakistan and India, and that most of the people who live in the Vale of Kashmir want to form their own independent state, even if people in the east of Kashmir would prefer to join Tibet and the ones in the west are already united with Pakistan. From the terrorists' point of view, that's real progress."

Verity nodded her agreement. "I'll grant you that the propaganda possibilities are great. In fact, I was really impressed by their brilliant choice of target when I first heard about the takeover—"

"It's low-risk, too," Andrew pointed out. "The foot soldiers of the Freedom Party aren't going to get killed invading a school. Instead, Yousaf has promised them that they're going to make lots and lots of money—"

"Stop right there." Verity leaned forward, her body tensing. "You just nailed what's bothering me, Andrew. Yousaf sounded like a diehard fanatic, but not like a lunatic, so he must know they're not going to make any money. Not a nickel. Surely he must know he hasn't got a chance in hell of persuading the United States government to hand over a hundred million dollars? It doesn't matter how many pictures he posts on the Internet showing little kids crying in their teachers' arms, it's not going to make any difference. Except to make Americans despise him and his cause, which is the exact opposite of what he's presumably trying to achieve.''

"Maybe he doesn't know that we have a policy of no negotiations with terrorists," Andrew suggested.

"How would that be possible? If you're going to be a terrorist, don't you need to learn a few of the basics? Like—the U.S. government won't negotiate."

Andrew shook his head. "You know that's not entirely true—"

"Okay, we do the occasional secret deal with rogue regimes we're trying to bring into the civilized world. But we sure aren't going to send Yousaf a check from Uncle Sam as a reward for terrorizing little kids and their teachers."

"Yousaf might not realize that. Fanatics like him operate within such closed social systems he could be totally ignorant of what the world outside Kashmir and India is really like. He could well be naive enough to believe we'll cough up the money. After all, the United States has an annual gross national product in the trillions. That's way too much money for an ordinary U.S. citizen to wrap their mind around, much less someone from an impoverished region like Kashmir. How much is a trillion, anyway? Ten billion? A hundred billion?"

Verity shook her head. "I haven't a clue."

"Neither have I, and I'm damn sure Yousaf doesn't, either. From his point of view, he must think we wouldn't even notice a little sum like a hundred million. And he's right, we wouldn't. It's probably less than the federal government spends on our annual program to save the panthers in the Florida Everglades.''

"Okay, but if Yousaf's not even informed enough to know that the U.S. government has a strict policy of not negotiating with terrorists, how could he have understood our national psyche well enough to grasp what a powerful impact he'd have in the States if he took over a school where lots of American students are enrolled? How did they know it would be *real* smart to upload heart-wrenching pictures onto the Internet? Those are both sophisticated judgments, so if he understands all that, how can he possibly believe the U.S. will send a hundred million bucks to a bank in Srinagar as a reward for terrorizing children? Especially since there would be zero guarantee that paying the money would ensure the release of those same children.''

Andrew tugged at his lower lip. "Jeez, I don't know, Verity. You're right, it seems incongruous. You're asking good questions, and I sure wish I had even halfway decent answers. My best guess is that these terrorists are a mixture of cunning and extreme fanaticism. They know what buttons to push to get their message across, but they haven't got a clue about what they'll do if their demand for money isn't met.''

He frowned, his eyes narrowing. "No, I take that back. Of course they know what they'll do, and so do we.''

"What?'' Verity's stomach knotted in anticipation of Andrew's reply.

"They'll kill themselves and all the kids in one giant explosion. Who the hell needs money in Paradise?''

"Maybe you're right.'' Verity sat back tiredly and rubbed her eyes. "You have to be right, I guess. Except if they don't really think they'll get the money, and if they know they're all going to die in the end, why go through the motions?''

"You know the answer to that one, too. We already discussed it. They want to die in front of an audience of millions. An audience of billions would be better, if they can spin out the hostage drama long enough to build really good international ratings. I'm sure there are a couple of British kids at the school. Probably even a few from countries in Europe. You can almost guarantee that this drama is being played out on TV screens around the world."

"You're right," Verity said, her stomach churning relentlessly as she realized what an inevitable and depressing path the situation was doomed to follow. She squeezed her eyes shut, trying to ease the headache that had started to throb with vicious force. The aftereffects of her concussion were starting to depress her.

An image of the slender terrorist holding up his giant placard danced behind her eyelids, teasing her with another nit-picking incongruity. "There's something about that damn placard Yousaf held up that's bugging me," she murmured, visualizing the name of the bank and its address, written in oversize printed capital letters.

"I thought the e-mail address was pretty wild," Andrew said.

Verity rose to her feet. "Oh, my God, that's it. That's the other thing that's been bothering me!"

"What?" Andrew demanded. "The e-mail address?"

"No, or not only that. The entire placard was written in English! Yousaf was speaking in Kashmiri, but the placard said The United Bank of Kabul, and even translated the street address, 44 University Plaza, Kabul, Afghanistan."

Andrew frowned and turned back to his computer monitor, scrolling through the cached film of the terrorist's speech until he reached the point where Yousaf held up the placard. "You're right," he said. "I hadn't noticed, but it's written in English."

"Why?" Verity demanded.

Andrew shrugged. "Well, it's a little strange, but it's not such a huge deal, is it? Almost every bank in India has stationery with its name and address written out in English. English is the universal world language these days, at least as far as commerce and finance is concerned."

"But English would never be the language of choice for a fanatical nationalist like Yousaf," Verity said. "He expected us to find somebody who could translate his speech, so why not his damn placard? Surely it would be a matter of pride for him not to utilize the language and alphabet of the United States?"

"Not necessarily. Remember all those demonstrations outside the embassy in Teheran? The signs the protestors carried were often written in English to make sure the American TV audience got the meaning. *Great Satan Go Home,* with pictures of Uncle Sam wearing horns to reinforce their message of hate." Andrew pushed his chair away from the computer again. "Anyway, what other significance could there be to having the placard written in English?"

"None that I can think of." Verity's mouth twisted wryly. "Except maybe Yousaf has a streak of practicality hidden beneath all that religious rhetoric. Whatever else we didn't understand, he wanted to be darn sure we got the message about where we have to send the money."

"Could be." Andrew gave a rueful smile. "Presumably our friend Yousaf picked a bank in Afghanistan because he knew the officers wouldn't cooperate with the States."

"And we don't have any meaningful diplomatic contacts with Afghanistan right now, so it's almost impossible to exert pressure on them to provide details about how the account was set up and so on.''

Andrew shrugged. ''Still, it won't matter whether the bank is willing to cooperate or not, because no money is ever going to get paid in. So the terrorists have been clever to no purpose.''

Dick Pedro stuck his head around the door. ''We're meeting in five minutes in the briefing room. Urgent.''

''What's up?'' Andrew asked.

''The young girl in the pictures, the one with the noose around her neck—she's just been identified. Her parents called the consulate in Bombay fifteen minutes ago and they patched her father through to us. The Secretary of State has already spoken to the parents.''

''Who is she?'' Andrew and Verity asked the question simultaneously.

''Mary Grace Klemper,'' Dick said. ''Fourteen years old, and the only child in the family. Her father, Matthew Klemper, is the founder and president of the largest privately owned plastics manufacturing company in the whole of India. He's just about ready to tear the world apart with his bare hands, he's so scared and angry.''

Dick broke off. ''I don't have time to talk. I have to return a call from the CTC. I'll see you in the briefing room in four minutes and fill you in on the details then.''

Verity stared after her boss's retreating back, the surface of her mind blank, but an idea was slowly bubbling up from the depths, still too far down for her to grasp. She jumped when she felt Andrew's hand tap her lightly on the shoulder.

''Come on, Verity. This probably isn't a real good moment to stand around daydreaming.''

She didn't respond, on automatic pilot as she followed Andrew along the corridor to the briefing room, which was already crowded with people waiting for Dick to fill them in on the latest developments. Andrew tugged her down into the seat next to him, then literally had to snap his fingers in front of her face before she realized he was talking to her.

"What's going on, Verity? You're concentrating so hard, you look as if you've just discovered a new theory of the universe."

"Not quite that." She drew in a shaky breath. "But I think I might have worked out why Yousaf took over the American School, and how he plans to make money."

"How?" Andrew gave her a startled glance.

"He's going to auction off the individual students to their parents. Then it doesn't matter if the American Government refuses to pay the ransom. Yousaf has got almost two hundred students held hostage in there, plus a few faculty members. If he can get each of the kids' families to send him half a million bucks, he makes his hundred million. That's why he gave the address of the bank in English. It was for exactly the same reason those protestors in Teheran didn't write their slogans in Persian— Yousaf had to be sure the parents of the kids he's holding hostage could read how to get in touch with him, and with the bank."

"Christ Almighty!" Andrew's eyes glazed with shock. Then he turned to look at her, respect replacing the shock. "You're suggesting that Yousaf wants the families to bypass the government and negotiate a direct deal with him?"

She nodded. "Think about it, Andrew. Yousaf has found a way to make the U.S. government policy of not negotiating with terrorists irrelevant. The American School in Bombay must be full of students whose parents are quite rich. It's a private school, and their physical facilities look outstanding, so we know the parents must be paying astronomical tuition fees. Or if the parents themselves aren't wealthy, a lot of them work for American corporations that would be more than willing to pay half a million to put an end to this nightmare.''

Andrew exhaled gustily. "Half a million or more. Why not? Hell, it's probably all covered in their corporate insurance policies. The companies can afford to be generous.''

Verity frowned. "There's only one thing still puzzling me. How does Yousaf plan to live long enough to enjoy his millions? He's obviously a very smart man indeed and so he must realize that the minute—the second—the last of those hostages is released, the Indian army is going to storm the school. They probably have the tanks drawn up outside, all ready and waiting.''

"That's easy," Andrew said. "Yousaf may be smart, but he's still a fanatic. He's got no intention of trying to stay alive. I'm guessing he's already made arrangements for his successor to collect the ransom money, so he doesn't care if the Indian army storms the school the moment the last student walks free. He plans to blow himself up anyway.''

Andrew shook his head, his expression one of grudging admiration. "The bastard's going to get his hundred million and a worldwide audience to watch him rocket off to Paradise. What more could any terrorist hope for?''

Fourteen

In Michael's line of work, success was often defined as nothing more than staying alive long enough to make your next report to headquarters, preferably within a day or two of the time you'd promised. By that standard, his months working undercover with the Kashmir Freedom Party had been outstandingly successful. He'd not only managed to report back to Langley on schedule each week, he'd even survived the ambush designed to kill both him and Farooq.

By every other standard Michael could think of, his mission to Kashmir had been one long, unrelenting fuckup. As of yesterday, Khalid was dead, along with a lot of good Americans who'd simply been trying to do their duty. Farooq had disappeared, and was quite possibly dead, too. Michael sure as hell couldn't get him to respond to any of his messages. Thanks to Verity, he had the key to Farooq's safety deposit box, but even that wasn't the bright spot it had seemed last night. He didn't have a clue as to where that box might be located, or how he was going to protect Verity from further attacks. To make matters worse, Yousaf was currently thumbing his nose at the world, selling off children and replenishing his coffers at breakneck speed.

And in an office somewhere in Washington, the son of a bitch who'd allied himself with Yousaf and turned the Kashmir Freedom Party into his own personal moneymaking machine was probably leaning back in his cheap, government-issued chair, laughing his ass off. Laughing his extremely *wealthy* ass off, Michael thought in exasperation, while no doubt making plans to hightail it out of the country the moment the parents of the school hostages stopped pouring ransom money into his and Yousaf's bank accounts.

True, there was one small cloud on this bastard's horizon: his client, Saddam Hussein, still didn't have functioning nuclear missiles to add to his arsenal, a fact that was undoubtedly pissing Saddam off big-time. And Saddam in pissed-off mode was not somebody you'd want to have breathing down your neck. Still, a hundred million bucks could buy a person a hell of a lot of privacy on some nice secure tropical island off the coast of South America.

Khalid's key and the guidance software that Farooq presumably still had were soon going to be only a minor blip on this man's mental horizon. Why would he care if some time in the far distant future Michael finally got his act together and found Farooq's damned safety deposit box with its incriminating evidence? By that time, their suspect would not only have a new name and a new address, he'd undoubtedly have a new face as well, courtesy of some South American plastic surgeon. Not to mention the latest in artificial skin grafted onto his fingertips, and a getaway helicopter purring on a landing pad tucked away on his personal island paradise.

And for this, Michael had spent eight months risking his life in Kashmir.

For all the good it seemed to be doing him or anyone else in the intelligence community, his time spent undercover had at least enabled him to provide the Counter Terrorism Center with a crystal-clear picture of how the Kashmir Freedom Party had been transformed from an inefficient protest group into a powerhouse player in the netherworld of fanatical Islam.

The transformation was largely due to Farooq Muhammad, who had lived to bitterly regret the mistakes of his youth. Seven years ago, when Farooq had been a hotheaded nineteen-year-old, full of testosterone and wild idealism, he had rebelled against the traditions of political moderation for so long embraced by his family. He had secretly joined the Kashmir Freedom Party and, after his initiation, had spent several exciting weekends with other young hotheads, lobbing grenades at police barricades. On one especially dazzling occasion they'd even managed to blow up a bridge across the River Vijil, producing a giant bang and a fiery plume of smoke large enough to satisfy even a reckless teenager's yearning for spectacle.

However, the bridge never got rebuilt, and Farooq was smart as well as foolhardy, so it didn't take too long for him to realize that blowing up the bridge had caused a lot more trouble for his fellow Kashmiris than it had for anyone in India's government.

Despite this flash of wisdom, Farooq still wasn't willing to give up on his adolescent dream of an independent Kashmir. His brother Khalid's dedication to the tedious path of moderation and negotiation merely annoyed him. More than fifty years had passed since Kashmir's dreams of independence had been obliterated in the chaos that followed the end of British Imperial rule. If fifty years of moderation hadn't won statehood for Kashmir, Farooq saw no reason to suppose that a few more years of quiet pleading was going to make a difference.

Since nobody else in the entire Vale of Kashmir seemed to be doing what was needed, Farooq decided that he would take on the task of building a mass popular protest movement, using the Kashmir Freedom Party as a base. He reasoned that the Indian government could resist terrorism, and fight skirmishes against Pakistani incursions, but no government on earth could stand up against the might of an entire people united to demand justice.

In his everyday life, Farooq was being intensively trained by his aging great-uncles to take charge of the family trading company. Troubled times in Kashmir limited the extent to which the company could grow internally, but Farooq was elated by the opportunities that existed overseas. Truth to tell, he was a trader at heart, and his ability to negotiate a successful deal brought him great pleasure. In Europe, demand for high-grade cashmere and pashmina products was strong, and he began to forge extensive links to various dealers in Germany, where his family had been doing business for years. Before long, overseas profits for the company had doubled, and even his great-uncles acknowledged that it was all due to Farooq's uncanny ability to piece together a deal.

His work with the family company helped Farooq to realize how many of the problems facing the Kashmir Freedom Party stemmed from the fact that the organization didn't have enough money. Most of the recruits were too poor to contribute funds, so the Party was never going to become rich through donations from its members. On the contrary, quite often the Party had to provide its recruits with extra food before they were strong enough to fight effectively. Farooq decided that the Freedom Party was never going to have a real impact on the course of events until they had a sound financial base to work from. In Farooq's not-at-all humble opinion, Yousaf and the other leaders needed to stop concentrating so hard on Islamic purity and the injustices perpetrated by India. Instead, they needed to turn their thoughts to methods by which the Kashmir Freedom Party could get itself some real money.

Farooq couldn't bankroll the Party from his personal funds. Even if he'd been willing to steal from his family, his great-uncles were much too astute to let him get away with milking their profits. Farooq didn't see this as a problem. With the arrogance of youth, he simply decided to utilize his overseas contacts to launch a parallel business that would keep the Kashmir Freedom Party floating on a healthy cushion of funds. Funds that would pay to recruit members and build the mass democratic movement he yearned to see.

Yousaf and the other party leaders were more than willing to give Farooq his head. An Islamic Muslim fundamentalist who genuinely believed America and India spent twenty-four hours a day working on a vast conspiracy to deny Kashmir its God-given right to self-determination, Yousaf nevertheless recognized that Farooq's genius for striking deals created a unique opportunity for him and the fanatics he'd gathered around him. If Farooq succeeded in making money, the Party would finally have the funds to buy arms and equipment to fulfill all their fantasies of destruction. If Farooq failed, then Yousaf knew exactly how to make sure that when Farooq climbed out on a limb, the leaders of the Freedom Party were nowhere behind him. Except, maybe, standing with saws in hand ready to cut off the branch he'd counted on to support him.

As for Farooq's ridiculous idealism about using the Kashmir Freedom Party to create a democratic mass movement... Well, Yousaf knew better than to argue about that up front. Farooq was still young, and he didn't understand hardball politics. When crunch time arrived, Yousaf knew he had plenty of allies who would help Farooq to see the light.

One way or another.

Having secured Yousaf's blessing, Farooq needed to find something to trade. Kashmir was hardly a hotbed of exportable products and selling cashmere wasn't an option, since that would be directly competitive with his family's company. After a few weeks of pondering this dilemma, Farooq found the answer one day on a sales trip to Dresden, a city in the eastern part of Germany that had once been under Communist rule.

Driving past a former army base that was being converted into a municipal park, he realized that it wasn't only the barracks and military hospitals of Communist Europe that were now obsolete. With the end of the Cold War and the disbanding of dozens of Communist armies, Farooq knew there had to be hundreds of thousands of excess weapons that were either being warehoused or sold off.

He decided to grab a piece of the action. He would become an arms broker, buying weapons from the countries of eastern Europe that no longer needed them, and selling them to his Muslim brothers struggling to gain freedom in countries all across the Middle East and Asia.

At first it had been hard for Farooq to get his hands on a supply of suitable weapons. After a while, he understood that his attempts to keep the deals legal and aboveboard were seriously interfering with his ability to make money. Many of the states that had broken away from the Soviet Union had no real national assets, and selling off stolen military equipment was just about the only way an entrepreneur in Kazakhstan or Chechnya could make money. Consequently, the best and most salable items never made it to the legal marketplace.

Farooq decided to discard his bourgeois obsession with legality and start brokering some really worthwhile deals. Starting out with small transactions that netted no more than two or three thousand dollars in total profit, he gradually built a reputation as an arms dealer who could be relied on. And once his suppliers saw he was trustworthy, they approached him to broker bigger, more important—and more blatantly illegal—deals.

It was during this slogging climb out of the minor leagues into the big time that Farooq first encountered The American. Gunther, an arms salesman from East Germany, developed an almost paternal interest in Farooq's skills as a deal-maker. A former member of the Stasi, who resented every centimeter of privilege that had been snatched from him since the fall of the Berlin Wall, Gunther got back at the world by putting together people who could maximize the mischief caused by the stolen military equipment he sold. Farooq only needed to be introduced to the right people, Gunther saw, and he could create one hell of a satisfying mess in the foothills of the Himalayas.

Accordingly, Gunther introduced Farooq to The American—if giving The American Farooq's cell phone number could be called an introduction. Farooq's first deal with The American was struck on the basis of this one cell phone conversation and a couple of follow-up e-mail messages, for which The American utilized the Internet account of a public library in Arlington, Virginia.

Farooq was by this time quite accustomed to dealing with people he hadn't seen and whose names he didn't know. Quite often even the nationality or residence of the dealer was a secret, so in that regard, Farooq already knew more about The American than about some of his other trading partners. He certainly had no desire to provide biographical details about himself, so he was 't si prised to find The American equally protecti... wn identity. Even after months of acquaintance Farooq k. no more about The American than that he cor all his business by cell phone, or by e-mail messages that were invariably piggybacked onto correspondence sent out from one of the public libraries in the Washington, D.C. area.

Farooq understood The American's need for secrecy. In the illegal arms trade, people didn't go around exchanging business cards. Or if they did, you could pretty much count on the fact that the name on the card you were given was fake, and the address no more than a hollow front that would lead to nowhere.

However, Farooq felt exposed and vulnerable vis-à-vis his new partner. Anyone as smart and connected as The American would have no difficulty figuring out that the Farooq who traveled around Europe brokering arms on behalf of the Kashmir Freedom Party was the same person as the Farooq Muhammad who traveled around Europe trading in high-end cashmere products on behalf of his family's company.

For his own protection, Farooq felt that he needed to find out what he could about The American's true identity, and he assiduously cobbled together such small scraps of information as he could glean. Interestingly, Gunther let slip on a rare occasion when he'd had too much to drink that The American was a State Department official, and they'd first met years ago at an embassy reception when the smuggler still held a position of honor with Stasi.

Unfortunately, as soon as Farooq pressed for more details, Gunther clammed up. Drunk or not, after thirty years with East Germany's notorious state police, it took more than a bottle of imported American bourbon to get the man to reveal any really dangerous secrets.

For a long time Farooq cared more about doing business with The American than about finding out his real name. Later, he wished that he'd found some way to shake the information loose from Gunther on the one night when he'd really come close to having the chance.

Farooq's partnership with The American started off well. The American had product that needed to be moved out of Kazakhstan and into China. The United Nations Disarmament Committee was sending frequent and annoying inspection teams into Kazakhstan, making it impossible simply to load the weapons onto a cargo plane and ship them out as had happened ever since the breakup of the Soviet Union.

The American decided that delivering his weapons via truck and mule might take longer, but would ultimately be safer. Kashmir not only made an excellent shipping route for the weapons, but Freedom Party soldiers would make excellent porters. They knew the terrain, and they knew how to avoid Indian government patrols. Best of all, United Nations inspections teams never stuck their long, interfering noses into Kashmir.

The American offered to pay Farooq a lump sum of thirty thousand dollars, provided the weapons arrived at their destination within three weeks. The penalty for late arrival was five thousand dollars a day. Farooq negotiated a bonus for early delivery of three thousand dollars a day.

Thirty thousand dollars was more profit than Farooq had so far cleared on any of the penny-ante deals he'd previously negotiated. It was summer and the transportation wouldn't be very difficult. His porters would be able to travel by moonlight, and by day they could blend in with the groups of nomadic sheep herders who roamed the hills of Kashmir from April to October.

The project turned out to be a resounding success from everyone's point of view, not only because The American upped their bonus to ten thousand dollars when the weapons were delivered three days early, but also because Yousaf was so enthusiastic. Yousaf had been disdainful of Farooq's moneymaking methods when the arms trades had been strictly legal, but now that there was a spice of the forbidden, he threw himself into the operation with boyish exhilaration. Ferrying arms across mountain pastures at the dead of night had all the elements of military planning combined with secrecy that were so appealing to him.

With Yousaf's support, Farooq made many more deals with The American, the risks becoming consistently greater, but the rewards rising at an even faster rate. The string of successes was finally broken when Freedom Party porters had an unexpected encounter with an Indian army unit on patrol in the mountains. Thanks to Farooq's profit-making abilities, Freedom Party foot soldiers all carried powerful weapons, but on this occasion the Indian troops were highly trained and effective, refusing to turn tail and run even when they realized they were outgunned. In the pitched battle that followed the initial clash, twenty Indian soldiers were killed before the surviving Freedom Party fighters were able to execute the wounded and make good their escape.

Even then, no long-term problems might have arisen if it not been for the fact that a second Indian army unit was lying in wait less than a mile away. Twenty-four Freedom Party fighters were captured, beaten, tortured for information, then taken off to federal prison in Bombay. However, they'd managed to hide their illicit cargo in a series of caves before they were captured, and the twenty-fifth freedom fighter managed to make it home alive to tell the tale. Yousaf mounted a successful rescue mission for the cargo before any of his men broke under torture and revealed its hiding place, and the shoulder-launched Sting Ray missiles made it safely to their illicit destination only a couple of days late.

At which point Yousaf declared the mission a resounding success. The weapons had been delivered and the Kashmir Freedom Party now had bona fide martyrs to help in their recruitment drive. In Yousaf's opinion, with certified martyrs there was no limit to the heights to which the Party could soar.

With a queasiness verging on horror, Farooq registered the fact that Yousaf's attitude to the massacre was almost playful, despite the number of men killed on both sides. Much too late, Farooq realized his own attitude had until now been similarly frivolous. For the past five years— even when the stakes were significantly raised by his deals with The American—he'd behaved as though trading in stolen weapons were simply an exciting game, conducted in partnership with interesting international players. The deadly nature of the product he brokered had been a matter of supreme indifference to him. The ethics of selling stolen military equipment had been something he'd considered only to dismiss.

Until now, in Farooq's mind, his actions had been entirely justifiable. He traded honorably, he guaranteed his products, and—considering the risks involved—he offered fair prices, thereby fulfilling all the obligations of an honest merchant. The people of Kashmir had been ignored by the great powers for so long, why should he care if he broke a few petty rules imposed by tyrannical governments that conspired with India to oppress his brother Kashmiris?

In retrospect, Farooq realized that he'd had to work hard to keep his conscience buried beneath such flimsy rationalizations. Twinges of reproach and regret had surfaced with increasing frequency over the years, but somehow he'd managed to ignore them all.

The capture of twenty-four Freedom Party members, including one of his own first cousins, left Farooq feeling as if he'd spent the past several years playacting in a movie. And now he'd suddenly woken up and looked around, only to discover the director had walked off the set and the knife in his hands was drenched in real human blood.

Even worse, Farooq realized he'd been so caught up in proving how smart he was at making deals that he'd paid only cursory attention to how the money he poured into the coffers of the Freedom Party was being spent. Now he recognized the truth. Far from being used to build a political party enjoying mass support from the people of his homeland, the Party had been turned into Yousaf's own personal, well-armed, well-paid, terrorist army.

Yousaf's religious belief was sincere, if narrow-minded, and he was genuinely dedicated to the cause of freedom and independence for Kashmir. He turned to Mecca, knelt and prayed three times a day for the well-being of his fellow Kashmiris, and for the peaceful establishment of a just Islamic society in his native land.

Justice and peace might be the ideals to which Yousaf theoretically subscribed. What happened in practice was that he and his fanatical followers spent most of their time maiming Hindu and Sikh civilians, killing Indian soldiers, and plotting the overthrow of the Indian government.

Farooq tried to reason with the man who had once been both his mentor and his inspiration, but Yousaf seemed deaf to any view other than his own. However many times and ways Farooq attempted to propose the idea that killing Indians didn't necessarily equate with making life better for the people of Kashmir, Yousaf never seemed to understand the distinction.

As for the concept of establishing Kashmir as an independent secular state where Hindus, Buddhists, atheists and Christians could live and work on equal terms with

Kashmir's Muslims, Yousaf considered the concept absurd. Islam was a generous religion, welcoming to everyone, no matter how badly they'd sinned in the past. Even Jews could be taken into the fold as long as they accepted the Koran, acknowledged the wisdom of the Prophet, and submitted themselves to the will of Allah. Since Islam was so generous in what it offered, why would Farooq or anyone else wish to live in a so-called secular state?

With a despair that was almost paralyzing, Farooq realized that he had single-handedly provided the funds that enabled Yousaf to dismantle the ramshackle, incompetent Kashmir Freedom Party and replace it with an efficient, terrorist monster. A monster that bore the same name but lacked any other meaningful resemblance to the organization that had gone before.

Pulling himself together, Farooq decided to make sure Yousaf's monster met a quick and certain death. He assumed that there would be no great difficulty in doing this. The monster required money to remain functional and Farooq was in charge of supplying the money. He therefore shut off the money spigot.

Without fresh funds, Yousaf soon faced the unpleasant truth that he could no longer afford to maintain his enhanced level of operations. Not surprisingly, he was furious. Having once tasted the power of wealth, he had no intention of allowing his newly aggressive Freedom Party to sink back into the impotence of poverty.

Yousaf needed the money to start flowing again, and for that he needed Farooq. At first he attempted to persuade Farooq to change his mind and resume the arms deals voluntarily. When that didn't work, he threatened.

His threats weren't very intimidating, however, since Farooq knew Yousaf couldn't afford to kill him. Yousaf was great at blowing up buildings, and brilliant at turning raw recruits into seasoned terrorists, willing to die for the cause, but he had no talent for making business deals. More to the point, he had no idea where to go or whom to contact in order to initiate a successful deal.

The American was by now the Freedom Party's business partner and chief financial officer in all but name. Despite this close working relationship, Farooq had no direct method of getting in touch with him, although such contact information as he had, he'd kept to himself. Even at the height of his devotion to Yousaf and the cause, some instinct for commercial caution, learned from running the family business, had warned Farooq to keep those crucial details secret.

In the end, though, Yousaf won the power struggle, because he'd been able to find the weapon he needed to coerce Farooq's cooperation. He'd kidnapped Khalid. Farooq could resist physical pain when it was inflicted on him. He couldn't watch his brother tortured.

Rather than run the risk that Khalid and his sons might be killed, Farooq went back to making money for the Kashmir Freedom Party. However, there were now two big differences in the way he ran his business. Farooq was no longer a happy-go-lucky believer in the integrity of the Kashmir Freedom Party, and Yousaf insisted on being informed about the details of every deal. Now, even if Farooq committed suicide, the trade in arms and terror wouldn't stop, because Yousaf knew how to get in touch with The American. At the moment, neither man fully trusted the other, and Yousaf knew that his bargaining skills weren't sufficient to negotiate the best deals on behalf of the Freedom Party. But Farooq could see the time coming when he himself would be cut out of the negotiating loop being forged between Yousaf and The American. And then it was almost impossible to imagine the mischief that would follow.

Tormented by the guilty knowledge that he had personally established a system that put deadly weapons into the hands of people who most assuredly shouldn't have them, Farooq finally plucked up courage to confess the truth to his brother, Khalid. The two of them spent hours discussing and discarding plans, desperately seeking some way out of the poisonous pit Farooq had dug himself into. They were two clever men, but search as they might, they could come up with no way to end Farooq's involvement in the Kashmir Freedom Party without bringing danger and death into the heart of their family.

Desperation finally brought inspiration, and Khalid came up with the suggestion that he and his brother needed to approach the American government and beg for help. Khalid had studied the U.S. political scene closely enough to know that the CIA had an over-stretched budget, and that the status of Kashmir only held their attention when India and Pakistan threatened to hurl nuclear bombs at each other. However, even though the Americans might be indifferent to the knowledge that Kashmiri insurrectionists were trading in illegal weapons, they would probably care a lot if they learned that one of their diplomats was actively involved in brokering the sale of stolen arms.

Since the man they hoped to expose was himself a U.S. government official, Khalid obviously had to be very careful about where and to whom he told his story. Fortunately, George Douglass had just arrived in Bombay to take up the post of U.S. Consul General, bringing his wife and family with him. Khalid had first met Maya Hardcastle when he studied for a year at the University of Virginia. He'd attended the wedding when Maya married George Douglass, and friendship among the three of them had flourished ever since. Flourished to the extent that Khalid was willing to risk trusting the man with his life, and the life of his brother.

George Douglass took Khalid's story seriously enough that he bypassed the usual State Department channels and sent in a top secret report directly to the head of the Counter Terrorism Center. It was a no-brainer to reach the conclusion that if a State Department official truly was helping China to sell weapons from the former Communist countries of Europe to buyers in the subterranean networks of Islamic fundamentalism, then that buyer needed to be stopped, and quickly.

Confirmation of a part of Khalid's story was available. Intelligence sources in the U.S. had already noticed a significant increase in the number and quality of arms reaching the hands of terrorists in an arc stretching from the northwestern borders of China, through Afghanistan, Kashmir, Pakistan and into Iran, but there was no evidence, other than Khalid's word, that those arms were being brokered with the help of an American official.

An urgent, top-level security investigation of State Department personnel was ordered. The investigation turned up a dauntingly long list of diplomats who had been posted to China, Afghanistan and Kazakhstan and therefore might have been able to make the necessary contacts. However, none of the diplomats on this long list had shown a recent splurge in their spending habits. None of them had taken off on unexplained trips to offshore banking havens. One of them had bought a luxury home in the high-priced suburbs around Washington, D.C., but it turned out that he'd just inherited half a million bucks from his grandmother. Two others had shown evidence of a costly drug habit, but both of these diplomats were heavily in debt, with second mortgages on their homes and credit cards extended to the limits.

Collin Krenz, head of the Counter Terrorism Center, had to ask himself if the American arms broker actually existed, or if he was a figment of Khalid's overheated imagination. If he wasn't going to indulge in lavish spending, or expensive vices, why would any American government official betray his country by helping former Communist scumbags sell weapons to some of the most destructive players on the world scene?

Khalid's story might have been dismissed in the wake of the abortive security investigation if George Douglass hadn't stressed what a moderate and reliable source of information he'd proven over the years. In addition, the activities of the Kashmir Freedom Party provided strong evidence that a great deal of money was suddenly pouring into the coffers of an organization that had previously eked out a sparse existence on the edge of penury.

If Khalid's traitor existed, he had obviously been operating without discovery for several years. It was more than two years since he'd started making deals with Farooq and the Freedom Party, at which point he'd already been an established player on the international arms dealing scene. The fact that he had escaped detection for so long suggested he was too smart to allow himself to be unmasked by routine security probes conducted within the United States.

Clearly, more dramatic measures were needed. Collin Krenz approached Michael Strait, who was not only uniquely qualified for a mission in Kashmir, he also happened to be the most effective agent working for the Counter Terrorism Center. Michael, who had officially been promoted to a desk job too senior to involve in-the-field assignments, was asked if he would volunteer for one final undercover mission.

Desperate to get away from Verity, Michael had not only been willing to accept the assignment, he'd been eager. With help from Farooq and Khalid, he would infiltrate the Freedom Party and participate in one of the deals supposedly masterminded by The American. With luck, he would gather sufficient incriminating evidence from the field to backtrack the threads of evidence to the States and make an identification.

That had been in May of last year. Without ever revealing his true name, or his exact position with the U.S. government, Michael had spent two weeks hidden in Khalid's home, studying genealogy charts and learning all the complex local history he needed to have at his fingertips. Then he had assumed the role of Abdullah Ghulam Nabi, the brother-in-law of a cousin of Farooq and Khalid. Abdullah had supposedly been raised in New York and—to make him more attractive to Yousaf as a Freedom Party recruit—Abdullah had supposedly spent the past five years working on Wall Street with a major American financial company, funneling much of the profit to various worthy Islamic political causes.

Once introduced into the Party, Michael had spent three months working on various small deals, waiting to be accepted by Yousaf, waiting to be invited into the inner circle of decision making. His faked credentials might be impressive, but Yousaf was leery of anyone introduced to the Freedom Party by Farooq, whose loyalty to the cause was now seriously suspect.

In the end, Michael won Yousaf's trust by a fairly simple process: he made money. He invested twenty thousand dollars of Freedom Party funds in a portfolio of Nasdaq stocks and managed to double the Party's stake in less than two months. Yousaf's disdain for all things American was suspended long enough to pocket the profits, and in September Michael was finally permitted to participate in his first deal that involved both The American and Farooq.

To his dismay, although Farooq shared with him every scrap of information about the deal, and Michael had access to the finest technology the Counter Terrorism Center could offer, he was able to discover nothing more specific about The American than that he sent his communications via a direct satellite uplink, ricocheting the message in such complex patterns that it was untraceable in the relatively brief amount of time he spent online.

Michael decided to up the ante. He recommended that Collin Krenz should send a highly classified memo to a few senior State Department officials in key positions, informing them that an unnamed CIA agent had infiltrated the Kashmir Freedom Party and was working to identify an American who was reportedly brokering arms for the Communist Chinese.

The memo had been sent and the ante had certainly been upped, Michael reflected grimly. On the very next deal that he and Farooq worked with The American, they had both damn near been killed.

And they still didn't know the name of the American traitor.

Fifteen

Michael broke off from his bleak reverie long enough to glance at the two TV monitors hung in opposing corners of his boss's office. One set was tuned to CNN, the other to MSNBC. Although the sound was muted, he didn't need to turn up the volume to understand the pictures he was seeing on both monitors.

Another two students were in the process of being released from the American School in Bombay. Dawn was at least a couple of hours away, but the security forces had the school buildings illuminated with powerful searchlights. Silhouetted against the harsh, artificial glare, a black-masked terrorist briefly loomed in the doorway of the main building, then disappeared from sight as he slammed the school door shut once again.

The children, two boys no more than eight or nine years old, appeared momentarily dazzled by the lights, and too terrified to move. Then they broke into a halting run, gathering speed when they realized there was no longer anybody to stop them.

As they neared the end of the school driveway, Indian security forces swung open a barricade. Two sets of parents, tears of joy and anguish running down their cheeks, simultaneously snatched their ransomed children into their arms. Other not-so-fortunate parents, whose own children were still inside, watched the reunited families with mixtures of helpless longing, happiness and envy.

Michael knew that the going price per child was six hundred thousand dollars, and already half a dozen children had been released. Which meant that Yousaf was now seven million, two hundred thousand dollars richer than he had been three hours earlier.

No, correct that, Michael thought bitterly. A treacherous American was now several million bucks richer than he had been three hours earlier, and Yousaf was congratulating himself on being allowed to take a relatively piddling ten or twenty percent commission.

Michael knew Yousaf well enough to be quite sure that he had neither the native smarts nor the organizational ability to pull off an operation like this without step-by-step guidance from someone with a profound understanding of the American psyche. Not to mention a good grasp of the international banking system, and insider knowledge of the precise way the U.S. government would handle a hostage situation of this sort. In Michael's opinion, everything pointed to the conclusion that the occupation of the American School in Bombay was the final master work of the American traitor. This was his swan song that would net him the money he needed to live out the rest of his days in complete luxury. Even Khalid's assassination yesterday had been no more than a prelude to this grand finale. Yousaf needed Khalid out of the way for political reasons, while The American needed Khalid out of the way because he knew more than he should. The American had used yesterday to dot his i's and cross his t's. Not only had Khalid been killed, Farooq had been falsely identified as the leader of the Kashmir Freedom Party to ensure that law enforcement agencies all over the globe would be searching for him. An action that suggested Yousaf and The American believed Farooq was still alive. A ray of hope for the good guys, Michael reflected. If Farooq was still alive, The American must be sweating bullets over what he might reveal—unless The American got to him first.

At an abstract level, Michael could admire the cleverness and simplicity of The American's plan. He and Yousaf didn't need to fear that the money supply would be prematurely cut off by a military assault designed to take back the school. On the contrary, Yousaf could count on being left undisturbed until every last student hostage had been bought and paid for. The distraught parents who still hadn't managed to arrange for the ransom of their children would never allow any military action against the school. Not surprisingly, the families of the hostage kids became almost hysterical with fear and outrage every time the Indian security forces so much as flew a helicopter over the roof of the school.

Who could blame them? Michael thought. What parent would want to see military action launched against the terrorists, when Yousaf was being smart enough to stick to his word? Every half hour, Yousaf lined up a row of half a dozen students, turned the cameras on their terrified faces, uploaded the resulting images onto the Internet, and then proceeded to auction them off to their families. As soon as the Bank of Kabul confirmed the arrival of the appropriate sum of money from a given set of parents, the doors of the school opened and a living, breathing, child ran out.

The U.S. government could fuss all it wanted about rewarding criminals, Michael reflected, but no parent could be expected to weigh abstract international concerns about terrorism against the life of his or her child.

Collin Krenz, Michael's boss, had finally tired of a half hour of brooding silence on the part of his most experienced deputy. He sent Michael a glance that was laced with sympathy. Sympathy that Michael was in no mood to appreciate. "If you don't stop pacing, Michael, *I'm* going to have a goddamn heart attack from nervous tension.''

With an effort, Michael stopped himself from taking another step. ''There's a way out of that building where Yousaf's holed up,'' he said, shoving his left hand under his right arm, hoping the support might do something to kill the throbbing pain of yesterday's bullet wound. Machismo had its limits, and for the past half hour, he'd actually been regretting the absence of his sling.

''I know Yousaf,'' he said, scowling at the TV set. ''He's not the stuff martyrs are made of. He believes in the cause, but he's no Osama bin Laden. He doesn't want to live in a cave and save his millions for the benefit of Islam. Yousaf wants to enjoy the good life.''

Collin shrugged. ''If he blows himself up, he'll go straight to Paradise. True, he misses out on a life of luxury here on earth, but on the other hand, he earns himself a bunch of real nice rewards in eternity. Dancing girls waiting to greet him, milk and honey flowing like rivers. And so on and so on.''

''Yousaf doesn't give a flying flip about *houris* waiting for him in Paradise,'' Michael said with utter conviction. ''He plans to get out alive. I've spent too many nights around the campfire with the guy and you can take my word for it, he hasn't any intention of committing suicide. He'll take his heavenly rewards later. Much later.''

''So how's he going to get out?'' Collin demanded. ''Sprout wings and fly?''

Michael was pissed enough to take the sarcasm seriously. ''The airspace over the school is being patrolled by the Indian air force, otherwise I expect Yousaf would do just that. He'd arrange to be picked up by a nice fast helicopter, then switch to a jet waiting on an airstrip somewhere nearby.''

"But the airspace is definitely being patrolled," Collin insisted. "I double-checked with the Pentagon."

"Yeah, I know." Hoping that he might spot something that he'd previously missed, Michael bent over the table where a computer printout had been spread out, showing the front and rear elevations of the school buildings, and their placement within the grounds. The campus was less than five acres in total, small by American standards, but in a city as crowded as Bombay, the space would be considered luxurious, especially in an area of town that was considered upscale.

He'd already studied the map a dozen times. It revealed nothing more to him this time than on the previous twelve. "Have we heard anything at all back from Josh?" Michael asked. Josh Edwards was the CIA station chief in New Delhi, but he'd flown to Bombay with his FBI counterpart as soon as word broke of the school takeover, so that the Bureau and the Agency would each have representatives on the spot.

Collin shook his head. "Nothing so far."

"Try him again, Col. Tell him I really need to talk to someone who worked on the most recent school rebuilding project in 1997. Or maybe he can put me in touch with the janitor. Anyone who knows all the nooks and crannies in the building. Anything that the blueprints might have missed."

With considerable restraint, Collin refrained from pointing out that he'd called Josh less than an hour previously with precisely the same message. More to avoid watching Michael resume his pacing than for any other reason, he put the secure phone into conference mode and dialed the number.

"Josh, this is Collin Krenz."

"Yes, Collin."

"Sorry to bother you again, but Michael and I have

studied the blueprints of the school you sent us every which way from Sunday. Michael is convinced Yousaf plans to get out of there alive, but I'm damned if I can see any way he could pull that off. The Indian security forces have the place surrounded with tanks, for Christ's sake—''

"Yes, I know. But Michael could be right." There was an unexpected note of excitement in Josh's voice. "Apparently it's possible that there's an underground escape route that would give Yousaf and his men a way out of the building."

Michael's expression didn't change, but he let out his breath in a sudden sharp hiss. "Yes! I knew the bastard wasn't planning to blow himself up! Yousaf's going to blow up the school, maybe, but not while he's still inside, and only to create a diversion that distracts the Indian military."

"Did you hear that, Josh?" Collin sounded amused. "Michael's once again reminding us what an obnoxious smart-ass he is."

"An obnoxious smart-ass who's made a real good guess this time," Josh said.

Michael leaned toward the speaker. "Tell us what you've got, Josh."

"I've got Mr. Karamjeet Singh, who is an architect, right here in my office. I tracked him down after your last message, and I was just finishing my conversation with him when you called. He's eighty-two years old and vividly remembers working on the construction of that main school building back in 1936. In those days the school was run by the Brits and it was known as Saint George's Preparatory School for Boys."

"Haven't there been extensive remodels since then?" Michael asked.

"Yes and no. The various satellite buildings shown on

the blueprints have been added at intervals since then, but the original building where Yousaf is holed up with his crew was designed and built by Mr. Singh's dad almost seventy years ago. What's more, Mr. Singh remembers the layout very clearly, since he was eighteen years old at the time, and St. George's was his first job as an apprentice architect.''

''That's great,'' Michael said. ''But cut to the chase, Josh. What's the escape route?''

''Disused water pipes. In the nineteenth century, the site was occupied by a British military fort that covered almost thirty acres of land, with the officers' mess situated right where the main school building now stands. The army engineers built a system of underground pipes designed to bring water from Lake Beatrice to the fort. The lake has long since been drained and built over, by the way, but it was apparently quite a large body of fresh water once upon a time. Anyway, back in the thirties when the military base was first being turned into a school, the board of trustees decided not to have the water pipes taken out.''

''Any reason why not?'' Collin asked.

''There was a real water shortage in the city in those days, and since the pipes had been maintained in top-notch condition by army engineers, the school board asked Mr. Singh's father to utilize them to ensure that the school had a plentiful water supply. So Mr. Singh senior shored up the existing foundations of the officers' mess with steel girders and some new concrete, installed a modern pump plus a filtration system—and left the pipes right where they were, syphoning hundreds of gallons of water from Lake Beatrice each day.''

''Even so, Josh, you're talking about a remodel that happened before the British left India. Before World War II, even.'' Michael felt deflated. ''Surely those pipes would have disintegrated or been filled in years ago, for safety reasons if nothing else.''

"Not according to Mr. Singh. When the Americans took over the school in the seventies, his firm was called in again to work on the renovations. Apparently the new board of trustees wanted to fill in the pipes, but there was a problem in that the tunnels don't stop at the school walls and other people were still using them, even though the lake was seriously polluted at that point. So the new board compromised and had the entrance to the tunnels sealed off with a cement block wall. That's a strong enough barrier to prevent students having an accident, but it sure isn't enough to keep out terrorists looking for an escape route.''

"What size are these pipes?" Michael asked. "Are we talking a big enough diameter that Yousaf and his men could realistically utilize them as an escape route?''

"Yes, according to Mr. Singh. He remembers the pipes as being three feet in diameter. Not big enough to walk along upright, obviously, but quite big enough for a slender man to crawl through, and at a spanking pace, too.''

"Where do the pipes lead to?" Collin asked. "Do we know?''

"Well, we know precisely where they go within the perimeter of the school grounds," Josh said. "They run across the sports field at the side of the main building, dip under the perimeter wall, and then continue under the foundations of the department store next door. After that, Mr. Singh hasn't a clue.''

Collin scratched his bald spot, a sure sign of tension. "Isn't there an engineering diagram for the pipes?" he asked.

"Yes, there is," Josh said. "Mr. Singh even brought me a copy. But his diagram only covers the school grounds. He also knows where the lake was that originally provided all the water. But he hasn't any idea what route the pipes took between the school and Lake Beatrice.''

Collin, who was a gifted linguist, let rip with his favorite curses in three languages. ''Okay, Josh, give us your opinion. Can we assume Yousaf knew those pipes existed before he ever attacked the school?''

''Absolutely.''

''So we can also assume that he and his men have demolished the cement block wall—''

''We sure can,'' Josh interjected. ''Yousaf has had both the time and the manpower to do it. In fact, the need to have his men clear their escape route is probably why he waited a few hours before making his first broadcast to the world. He wanted to be damn sure he could get away with the loot before he started collecting it.''

''Bottom line,'' Michael said. ''This system of tunnels allows Yousaf and his men to travel underground for the equivalent of several city blocks, in a direction we're not sure of, with an egress—or possibly multiple egress points—that we can't identify.''

''That about sums it up,'' Josh agreed, his voice bleak.

''Then we're totally screwed,'' Collin said. ''You can bet Yousaf hasn't just knocked down the cement wall at this end of the tunnel. He's already sent a couple of men clear through the system to make sure that the other end of the pipe is free of anything that might block his exit. In fact, he probably started preliminary work on a passage through those tunnels weeks ago.''

''Yes, he probably did,'' Josh said. ''The janitor is a relatively new hire—he started work at the school a couple of months ago. He's originally from Kashmir, and he's currently missing. At this point, the Indian authorities are assuming he's a member of the Freedom Party.''

''Just because he's from Kashmir?'' Michael asked,

although for once he had to admit that the government's instant suspicion was most likely justified.

"No, there's more to it than that. The Indian government isn't saying anything publically about how the school was taken over, but I have a source who informed me that the terrorists gained access to the school through the basement. The working theory is that the janitor stayed behind after hours, dismantled the security systems, and let Yousaf and his men into the building during the night, so that they were ready to launch their attack as soon as the faculty and students arrived the next morning."

It was terrifying how vulnerable the school had been, Michael thought. Even more terrifying to contemplate how vulnerable any public institution was when you got right down to it. In the case of the American School in Bombay, one fatal mistake in hiring a janitor, and the rest of the disaster had flowed with all the inevitability of a Greek tragedy.

He massaged his arm, which felt as if it were on fire from the elbow up. "At their last briefing, the FBI told us that Indian army intelligence estimates there were twenty-five terrorists inside the main school building at the time it was taken over. As more and more children are ransomed by their parents and set free, the number of terrorists needed to guard them will decrease. Presumably by the time the last of the hostages walks out the front door, most of Yousaf's men will be long gone into the tunnels."

Collin nodded. "I can't see any reason why they'd try to defend their position inside the school at that point."

Michael resumed his pacing. "I'd be willing to place a large bet that three or four of the men who helped Yousaf take over the school have already made their getaways. By now, they're probably not even in the city of

Bombay. And unless we can find out precisely where the exit points are from the tunnels, every hour or so is going to see another of Yousaf's men escaping.''

''Jesus.'' Collin gave his bald patch a major workout. ''Jesus, I hope you're wrong.''

''But you know in your gut that I'm not,'' Michael said grimly. ''In fact, we can make a damn good guess as to how this whole charade is going to play out. The moment the last ransomed kid is swept into its parents' arms, the Indian top brass will send in their elite special forces team to take back the school. The troops will storm up the drive, thinking they're about to capture the terrorists, or at least annihilate them, and—kaboom! Yousaf sets off a remote-controlled explosive device that blows up the school and takes out scores of highly trained Indian soldiers in the process. There's mass confusion for a good fifteen minutes or so. Meanwhile, Yousaf and the last few of his men have already made it through the tunnels and emerged at the other end. Wherever the hell *the end* may be.''

''We know where Lake Beatrice once lay,'' Josh pointed out. ''We can advise the Indian government to have their security forces scattered throughout the likely area where the tunnels might run.''

''They'd have to seal off at least fifty city blocks to be effective, and even that might not be enough to ensure that we have the appropriate area covered,'' Michael said. ''How do you evacuate fifty blocks in the center of a city like Bombay? And unless you get rid of all the other people milling about, how are the security forces going to spot Yousaf and his men? When they come out of the tunnels they won't be wearing black hoods and they won't look anything like wild Kashmiri terrorists. They'll look like regular guys going about their lawful business. Plus, Yousaf has enough experience planning getaways that you can be sure his men won't make the mistake of staying together. He'll have arranged getaway cars—two, four, however many it takes to have his men scattered all over the city within half an hour.''

"The son of a bitch has found a way to get the money and get away with it,'' Collin muttered. ''It would fucking work.''

Michael let out a long, slow breath. ''Yeah, it would. Less than thirty minutes after the school blows up, it's all over. And Yousaf has gotten away with a hundred million dollars.'' He gave a laugh totally without humor. ''If he makes a big enough bang—and God knows, he has the supplies to do it—we'll never know how many people died in the explosion. If we hadn't found out about the water pipes, not only would he and his men have gotten away, we'd never have known they survived.''

''Damned if we're going to let that happen.'' Collin let rip with a few more choice obscenities. ''There has to be a map of those underground tunnels,'' he muttered. ''Somebody in the government must have one.''

Michael gave a laugh that contained no trace of mirth. ''In Bombay? Where they barely have a map of today's bus routes? You're hoping to find a map of tunnels built some time in the middle of the nineteenth century? Dream on.''

''Before you get too depressed, there's something you should know,'' Josh interjected.

''What's that?'' Collin snapped.

''I just brought Mr. Singh back into my office and explained what we needed. He's given me some good news. He says he has a friend, Mr. Naipul, who is a military historian. He knows Mr. Naipul has a map that shows the location of the old British military base, complete with all the buildings. He thinks there's a good chance his friend also has a map that shows exactly where and how the water pipes were laid out. Of course, the map will show the location of the pipes relative to the city as it was in the nineteenth century, but his friend is an expert on the history of Bombay. According to Mr. Singh, Mr. Naipul should be able to impose the modern topography of the city on the outlines of the old map.''

Collin let out a whoop of relief. "Yes! Thank you, Jesus!''

Michael was more restrained, but no less relieved. "How far away does Mr. Naipul live?'' he asked.

There was a brief silence while Josh and Mr. Singh conferred. "About twenty minutes by car from the consulate,'' Josh reported. "Traffic permitting.''

"Go get him,'' Collin said. "And when you've found him, don't let him out of your sight. We're going to stop those bastards from making a getaway.''

Sixteen

It took Josh Edwards, Mr. Singh and a hastily assembled team of helpers two hours of frantic searching to track down Mr. Naipul. He was eventually found in a distant suburb enjoying a cup of fine Darjeeling tea with his favorite chess partner, another insomniac who enjoyed socializing at the break of dawn.

The effort to find Mr. Naipul was well worth the use of valuable manpower, since it turned out that he owned what was almost certainly the only map still in existence of the route followed by the British military when digging the tunnels and laying down the pipes that brought fresh water from Lake Beatrice back to the army base.

The system proved to be more elaborate than Michael would have expected from Mr. Singh's preliminary description, with one major pipe that traveled in a remarkably straight three-mile line to the area where Lake Beatrice had once flourished, and two other tunnels meandering off at right angles for a distance of about a mile each. The British army engineers, Mr. Naipul explained, had decided to provide water not only to their own base, but also to the parish Church of Saint George, at which the local British community worshiped, and the courthouse at which the British magistrates dispensed Imperial justice to the bemused natives.

Mr. Naipul and Mr. Singh both seemed confident that even prior to the 1970s only the three miles of main pipeline had been consistently maintained in a state of good repair. They were also confident that side tunnels were now, and always had been, too small to permit men to pass through. To be safe, however, Michael asked Mr. Naipul to draw a map of all the tunnels, including the side routes, indicating exactly how they were positioned under the modern city of Bombay.

Michael was determined that this time the U.S. government wouldn't be caught with its institutional pants down. He could just picture Yousaf and his band of terrorists sneaking through a "too narrow" side tunnel and making good their escape, while television stations around the world carried film of military assault vehicles and special forces commandos storming the end of the main pipeline—and coming up empty.

The American traitor sitting in his State Department office would be chortling out loud over that one, Michael thought grimly.

Fortunately, the military brass and the FBI were in the mood to be persuaded by Michael's arguments, and he felt a slight lowering of his overall anxiety level as he presented his findings and got an immediate positive reaction. With impressive efficiency, the commanding general pulled together a plan with his counterpart in the Indian army that would get highly trained troops and powerful weapons in place with maximum speed. Obviously they were too late to capture any of the terrorists who might already have sneaked out of the school, but at least they would have forces in place in time to prevent Yousaf and his most senior aides from making good their escape.

Meanwhile, contingency plans for a frontal attack on the school went ahead with a lot of public hoopla, chiefly because it was essential to deceive not only the world's media, but also the American traitor. A media report about the existence of tunnels under the school would be disastrous, since anything that appeared either on the Internet or on television would presumably be viewed by the American traitor, if not by Yousaf himself.

And if Yousaf found out that his escape route had been cut off, Michael had no doubt he would indulge in a temper tantrum to end all tantrums. If he couldn't escape, Yousaf would make sure nobody else escaped, either. There would be no more hostages released, and the lives of the children remaining inside the school would come to a swift, violent and bloody end.

To make sure that Mr. Singh and Mr. Naipul didn't leak their stories to an enterprising journalist—courteous, naive civilians were unlikely to be a match for the devious sharks of the international media—Josh Edwards was assigned the task of keeping the two elderly gentlemen happy, with every comfort provided, except that of leaving the consulate compound.

As dawn brightened to midmorning in Bombay, and evening faded to night in Washington, D.C., a new mood of cautious optimism swept through the Counter Terrorism Center. Even the FBI agents, usually quick to heap scorn on CIA operations, seemed to feel that the months Michael had worked undercover with the Freedom Party were paying off a big dividend. Without his insights into Yousaf's character, the Center's other terrorism experts would have assumed that Yousaf planned to blow up the school in a typical attempt to attain glory through death. Because of Michael's persistence, the military's plans had been adjusted in time to prevent disaster.

Michael wasn't quite as happy as people seemed to think he should be. Driving back into the District in order to pick up Verity from the State Department, he tried to feel gratified that at least Yousaf and some of the other leaders of the Freedom Party seemed unlikely to escape punishment. Despite that limited success, nothing he'd done today would help to reveal the name of Yousaf's American partner. Even if Yousaf and his men were captured alive, the American traitor would still go free, since Yousaf didn't have a clue as to the man's real identity. The treacherous son of a bitch would soon be flying off to some luxury hiding place, along with a hundred million dollars' worth of blood money sucked from desperate parents.

He had men searching all over Germany for Farooq, but so far they were coming up empty on every lead Michael had given them. If they didn't find Farooq, The American was going to get away. That inescapable reality stuck in Michael's craw, refusing to be dislodged.

It was almost nine o'clock when he found a space to park his car near the State Department, at which point he finally realized he'd given Verity no warning of his impending arrival. At some subliminal level he'd been thinking about her all day, but it had never occurred to him to pick up the phone and call. One of the many things he loved about Verity was the fact that she approached her work with a dedication he recognized as identical to his own. Far from feeling the need to call and chat with her this afternoon, he had found something deeply satisfying in the certainty that she had spent the past few hours as intensely focused as he himself.

A little late, it occurred to him that he had been insufferably arrogant to assume that Verity would be meekly waiting for him whenever he deigned to arrive. With a flash of panic, not an emotion he was accustomed to feeling, he recognized that it would serve him right if Verity had ignored their agreement and gone home by herself. For most of the past three years, they'd barely acknowledged each other's existence, and rarely spoken to each other except through gritted teeth. With that background to their relationship, how in the world had he convinced himself that he understood Verity so well that he didn't need to pick up the phone to discuss their plans like any normal person?

Michael waited, fists bunched with tension, while one of the State Department night duty guards called Verity to confirm that he was expected. She took far too long to answer the phone, and Michael began to run through a mental list of horrors that might have befallen her. In retrospect, he wondered if he'd made it crystal clear how much danger she was in until word reached The American that she no longer had Farooq's key. At the time, he'd thought they understood each other. Now he wondered if the clarity had all been in his mind, not in Verity's.

He let out a quick sigh of relief when the guard finally got a response to his repeated buzzing. "Ms. Marlowe? You have a visitor." The guard had already put Michael's ID badge through an electronic reader, and he recited the name from his computer screen. "Michael Brown is here from the Department of Defense. He has clearance for entry to the State Department." The guard paused for a beat. "Yes, ma'am, I'll send him up right away."

The guard handed Michael back his ID badge and security passes, one of several sets of fake identities provided courtesy of the Agency. "Ms. Marlowe says to go on up, Mr. Brown. Her office number is 327. That's on the third floor and there's only one elevator working at this time of night. The security guard in the lobby will unlock the elevator for you."

When Michael finally walked into Verity's office, he discovered that the mental picture he'd carried of her all day was uncanny in its accuracy. She was seated at her desk, massaging her left temple in a gesture of mingled pain and fatigue, while staring at her computer monitor with such fierce concentration that she didn't even notice his arrival.

He wanted very much to kiss her into awareness, except that he'd waited more than three years for the moment when he could make love to her without guilt, and a quick embrace in her office didn't seem to do justice to the momentous nature of the occasion. So instead of sweeping her into his arms, he took a firm grip on his willpower—God knew, he had plenty of experience exercising that where Verity was concerned—and merely said a quiet hello. He'd practiced looking impassive in her presence so many times that he sometimes wondered if his features even knew how to relax into a normal friendly expression when he was in her company.

She looked up, startled. Her frown smoothed out as soon as she saw him, and she gave him a warm smile, accompanied by a friendly but somewhat absentminded greeting. Almost at once, her gaze returned to the screen.

A surge of wry affection washed over him. Oh, well, he thought. At least he'd been dead-on in his assessment of Verity's attitude about phone calls. It sure didn't look as if she'd spent too much of the afternoon pining to hear from him.

He crossed the room and stood behind her, resting his hands on her shoulders and pressing his thumbs against the base of her neck, massaging gently. When Verity had phoned him from the bar in Georgetown last night, some profound barrier in their relationship had been breached. Even so, it was amazing to discover that he could indulge in the luxury of touching her without provoking instant rejection. He felt a deep-seated satisfaction when she tilted her head back and closed her eyes, letting out a sigh of sheer pleasure. She even reached up for a moment and covered his hand briefly with hers.

The age of miracles, it seemed, was not yet past.

"Rough day?" he asked softly.

"Mmm." She drew in a slightly unsteady breath. "You're one of the few people who can imagine just how rough."

"Yeah." Her muscles cramped beneath his fingers, and he pressed gently, soothing away the knot of anxiety and fatigue. "Ready to come home?"

She wheeled her chair around to face him, her eyes suddenly wide-open and her spine straight. "With you? To your house?"

Their relationship, Michael realized, hadn't yet surmounted every obstacle. "It would be best, don't you think?" He held her gaze. "It isn't safe for you to be alone right now—"

"Because of Khalid's key?"

"Yes. I haven't done a thing today to get the word out that you don't have it anymore—"

"Me, either," she admitted. "There's barely been time to breathe."

"And then, apart from the safety issue, your house still hasn't been cleaned up after last night's intruder, and the invasion of FBI technicians earlier today won't have helped with the general level of mess."

She was silent for a moment, debating the implications of his suggestion. Then she gave a quick nod of acceptance and swung around so that she could close down her computer. But as soon as she turned back to face the monitor, she forgot about him again, caught up in staring at the chart on her screen.

With a touch of self-mockery, Michael wondered if he hadn't preferred it when Verity was so tense in his company that she could never ignore his presence, even for a moment.

She scowled at her computer, fiddling with her mouse,

but not executing any command, as if the list of names in front of her was already familiar to the point of irritation and the problem posed by it one that she'd been struggling with for hours. Eventually she clicked on a couple of icons, bringing up a picture that Michael recognized. It was a frontal shot of two hostage students, standing one on either side of Yousaf, their heads jerked back by their captors, nooses taut around their necks, their faces fully exposed to the camera.

"Speak to me," she muttered, staring at the photo. "Tell me what I'm missing, damn you!"

"What's the problem?" Michael asked, leaning across the desk so that he was in her line of sight. "Other than the obvious fact that you're upset each time you think about those kids at the mercy of Yousaf and his band of not-so-merry men."

Verity blinked, registering his presence again. "Oh, Michael. Sorry. I've been staring at this photo for so long, I've lost all sense of perspective."

"Maybe I can help."

"I need your honest opinion. If I'm obsessing about nothing, tell me, okay?"

"Deal."

She keyed in a command so that the screen simultaneously displayed the list and the photo, side by side. "The chart on the left shows the names of all the students Yousaf has already offered to ransom back to their parents. At last count, fifteen students had actually been released. That little box in the upper left-hand corner of the screen shows their names. Forty-five more families are in the process of trying to raise the funds, or they've raised the funds already and now they're making arrangements to transfer the ransom money to the bank in Afghanistan."

Michael ran his eyes down the list, which was identical

to one he'd seen right before leaving Langley. "It's no surprise that the families of the hostages are moving fast to get their kids released."

"Is that how it strikes you? As fast?" She sighed. "In an emergency situation like this, I hoped the banks and insurance companies would wave a magic wand and say to heck with the paperwork. But I guess that was unrealistic. It was bound to take a while to actually get the money wired to Yousaf's account."

"I know fifteen students released seems like an unacceptably low number, given that Yousaf and his men are holding a hundred and thirty-five kids hostage, not to mention a dozen faculty members. But you have to remember it's less than twelve hours since Yousaf sent out those very first pictures of the little kindergarten children huddling in their teacher's arms. Realistically, fifteen freed hostages in less than five hours isn't bad. In fact, given the time difference, and the fact that the families are trying to send funds to Afghanistan of all places, it's close to a miracle."

"I know that, really." Verity pushed a loose strand of hair back into its clip, the gesture impatient. "I also keep reminding myself that since there are almost seven hundred students enrolled in the school, the situation could have been a lot worse."

"Then what is it that's worrying you?"

"I'm hung up on the inconsistency of Yousaf's behavior." She clicked swiftly through a succession of photographs. "You must have seen most of these pictures already. And I expect you're aware of how Yousaf is handling the practicalities of ransoming the kids?"

"Sure. I'm a well-informed secret agent." Michael sent her a wry half smile. "My office has access to CNN just like everyone else."

"Then you must have realized that Yousaf's system is

highly efficient. It's the wee hours of the morning in Bombay, but that isn't slowing him down at all. Every thirty minutes he marches a set of seven kids into the school's computer lab and films them. Their hands are bound, and the girls are all wearing veils, but they appear basically unharmed. Scared, but not bruised or bloodied. He informs the parents that the price of freedom for each student is six hundred thousand dollars. To prove that the child is alive and well, and that the scene wasn't prerecorded, he allows each kid to step forward and say his or her own name, their age, and their address, followed by the date and the exact time. The first few students reminded their parents that they had only twenty-four hours to send the money. This last group told their parents they have only eighteen hours. By the time the last unlucky student gets his turn on TV, Yousaf could be demanding the money in less than twelve hours.''

Michael felt savagely angry all over again, although how much of that rage was directed at Yousaf, and how much at himself and his failed mission in Kashmir, he wasn't entirely sure. ''Presumably the parents of all the hostages have been working to get their ransom money together from the moment Mary Grace Klemper was released,'' he said. ''Everyone has realized from the beginning that we're working with a terrifyingly tight schedule here. At the rate Yousaf is going, he'll have all 135 hostages auctioned off before morning.''

''He's a regular Speedy Gonzales, isn't he?'' Verity said with a touch of her own bitterness. ''Which brings me to the point that's been gnawing at me for the last two hours. Yousaf has a very efficient system worked out for ransoming off the hostages, and time is obviously of the essence from his point of view. After all, he has to worry about when the Indian government might get pissed off enough to send in the tanks and blow him and his nasty little scheme all to hell.''

"Yes, I agree."

"Okay, then since you agree with me, explain this. Why did Yousaf waste everyone's time by bringing out those two unidentified students when he made his very first speech? Why not trot out seven students, give their names, and set the ball rolling in the pattern he intended to continue with?''

"I can think of two good reasons," Michael replied promptly. "First, knowing Yousaf, I'd say that he feels a real need to pay homage to the rhetoric of Islamic fundamentalism. He truly believes that the United States is the enemy not just of Kashmir, but of all devout Muslims everywhere, and it doesn't surprise me at all that he felt a need to make at least a token gesture toward having the hundred million dollar ransom paid by the wicked American government. Payments by individual parents fatten his bank balance just as efficiently, but they don't have the symbolic impact that a payment by the U.S. government would have.''

"But he knew the States wouldn't pay up, so demanding payment from the government basically amounts to nothing more than a silly waste of time.''

Michael shrugged. "Impassioned rhetoric can convince the person spouting it as well as the people listening, you know. The whole point is that Yousaf honestly believes the U.S. government is the Great Satan.''

"Maybe.'' Verity sounded far from convinced. "Okay, that's your first reason. What's the other one?''

"Yousaf is being really smart about the psychology of this situation. He realizes that unnamed victims with nooses around their necks make for great theater. Much better theater than lining up half a dozen kids and having them recite a standard plea for money. It was more compelling, and much more threatening, not to identify those first two students, and not to let them speak out, so that the whole world waited with bated breath to find out more.''

"You're right," Verity admitted. "But Yousaf strikes me as a man with a practical streak beneath all his fancy oratory. I'll concede that he may have decided to sacrifice a little bit of speed for the sake of maximizing the psychological terror. Even so, I'm quite sure he didn't randomly select those first two students he trotted out for display. He had reasons for choosing them. Reasons for singling them out and giving them special treatment."

"I'm sure he did," Michael assented. "Mary Grace Klemper comes from a very wealthy family. I wouldn't be surprised to learn that the Klempers have more money than any other family with kids attending the school. Mr. Klemper probably considers six hundred thousand dollars a bargain basement price for the safe return of his only child and Yousaf would have known that up front. He knew the instant Mr. Klemper saw his daughter on TV the man would call the bank in Kabul and try to work out a private ransom deal."

"Yes," Verity said swiftly. "I'm in complete agreement with you. But if we agree that Mary Grace wasn't a random selection on Yousaf's part, then logically we have to conclude the boy who appeared with her wasn't a random choice, either."

"True—"

Verity pounced. "So who is he, and why was he chosen?"

Michael opened his mouth to respond, then shut it again when he realized he had no answer. "That's a damn good question," he said. He reflected for a moment. "Maybe Yousaf chose him in part because he's a total contrast to Mary Grace. She's female, he's male.

She's American, he's Indian. His family is maybe poor, whereas hers is rich—'' He broke off. "No, that wouldn't work. Yousaf wants these kids ransomed, so he isn't going to waste valuable media exposure on a poor student. Hmm…what information do we have about this boy so far?''

"Almost nothing, except that he isn't a scholarship student, so his family can't be poor. The dean of students identified him as Kalil Mustafa, a new student who only enrolled at the school a few months ago. Apparently he's seventeen years old and a senior. He's also one of only twenty students who board at the school, living in a small dorm that's a converted Victorian house. I called Archie Bree—you know he's our acting Consul in Bombay now that George Douglass has been killed?—and he managed to arrange for me to have a short phone conversation with the dean of students. It wasn't much use, though. The dean says he's never met Kalil's parents. In fact, he doesn't remember any details about them, except that the family comes from New Delhi. He remembers their home city because most of the kids are day students, who all live in Bombay, of course, so New Delhi stuck in his mind.''

Michael frowned. "It seems very impersonal information. Didn't the dean interview the parents before Kalil was first enrolled in the school?''

"He says not. The principal dealt with the enrollment personally.''

Michael put his right hand under his left elbow, unobtrusively supporting his aching arm. "There must be official records available, though, even if the dean doesn't recall the details off the top of his head. The name of both Kalil's parents, and their address. A contact phone number. Health records.''

"Yes, but the dean can't access those records because

the files are all stored in the main building. The one You-saf is occupying."

"Damn! How about computerized records?" Michael answered his own question. "No, of course not. Yousaf has commandeered the computer system and changed all the password codes, so the dean can't access those, ei-ther."

Verity nodded. "That's why it took so long to deter-mine which students had been taken hostage and who had escaped. There was no master list available for any-one to consult."

"What a god-awful mess this is." Michael massaged his arm. "And we can't talk directly to the school prin-cipal because he's one of the faculty members Yousaf is holding hostage."

"Right." Verity made a quick, restless gesture. "I have to say the dean of students didn't strike me as one of India's very brightest brains, so I'm not too bothered by the fact that he can't remember the home address of one of his students. What's bothering the heck out of me is the fact that Kalil's parents haven't stepped forward to ransom him. They've had almost an entire day to learn that their son's school is under siege. They've had since four o'clock this afternoon to come forward and agree to pay a ransom to get him set free. Two minutes after You-saf was off the air, Mr. Klemper was on the phone, iden-tifying his daughter and demanding action. Why were Kalil's parents silent? If they can't raise the money, why haven't they sent a desperate message saying just that? In a hostage situation like this, five hours is a lifetime for anxious parents. Why hasn't anyone heard from them?"

"Because they're vacationing somewhere and haven't switched on a television set?" Michael suggested.

"They're going to be frantic when they come home and realize what's been going on while they were away—"

Verity shook her head in fierce denial. "That's no explanation at all," she said. "Doesn't Kalil have grandparents? What about uncles and cousins? You know what the extended family system is like in India. I'll accept that maybe his mother and father are on a private yacht in the middle of the Pacific, or trekking through the jungles of Peru—which is just about where they'd have to be to avoid hearing about this. Even so, why haven't other members of Kalil's family called the school? Why hasn't anyone in authority been approached by a frantic uncle or cousin begging for the government to step in and find some way to reach the missing parents? Good grief, there should have been a minimum of twenty distraught relatives pounding on the school gates by now. You know there should."

"Can you be sure that the Indian government hasn't been approached?" Michael asked. "Have you checked your sources?"

Verity nodded. "I've checked all of my sources, from staff at the consulate, through a reporter at CNN, all the way up to the FBI. I even called in a favor from a friend at the Indian embassy and had him check out *his* sources back in Bombay. As far as I can tell, there's been no communication of any sort from anyone claiming to be a relative of Kalil Mustafa. Either the kid has no family, or his family doesn't care that he's being held hostage by vicious terrorists. What other explanation is there?"

As she spoke, Verity clicked on the picture of the two hostage students, enlarging the face of Kalil Mustafa until it filled her screen. "From his name, we have to assume he's from a Muslim family. So why the heck did Yousaf pick on him, a Muslim brother, with four hundred other boys in the school to choose from?"

"Could that be the reason?" Michael asked. "Is he the only Muslim in the school by any chance?"

"No, I thought of that and asked the dean of students about the religious and ethnic mix in the school. He says the school prides itself on its diversity. Three-quarters of the kids are Hindu or Christian, but there are several Sikhs, quite a few Muslims, some Jains and even a dozen Buddhists."

Michael studied the photo on the screen with narrowed eyes. "Mary Grace is very pretty and Kalil is handsome. Extremely handsome, in fact. It could be as simple as that. Yousaf decided these two would look good in pictures."

Verity made a frustrated sound. "Even if Kalil's good looks explain why Yousaf chose him, it doesn't begin to explain why Kalil's parents haven't attempted to ransom him. Yousaf hasn't put a foot wrong in this operation so far. Why would he screw up by singling out a boy whose family cares so little that they haven't even bothered to contact the school and say *Hey, that's our kid with a noose around his neck.*"

What Verity was saying made perfect sense, Michael acknowledged. She had spotted a discrepancy that everyone else seemed to have glossed right over in the inevitable confusion of events. The Counter Terrorism Center, the State Department and the FBI had all honed their procedures for dealing with terrorist attacks to a point of impressive efficiency. Contingency plans in case foreign terrorists attacked a school on American soil had been developed. Ditto for terrorists attacking a U.S. embassy or consulate on foreign soil. Unfortunately, nobody had ever envisaged dealing with a school hostage situation involving American kids taken captive in the middle of a foreign city. A foreign city, moreover, where every move by the U.S. had to be approved by officials in the

Indian government who were touchy as hell about issues
of sovereignty. In the circumstances, it was inevitable
that some details would fall between cracks in the hastily
cobbled-together response system.

"I'm going to make a couple of phone calls and get
some people working on finding Kalil's family," Michael
said. "Our resources are stretched close to their limits
right now, but you're absolutely correct. We need to
know both why Yousaf singled out this student and why
his parents have made no effort to ransom him."

"Who will you call?" Verity asked. "Archie Bree, the
acting consul in Bombay, sounded punch-drunk when I
tried to talk to him about this. I don't think you can ask
him to take care of another single thing. Dick Pedro is
the same. He's so overloaded, he's approaching meltdown."

"This isn't a State Department issue," Michael said,
dialing as he spoke. "We need to get the FBI working
on it. The Bureau has people on the ground, already in
place, and they have more agents flying over there as we
speak. The Bureau will at least know how to set about
questioning some of the faculty and students who might
be friends with Kalil. The other kids who share his dorm,
for example. Somebody must know more about him than
the fact that his family is from New Delhi."

Verity's shoulders slumped in relief. "Thank you,"
she said, pushing her chair away from the computer. "I
was beginning to wonder if I was making a huge mountain out of a very small molehill. I'm glad you agree that
I wasn't."

"On the contrary," Michael said. "You spotted a big
hill the rest of us shouldn't have overlooked."

He watched her as he made his phone calls, pulling
rank to make sure that the investigation into Kalil's family was given top priority despite the pressures currently

straining everyone's temper and resources. During the past three years he'd tried every tactic he knew to transform his stubborn desire for Verity into indifference. His failure rate had been spectacular. As he waited for the appropriate people to be found to take his calls, he thought about the many occasions he'd been forced to deny himself the pleasure of looking at Verity. Not to mention the countless times he'd walked clear across the room to avoid taking a glass from her because there was a danger their fingers might accidentally touch. Or the rare occasions when their eyes had met and he'd allowed himself the secret luxury of holding her gaze. He'd always regretted those split second moments of intimacy because they'd invariably reignited fantasies he'd spent weeks wrestling into submission.

Tonight he was finally free to look his fill, and the pleasure was all the greater for having been so long denied. He could see that Verity hovered on the brink of total exhaustion, but the classical perfection of her features seemed almost enhanced by the pallor of her skin and the rumpled disorder of her hair. He had always admired her beauty, but that feeling was abstract, the same sort of aesthetic admiration he would feel for an oil painting by Botticelli, or a statue by Henry Moore. What touched his heart and stirred his senses was the glittering fire of Verity's intelligence and the subtle lure of her sensuality. A sensuality that he knew in his gut had never been fully awakened.

From the night of their first meeting, he had forbidden himself to picture what Verity might look like when she was sexually aroused. Now he could finally indulge his fantasies. He imagined her skin flushed in the aftermath of desire, her long hair wildly disheveled, her mouth red and swollen from the impact of his kisses. The images rapidly became much too vivid, and Michael stumbled in the supposedly crisp explanation he was giving to the FBI Asian division chief, caught off guard by a rush of sexual arousal strong enough to annihilate any hope of higher brain function.

He turned his back on Verity, recovering his composure enough to complete his phone calls and make his points—although now that his desire had slipped its leash, he knew he would have a hard time bringing it under control again. He was afraid that fatigue and the throbbing ache of yesterday's bullet wound might be just enough to take the edge off his self-control, without being nearly enough to prevent him feeling his usual overwhelming need for Verity. However much his intellect might tell him that a night when they were both wounded and exhausted wasn't the perfect occasion on which to consummate three years of forbidden desire, the rest of him didn't give a damn about anything except making love to her. As soon and as often as possible. Hell, last night he'd played the gentleman. Tonight he was ready to revert to full caveman mode.

He finally finished his phone calls and hung up the phone. Verity gave him a tired smile. "Thanks for your help, Michael. I'm really grateful. Not to mention impressed by the number of high-powered people you managed to get on the other end of the phone. I'm sure it's important to find Kalil's parents, even though I can't figure out exactly why at this point."

"I agree," he said, holding out her coat. He sent her a smile. "And I'm really glad that I managed to impress you."

"You sure did that." She stood up, almost reeling from fatigue. If Michael hadn't helped guide her arms, she wouldn't have been able to direct them into the sleeves of her coat.

He twisted her around to face him and fastened a cou-

ple of the buttons. Using up the final dregs of his willpower, he managed to avoid kissing her. At least he retained just enough smarts to realize that once he started
kissing her, he wasn't going to stop until they were naked
and horizontal. "Okay, honey, we're done here for the
night. Now let's get out of here and go home."

At home there were beds. Thank God.

Seventeen

If it had been strange to wake up this morning and find herself eating breakfast in Michael's kitchen, Verity found it little short of bizarre to be driving home with him again tonight. Not only driving home with him, she reflected, but feeling so much at ease in his company that it was hard to resist the temptation of resting her aching head on the enticing cushion of his shoulder. She probably would have done just that if she hadn't noticed how he was favoring his left arm, which suggested that he needed all the flexibility he could get in his right one.

They stopped for a traffic light and Michael turned to look at her. "Are you hungry?" he asked. "My stomach has been growling for at least the past four hours."

"I'm starving." She cast her mind back over the day and realized that all she'd consumed since breakfast was a yogurt Andrew had brought her from the cafeteria, washed down by a carton of tepid apple juice. Her stomach rumbled to reinforce the message that food would be appreciated.

"Where would you like to eat?" Michael asked. "There's a sushi bar in the next shopping strip that my neighbor swears is the best in McLean. Or there's a Lebanese deli in the same strip that has a decent take-out menu. They do a stuffed pita bread with chicken and roasted vegetables that's quite tasty."

"Stuffed pita bread sounds perfect," Verity said. "If

we went to the sushi restaurant, there's a real danger I'd
fall asleep facedown in the raw tuna.''

"I'd prefer to eat at home, too." Michael swung the
car into the small shopping center and parked outside the
brightly lit deli. He put the gear into park, but left the
engine running. "The wind is really cold," he said.
"There's no need for you to come in with me unless you
want to."

"You go ahead." She smothered a yawn. "I'm much
too comfortable to move."

"Don't talk to any strangers." Michael gave the instruction without a trace of flippancy. "Blast on the horn
if anyone approaches the car."

She smiled tiredly. "Don't worry, Michael. I'll summon you at the first sign of any villain searching for
Khalid's key. Trust me, I haven't the smallest desire to
play heroine."

He touched her lightly on the cheek. "I think you
played that role a couple of times this week already."

Coming from Michael, this was the equivalent of a
two-stanza poem of praise, and Verity flushed with pleasure. He brushed his hand lightly across her cheek, then
slammed the door shut. She watched him as he walked
across the parking lot, his stride fast and long despite the
fact that she was sure his wounded arm was giving him
a lot of pain. A gust of wind caught the hem of his ankle-
length leather coat and it billowed out behind him in a
black cloud. Her body reacted with a shiver of primitive
sensation, a desire so intense and so immediate that her
nipples puckered as if they'd been touched. How was it
possible for her body to ache with exhaustion at the same
time as she yearned to make love to Michael?

*Well you know, sweetie, I've told you this before. Mi-
chael wants to make love to you every bit as much as
you want to make love to him. I say go for it.*

Verity's head jerked around, heart hammering. Sure enough, Sam was sitting behind the wheel of the car, his body quite solid tonight, although there was a shimmery glow around the edges of his favorite sweater and his facial features appeared a little blurred.

Verity didn't feel frightened or sad at this latest appearance of her dead husband. What she felt, she realized with surprise, was irritation. She remembered what she'd been thinking before he materialized and her cheeks burned with humiliation. She felt naked in his presence, stripped and exposed, and she had to fight the urge to cross her hands over her chest. Good grief, what if he could see the puckered state of her nipples? Or worse yet, what if his X-ray ghost vision could accurately translate that weird clenching feeling in the pit of her stomach into a pictorial image of sexual desire?

"Sam, you have to stop this, dammit! You were a sensitive man when you were alive, and you should have more wisdom now, not less. Surely to goodness you can understand how embarrassing it is to have my former husband popping up like a jack-in-the-box and commenting on my sexual feelings for his best friend!"

Sam tipped his head to one side, in the achingly familiar gesture that indicated deep thought on his part. *I guess it might seem humiliating from your perspective,* he said at last. *But I promise you it doesn't seem at all embarrassing or difficult to me. When you're dead, you'll understand that love is love, whether it's expressed sexually or any other way.*

"But I'm not dead!" she yelled. "I'm very much alive. It's you that's dead, for heaven's sake!"

Sam sent her a smile, a hearty smile with no tinge of sadness. *I'm glad you've finally realized that, Veri. For a few months there, it looked like you were determined to bury yourself in my grave.*

"It did take me a long time to come to terms with your death," she acknowledged, "but I've gotten there, finally. And I have to tell you, Sam, having your dead husband turn up to give his approval for your prospective sex life is spooky."

Well, yes. He sent her a sly grin. *What can you expect? I am a spook.*

He surprised a tiny laugh out of her. "Oh, Sam, you're hopeless. Now that you're dead, I'd have thought you had better things to do than play silly word games."

Of course I have better things to do—

"Then do them," she said simply. "Sam, I loved you with all my heart when you were alive, but now it's time for me to move on. I need you to stop materializing every time I'm tired, or my mental guard is down." She drew in an unsteady breath, hardly able to believe what she was about to say. "If...when...I make love to Michael, I don't want to be wondering if you're going to sit yourself down on the bed between the two of us and start delivering helpful hints on ghostly techniques for making orgasms more exciting. I couldn't bear that, Sam."

Then it won't happen. Anyway, sweetie, I have nothing useful to say on the subject of orgasms. As far as I know, there's no ghostly how-to manual for making human sex more exciting.

"But will you be there, watching us?" Verity flinched mentally at the prospect.

No, I promise. You and Michael will be alone, Verity. Always, from now on. This is our time to say a final goodbye.

"Goodbye, Sam." She pressed the back of her hand to her mouth, swallowing to hold back the tears. He was so very dear to her that it was hard to imagine never seeing him again. Even harder to imagine that she was the one sending him away.

He reached out his hand, his fingers not quite touching hers. For some reason, Verity's hand felt too heavy to lift, so that she couldn't move her hand to close the tiny gap that separated them. Looking at him, she realized that Sam's face, which she would have sworn she knew in every mood, and recognized from every angle, no longer seemed familiar to her.

Sam smiled, or at least that was the closest word she could come up with to describe his expression. *I was only here because you wouldn't let me go, Veri. Now that you don't need me anymore, I can move on, too. Thank you.*

"Move on to…heaven? Isn't that where you are already?" she asked.

His eyes twinkled with Sam's habitual mischief and for an instant he looked familiar again. *You can't expect me to give away all the secrets of the afterlife, Veri. But don't worry, I'm happy now that I'm dead and you will be, too. Although your death isn't going to happen for a long time, measured in earth years. I have it on good authority that you and Michael are going to get married next month. In a couple of years, you're also going to have a beautiful baby boy, named Sam.*

"We are?" The news brought her as much pleasure as surprise. "How do you know?"

He gave a patented Sam grin. *Trust me, sweetie. Nowadays, my sources are the best.* The shimmering glow of his sweater spread, until there was only a glow and no more Sam.

"Sam, don't go for just a minute. Stay, please! If your sources for information about the future are so wonderful, tell me who that boy is that Yousaf paraded out with a noose around his neck."

Sam didn't reappear, but his voice echoed in her head. *You know him, Veri. That's why his face is haunting you.*

Reach back into your past. To Kashmir. Goodbye, dearest one. I love you forever and always.

Michael opened the door, a paper sack nestled in the crook of his right arm. "Brrr…it's freezing in here." He slipped into the driver's seat and leaned over the back to put a large brown paper sack on the rear seat. He rubbed his hands together. "That's strange. I left the engine running, but it's almost as cold inside the car as out."

Verity didn't reply at once and Michael turned to look at her. "You look sleepy. Did you doze off? Sorry if I woke you."

"I don't think I was asleep. I'm not sure."

He grinned. "That's what I like. A woman who knows her own mind."

It would be so easy to let the conversation slide away into new topics, Verity thought. But it occurred to her that while Sam was alive, she'd never been able to talk honestly with him about Michael, and she didn't want to reverse that problem and start off her new relationship with Michael by concealing the truth about her encounters with Sam's ghost. She was smart enough after eight months of intense mourning to realize that an intimate relationship with a secret at its heart could never be entirely satisfying. Not just to the partner keeping the secret, but to the other partner as well.

She decided to tackle the problem right now, before she could lose her nerve. "Do you believe in ghosts?" she asked Michael.

"It depends whether I'm anywhere near my father when the subject comes up," he said, not showing any particular surprise at a topic that must have seemed to him to come straight out of left field.

"How does being near your father affect your opinion about ghosts?"

Michael's smile was tinged with affection. "Well,

every so often, when he starts to look really hounded, I feel the need to give the poor guy some moral support. He's an engineer, remember, with a highly rational view of the world. One that for sure doesn't include ghosts, demons and other assorted spirits. My mother, on the other hand, sees the universe in more colorful terms—''

"Define *colorful*.''

"Well, for example, she had a sister called Dayita who died three months before Mom was born, but my mother insists she grew up having regular conversations and play sessions with her dead sister.''

Verity pulled a face. "My sympathy is with your dad on that one. A dead sister for a playmate is a little creepy, isn't it?''

"Not according to my mother. She and Dayita had a grand time together. I remember on one occasion Mom started to describe some kid's game she had supposedly been taught by her sister, and Dad suggested quite sternly that she hadn't been taught any games by a ghost. She'd simply had an imaginary friend nobody else could see, as many lonely children do.''

"What was your mother's response to that?''

Michael smiled. "My mother informed my dad very sweetly that he was absolutely right. She *did* indeed have a friend nobody else could see—Dayita, the ghost of her dead sister.''

Verity laughed. "Your poor father didn't have a hope of winning that argument, did he?''

"Not a hope,'' Michael agreed. "But it wasn't the dead sister who really ticked off my dad because she stopped visiting as soon as my mother moved to America—''

"Dayita had geographic prejudices?'' Verity inquired.

"Hey, she was a kid, no more than seven or eight. Cut her some slack. She wanted to be near her family, according to my mother, and she was scared of crossing the Atlantic Ocean.''

''Right. A ghost with a water phobia. I'm with your dad on this one. Your mother had an imaginary playmate.''

''Whatever. Anyway, Dayita was replaced in America by the ghost of Great-aunt Varja, who had no fear of the water, or anything else as far as I can tell. My mother would consult Aunt Varja about everything from the best cure for a sore throat up to and including whether my sister should marry the lawyer from Boston or the pediatrician from Los Angeles.''

''What did Aunt Varja advise in that instance?'' Verity asked, sufficiently amused to be diverted from her own problems.

''She strongly advised against marrying either one.'' He grinned. ''Which was probably fortunate, since my sister had already decided she was going to marry a college professor from Chicago.''

Verity laughed, then sobered, realizing that she still hadn't broached the subject of Sam's ghostly visits. ''Before I get too distracted by Aunt Varja, there's something I need to tell you, and I honestly don't know whether I want you to react like your mother or your father right now.''

''I could try just reacting like me,'' Michael said. ''Seeing as how we're the only people here, and I don't need to placate either of my parents.''

''I sure as heck hope we're the only two people here,'' Verity muttered beneath her breath. She waited for a beat, half expecting to see the shimmer of Sam's sweater, or the flicker of his facial features, but the car remained reassuringly empty.

''Who else might we be expecting?'' Michael inquired.

"I assume you'd have mentioned it by now if we had intruders with guns hiding under the back seat?"

"Of course. It's nothing like that, nothing dangerous." Verity drew in a calming breath, which did absolutely nothing to calm her. "It's just that I've been seeing Sam's ghost ever since New Year's Day." She blurted out the truth before she could rationalize herself into keeping silent. "I've been chatting with him quite regularly. In fact, his most recent appearance was just now, while you were in the deli."

"I'm sorry I missed him," Michael said politely.

"Don't mock!" Verity said through clenched teeth. "If you think I've gone totally and completely crazy, say so. But don't make a joke of it."

"Why would you assume I was making a joke, much less mocking you?" Michael asked.

"Because obviously I'm not really seeing Sam!" Verity realized she was yelling and lowered her voice. She rubbed her forehead, where her headache had returned. "Despite your cute stories about Dayita and Great-aunt Varja, I know you don't believe in ghosts. Nobody sensible does. Obviously I'm so damn neurotic, my subconscious is sending out full-blown hallucinations, complete with auditory accompaniments."

"Oh, okay, I understand now." Michael's voice was deceptively mild. "You've confided in me that you saw Sam's ghost, but I'm not allowed to believe this is an actual possibility. That being the case, can you give me a hint about my role in the conversation? Am I supposed to recommend the name of a good psychiatrist? Suggest that you take more vitamins? Get an X ray of your skull? Let me know, will you? I'd like to play my part to your satisfaction."

"I hate sarcastic people," Verity said, crossing her arms and huddling as far away from Michael as possible.

"Mmm...so do I. I'm glad we agree about that."

"You're sometimes so...so infuriatingly...Indian."

"Quite often, I expect." Michael smiled tightly. "Almost all the time I'm not being infuriatingly American, in fact."

Michael's low-key responses merely made Verity more determined than ever to feel ill-used. "Admitting that I spend time chatting with dead people wasn't exactly easy for me, you know."

"I can see that. If I ask another question about Sam, am I going to get my head snapped off again?"

"I don't know," she mumbled. "It depends on the question."

"Since I'm a brave man, I guess I'll chance it. What does Sam's ghost have to say when he pays you these visits? Does he talk about life after death? Suggest solutions to the problems of world hunger? What? Hell, if Sam's giving away insights into the mysteries of the universe, I definitely want to share the wisdom."

Verity decided that she'd been supersensitive long enough and it was time to revert to a state that could be considered at least semirational. "I'm not sure that Sam has revealed anything very profound or shocking during our conversations," she said, "The first time he appeared was right after midnight on New Year's Day, and we definitely didn't discuss the secrets of the universe. Not that I would have been in any fit shape to absorb them at that point. That night, he just told me to stop feeling sorry for myself and to stop drinking so much."

"Had you been drinking too much?"

She nodded, relieved to finally admit the truth. "Yes, way too much. Not just that night or even that week. I'd been on some sort of low-grade binge at least since November. With a few high-grade drunks thrown in for good measure."

"Why only since November? Sam died in July, after all."

"I've asked myself the same question. When Sam first died, I think I was too exhausted and too numb to feel the full pain of his loss. Then, as everybody started to get ready for the holidays, the numbness wore off. I thought about how happy Sam and I had been our last Thanksgiving together, and before you could say Happy Holidays, I'd spiraled down into a dark hole of self-pity. I had days when I was honestly convinced that nobody in the world had ever felt as miserable as I did."

Michael's voice was sympathetic rather than condemnatory. "Didn't your family and friends step in and try to help?"

"Sure they did." Verity had been surrounded by love and concern from the moment Sam's tumor was diagnosed. She'd discovered that when grief was intense enough, other people's concern didn't even smooth the surface ripples of your pain. She tried to explain. "People had been kind and considerate for months, and they must have been getting sick of walking on eggshells whenever I was anywhere in the vicinity. Even so, Sam's brother and his wife invited me to spend Thanksgiving with them and their children, so did my mother, so did Andrew Breitman, but I said no to everyone. I just wanted to stay home by myself and wallow in how lonely and dreadful my life was and how nobody understood the agony I was going through. Sam was dead, my mother had won a prize from a local TV station for the best flower garden in North Carolina and all she ever seemed to talk about was her damn tulips—"

Despite his best efforts, Michael's lips twitched. "I'm not absolutely convinced that Sam's death and your mother's love of gardening are tragedies of equal proportions, honey."

"Maybe not." Verity laughed when she realized she was still reluctant to concede the point. "Obviously I was getting to be a tad irrational by last November. Not only was Sam dead, but you—" She stopped abruptly.

Michael braked for a traffic light. He turned to look at her. "And I...?" he prompted.

"You were gone," she said, her voice low. "Except for the formal condolence letter you wrote, I didn't hear a word from you. I was mad at Sam for dying. Mad at my mother for not bringing her life to a halt because my husband was dead. Most of all, I was mad at you for staying in Kashmir when I...needed you so desperately."

Michael's voice was husky. "God knows, if I could have come home, I would."

"I recognize that now, but during the holidays I felt so...abandoned."

"By Sam?" He hesitated for a moment, then added, "By me?"

She nodded, looking down at her hands. "I was grieving for Sam, but underneath it all I was furious with you. Remember, I thought you were a salesman. How could buying cashmere, or selling water purification plants, be so important that you couldn't spare two weeks to fly home and see me? Drinking myself into oblivion each night suddenly seemed to make a lot of sense."

Michael's profile was momentarily grim. "I'm glad I didn't know how badly you wanted me to come home."

"Why?"

"Because I would have come," he said simply.

"And blown your cover with the Kashmir Freedom Party?"

"Not just my cover," he said, tacitly acknowledging how he'd spent his months in Kashmir. "It would have blown the entire operation sky-high. It would have been criminally irresponsible."

"Then I'm glad you didn't know," she said. "At least in retrospect."

He took his gaze briefly from the flow of traffic. "Maybe Sam realized that he had to take up the slack. Otherwise, why do you think it took him until New Year's Day to put in an appearance?"

"Maybe ghosts hope that their loved ones won't need them to come back and visit so they hang around and wait for a while before putting in an appearance? But by the end of last year, I sure needed something or somebody to knock some sense into me. Looking back, I can see that by New Year's Eve I was in danger of doing myself real physical harm. It must have been a couple of days since I'd last eaten anything, and it was a lot longer than that since I'd been fully sober. Then Sam appeared and told me in no uncertain terms to stop being an idiot and to quit drinking."

"Thank God he did."

She couldn't quite keep the hope out of her voice. "Then you believe it really is Sam I've been seeing?"

Michael was silent for a moment before answering. "Given the circumstances, does it matter whether Sam's ghost was real or not? The point is that you snapped out of a desperate situation and pulled yourself back onto your feet with amazing speed. Maybe you managed to stop drinking because Sam's ghost came back from beyond and gave you the necessary kick in the pants. Or maybe your subconscious knew you needed a crutch to lift you over the initial hump of getting sober, and so it provided an image of the person you respected most in the world in order to deliver the message. Why does it matter which?"

Verity tried for a smile and didn't quite make it. "I guess it does to me. I'd like to know if I'm crazy or merely possessed."

"Neither. You were grieving, you were stressed to the max and now you're recovering. Thanks either to Sam's ghost, or to your own subconscious. Or maybe both."

"That's another one of those weasel answers we diplomats have been trained to pounce on, Michael."

He shook his head. "I'm not avoiding giving you an answer, far from it. I'm suggesting that sometimes—more often than we'd like to believe—the question isn't valid and so the answer doesn't matter."

"Your father wouldn't agree with that," Verity pointed out. "Neither would your mother."

"True. But despite their fervor, neither one of them can ever produce any evidence that would persuade the other. We can prove that when people keep surgical instruments sterile and treat wounds with antibiotics, people heal faster. We can prove that the moon isn't made of green cheese because we've sent rockets there. But we can't ever prove to my mother that she didn't see a ghost, or convince my father that she did."

"I guess you're right. If your father ever caught a glimpse of Aunt Varja, he'd get his eyes tested for new glasses. If your mother was told she had a lesion on the brain that caused visual hallucinations, she'd say the lesion was what enabled her to see the ghosts who are always there, but normally invisible to humans."

Verity rose above her own problems just long enough to realize how difficult it must have been for Michael to grow up wedged between two such conflicting philosophies. "When you were a child, how did you stay sane trying to find a balance between your parents' differing beliefs?" she asked him.

He hesitated for a moment, and she sensed that he normally brushed aside questions like hers with a standard reply designed to shut people out rather than invite them into a deeper understanding of his personal beliefs.

She realized it was an important compliment when he chose to answer her.

"I respected both my parents," he said finally. "So I was never tempted to think either one of them had a lock on the ultimate meaning of the universe. By the time I was in high school, I'd decided that my mother and father both had equally imperfect explanations for profound truths that we human beings can only grasp dimly, usually through metaphors. And by the time I was done with college, I realized that poking and prodding at the metaphors almost never takes you to a clearer understanding of anything, it just makes you either irrational or dogmatic. So I learned to accept the metaphor and to quit prodding." He flashed her a quick grin. "Which is basically a long-winded way of saying I have a personal philosophy of deeply confused ambivalence."

She laughed. "*Confused ambivalence* describes my world view with startling accuracy."

"It's not surprising that we should have similar outlooks, is it? As a child, you must have experienced a lot of the same bewilderment that I did. After all, you grew up in Kashmir, among people who had completely different cultural and religious systems from your parents."

"Yes, that's true. But at least within the walls of my own home there was no confusion. My parents were both dedicated Baptists, in total agreement about what I should be taught. Not like yours."

Michael pressed the button on his car visor to open the garage, and drove inside. "My home life was a lot easier than you're making it sound. Kids are adaptable. My parents loved us and loved each other, and most of the time, that was all we needed from them. My chief memory from childhood is how lucky I considered myself because our family got to celebrate all the regular American holidays, plus a bunch of Hindu festivals as well. Every month was party month at our house.''

She followed him through the garage into the kitchen. The sunny yellow walls that had seemed so welcoming this morning looked equally inviting at night, but Verity felt a sudden flare of tension that hadn't been present at breakfast time. Not because of anything that had happened between her and Michael, she realized. On the contrary, the edginess of her mood sprang from everything that hadn't happened between them over the past twenty-four hours.

For three years she hadn't dared to imagine being alone with Michael. Now she was alone with him for the second night in a row, and her imagination seemed to have skittered to a dead halt. Having forbidden herself ever to associate Michael and making love in her mind, she found that the barrier was too effective. Her nerve endings might jump with all their familiar awareness of his presence, but deep inside she felt no great stirring of passion. On the contrary, she felt numb. Empty. Utterly removed from any possibility of sexual desire.

Michael, thank heaven, seemed ready to play the polite host, which postponed the problem at least temporarily. He hung her coat in the hall closet, showed her the downstairs guest bathroom, set out their overstuffed pitas on heavy, stoneware plates, made them glasses of spicy hot *chai* and generally managed to keep a conversation going while her mind gnawed over the dire problem of what they would do when they had finished eating, when their plates were in the dishwasher and their paper napkins tossed in the garbage. It was late—heading toward eleven—after an exhausting day. Any attempt to delay bedtime would not only appear idiotic, it would be idiotic. Which meant that in just a few minutes, she would have to walk upstairs and pick a bedroom for the night.

Should she choose the one she'd slept in yesterday? Or should she choose Michael's?

In Kashmir, in the Palace of the Wind, when she had marriage vows to constrain her, it had taken all her willpower to resist making love to Michael right there on the veranda, her back thrust against the carved stone pillar, and with servants within hearing range. Tonight, with a soft bed beckoning, and Michael no longer forbidden, she felt paralyzed by fear. Devastating as it would be if the heat between them burned out the moment the sex was over, it would be even worse if it vanished before they managed to make it through to the end.

If she was ordered to choose one word to describe the sexual relationship she and Sam had shared, she would choose *friendly*. She was one hundred percent positive that where sex was concerned, friendly wouldn't cut it with Michael. Unfortunately, she wasn't sure she could do any other sort. Besides, she didn't want to have friendly sex with Michael. She wanted to have hot, sweaty, earthy sex with him. She wanted him to be wild with desire for her. As for herself, she wanted to scale the heights, soar in the clouds and romp through a few dozen other clichés that had never before seemed within her reach.

Sadly, she didn't have an idea in the world how you set about driving a man wild with desire, much less a cosmopolitan, experienced man like Michael. And unless Michael was wild with desire, she didn't see how she was going to soar in the clouds. She wouldn't describe herself as inhibited, but she wasn't somebody who could swing naked from the chandelier, or hook herself to the bedpost with a jeweled handcuff, either. And there were only so many variations you could work on normal, straightforward sex.

Michael reached across the table to take her dinner

plate and their hands touched. Verity jumped, snatching her hand away as if it had been scalded, and he sent her a puzzled look.

"I'm sorry." She struggled to find her voice. "I don't know why I did that."

"Old habits?" he suggested softly, putting down the plate.

"Must be."

He held her gaze, his dark eyes gleaming with sympathy and only the slightest touch of frustration. "Don't, Verity. Don't look at me as if you're afraid I'm going to fall on top of you and rip off your clothes the second you let down your guard. I've waited three years to make love to you. If you're not ready tonight, I can wait another few days, or even another few weeks." He smiled grimly. "Of course, I wouldn't want to be around me while I'm waiting, but I could do it."

"It's not so much that I'm not ready. I want to make love to you, Michael. Honestly." She flushed, realizing she sounded slightly less sophisticated than your average high school cheerleader. She only needed some gum to snap and she'd be picture-perfect. She moistened her dry lips, preparing herself for another embarrassing bout of honesty. "The fact is…I'm afraid you may be disappointed. It occurred to me that you've been waiting a long time for something that might not be too wonderful when it actually happens. Suppose I can't give you what you want? What you need?"

"I'm absolutely sure you can give me everything I've ever wanted or needed."

"How can you be sure?" She was so nervous, she forgot to be annoyed by his inevitable, arrogant confidence. Trying to get her point across, she rushed on. "I'm a boring, white bread kind of lover, Michael. I don't do chandeliers, and jeweled handcuffs, or any of the exotic stuff you might be accustomed to."

His eyebrow quirked. "Jeweled handcuffs?" he murmured. "Chandeliers?"

She flushed deeper. "Well, you know what I mean. *Chandeliers* was just a code word." She looked down at her paper napkin, which she'd somehow managed to shred into about twenty pieces. "I meant that I don't know how to act out weird fantasies or perform oral sex hanging upside down and...and stuff."

He smiled at her without a trace of his usual reserve, then walked around the table and took her into his arms. "Verity, my dearest love, I promise you we aren't going to need chandeliers to make this wonderful. Or even weird fantasies. Much less *stuff*."

It felt so good in his arms, she was willing to be convinced. She drew a random design on his chest, not looking at him as she spoke. "I want you to want me," she said huskily.

His smile was wry. "Trust me, there isn't a problem." He wrapped his arms around her waist as he spoke, urging her up onto her toes. If he heard the quick intake of her breath, or felt the tremble that accompanied it, he made no comment. He simply bent his head and slanted his mouth across hers.

Verity went from nervousness to raging desire in about three seconds flat. She had often wondered if their kiss at Hawa Mahal, the Palace of the Wind, had been made powerful by some special magic, unique to that night. She'd gradually convinced herself that her response to Michael's kiss had been a one-off type of event that would never be duplicated. That her wild flaring of sexual need had been caused by nothing more than a combination of time, place and circumstance, spiced with the thrill of the forbidden.

Tonight's kiss proved her conclusively and unmistakably wrong. Clearly, they didn't need moonlight and palaces to ignite their desire, they just needed each other. As Michael kissed her, the same incredible blaze of sexual yearning began to burn, even though the setting was nothing more romantic than the kitchen, with the dinner dishes still stacked on the table. Nerve endings that had been tense with anxiety quickened with an entirely different sort of anticipation. The fire of passion warmed her blood and simmered through her veins until her skin dewed with heat and her breath shortened with desire.

They broke away, then came together again almost instantly. He slid one hand caressingly down her spine, spreading possessive fingers over her too thin hips as he held her pressed against his thighs. She felt the hard, lean, muscled length of his body touching her from shoulder to knee, and she relaxed against him with a little sigh of pleasure, as if she were coming home. His mouth moved against her lips, tempting and teasing, and the taste of him poured through her, filling all those empty places that only moments ago had felt numb.

Their kiss at the Palace of the Wind had been consuming, even devastating, but a part of her had held back that night, horrified at how her body was betraying her. Betraying her marriage, and betraying Sam. Now she had no reason to hold back anything, and she surrendered with total abandon.

"Verity." Michael murmured her name against her mouth, before drawing slightly away from her. "We can't do this here."

She didn't want to talk, didn't want anything to break the fabulous spell they were weaving between them. She shook her head in silent protest, and reached out to trace the outline of his mouth with her forefinger. He opened his mouth to say something, and she slipped her finger inside, teasing his tongue, mimicking the act of love.

He closed his eyes, then bit down on her finger, but she twisted away and linked her hands behind his neck. As she pulled his head down, she arched up toward him, moving her mouth beneath his with deliberate provocation, kissing him with all the force generated by three years of pent-up passion.

He returned her kiss with a savage intensity that satisfied her for a little while. But only for a while. Her fingers dug into his shoulders, then moved up to tangle in his hair. It felt sleek and thick and soft against the palms of her hands, the only part of him that retained any measure of softness. He reached under her sweater and unfastened her bra, cupping her breasts in his hands, soothing a little more of her need.

Still, it wasn't enough. She wanted to be closer. She wanted to feel her naked skin against his skin, and to feel his erection thrusting against the flat plane of her belly. It took her several seconds to realize there was no reason why she couldn't act on her wishes. Trembling a little with shyness as well as longing, she fumbled with the buttons of his shirt, her fingers made clumsy by desire. She registered only a fleeting moment of surprise when she heard his shirt buttons pop off and tumble to the floor. Verity had never really believed that people actually tore off each other's clothes in their haste to have sex. Now she understood exactly how it could happen. She tugged Michael's shirt out of his pants, pushed it off his shoulders, and flung it onto the floor.

Michael gave a shuddering sigh, then his hand brushed over her breasts again, lingering on her nipples. Her knees went weak and she stumbled against him. He gave a laugh that was part groan. "We need a bed, Verity. God, have you any idea what you're doing to me?"

"Yes." She wasn't sure what she was agreeing to. Didn't much care. She closed her eyes but otherwise she didn't move, drowning in the sensations created when he grazed his thumbs over her nipples. Each new place Michael touched ignited a shower of sparks on her skin. By now, the sparks had erupted in so many places that they flamed across her entire body, making her burn with a sensation halfway between pleasure and pain. Her muscles began to quiver with the strain of wanting, and Michael's mouth grew more urgent, his hands more demanding.

"We have to go upstairs." Michael pulled away for the second time, his forehead resting against hers. "You're covered in bruises and I can barely move my left arm. We can't do this on the floor. We need a bed."

This time she registered the meaning of what he was saying, instead of just hearing a jumble of words. Blinking, she focused on the bandage wrapped around his left forearm. A spot of new, bright-red blood had seeped through the whiteness.

"Did I do that?" Horrified, Verity reached out and touched her fingertips to the blood.

"No. Anyway, it doesn't matter. It's nothing." Michael lifted her hand away and put his right arm around her waist, leading her out of the kitchen and urging her up the stairs to the bedroom.

There was a night-light burning in a wall outlet, and he didn't switch on any more lights. Verity had a blurred impression that this most personal and intimate room was decorated in a style that owed almost everything to the heritage of his mother's people, almost nothing to his Yankee fathers. Dark, exotic, with a carved sandalwood chest beneath the window and an exquisite antique Kashmir silk carpet in the Tree of Life design hanging on the wall behind the bed, the furnishings could have come straight from the Hawa Mahal. Even the bed, which was American and king-size, was stacked with multicolored silk cushions.

She might have been amused, or even irritated, by this haremlike touch, but Michael left her no time for reflection, no time for the heat of desire to cool. He undressed her, muttering a string of curses when he saw the full extent of the bruises on her rib cage and her shins. He ran his mouth along the trail of her bruises, his touch gentle, his hands almost unbearably tender as he led her to the bed. She knew she was still too thin after the months of neglect and drinking, but his gaze told her that he found her body beautiful and somehow she believed him.

She lay down in his arms, bewilderment and desire mingled almost equally. How was it possible that she was here, in Michael's bed? Even three nights ago, such an outcome would have seemed impossible. Now it seemed entirely right and natural.

Supporting himself on his right arm, Michael turned on his side and looked down at her. Even in the dim glow of the night-light, she could see that his eyes were filled with a wonder and a longing that mimicked her own.

"I never dared to dream of having you here," he said. "So I can't say that this is the fulfillment of my fantasies. It's more than that. It's the fulfillment of all the fantasies I never allowed myself to have."

The part of her brain that supplied words and speech seemed to have gone on strike, so she reached up and cradled his cheek with her hand, at the same time as her legs twined intimately with his. He turned his face to press a kiss into her palm, then he pulled the clips from her hair and dropped them onto the floor. Her hair tumbled over the pillow in a light-brown cloud. She felt a primitive sense of triumph when she saw his breath visibly catch.

It was a moment before he spoke, and then his voice was husky with emotion. "I want you, Verity, more than I ever imagined I could want any woman."

Desire leapt and danced in her belly. "I want you, too, Michael." She said his name softly, but with all the longing she felt deep inside. "I want you more than I thought I could ever want a man."

His gaze burned into her, searing in its intensity. "I love you, Verity."

"I love you, too." She smiled at him, her eyes a little misty, her breathing a little uneven. She would never in a thousand years have expected to find so much joy in making such a declaration.

His breath escaped in a long, harsh outpouring. "Say that again, could you? Just to be sure I didn't dream it."

"I love you, Michael. With everything that I am, for everything that you are."

For a single moment he closed his eyes. When he opened them again, tenderness and gentleness were forgotten. His mouth and hands roamed with urgent demand over her body, driving her toward a peak she recognized only dimly. The thud of her heartbeat echoed in her ears, drowning out all sounds except the rasp of Michael's breathing and the pounding roar of her pulses as they sent fiery hot blood coursing through her veins. The air felt heavy around them, too thick to draw into her lungs. She writhed on the bed, struggling to find release from a torment she wasn't sure she wanted to end. Not quite. Not yet. Not when Michael could touch her and kiss her so that her whole body vibrated with the intensity of her longing.

But it had to finish soon, Verity thought frantically, or she would be insane by the time it was over. She gasped, her hips arching off the bed as Michael entered her at last. His mouth took hers in a final demanding kiss and her entire body convulsed with a pleasure too intense to bear. She groaned his name and clutched his hands, clinging to the rock solid reassurance of his presence before she slid out of the clouds, down the rainbow slope into total and consuming bliss.

Eighteen

Michael's sleep was so deep, and his dreams of Verity so captivating, that it took a while for him to realize that the noise he heard was the ringing of his phone and not some fantasy bell he could safely ignore. Still half-asleep, he rolled over to grab the receiver before the noise woke Verity, and a stab of gut-wrenching pain in his arm brought him instantly to a state of full alert.

He smothered a groan and clicked the talk button on the receiver, automatically noting that the time was 4:20 in the morning, and that the caller ID displayed an unknown number in the Washington, D.C. area. He said hello quietly into the receiver as he walked toward the bathroom. He chose the bathroom partly to avoid disturbing Verity and partly because his arm had hot, fresh blood on it and he needed to find something to use as a bandage.

He was reaching in the medicine cabinet for one of the prepacked sterile dressings they'd given him in the hospital when a voice with a distinctive Indian accent spoke at the other end of the phone. "Michael? This is Farooq. Are you alone?"

"Yes, I am alone." He was in the bathroom with the door shut, so it was almost a truthful reply. "Where the hell have you been for the past two weeks?"

"In Germany, keeping my head down, while I have been waiting with much impatience for Gunther to show up." Farooq spoke excellent English, but his word choice and intonation sometimes sounded a little quaint to American ears.

"Why didn't you answer any of my e-mail messages?" Michael took off his bandage and slapped on another one, using his teeth to tear off some strapping tape to hold it in place.

"I was afraid to break my cover. You know Internet contacts can be traced."

"You didn't have to respond in real time—"

"I know, I know. But only Allah knows how many people are trying to kill me and it hasn't been easy. I seem to have caused grievous annoyance to many and diverse groups of people."

"Where are you now? Have you spoken to Gunther?"

"Yes, and I have the answer that we both sought with such eagerness. You will be pleased to hear, Michael, that I know the name of your American traitor."

Michael's breath exhaled in a sharp hiss. "Give it to me."

"Yes, I will do so. And now, over the phone. His name is Dick Pedro, who is Deputy Assistant Secretary for Asian Affairs in the State Department. Do you know him?"

Michael was silent for a second or two, as his brain raced to sort out the implications of what Farooq had just told him. "Yes, I know him," he said finally. "And I can't say that I'm entirely surprised. He was on my list of suspects. Do you have any proof of Secretary Pedro's treachery that I can take to the authorities? He's obviously a very senior diplomat and a long-term employee of the State Department. My people are going to need a watertight case before we can move against him."

"I might be able to provide you the proof your people will need." Farooq's voice became cautious. "But I am a trader by nature as well as profession, and I need to receive something of value in exchange for this proof.''

"I'm sure you have something in mind.'' Michael didn't attempt to hide his irony.

"Indeed I do. My brother Khalid took the key to the safety deposit box where I had placed certain items of great value to a customer of the Kashmir Freedom Party. He gave that key to Verity Marlowe.''

Shit, what should he say now, Michael wondered. There wasn't enough time to think through the implications of Farooq's statements, much less his own answers. "I am aware of the existence of such a key,'' he admitted.

"Good. The key is very important because without it, the safety deposit box cannot be opened.''

"There are drills—''

"No, not in this case.'' Farooq's denial was swift. "It so happens that the safety deposit box is wired in such a way that without the key, anyone who attempts to open it will—most sadly—find himself blown into a multitude of very small pieces. Taking, of course, the contents of the box with him into eternity.''

"I understand.'' At which point, a seriously pissed Saddam Hussein would be permanently without guidance software for his stolen missile system.

"This key is therefore extremely valuable to me,'' Farooq continued. "It goes without saying that I need it returned. If you will meet me now, within the next thirty minutes, bringing the key with you, I will give you the proof you need that Dick Pedro has been working in alliance with the Kashmir Freedom Party to buy and distribute arms to terrorists around the world.''

Michael couldn't appear too willing, or suspicions would be raised. "You're asking a lot, Farooq. You promised me that you would find out the name of the

American traitor and give it to me as a free gesture of your goodwill—''

"And you promised me that you would protect Khalid." There was bitter mockery in Farooq's reply. "We all break our promises in this business, even if we would prefer not to."

Michael winced at the unpalatable truth of Farooq's statement. "I saw from my caller ID that you're in the Washington, D.C. area," he said. "Where do you want us to meet?"

"I thought a supermarket parking lot would be a good, all-American choice. I have selected one not too far from your home, a Safeway on Dolly Madison Boulevard, at the intersection with Green Farm Road." Farooq's voice deepened. "Be there by five-thirty, Michael, and bring my brother's key. Many lives depend upon your timely compliance to my instructions."

"What if I don't have the key in my possession?"

"Then I will meet you in the parking lot and we will travel together, in my car, to retrieve it. I trust, Michael, that you haven't been foolish enough to leave my brother's key anywhere in Langley where official signatures are required to reclaim it?"

"No, it's not in Langley. I want to nail Dick Pedro a lot more than I care about you retrieving weapons guidance software from a safety deposit box. Especially since I don't have a clue where the box is located. In fact, I have the key, and I'll bring it to the parking lot. I'm willing to make a deal."

"I am most relieved to hear it. And Michael—"

"Yes?"

"There is, of course, a surveillance team watching your house. Despite your claim to the contrary, I know that you are not, in fact, alone. There is also a wire tap on your phone. If you should attempt to contact your colleagues, or arrange for an FBI team to be waiting at the designated supermarket when you arrive there, you will die. It is just possible that your own death might not concern you, but be advised that if you betray me, Verity Marlowe will not survive long enough to mourn at your funeral.''

Rage and terror formed a physical lump that momentarily choked Michael, making speech impossible. Then his years of training took over and he turned away from the phone so that he could draw in a deep, calming breath that wouldn't be audible to Farooq, or anyone else listening in on their conversation. In less than two seconds he had himself sufficiently under control to speak in a tone of voice that approximated his normal professional detachment.

"Let's stop playing games here, Farooq. You know as well as I do that cell phone calls can't be traced. You also know that there's no way in hell I'm going to leave this house without informing one or more of my colleagues that you have accused Dick Pedro of being a traitor, and that you claim to have the documentation to prove it."

"I accept that you will do this," Farooq said. "But be warned, Michael. We both know how the government operates. Do not let them know that you are meeting me. Do not mention the key given to Verity by my brother. Your colleagues will lie to you. They will pretend to agree that you can meet with me alone. In truth, knowing what is at stake, they cannot permit such a meeting to take place. You know that they will rush and scramble to put a team together in time to arrest me. With luck, such a team would not make it to our meeting place in time. With very bad luck, they would. And then, my friend, you and I are both likely to die in the ensuing gun battle. And only a very little later, your much loved Verity Marlowe would meet the same fate.'' He paused for a beat, then added. ''Now that you have finally bedded her, it would be a shame if she were to die, would it not?''

The sons of bitches had wired his house! Michael thought, and a red haze of fury blinded him. When his brain cleared, he realized Farooq had said nothing that suggested specific knowledge of what had passed between him and Verity last night. If his house was under surveillance—and how the hell had he missed that, for Christ's sake, except that he'd been so damn busy mooning over Verity that he'd been blind and deaf to everything else—then Farooq would know that she had spent the past two nights here.

Farooq was probably guessing that he and Verity were lovers, but Michael wasn't about to make the mistake of denying a sexual relationship just in case the bastards had every room in the house wired for sound. And pictures. Christ, did they have pictures? No, he wasn't going to go down that sickening road.

He gave a mental shrug, forcing himself into character, although the words burned acid in his throat as they emerged. ''Hey, Verity's a good-looking woman and she's willing to put out. What can I say? She turns in a hot trick. But you and I are old buddies, Farooq. You know my views on women. In the dark, under the sheets, who can tell the difference?'' He injected a leer into his voice. ''Fat, thin, tall, short, the essential equipment's the same, right?''

And if he didn't have any other reasons for killing The American, being forced to utter such crudities about Verity was sure as hell grounds for murder, Michael reflected bleakly.

''About women, you know we are in total agreement,'' Farooq said. ''And now, to business. The time is cur-

rently 4:26. You need to be at the supermarket no later
than 5:00 a.m. With the key, of course. There is no traffic
to speak of on the roads at this hour, so there is no reason
for you to fail to keep your appointment. If you are not
here by the time agreed, I am sure I need not remind you
that there will be unfortunate consequences for Ms. Marlowe.''

Michael hung up without saying goodbye, a petty gesture that did little to relieve his general state of fury. A
fury generously spiced with high-quality terror. Since he
was in the bathroom, he splashed hot water on his face,
followed by cold. The water did nothing to alleviate his
rage or terror, little to improve his brain functioning.

He returned quietly to the bedroom, but Verity was
awake, and with an alchemy he could have done without,
she knew that something was wrong. "I heard the phone
ring,'' she said. "What's happened?''

Was the bedroom wired or not? Did it make a difference to what he would tell her anyway?

"That phone call was from Farooq,'' he said.

She shot up in the bed. "Khalid's brother? That Farooq?''

He nodded, pulling on clothes as he spoke. "He's been
in Germany, trying to make contact with an illegal arms
dealer, a man known only as Gunther. Gunther is ru-
mored to know the name of the American traitor—the
man Khalid told you about.''

"Did Farooq succeed in making contact?''

"Yes, apparently so.'' He was going to tell her about
Dick Pedro, Michael decided. As far as he could see,
there was no reason to keep the information secret, and
no added danger to Verity in revealing it. "Farooq spoke
with Gunther, and somehow extracted the information
that Dick Pedro is the State Department official we're

looking for. According to Farooq, he's the man we need to put behind bars."

"Dick Pedro is a traitor?" Verity sounded incredulous, as well she might. "You're suggesting that *Dick Pedro* is Yousaf's American ally? The mastermind behind the terrorist takeover of the school in Bombay?"

"Yes." Michael had no idea if the bedroom was wired, but he was conducting this conversation as if hostiles were listening to every word. He didn't want to sound too credulous, or too easy to deceive, but he did need to convince any possible listeners that he believed Farooq's story. Walking into the closet, where Verity couldn't see him, he took Khalid's key from its hiding place, taped to the inside of one of his ties, and used a fresh Band-Aid to stick it to his rib cage.

"Dick's always been on my short list of suspects," he said, emerging from the closet. "He's got all the necessary contacts among renegade diplomats overseas, he's been divorced twice, his wives both took him to the cleaners and yet he always manages to find the spare cash to take regular vacation trips abroad. We know he doesn't have any money squirreled away in bank accounts here in the States, because we've checked. Carefully. But God knows what he must have overseas."

"But he's such a dyed-in-the-wool bureaucrat," Verity protested. "And he's not even all that smart. Every time there's a crisis in Kashmir, I have to remind him about the location of the cease-fire line, and the fact that Pakistan and China both claim part of the territory now governed by India—"

"It's the easiest thing in the world to pretend ignorance, Verity. Dick probably spends a great deal of time laughing at us behind our backs."

"It just seems so incredible," she muttered. "I mean, Dick Pedro. My God!"

"Yes, it does. But it would sound incredible whoever Farooq had named, wouldn't it? We don't expect our colleagues to be traitors."

"No, I know, but still—"

"Honey, I'm sorry, but we can't talk anymore. I have to get out of here."

Michael grabbed his cell phone from the night stand. He would call Collin Krenz when he was almost at the designated intersection. That way, he could reveal where he was going without risking the arrival of an FBI team before he and Farooq concluded their deal. Whatever the real deal might be.

"Where are you going? Why do you have to leave?" Verity was already pushing back the covers on the bed and looking around for her clothes. Any minute now she'd insist on coming with him. Fortunately, he seemed to have tossed her clothes far and wide. An unexpected bonus, courtesy of last night's mind-blowing sex.

He shook his head, clearing his mind of images he couldn't allow to intrude. "I have to meet with Farooq—"

Her eyes blazed at him. "You're going to meet the man who's been identified by Interpol as the head of the Kashmir Freedom Party? Are you crazy, Michael, or do you just have a death wish?"

She was sitting on the bed, so he leaned down and kissed her forehead, unable to resist. "Honey, I spent eight months undercover with the Kashmir Freedom Party. I assure you, Yousaf is the big cheese, and Farooq is merely the money man. Farooq is going to give me the documentation I need to prove that Dick Pedro is a traitor to our country. That's all."

"Oh, sure, I can see why you'd believe that just because somebody claiming to be Farooq calls you at four in the morning. Don't leave yet. I need to find a Sucker label to stick on your forehead.''

"It was definitely Farooq. I recognized his voice. And I have no reason to believe he wants to harm me. It's going too far to say that Farooq is my friend, but we've been in some tight spots together, and I trust him, up to a point. I'm accustomed to assessing risk—that's my job. Farooq wants Pedro behind bars as much as we do, so it's in his own self-interest to get the documentation into the proper hands. Believe me when I say this isn't a dangerous situation.''

Her mouth firmed into a stubborn line. "Nobody expected it to be dangerous when Khalid walked out of the Creighton Hotel, either.''

She was too smart, too perceptive and too knowledgeable about the situation to be easy to deceive and he didn't have time to invent lies that might be more convincing. "Don't worry so much, Verity. Farooq and I are meeting in a public place, the Safeway parking lot on Green Farm Road—''

"You can't get more public than a hotel entrance in Washington, D.C., but Khalid and three other people died right there, in front of dozens of onlookers.''

She wasn't going to believe him when he said it wasn't dangerous, so he might as well quit protesting. He spoke briskly, as if there were no room for discussion. Because, in fact, there *was* no room for discussion. "My current job comes with a degree of risk attached. Bottom line, I'm going to meet Farooq because that's my job. I don't anticipate any danger. But I'm armed—'' He touched the Glock, which was in the shoulder holster he'd just finished buckling. He hoped to God that if he needed to use it, the two-day-old bullet wound wouldn't slow him down too much. "Trust me, Verity. After what happened to

Khalid, I'm sure as hell alert to the possibility of traps or ambushes."

"Yes, of course you are. However, it's the traps and ambushes people don't see that tend to kill them."

He drew in a frustrated breath and made for the door. "I don't have time to argue this with you anymore. I have to go, but I should be back in an hour, maybe less. Wait for me here, Verity. Don't leave the house, promise me?"

She shook her head. "I can't promise that."

"You have to." His voice hardened. "I need to know you're here, safe, while I'm meeting with Farooq. Promise me you won't leave the house. Dammit, Verity, I need your word." He hesitated for a moment, then added, "Please."

"All right," she said slowly. "I promise." Her gray eyes were still troubled, and he turned away, knowing that he'd never be able to focus on his upcoming meeting if he allowed his mind to be filled with images of Verity sitting forlornly on the side of his bed. With ruthless efficiency, honed over ten years of life-and-death undercover missions, he switched off all thoughts of the woman he loved and focused his attention exclusively on the American traitor. And on Farooq Muhammad.

Who, by the simple process of speaking in English instead of Kashmiri, had activated one of their coded warning systems, and alerted Michael to the fact that everything he said was spoken under duress, probably with a gun pointed at his head.

Nineteen

Not to put too fine a point on it, Verity was majorly pissed with Michael. Since she was also hopelessly in love with him, the state of her feelings could only be described as confused. He had clearly been lying to her, or at least holding back something important. She didn't have to be acutely sensitive to his every mood to figure that one out. But why had he lied? Why would he tell her Farooq had called if he hadn't? And there couldn't be any purpose at all to telling her Dick Pedro had been identified as a traitor if that wasn't really the case.

Sleep seemed to be a lost cause at this point, so she hunted around the bedroom for her clothes. She found her underwear behind a chair, her bra under the bed, her sweater between the sheets, and her twill pants draped over the sandalwood chest. Tossing the crumpled collection on the comforter, she went into the bathroom to take a shower. Maybe the hot water would pound some inspiration into her addled brain.

Was Michael walking into a trap? Verity didn't see how it could be otherwise. Michael probably assumed that he was smart enough, and wary enough, to spring the trap before it cut him in two. Verity wasn't so confident. When you stacked courage, integrity and fierce intelligence up against brute force, cunning and desperation, the good guys didn't always win.

Michael claimed that he'd recognized Farooq's voice,

but these days, with voice synthesizers, it was dangerous to believe everything you heard. Look at the all too male intruder who'd menaced her in a soft, feminine voice. With that sort of technology readily available, how could Michael be sure what he'd really heard? More to the point, how could he be sure that Farooq didn't want to harm him? The pressure cooker of Kashmiri politics produced twists and distortions that seemed little short of bizarre to people who'd never endured multiple generations of violence and repression.

Verity rubbed shampoo into her scalp and thought about Farooq. It had to be at least six years since she'd last seen him, during the one trip she and Sam had made to Kashmir together. Farooq had been a mere youth in those days, no more than twenty, with laughing eyes and an enthusiasm for life that was contagious.

Despite his easy laughter, he had all the arrogance that was natural for the exceptionally handsome son of a wealthy father. In fact, he'd been almost movie-star handsome, Verity thought, so caught up in her memories that she slathered shampoo instead of soap over her body.

Khalid had also been quite good-looking, but he wasn't in the same league as his younger brother. She remembered that the boys' father had once announced to her parents, when she was within hearing range, that Allah had gifted Khalid with brains and Farooq with good looks, but that Ali had received both good looks and a sharp mind in full abundance. It was Allah's way of compensating Ali for being the youngest child in the family, his father had claimed.

The American ideals of building self-esteem in children and not making comparisons among siblings still had a way to go in Kashmiri households, Verity thought wryly.

Ali must be about seventeen or eighteen now, since he

was at least eight years younger than Farooq, and thirteen years younger than Khalid, separated from his brothers by a trio of sisters. The age difference meant that Verity didn't know Ali in any meaningful way, but on the one occasion when she and Sam had met him, she'd been struck by how much he looked like a younger version of Farooq....

Slides clicked together inside Verity's head. Snapshot memories of Khalid, Farooq and Ali standing together in the garden of their uncle's house. After a moment, she heard a thud. She looked down at her feet and realized the bottle of shampoo had slipped through her fingers and dropped on the floor of the shower. Fortunately, it was plastic, so it hadn't broken. She picked it up and returned it to the niche in the wall, but she missed the ledge and it fell again.

This time she didn't even bother to bend down and pick it up. Didn't fully register that it had fallen. Because she was suddenly quite, quite certain that she'd identified the Indian student from the American school, the one with the noose around his neck who'd been put on display alongside Mary Grace Klemper.

He wasn't Kalil Mustafa, mysterious orphan. He was Ali Muhammad, youngest brother to Farooq and Khalid.

Verity stood in the shower, water beating down unheeded on her head, as a ball of panic inside her stomach exploded, sending chills racing over her body. The tangled threads of assassination and terrorism that had previously seemed so random suddenly wove themselves into a complex but discernible pattern, like the elaborate design on a Kashmir paisley shawl that became more clearly formalized the longer you looked.

In an effort to keep Ali safe, away from the political nightmare swirling around their family, Khalid and Farooq had sent their youngest brother to the American

School in Bombay. He had been registered there under an assumed name and, from the fact that George Douglass had been assassinated before Yousaf captured the school, Verity concluded that the American consul might well have been involved in making the arrangements for Ali's enrolment.

But somehow Ali's false name had failed to protect him and his true identity became known to Yousaf. Had undoubtedly been known to Yousaf long before the first of his terrorist minions stepped foot on American School property. Yousaf would have plenty of obvious motives for plucking Ali out from the mass of student hostages and parading him before the world, not least revenge against Khalid for his moderate political views. But could Yousaf have had a more urgent and more secret motive for his choice?

The answer came as soon as Verity asked herself the question. Ali wasn't just being used as a vague general threat to the philosophy of peaceful negotiations over the future of Kashmir. Of course not. He was the powerful weapon Yousaf and the American traitor were using to smoke Farooq out of his hiding place. Only Farooq knew where he had hidden his infamous safety deposit box, the one to which Khalid had given her the key. Khalid had warned her that people were willing to kill to access that box, and Yousaf would have no qualms about using Ali's life as a bargaining chip. Yousaf and his treacherous American partner wanted—needed—the contents of that box badly enough that they were using every weapon at their command to flush Farooq out of hiding.

And they'd succeeded brilliantly. Khalid's death hadn't provoked any discernible reaction from Farooq. Perhaps he'd felt that he could best honor his dead brother by keeping safely hidden. But it had taken less than twelve hours after pictures of his younger brother flashed across the world's television screens before Farooq surfaced and made contact with Michael.

Verity coughed, choking on a spray of shower water she accidentally swallowed. When she could breathe again, she pushed her dripping wet hair out of her eyes, turned off the faucet and wrapped herself in a towel. She meant to walk back into the bedroom and get dressed, but her thoughts were churning so fast that there didn't seem to be any room in her brain for giving automatic commands like putting one foot in front of the other. So she stood half in and half out of the shower stall, staring blankly at the tiled wall, until the fact that she was darn near freezing finally penetrated her consciousness.

Shivering, she walked back into the bedroom and pulled on yesterday's wrinkled clothes. As soon as she started to warm up, her mind raced off again. Why had Farooq made contact with Michael? Since Farooq's primary concern was saving his brother, it seemed logical to conclude that when he decided to break cover his first contact would be with Yousaf. But unlike the families of the other student hostages, Farooq wouldn't have offered Yousaf money in exchange for his brother's life. No, he would have offered Yousaf and his American partner whatever it was he had hidden in the safety deposit box.

That damned life-and-death box to which she had given Michael the key.

Twenty

Whenever the agents assigned to the Counter Terrorism Center discussed the identity of the American traitor, Dick Pedro's name always appeared high on the list. At their last interagency meeting, right after the New Year, Michael had been one of the participants who argued most forcefully for Pedro's guilt. Here was a man embittered by his two divorces, who complained constantly about being underpaid. A man, moreover, who showed a blundering lack of any diplomatic skill save that of brownnosing his superiors and failing to give credit to his juniors.

Dick was such a perfect stereotype of the rigid bureaucrat that he had to be faking it, Michael had argued with a passion that convinced many of the other attendees at the meeting. Beneath the bumbling, by-the-rules facade lurked the brilliant brain and ice-cold heart of a traitor. Now, only a week later, Farooq had validated Michael's suspicions by promising to provide documentary proof that Dick Pedro was indeed guilty of using the Kashmir Freedom Party as a conduit through which to buy and sell illegal armaments.

It was ironic, Michael thought, that the one rock solid certainty to have emerged from this morning's phone conversation with Farooq Muhammad was the complete innocence of Dick Pedro.

He was already less than a mile from the intersection

that Farooq had designated as their meeting place, and it was only 4:50. Ever since turning out of his driveway, he'd been followed by a green Chrysler Concorde, its license plate conveniently obscured by splatters of mud. Other than the license plate, the driver was making no attempt to conceal what he was doing, which suggested that the purpose of the tail was simply to ensure that Michael arrived at the meeting alone, as promised, without a SWAT team escort. Giving a mocking salute into his rearview mirror, he turned into a side street and waited for the tail to follow.

Cruising the quiet, residential street, he flipped open his cell phone and dialed the number for Collin Krenz. His boss, probably on tenterhooks because of the situation in Bombay, picked up the call on the first ring. "Yes?"

"It's Michael. Farooq Muhammad contacted me this morning by phone. I'm en route to a rendezvous with him now. Farooq's chosen the parking lot of a Safeway supermarket at the intersection of Dolly Madison and Green Farm Road."

"Supermarket parking lots are the most likely place to get robbed and mugged."

"Yeah, well, I don't think Farooq's planning to mug me. They're not going to kill me unless I do something real stupid."

"I'll send backup—"

"Don't even think of it, Collin. Sending in backup is the one sure way to get me killed. Farooq and I have negotiated a deal and there's no reason for him to break it. He wants to get back the key to his safety deposit box. No surprise there. We both know how badly Yousaf and his American partner need to get access to the contents of that box. In exchange for the key, Yousaf's going to provide me with watertight evidence that Dick Pedro is the State Department traitor we've all been looking for.''

"Dick Pedro, eh?" Collin's breath exhaled in a long, low sigh. "So you were right after all. Dick Pedro is the bastard who's been selling us down the river. The son of a bitch who masterminded Yousaf's terrorist attack on the American School.''

"That's what Farooq tells me." Michael kept his voice deliberately bland.

Collin let rip with his own trilingual brand of obscenities. "I'm going to make sure the prosecutors go after him with every charge they can scrape out of their law books.''

Collin was accepting Farooq's accusation at face value, which wasn't surprising. He had no way of knowing that Michael had given Farooq several opportunities to say something that would indicate he was telling the truth, despite the fact that he was speaking in English, their agreed code for indicating trouble. On each occasion, Farooq had delivered clear indications that he was lying. As, for example, when he expressly pointed out that he was revealing the traitor's identity over an open phone line. Or the outrageous claim that Farooq, the ultimate male chauvinist, shared Michael's views on women.

Michael had already decided that he couldn't risk letting Collin in on the truth about Farooq's call. Because of his position as head of the Counter Terrorism Center, Collin's phone line was swept weekly for bugs and line taps and Michael's cell phone couldn't be monitored except by chance. Still, on the faint off chance that someone was listening in to their conversation, Michael knew he couldn't afford even to hint at what was really going on. Which was that he would bet his ass—in fact he *was* betting his ass—that Farooq had made the arrangement for this meeting under pressure from the real American traitor.

"It should be fairly easy for Justice to put together a case that will hold up in court," Michael said. "Farooq claims to have all the proof we could possibly need to put Dick Pedro behind bars for the rest of his life."

Collin was a smart man, a really smart man. When he hung up the phone and had a moment to reflect, he might realize that Michael's end of their conversation had been off-key. Collin had never been persuaded of Dick Pedro's guilt. He and Michael had argued the pros and cons several times over the past couple of weeks. Given that background, if Michael really believed Farooq's claims, he would have squeezed out a few seconds to deliver a couple of zingers, reminding his boss that he'd been right all along.

It was a slender hope that Collin would pick up on the discrepancy. For Dick Pedro's sake, if for no other reason, Michael knew he had to get out of this damn meeting alive, or the poor guy might end up spending the rest of his life in federal prison for crimes he hadn't committed. While the real traitor laughed and chortled his way through a life of luxurious beachfront exile.

Whatever Collin might pick up on after the call ended, right now his attention was fixed on Michael's safety. "You're taking a huge risk meeting Farooq without backup," he said. "I know you trust Farooq, but there's Dick Pedro to worry about. How do you know he isn't hot on Farooq's trail? You could end up right in the middle of a battle between the two of them."

Dick Pedro wasn't hot on Farooq's trail because Dick Pedro was a dumb-ass bureaucrat who was so far out of the loop that he didn't have the faintest clue he was being set up. The poor guy wouldn't have taken even a baby step to protect himself from a false accusation. Michael was quite sure that the documents Farooq was about to give him would show that Pedro had an offshore bank account in his name with at least half a million bucks in it. Half a million, or even a million, to set up a scapegoat would be no more than a piddling drop in the bucket to the real traitor. The bastard was, after all, currently racking up tax-free profits at the rate of a couple of million dollars an hour.

No, Michael thought. He wasn't in any danger from Dick Pedro. And the real American traitor wasn't going to kill him for a very good reason: he needed somebody to carry all his carefully manufactured pages of "proof" back to the authorities. If the real traitor was going to enjoy his retirement free of even a breath of suspicion, he needed to have a substitute traitor identified and convicted. That meant he needed to have somebody alive who knew Farooq well enough to swear in a court of law that the documents proving Dick's guilt were authentic and came from an impeccable source. All things considered, Michael was confident he wasn't facing much of a risk at this meeting, provided he managed to perform the delicate balancing act between appearing too gullible and too skeptical.

The person in danger of dying was Farooq.

Even at five in the morning, the supermarket parking lot had thirteen cars in it, reinforcing Michael's view that he wasn't being set up for an assassination attempt. If they wanted to kill him, there were a lot of better places to have chosen as a meeting place.

He got out of the car and the wind whipped around him, carrying the sting of snow on its breath. The tall perimeter halogen lamps cast a harsh, yellow glare but not much light, increasing the impression of chill desolation. Michael stood by the car door, not moving, his gaze raking the lot. After a three-minute wait—he could see the clock on a nearby bank building—the driver's door on a white Toyota Camry parked in the next aisle opened.

Farooq stepped out, a briefcase in his left hand. He held his right arm well away from his overcoat, his gloved hand extended to show that he carried no weapon of any sort. Slowly, he walked away from the supermarket building, toward the end of the short row of vehicles.

Michael squinted, trying to get a glimpse inside the Camry, but the windows were tinted to obscure all view of the interior. Even without seeing inside, though, it was a safe bet to conclude that Farooq might have driven the car, but he hadn't come here alone. Pretty safe to conclude also that Farooq would be wired for sound, so that The American could be sure he said just what he was supposed to say and nothing more.

Michael could have slid between two cars and immediately been in the same parking aisle as Farooq. Instead, he avoided making any movement that might seem unpredictable and walked the longer way around the cars, heading toward the same point as Farooq, both his arms held away from his body, his gloved fingers spread wide to prove that his hands were empty. Just as if neither he nor Farooq knew that there was room in the bulky sleeves of their coats to hide enough explosives to blow away the entire parking lot and half the neighboring street as well.

This encounter had definitely been set up and choreographed by The American, Michael thought with morbid humor. Only a desk jockey who'd watched too many Cold War spy movies could possibly think that this was the way twenty-first century terrorists and undercover agents conducted their business.

By unspoken consent, Michael and Farooq stopped

when they were about six feet apart. Michael slowly lowered his arms. "I've been wondering what happened to you," he said quietly. "How long have you been back in the States?"

"Not very long. The information I sought in Germany was difficult to find."

"Yes, I'm sure it was." Had Farooq actually met with Gunther, Michael wondered. Did he know who the American traitor really was? "I'm sorry about the death of your brother," he said, hoping Farooq would understand that, at least in this, his comment was entirely sincere. "You know that if I could have prevented it, I would have."

"Yes." Farooq's voice was a bleak as his expression. He made an abrupt gesture, changing the subject. "To be honest, Michael, I'm surprised you're here. I wasn't sure you would be willing to hand over the key, even in exchange for the documents I've managed to acquire."

"Precisely how did you acquire them, by the way? Their provenance will be important in the case my government will bring against Pedro."

"I got them from Gunther. He called them his insurance policy."

"How did you persuade Gunther to part with them?" He needed to ask these questions, Michael decided, or he would sound much too trusting.

Farooq shrugged. "I pointed out that if he was dead, his insurance policy would have no value to him."

Michael gave a humorless laugh. "And no doubt you explained that if he didn't hand them over, he would be dead very soon."

"Precisely." Farooq gave a fleeting smile, but the cloak of sadness soon draped over him again. "Did Verity Marlowe give you the key to my safety deposit box?" he asked. "Is that how you acquired it?"

"Yes. She has absolutely no idea what it's worth, or what is in the box."

"Unlike you. Since you know precisely how much the key is worth, even if you don't know where the box is located, I repeat that I am surprised at your willingness to cut a deal." Farooq tipped his head to one side. "Facilitating the sale of nuclear weapons to Iraq? That hardly fits your squeaky-clean image, Michael."

"It's been a good few years since I believed choices were either all good or all bad. Nowadays I realize that most of the time we're simply choosing between the lesser of two evils." Michael shrugged. "If Saddam Hussein doesn't get functioning nuclear missiles from you, he'll starve a few more thousand children and get them from somebody else. On the other hand, I want Dick Pedro behind bars, and I want it bad. The slimy little son of a bitch has been making a horse's ass out of the United States government quite long enough. Besides, he must be the man who gave Yousaf the orders to have us killed. That makes it real personal."

Farooq pushed the briefcase over the gritty surface of the parking lot toward Michael. "It is not locked," he said. "Do you want to check out the material?"

"Of course." Never taking his eyes from Farooq—and he wasn't sure how much of that was playacting for the benefit of any possible watcher in the Toyota, and how much of it was instinctive caution—Michael bent down and picked up the briefcase. He set it down on the trunk of the nearest car and gestured for Farooq to open it. If it was wired to explode, he didn't want to be the person blown away.

Farooq opened the case with an ironic flourish, then stepped away, leaving Michael to rifle through the contents. The very top sheet was a copy of a September 1999 statement from a bank in the Cayman Islands, showing a balance of $2,870,000. Michael had no doubt that the papers stapled to the back of this incriminating document proved that Dick Pedro was the name behind the anonymous account number. No doubt, either, that the almost three-million-dollar balance had been whittled down by now to a modest half million or so. But that wouldn't weaken the case against Pedro; it would merely convince the prosecutors that good ole Dick had been living high on the hog.

There were plenty of bills in the package, evidence of Dick's supposedly extravagant spending habits, and—as if that weren't enough—the stupid prick had managed to get himself photographed in a sexual situation that involved himself and two very young naked women. There were also pictures of Dick going into a bank building in the Cayman Islands, and another shot of him going into a bank in Zurich, Switzerland. Those two photos were dated the previous January and mid-July and the negatives were attached to prove they weren't the result of electronic wizardry.

The poor shit had obviously been in The American's sights as fall guy for at least a year, Michael reflected.

"These are amazing documents," he said, lowering the lid of the briefcase and snapping the locks closed.

"Yes." Farooq inclined his head. "Even I had not expected Gunther to be so very well-informed. Anyway, you see that I have lived up to my part of the bargain. Now, if you please, I need my key."

"It's stuck to my rib cage with a Band-Aid." Michael moved his hand slowly toward the front of his coat. "Do you want me to reach under my clothes to get it? Or will you?"

"Either option poses risks," Farooq said. "If you reach inside your coat, you could pull out a gun. If I approach you closely enough to take the key, you could attempt to overpower me.''

"True, I could do either of those things, but I won't.'' Michael spread his hands. "Your choice, my friend.''

A gun suddenly appeared in Farooq's left hand, slipped from his sleeve in a fluid maneuver they'd both learned from Yousaf. The gun was rock steady, and aimed straight at Michael's heart.

"Open your coat slowly,'' Farooq ordered. "Then raise your sweater and allow me to see the key before you attempt to hand it to me.''

Michael followed the instructions with slow, careful movements. Willing himself not to shiver, he lifted his sweater and T-shirt, revealing the Band-Aid taped to his rib cage and the key protruding on either side. "Satisfied?'' he inquired laconically.

"Satisfied.'' Farooq's gaze locked on to Michael's, and if they had not spent months together evading Indian soldiers in the mountains of Kashmir, he would never have noticed the almost nonexistent jerk of Farooq's head, much less the swift flick of his gaze toward the Toyota and then back to Michael.

As it was, accustomed to silent signals in the pristine, rarefied air of the Kashmir mountains, where every sound carried for miles, Michael could guess what he was silently being asked to do. If he stepped to his left and twisted his body angle just fractionally, he would be facing squarely toward the side of the Toyota. Which meant that when Farooq stretched out his right hand to receive the key, his back would block any view of the actual transaction for an observer seated in the rear of the Toyota.

Michael made the slightest turn and eased leftward. "I'm freezing my fucking balls off here, Farooq. Will you take the damn key already?''

"Make no sudden moves," Farooq ordered, using his teeth to tug off his right glove. He would need the added flexibility of bare fingers in order to take the key without fumbling. "We neither of us want to precipitate an unfortunate accident."

Michael ripped off the Band-Aid and held out the key in the palm of his hand. Farooq stepped forward fractionally, then reached out and grabbed the key. In its place he left a tiny, damp wad of cellophane that he had taken from his mouth when he removed his glove. Michael didn't allow his expression to alter by so much as the shimmer of an eyelash as he let his hand drop, the cellophane wedged between his index and middle fingers.

Farooq changed position again, the movement subtle and seemingly unstudied. The man in the car could now see him examining the key. "It looks like the correct one. You know that there will be consequences for both you and Verity Marlowe if you've tried to deceive me."

"Yeah, I understand. Can I pull my sweater down before the supermarket manager comes out and tells us to rent a room?"

Farooq inclined his head. "You may button your coat now. I will escort you back to your car."

"I suppose it's useless to suggest that you should turn yourself in and allow me to request political asylum for you."

Farooq laughed. "So that I can be slaughtered like my brother, Khalid? I thank you for your generous offer, Michael, but I regret I must refuse." He tapped the key against the side of his gun. "Besides, I have a customer waiting for a delivery. As you very well know."

"The fact that you've given me this material on Dick Pedro is only going to buy you so much protection," Michael said. "You know that the U.S. government is going to be looking for you in force. Along with Interpol and half the armed forces of India.''

"Yes, I know.'' Farooq's tone of voice was as abrupt as his words.

Michael's offer of political asylum had been genuine. The bitterness of Farooq's response had probably been equally genuine. Two rare moments of honesty in a conversation filled with half truths.

Michael picked up the briefcase and walked the thirty yards to his car, Farooq following a couple of paces behind. He assumed Farooq now had the gun aimed at his spine, but he had no way of knowing for sure. Anyway, he was convinced Farooq would do everything in his power to avoid firing.

Just as they reached Michael's car, two trucks pulled into the parking lot, engines revving. Jesus, Michael prayed. Don't let Collin Krenz have gone crazy and sent in the Marines.

He froze, and felt Farooq freeze behind him, until the trucks came to a stop near the supermarket entrance. A couple of scrawny young men climbed out of the cabs. One of them tossed the other a pack of cigarettes and the two of them walked into the supermarket without sparing either Farooq or Michael a glance. Farooq made no sound, but the wave of relief coming from his direction was almost tangible.

In other circumstances, Michael would have laughed at how hard they were both playing tough guys to impress the watcher in the car, while simultaneously trying to make sure that nothing happened to precipitate violence. "Do I have permission to get into my car?'' Michael asked dryly. "I hate to break up the party, but time is marching on. We need to say goodbye before this place is swarming with the coffee-and-donuts crowd.''

"Please, be my guest.'' Farooq swept his hand toward

the car, indicating Michael should get in. For a second
he allowed Michael to glimpse the rage that was consuming him, barely held in check. Confirmation, if Michael
had needed it, that his former partner was participating
in this charade under extreme duress. Farooq's voice,
however, was mild as he said goodbye. A necessary concession if he was wearing a wire. "Good luck in your
prosecution of Mr. Pedro. Forgive me if I take this opportunity to remind you that if he isn't convicted, my life
isn't worth a bucket of spit. I sincerely hope you nail the
bastard."

"You can count on me." Michael said. An answer
loaded with multiple layers of meaning.

"I know I can." Farooq sent him one last intense look,
then turned and walked back to the Toyota.

Michael didn't seem to have a tail for the homeward
journey. Even so, he waited until he was safely inside
the garage before he unwrapped the little wad of folded
cellophane that Farooq had given him. Inside the cellophane was a scrap of paper the size of a postage stamp.
On one side the word *Andrew* was written across the
diameter. On the other side was written the word *Breitman.*

Andrew Breitman. The real American traitor.

Twenty-One

Verity had gone through some trying times over the past few months, but the hour while she waited for Michael to return from his meeting with Farooq ranked right up there among the most unpleasant. Michael had left the house believing that Farooq could be trusted; Verity knew that he couldn't. The noose that held Ali captive was heavy-duty, double-purpose, snaring Farooq along with his younger brother. What did that mean in terms of Farooq's likely behavior?

Just thinking about Dick's treachery made Verity wild. She visualized the death of George Douglass and the terrified students held hostage at the American school in Bombay. Then she recalled the assassination scene outside the hotel, with Khalid dying in her arms, and three other people losing their lives simply because they tried to do their duty. Her hands turned to claws as she paced. Knowing that Dick had manipulated fanatical members of the Freedom Party into carrying out his murderous plans made her want to run screaming to his house to confront him. For the first time in her life, she could understand how one human being could knowingly choose to inflict pain on another. Right at this moment, she didn't think it would be safe to leave her alone in a room with Dick-the-infamous-Prick.

Since she couldn't attack Dick Pedro, she cleaned her teeth, tidied the bathroom and then made the bed, simply because she had to do something physically active or jump out of her skin. With those chores completed, and at least another twenty minutes left before she could hope to see Michael again, she went down to the kitchen to brew a pot of coffee. Anything to distract her too vivid imagination.

The ritual of brewing coffee was soothing and, as she took her first scalding sip, her thoughts stopped skittering in twenty different directions and suddenly focused on a huge flaw in her theory that Kalil Mustafa was simply a false name for Ali Muhammad. If Dick Pedro had been working in partnership with the Kashmir Freedom League for several years, he was not only totally amoral, he was also brilliantly clever. He was also the puppet master pulling Yousaf's strings. But if Yousaf was holding Ali Muhammad prisoner at the American School, why in the world had Farooq arranged to hand over evidence that would prove Dick Pedro's guilt? If Farooq was in Dick Pedro's power, surely they should both be striving their utmost to divert suspicion from Dick, not attract it.

How had she managed to overlook such an obvious defect in her theory? Verity set down her coffee mug, cradling her hands around its reassuring solidity. If she was correct in her identification of Ali, there was only one reason for Farooq to hand over "conclusive" proof of Dick Pedro's guilt. Poor old by-the-book Dick was not only innocent, he was being set up to take the fall for the real traitor.

Her logic seemed inescapable, however many times Verity tested it. Should she call Dick and warn him what was going on? She dismissed that idea in a couple of seconds. No, of course she couldn't call him. Her conviction that he was an innocent man was derived solely from the fact that Farooq's brother was being held hostage at the American school. If she happened to be wrong about Kalil's true identity, then calling Dick Pedro would be a disaster of major proportions. There was nobody else she could call, either, since if Dick wasn't the traitor, then anybody she chose to confide in could be precisely the wrong person.

Verity finally understood at firsthand something of the dilemma Khalid had faced, and why he'd insisted on having her brought to the hotel. It was almost impossible to function in a world where you had to question every premise and suspect everyone around you of treachery.

It was some consolation to realize that if she was right in her deductions, at least Michael wasn't at all likely to get killed this morning. Still, doing nothing when she had so many new insights percolating was almost more than she could handle. She paced the kitchen, drank another mug of black coffee which her churning stomach turned into instant acid, and was just about ready to explode from nervous tension when she heard the sounds of the garage door opening.

She opened the connecting door into the garage and saw Michael still sitting in his car. He got out at once and strode toward her. "Thank God you're back safely. Michael, I've got so much to tell you—"

"My meeting with Farooq went fine," he interrupted. "I told you there wouldn't be a problem." He took her into his arms and propelled her back into the kitchen, whispering in her ear as they walked. "Watch what you say. The house may be bugged. Possibly a camera, as well."

Bugged? *With cameras?* Verity stepped back from him, trying so hard to act naturally that even her breathing felt stilted. "I...er...made some coffee. Would you like some?" Acting, she thought wryly, was probably not her strongest suit.

"Love some. Just a quick mug, though." Michael sounded a tad overhearty as he crossed to the fridge and found milk, although he was presumably much more accustomed to role-playing than she was.

Michael poured himself coffee. "Well, I have good news to report. Farooq and I skirmished a bit, but on the whole, the meeting went great. He's really delivered the goods for us." Michael patted the briefcase he'd brought in with him from the car. "Inside this baby is everything the Justice Department could need to bring a really strong case against Dick Pedro." His eyes sparked with momentary laughter. "You might say his conviction is in the bag."

Camera or no camera, Verity rolled her eyes. "That's great, honey. I'm so glad you were right when you told me there wouldn't be any danger for you."

Their dialogue sounded like a cross between a B movie and an episode of *The Honeymooners,* but anybody listening in to their conversation wasn't likely to be a member of the Good Guy team and they needed to play safe. Stifling a sigh, Verity realized it wouldn't be smart to mention the great revelation she'd had in the shower until after they left the house.

She sent Michael a smile that she hoped didn't look as fake as it felt. "I expect you're anxious to get to the office and hand the material over to the right people. After my experience with having my home ransacked, you won't want to run the same risk."

"I sure don't. In fact, we want to avoid any possible mishap now that we're this close to nailing Dick Pedro."

"Could you drop me off at Foggy Bottom before you go on to Langley? I know it's miles out of your way, but I need to get into the office and get a head start on the day. Unfortunately, the school hostage situation won't resolve itself just because we know Dick Pedro is the mastermind who planned it all.''

"Of course I'll drop you off," Michael said, draining his coffee. "It would cost a fortune to get a cab from here. Are you ready to leave right now? Traffic was already starting to build up."

She nodded. "I'm ready. I'll get my coat."

"I need to get gas," Michael said, as soon as they were in his car. He pointed to his gas gauge, which indicated a nearly full tank. "There's a service station at the end of the block, and I'll stop there."

Was it really possible that his car was bugged, too? Or had Michael developed a sudden raging attack of paranoia? Verity decided to err on the side of caution and talked about nothing except the weather for the two minutes it took to reach the service station, which had a small attached coffee shop.

Michael and Verity each picked up a bottle of water and a dubious-looking packaged muffin. "Sorry," he said, sliding into the seat on the other side of the rickety plastic table opposite her. "I know we both sounded like idiots back at the house, but when Farooq called this morning he claimed that both my house and my phone line were bugged. I think he was lying, but I couldn't take the risk."

"I understand. I'm glad you stopped me saying anything because I have some big news." Verity realized she had goose bumps she was so anxious to explain her theory. "Michael, I know—I think I know—who Kalil Mustafa really is. He's Ali Muhammad, brother to Khalid and Farooq."

"My God." Michael stared at her with a gratifyingly stunned expression. "How sure are you?"

"Pretty damn sure. Remember, I spent hours studying Ali's picture yesterday, trying to remember where I'd seen him before. In fact, I hadn't seen him since he was a little kid. What was haunting me wasn't a memory of Ali himself. It was his family likeness to Farooq at the same age.''

Michael appeared more dubious now that he knew what her identification was based on. ''I've worked alongside Farooq for months, and I didn't pick up on any massive family resemblance.''

''I understand why. I saw the picture of Farooq put out by Interpol, and I agree he doesn't look much like Ali now. But I knew Farooq when he was eighteen or nineteen, and I'm telling you the similarity is striking. Think about it, Michael. It would explain why Kalil's family never stepped forward to ransom him. The instant Farooq heard that Yousaf had taken over the American School in Bombay, he would have known that his brother was doomed unless he took action. Farooq probably sent frantic messages to his relatives telling them not to react, not to reveal that Kalil was really Ali. He must have contacted Yousaf at the same time, promising to do whatever it took to get his brother released. Don't you see? It all makes perfect sense.''

''Yes, it does.'' Michael looked at Verity with undisguised admiration. ''You're one very smart woman, you know.''

''But wait, there's more!'' She hadn't meant to sound like a TV commercial, but she was so anxious to explain the rest of her theory that she could feel the words jostling and shoving to order themselves in her brain. ''Michael, this is the really important part. If Farooq is trying to ransom his little brother from Yousaf, why in the world would he give you proof that Dick Pedro is a traitor? There's only one possible reason. He's being blackmailed into doing it. Which means that whatever so-called proof

Farooq may have given you, however damning it may appear on the surface, Dick Pedro has to be innocent.''

"I completely agree—''

"No, honestly, Michael, if you think some more you'll see it all makes sense—'' She broke off. "Did you say you agree with me?''

"Yes. In fact, from the moment Farooq first called me, I already had an idea he wasn't arranging this meeting of his own free will because he spoke to me in English, which was one of our agreed codes for indicating trouble. Then, at the actual meeting, everything about his behavior was designed to let me know that the information he was giving me couldn't be trusted.''

"Oh.'' Verity felt a trifle deflated. "And here I was thinking I was galloping to the rescue with my brilliant deductions—''

"You were.'' Michael briefly covered her hand with his. "You provided an explanation and a motive as to why Farooq would do this. And your insights *were* brilliant.'' He shot her a tiny smile. "Are you sure Sam didn't pay you a visit and give you a few hints?''

She returned his smile. "Not this time.'' She finally ate a piece of muffin, ignoring the cardboard taste as part of her campaign to gain five pounds in the next month. "Dick Pedro is a pain in the rear end, but he doesn't deserve to be arrested on trumped-up charges. On the other hand, you've got a mass of documentary evidence that can't be ignored. How are you going to handle this?''

"That's easy,'' Michael said. "I'm going to take you to meet my boss. I need to tell him that before our meeting was over, Farooq had managed to slip me a scrap of paper that identified Andrew Breitman as the real traitor we've been looking for.''

Verity choked on her muffin.

* * *

If Verity had expected the head of the Counter Terrorism Center to look even remotely like James Bond in any of his incarnations, she would have been seriously disappointed. Collin Krenz looked like a balding jockey who'd lost the battle of the waistline bulge. However, the energy of his quicksilver movements and the powerful intelligence of his gaze more than made up for his small stature. He listened without comment while Verity explained how and why she believed Kalil Mustafa was really Ali Muhammad, and that with his brother held captive, Farooq's identification of Dick Pedro as a traitor couldn't be trusted.

Collin thanked her for her input, then turned to Michael. "I assume you agree with her speculations, otherwise you wouldn't have brought her here."

"Yes, I strongly agree with Verity's conclusions."

A raised eyebrow suggested that Collin was quite well aware that Michael had substituted the word *conclusions* for *speculations,* but he made no verbal comment. "Tell me what happened this morning with Farooq," he said.

Michael gave a crisp report and Collin again listened in silence, at least until Michael reached the point where he explained about the note with Andrew Breitman's name on it, and then pushed the tiny cellophane package across the desk so that Collin could examine it himself.

Collin perched a pair of glasses on the end of his nose, which gave him the appearance of one of Santa's elves, posing for a Christmas card. He extracted the postage-stamp-size note from the cellophane with a pair of tweezers, reading first one side, then the other.

He put the note carefully back in its nest of cellophane. "So let me get this straight," he said with ominous mildness, peering over his glasses first at Michael and then at Verity. "On my left side here, I have a briefcase stuffed to the brim with documents indicating Secretary Pedro is guilty of treason. There are photocopies of illegal bank accounts, compromising photos, deeds showing that he owns property in at least five different countries. And on my right here, I have a scrap of something that looks like birdcage liner on which the name Andrew Breitman is written in blurred ink. According to both of you, the birdcage liner is proof positive of Mr. Breitman's guilt. The comprehensive collection of incriminating documents, however, merely underscores Secretary Pedro's total innocence.''

His sarcasm was acid enough to etch metal, and Verity barely avoided squirming in her chair. Michael, however, flashed his boss a friendly smile. "Yeah, you got it, Coll. Breitman's our man."

"Hmm." Collin steepled his fingers under his chin. "Then what the hell are we going to do about it?"

Michael leaned forward in his chair. "Arrest Dick Pedro would be my first suggestion."

Collin nodded. "I don't see any way to avoid that. Breitman will be waiting to hear that we've acted on this impressive pile of evidence he's provided for us. He'll know his ruse hasn't worked if Pedro isn't arrested by the end of the day, and that would spook him into running."

"There's also the matter of Farooq and the guidance software for Saddam Hussein's nuclear missiles," Michael said. "With all the money Breitman is raking in right now from the hostages, I assumed he wouldn't give a damn about a failed deal that was never going to net him more than half a million bucks after expenses. I've revised my opinion on that. We all know Saddam's military men have been demanding nuclear toys to play with, so the Iraqis may be harassing Breitman enough that he's worried about his chances of survival if he doesn't deliver the goods. The fact that Ali was paraded in front of

the world with a noose around his neck suggests Breitman was real anxious for Farooq to break cover.''

Scowling, Collin reached for a pack of antacid tablets.
He stuffed a half dozen into his mouth and crunched.
''Obviously, it would be very bad news if Breitman man-
aged to get that particular package to Baghdad.''

''You mean the key Khalid gave me has something to
do with Saddam Hussein's arsenal of nuclear weapons?''
Verity nearly choked. ''Oh, my God.''

Michael gave her back an encouraging pat or two.
''The good news is that Saddam's missiles are currently
nonoperational because they have no guidance software.
The guidance software is in Farooq's box, which is hidden God knows where, protected by an explosive device
wired to the lock. The rest of the good news is that the
key I handed over to Farooq this morning was a duplicate, not the original one Khalid gave you.''

''What difference does it make if it's a duplicate?''
Verity asked.

Michael and Collin both looked pleased with themselves. ''We had the duplicate cut here on the premises
as soon as Michael brought it in to me yesterday,'' Collin
said. ''Our senior locksmith assures us that the key Michael gave Farooq this morning was just enough off the
mark that it won't open his box.'' He reached in his
drawer and pulled out a plastic tray containing four identical keys. ''As you can see, we thought ahead and got
the locksmith to make us a handy collection of nonfunctional duplicates if we should happen to need them.''

''But you just said the box is wired to explode if it's
tampered with,'' Verity protested. ''Won't it blow up if
Farooq tries to insert the wrong key?''

''It could.'' Michael said tersely. ''It depends on the
type of trigger used in the explosive.''

''But that means Farooq...'' She stopped.

"Might get killed," Collin said. "I'm sorry, but I consider the death of one man with a murky past a preferable alternative to giving Saddam Hussein the guidance software for a nuclear weapons system."

Verity, who had a hard time setting mousetraps, knew that Collin and Michael had made the right decision. Still, she hoped very much that she wasn't going to hear in a couple of days that pieces of Farooq had been scraped off the walls of some bank vault or other.

"Where's the real key to Farooq's box?" she asked. "The one Khalid gave me."

"In an Agency safe with a time lock, and strictly limited access," Collin said. "After all, we're talking about software that can activate weapons of mass destruction. Obviously we weren't going to allow Michael or anyone else to wander around the city with the real thing, even if we don't have a clue where Farooq has hidden the damn lockbox."

"Okay, bottom line," Michael said. "We have two problems here. First, we need to think of some way to get proof that Andrew Breitman is our traitor. Proof that a court would find a little more convincing than a scrap of paper with his name scratched on it. Second, we need to find Farooq's box before Andrew can get to it. Do either of you have an idea in hell how we might accomplish those two things?"

Collin looked glum, but didn't speak. Verity cleared her throat. "I have an idea," she said.

Twenty-Two

The three of them spent half an hour brainstorming the various problems and loopholes that had to be covered before Verity's plan might work. "We're discussing this to death," she said finally. "You have to trust me to wing it if I need to. It's already nine-thirty and at last report, there were only twenty-six students still waiting to be ransomed. Andrew's raked in millions by now. He could decide to cut his losses and make a run for it at any moment. Literally any moment."

"I agree," Collin said with sudden firm decision. "We have an extremely narrow window of opportunity here, so I'm going to give Breitman what he wants. I'm going to set the wheels in motion to get Secretary Pedro arrested."

Verity turned to Michael as soon as his boss left the room. "What's wrong, Michael? You've been unusually silent these last few minutes."

He walked over to the window and stared at the wintry landscape for a few seconds before replying. "I'm letting my imagination run riot. Visualizing all the possible ways in which Andrew might be able to surprise us all and do you harm."

Verity closed the gap between them, laying her head against his chest. His arms tightened around her and she felt his lips brush against her hair. "Give your imagination a rest," she said softly. "I'm not meeting with Yousaf out in the high plains of Kashmir. I'll be dealing with Andrew Breitman, within earshot of a dozen people. He can't possibly get into the State Department buildings carrying a weapon, so what could happen? Besides, Andrew seems to like his violence and killing at a safe distance, with other people doing the dirty work. Don't worry, Michael. Everything will be fine.''

At two-thirty that afternoon, the chief of security for the State Department called an urgent meeting of the people who reported to Dick Pedro: diplomats, clerks, the division accountant and Dick's personal assistant, an elderly woman approaching retirement. There were a total of thirty-eight people crowded into the small room as the security chief announced the shameful news that Secretary Richard T. Pedro had been arrested, charged with committing acts of high treason. The precise charges leveled against him were classified, but the security chief indicated that Mr. Pedro had allegedly been involved in brokering illegal arms sales to hostile nations, and also to aiding and abetting the hostage taking at the American School in Bombay.

The scope of Pedro's treachery was huge and the security breaches enormous—and all too newsworthy. The chief warned that the media was likely to descend on the State Department in force. People who had worked with Secretary Pedro would be hotly pursued for interviews and comments. He instructed everyone in the room to refuse all interviews and to direct any journalists to his office.

Dick wasn't a popular man but, not surprisingly, his staff was devastated by the revelation of his treacherous double life. His secretary, whose husband had died in Vietnam thirty years earlier, was in floods of tears, protesting that there had to be a mistake, her boss wasn't capable of betraying his country. Andrew Breitman also seemed to be taking it hard, which was only to be expected, staffers agreed, given the number of years the two men had worked together.

Verity caught up with Andrew as the disconsolate group filed out of the briefing room. "I'm not sure if I can take any more bad news this week," she said. "First George Douglass dies, then Khalid is gunned down along with three other victims. Then those poor kids in Bombay are taken hostage. Now this. What more could possibly happen?"

"India or Pakistan could accidentally launch a nuclear weapon?" Andrew suggested. He rubbed his hand across his forehead. "Jesus, this has really knocked me for a loop. I can't seem to wrap my mind around the image of Dick Pedro brokering arms deals with terrorists and criminals. Can you?"

She shook her head, then couldn't resist adding, "To be honest, he never struck me as smart enough to lead a double life."

"He sure fooled both of us, didn't he?" Andrew sounded convincingly bitter.

They'd reached the door of Verity's office, which was across the hallway from Andrew's.

"Come down to the cafeteria and have a cup of coffee with me," she said, trying to make the request sound like a spur-of-the-moment impulse. "I can't face going back into my office right now and you don't look as if you're doing too well, either."

"No, I'm not. To be honest, I'm...shattered by the news about Dick. We've worked together on and off for the best part of ten years and I didn't have a clue about the man he really was. But we both have desks piled high with work, so we can't let Dick's treachery get to us." He sent her a brave smile that was picture-perfect. "You know me, I'm the first person to mock all the boot licking and pomposity that infects this place. Still, at the end of the day, most of our colleagues are fine public servants and we can't allow ourselves to go to pieces because Dick Pedro betrayed us."

The skunk was going to make her vomit any minute now. Verity drew in a shaky breath. "I guess you're right." She was finding it a lot harder than she'd anticipated to keep her cool. She fought the urge to scream out accusations and aim blows anywhere she could land them on Andrew's murderous body.

"I don't seem to have as many emotional reserves to draw on as you do. Despite all the work waiting for us, I need to get away from my office, at least for a while." She forced herself to meet his gaze with an ingenuous smile. "Besides, I need to talk with you about a conversation I had with Khalid. And I'd like to keep it off the record."

She had to hand it to him. Andrew was looking straight at her and she detected nothing—absolutely nothing—in his gaze beyond professional interest. "You want to talk to me about Khalid Muhammad?" he queried mildly.

She nodded. "As you know, I spent a long time in the bedroom with him, supposedly talking to his wife. In actual fact, Miryam and I barely exchanged a greeting. I was talking the whole time with Khalid."

"You really should have reported this when it happened, Verity." Andrew arranged his features to project the image of a stern, but kind, boss. She had never noticed before how cleverly he managed always to express exactly the emotion and the image that was expected.

"I know." Her gaze was limpid. "But I've been so busy. I could have used a few thirty-hour days this past week."

"Me, too. Which is a reminder that we need to get back to work—"

"Don't be such a workaholic, Andrew. This building and the Counter Terrorism Center are crawling with people worrying about the situation in Bombay. They can spare us for twenty minutes." She forced herself to produce a cajoling smile and actually hooked her arm through his. "Come on, you could use a break as much as I could."

"Okay, you win." He gestured to indicate they should head toward the elevators. "You're right. I could use a break every bit as much as you."

She looked away from his smile because she couldn't bear to remember the respect she'd always felt for him. Not to mention all the times she'd sat around with this man—this monster—happily sharing the mundane events of her daily life. Fortunately there were other people in the elevator, so she didn't have to find anything to say to him as they rode down to the cafeteria.

Once at their destination, she couldn't prevent a quick glance around, wondering which of the customers were from the Counter Terrorism Center. She couldn't pick out anyone who shrieked FBI or CIA and she hoped like hell that Andrew couldn't, either.

They bought coffee and granola bars, and Verity led the way to a table in a corner. She'd been told to pick this one because it had been prewired to record their conversation. She'd also been reassured that security personnel would be stationed in close proximity, and have her clearly in view at all times. She tried not to let her thoughts wander in the direction of Khalid, who had also been under constant surveillance, right up to the second when he was shot dead.

Andrew bit into his granola bar, took a couple of

chews, then pulled a face. "This cafeteria is the pits. How do they manage to ruin food that comes in a package?"

"I don't know. They probably take special courses." Verity leaned across the table, lowering her voice. "How would you like to buy the guidance system for some nuclear missiles?"

Andrew didn't say anything, he merely looked puzzled. After a second or two of silence, he gave her a tentative smile. "Okay, Veri, go ahead. I'm waiting for the punch line."

"There is no punch line. I asked a serious question. I'd appreciate a serious answer."

His expression hardened. "I hate to ask this, Verity, but have you been drinking?"

"Yes. This is my third cup of coffee today."

He took another bite of granola bar, then tossed it aside. "This is really disgusting and the coffee isn't much better." He pushed his chair away from the table. "We should get back to work, Verity."

"You can't leave now," she said. "I have a story to tell you. Once upon a time there were three brothers. Their names were Khalid, Farooq and Ali Muhammad. They lived in a big house at the foot of a mountain. One day, Khalid came to Washington, D.C. and he insisted on speaking with his childhood friend, Verity, who worked for the State Department."

Andrew appeared bored. "If there's a point to this, please get to it."

"When Khalid first arrived at the hotel, he had his master bedroom professionally swept for electronic eavesdropping equipment. Then he installed his wife in the bedroom and forbade her to come out, even for a moment. That way, he could be sure whatever he said in the master bedroom would remain secret."

Andrew shrugged. "As it turns out, we know Khalid

had a right to be paranoid. After all, somebody was trying to kill him.''

''That would be you, of course, but you have to stop butting in, Andrew. You're spoiling my story. Khalid soon made an excuse to take me into his secure, bug-free master bedroom. Once we were there, he told me something very shocking. He told me that Andrew Breitman was a traitor who had been using the Kashmir Freedom Party to help in the purchase, sale and delivery of stolen weapons. Khalid also instructed me to say nothing about this to anyone until he could provide documentary proof. His brother, Farooq, was conferring with an arms dealer called Gunther in Eastern Germany, and would soon be able to provide all the evidence needed to put this traitor behind bars.''

''And that evidence obviously came into the government's hands today,'' Andrew said. ''Except that your friend Khalid made a mistake about the identity of the traitor. We know now that it's Dick Pedro.''

''Khalid made no mistake,'' Verity said flatly. ''Which is why I asked if you would care to purchase the guidance system for a set of nuclear missiles that were delivered to Saddam Hussein early in December and are now stored, depressingly nonfunctional, in one of his many secret military storage depots. I have a missile guidance system for sale if you're interested.''

Andrew's gaze rested on her consideringly. ''The charitable thing to say at this point is that you're mentally unbalanced.''

''Let's not play games, Andrew. You're desperate to get back the software Farooq took with him out of Kashmir when Yousaf bungled the orders to kill Farooq and Michael Strait.''

''I have no idea what you're talking about.''

''Oh, please! You know exactly what I'm talking

about.'' Verity pushed her hand across the table, palm down, stopping when the tips of her fingers reached halfway. ''This morning you got a key from Michael Strait in exchange for a briefcase full of documentation that supposedly proved Dick Pedro is a traitor.'' Slowly, she lifted her fingers just sufficiently to afford Andrew a glimpse of the oddly shaped, stainless steel key concealed under her hand. ''I find it ironic that the key you got was as fake as the documentation you invented to incriminate Dick Pedro.''

She had finally—finally!—managed to say something that caused Andrew to react. For a moment, his gaze narrowed and his jaw clenched. ''Did Michael know the key he gave me was fake?''

''No.'' She sighed. ''It never crossed poor Michael's mind that I might deceive him.''

''I heard that you and Michael were passionately in love. Why would you deceive him?''

''Because you heard wrong,'' Verity said. ''I was deeply in love with my husband, and I have no hope of ever replacing him. A woman is lucky to fall in love once in a lifetime and I've had my allocation of good luck. Michael is great in bed. End of story as far as he's concerned.''

Andrew dropped his gaze from her face to the key nestled beneath her fingers. ''I would like to examine that key you're holding more closely.''

''Be my guest.'' She pushed the key across the final few inches of table to his side. ''Look your fill. You can see that it's seemingly identical to the one Farooq acquired this morning. I assure you, however, that this is the key Khalid gave me. The one and only genuine original.''

Andrew snatched the key, holding it tight in his fist as if expecting her to grab it back. He realized belatedly that

he'd delivered a serious blow to his aura of imperturb-
ability and he tilted his head in a mocking salute, trying
to recover ground. "I appreciate your generous gift," he
said. "Thank you."

She smiled, although sweat was starting to pool in the
small of her back. This was the moment when Andrew
had to buy into her story. "Do you really think it's so
easy to outwit me, Andrew? You need to start taking me
more seriously. I wouldn't have let you anywhere within
touching range of that key if it still retained any useful
purpose whatsoever. It's the one Khalid gave me, but it
won't do you, or Farooq, or anyone else a lick of good."

"Why not?" Andrew demanded.

"Because I already went to the box, unlocked it and
removed the guidance software."

"How could you have gone to the box?" Andrew's
voice was low, but it throbbed with fury. "You have no
idea where it is."

"On the contrary. Khalid told me the location before
he died."

"No." Andrew's face tightened with suspicion. "No,
he couldn't have. In the hotel, when Khalid gave you the
key, you were baffled, you didn't know what it was for.
And there was no opportunity for him to speak to you
alone again after that."

"Listening in on Khalid's conversation with me, were
you, Andrew? What a nasty habit."

Verity kept her voice matter-of-fact, as if she weren't
desperately trying to explain away inconsistencies in her
story. "Khalid was terrified of being killed, you know
that. He was desperate to deflect some of the heat away
from himself and his family, and he begged me to help.
I agreed, partly because we're old friends, but mostly
because at that point I thought he was exaggerating the
problem. If you recall, Khalid deliberately transferred me

from the master bedroom to his sons' room, which we both knew was bugged. We'd been speaking in Kashmiri before, but we switched to English to make sure that you'd understand he no longer had the all-important key. For my part, I gave him an opening to say that he had no idea who the traitor was. Sadly, it was too late for our ploy. Your assassination orders were already signed and sealed and about to be executed.''

Unfortunately, Andrew didn't confirm that he had indeed ordered Khalid's death, which would have been enough for the FBI agents to move in and arrest him. In fact, although he hadn't exactly denied Verity's various accusations, he hadn't acknowledged them, either. Verity could almost hear a defense attorney pointing out that Andrew, as a loyal civil servant, had simply been trying to find out what Verity had done with a highly dangerous piece of military equipment. Nothing could have been further from his mind than treason.

''If you've opened Farooq's box, tell me where it was located,'' Andrew said.

''In a storage locker at Dulles Airport. Khalid put it there the moment he cleared Customs when he flew in from Frankfurt. Khalid gave me the key for the storage locker, too, but not when anyone was listening.''

''Dulles airport is not where Farooq claims the box is located.''

That surely inched a little closer to having Andrew say something incriminating. Verity spread her hands in a what-would-you-expect? type of gesture. ''Farooq is desperate to get his younger brother freed from Yousaf's clutches, as you and I both know. Ali with a noose around his neck makes for a pretty compelling reason for Farooq to try to please you.''

A hitch in Andrew's breathing was quickly covered, but Verity could see she'd scored another point. Andrew must be feeling that his clever secrets were unraveling in front of his eyes.

"Farooq isn't going to admit to you that he handed the guidance system over to Khalid while they were both in Germany," Verity continued. "And he certainly isn't going to admit that with his older brother dead, he no longer has any clue where that system might be. In fact, when you think about this from all angles, Andrew, you'll realize it's darn lucky Khalid decided to take me into his confidence. The result is that I have what you need to get Saddam Hussein's henchmen off your back. Best of all, I'm willing to sell it to you at a reasonable price."

"Why?" Andrew said. "Why are you willing to put yourself at risk of years in prison? Why not go for the glory of turning me in to the authorities?"

She stared at him as if she were having trouble comprehending the question. "For the money, of course. What else?"

"Didn't those missionary parents of yours instill any conscience into you at all?"

"Yes, they did, but you and I have often talked about how I never did accept their values. Besides, what's to feel guilty about? I don't believe Saddam is actually going to use these missiles. He just wants to have them so that he can swagger around the Middle East claiming he's got more dangerous toys than all the other little boys."

Andrew actually seemed to accept that she would believe something so ridiculous. Presumably because he'd started out in the illegal arms trade making precisely that sort of limp rationalization to himself.

"Okay, I agree that I might have some interest in what you're selling," he said finally. "What's your price?"

"One point five million dollars."

He gave a bark of laughter. "All right, Verity. Try again."

"One point seven five million dollars."

"Are you insane?" he asked, his voice biting.

"No, I'm a generous and reasonable woman, who would like to have a little bit of extra money to fix up my house, take a long vacation, and maybe buy a new car. Top up my retirement fund. I have you over a barrel, Andrew, but I'm not taking advantage of my leverage. If you don't get this guidance system shipped to Iraq within the next few days, you're going to find yourself stretched out on some pavement with a bullet in your head, deader than Khalid Muhammad. Don't be a fool and try to nickel and dime me. You and Yousaf have made millions of dollars over the past couple of days. Spend a tiny percentage of that to buy back the damn guidance system."

Andrew scooped the crumbs of his granola bar into a neat pile on top of its wrapper. Verity realized just how bizarre it was to be sitting across a Formica table in a dowdy cafeteria conducting a serious negotiation for the sale of nuclear weapons.

Andrew finally had the crumbs arranged to his satisfaction. "How soon could you deliver the guidance system to me?"

"How soon could you get me my money? I guess you must have a good system going. After the last couple of days, you ought to be quite accomplished at secret, illegal electronic money transfers."

Andrew glanced at his watch. "The banks will be opening soon in Australia, so I could take funds from an account there, but you don't want to bring the money into the States. That's asking for trouble for both of us."

Hallelujah! They had finally exchanged three or four sentences that Verity thought would be legally compromising. "No, of course I don't want you to send the money to a bank here in the States," she said. "I want you to set me up one of those nice, numbered accounts like you did for Dick Pedro."

"You're asking the impossible, Verity. Those accounts can't be set up on the basis of a few e-mails, and you want the money right away. I sure as hell want my guidance system right away."

"Then you tell me how we can make this work. I'm the novice here, and you're the expert."

"I have a numbered account at the Joffrey Bank in the Cayman Islands. Its current balance is right around a million five. Might be a hundred thousand more, or a hundred thousand less. I'll give you my pass codes, and you'll have immediate access to the funds. No questions asked." Andrew gave a smirk. "Post office box address okay. Fake names for the account holder not only accepted, but even expected."

Verity drew in a deep breath. "Okay, I accept, even though I'm taking the risk of getting a hundred thousand less than I hoped for. Do we have a deal? Approximately one point five million dollars from you in exchange for the nuclear missile guidance system from me."

"We have a deal," Andrew said.

Verity was facing out into the cafeteria and she saw two men appear in the doorway, blocking the exit. At the same moment, two African American women who were seated at a table in the center of the room sprang to their feet. A young man who was mopping the floor dropped his mop and pushed aside his pail. All three of them converged on Verity's table at a fast run.

One of the women got there first. She held up her badge. "I'm Agent Johnson, FBI, Counter Terrorism Center. Andrew Breitman, you're under arrest."

Twenty-Three

Michael and Collin were both waiting for Verity in the office of the State Department's Chief of Security. All three men wore beaming grins as she entered the room. Michael enveloped her in a bear hug. "You were wonderful, Verity."

"You seem to have a real talent for making lies sound like the truth," Collin said.

She laughed, feeling a little giddy. "Right now, I'll take that as a compliment."

"You should. That was impressive. Congratulations." Felix Mahler, the security chief, walked around his desk to shake her hand.

"Did I get strong enough statements from Andrew to ensure a successful prosecution?" Verity asked. "It was hard to get him to commit to saying anything compromising."

"What you got was enough to justify the arrest. Now we have to work on getting more evidence. We've already seized his laptop and we have agents en route to his home right now to start searching for anything more they can find."

Collin spoke up. "On a related front, you'll be pleased to hear Felix and I have approached the Justice Department and arranged for the charges against Dick Pedro to be dropped. His lawyer has already left to pick him up from jail."

"That's great. Although knowing Dick, he'll spend the rest of his life complaining about the fact that he was wrongly accused."

"Possibly not," the security chief said dryly. "As soon as he gets out of jail, he's going to be informed that he's been appointed ambassador to Spain. His grandparents immigrated from Barcelona and apparently this has been his lifelong career ambition, so he may consider a few hours in jail an acceptable down payment on the deal."

And his plodding approach to diplomacy could do very little harm in Spain, which wasn't exactly a flash point for world problems. Verity realized Michael still had his arm around her, and she leaned back against him, recognizing that she was close to exhaustion. The past several days had been seriously overcrowded with events and under-provided with sleep.

The security chief responded to his speakerphone's summons and a woman's voice spoke into the room. "Turn up the volume on your TV, Felix. They're broadcasting live from the school."

Felix complied and the sound of the CNN reporter's voice filled the room. "As you can see, Bernie, there's mass rejoicing here outside the gates of the American School. Family members are hugging and kissing the Indian soldiers as they escort the faculty members and the last of the hostage students to freedom. One of the female teachers seems to have a broken arm, several of the male teachers have black eyes and bloody noses, but they are alive, and that's cause for celebration. As you can imagine, the Indian army is euphoric at their success in liberating the school without any loss of life to the hostages."

"Is there any word yet on what's happened to the terrorists, Christianne?"

"We understand that Yousaf and seven other terrorists were captured alive. They're in custody at an unnamed location. Four of the terrorists were killed when the Indian special forces troops stormed the school. Seven Indian soldiers were wounded, but there are no deaths reported at this point among the rescuers."

"That's amazing, and it's certainly good news. Do we have any official statement on how this rescue was organized?"

"No official statement as yet, Bernie, although there are plenty of rumors! A senior military officer tells me that the Indian army learned of a system of disused water pipes that tunneled under the school. The army infiltrated special forces soldiers into these former water conduits, and the troops were able to exit from the tunnel system into a closet in the basement of the school building."

"It turned out great, but the army was taking a huge risk, weren't they?"

"Apparently the reason the army decided to risk sending in troops was concern for the safety of faculty members. Teachers are not people who have access to large sums of money, and hostage students who have been released over the past twenty-four hours reported that Yousaf and his men had not only refused to give the teachers food and water, they were beating them as well."

"The remaining student hostages are all in good shape physically, Christianne?"

"Tired, stressed and dehydrated, but otherwise okay. One student—" She glanced down at her notepad. "A student named Kalil Mustafa, the young man we first saw two days ago with a noose around his neck, seems to have been singled out for special punishment by Yousaf. Kalil is in the hospital, but he's reported to be in fair condition, with no lasting consequences from his injuries expected, according to a hospital spokesperson."

"We'll talk to you again soon, Christianne. Thank you." The link with Bombay was cut and the CNN desk anchor looked straight into the camera. "Good news for a lot of people coming out of Bombay, India at this hour. Stay with us. We'll be right back with more on the stunning climax to the school hostage situation."

Collin Krenz let out an unabashed whoop of sheer delight. "The Indian military must have brass balls. They sure were crazy to authorize a mission like that. Thank God they did."

Verity slumped against Michael, limp with relief and joy. "I didn't think there was any way we were going to save Ali," she said. "I've never been so happy to be wrong."

Michael's arms tightened around her. "You're trembling," he said quietly.

"Am I?" There was a little catch in her laughter. "It's been a rough few days, Michael. I think I'm about twenty minutes away from passing out from sheer exhaustion."

Michael gave a mock salute to his boss. "We're out of here, Collin. We'll check in with you again in a couple of days. Right now, Verity and I are going home."

"That sounds wonderful," she said.

Epilogue

Early February, 2000

Sunshine and brilliant blue skies gave the town of Asheville, North Carolina, a welcoming appearance, despite the withered grass and occasional patches of dirty, roadside snow. While Michael paid off the cab, Verity ran up the steps to her mother's house. Most people had barren yards at this time of year, but not Phyllis Hullman. Bright-red berries glowed on the holly bushes at the end of the path, and her narrow front porch was decorated with tubs of flourishing evergreens. A fragrant wreath of ivy, pine cones and eucalyptus circled the antique brass knocker, but before Verity had time to use it, her mother opened the door.

Phyllis, never demonstrative, gave Verity no more than a quick peck on the cheek, but her voice was husky with affection as she welcomed her daughter to Asheville. "You're looking a bit better than the last time I saw you," she said, stepping back and gesturing for Verity to follow her into the warmth of the tiny entrance hall. "The prospect of getting married seems to agree with you."

Verity grinned. "It does. The truth is, Mom, I'm head over heels in love with the guy."

Phyllis cast an openly curious glance to the end of the driveway where the cab had just driven off and Michael was walking at his usual fast stride toward the porch. "Hmm. Well, you've picked a handsome one this time, that's for sure. You said on the phone that he and Sam had been friends?"

"Close friends." Verity linked her arm through her mother's. "Michael's more than just a handsome face, Mom. He's a good man, too."

"I'm pleased to hear it." Phyllis's crisp, schoolteacher voice softened. "You certainly deserve some happiness after what you've been through recently."

Michael took the steps leading up to the door at a run, but Verity smiled to herself when she noticed that there was a momentary hesitation in his confident stride as he approached her mother. Michael might be able to face down terrorists and assassins without a blink. Meeting his prospective mother-in-law for the first time was a significantly more terrifying proposition.

Phyllis extended her hand, her gaze so intent she forgot to smile. "It's good to meet you, Michael. Welcome."

"It's good to meet you, too, Mrs. Hullman. Thanks for suggesting we should have the wedding ceremony here, even though it's such short notice. I know how happy Verity is about that."

"It's my pleasure." Phyllis finally smiled. "I'm looking forward to meeting your parents at dinner this evening. And one of your sisters is coming to the wedding, too, is that right?"

"Yes, my youngest sister, Sophie. She's taking the same flight out of Chicago as my parents."

"Have they arrived in town already, do you know?"

"Their plane should have landed about an hour before ours did," Michael said, following Phyllis and Verity into the living room. "I'll call the hotel in a moment and find out if they've checked in."

"Come into my garden room first to take a quick look

around. That's where I thought you'd like to hold the ceremony tomorrow.''

The glass-walled room that led off the tiny living room was heady with the scent of flowers and Verity drew in a deep, pleasurable breath. ''It's the perfect setting, Mom, thank you. You've worked miracles since I was here last. I can't believe you have daffodils blooming already. And hyacinths. And azaleas, too! How lovely everything looks.'' She sent her mother a rueful smile. ''I wish I'd inherited your green thumbs—or even a few cells from your green thumbs. Instead, I'm a certified plant killer.''

''I have been working quite hard,'' Phyllis acknowledged, pink-cheeked with pleasure at her daughter's compliments. ''This room has turned out rather well, hasn't it?''

''It's great. Dad would be so pleased.''

Phyllis turned to Michael to elaborate. ''When my husband and I bought this house four years ago, where we're standing now was nothing more than a ramshackle porch closed in by rusted screens. Right before he died, Jeremiah made me promise to go ahead with our plans to make this into the garden room of our dreams.'' Phyllis smiled a little wistfully. ''I like to imagine Jeremiah taking a peek at your wedding ceremony tomorrow afternoon and admiring the flowers—''

''Of course he will.'' Verity gave her mother's arm a quick squeeze. ''And he'll be admiring your azaleas, for sure. Remember how much he loved to sit in your garden in Srinagar?''

''Oh, yes, he did love that, didn't he? Especially in spring when the almond trees blossomed, and the azaleas were in full bloom...'' Her voice trailed off a little wistfully.

''Mom's azaleas were famous,'' Verity explained to Michael. ''She transformed the school gardens, too. She laid out a big vegetable patch, and all the students were required to spend at least half an hour a week working there. For a lot of the students, it was the only manual labor they'd ever been expected to do in their entire lives.''

''Speaking of Srinagar,'' Phyllis said, absentmindedly nipping a dead head from a cluster of daffodils, ''I must tell you before I forget. I had a visit last week from Farooq Muhammad.''

''From *Farooq?*'' Michael and Verity both spoke at once.

''Farooq was here with you?'' Michael said, looking stunned.

''What did he want?'' Verity asked.

''He wanted to reclaim a package he'd left in my keeping. Ah, that's where you got to, you wretched things.'' Phyllis picked up her garden shears from a spot on the windowsill partially obscured by budding tulips. She shook her head in exasperation. ''It's an absolute curse of growing older, you know. Somebody calls, you answer the phone, and before you know it, you've completely forgotten what you were doing before you took the phone call. These poor garden shears of mine end up in the oddest places.'' She snipped at an azalea, by some alchemy managing to make the foliage look thicker by cutting some leaves away.

''Mother, could we stick with the subject of Farooq Muhammad for a while?'' Verity tried not to sound brusque. ''You said he came to visit you last week. To reclaim a—package?''

''Yes, he did.'' Phyllis smiled. ''I always had a soft spot for Farooq when he was a student, you know, even though he exploited his good looks quite shamelessly. He's become even more charming as he's grown older.'' Her smile faded. ''Poor boy. He's facing a lot of trouble right now. He's taken the assassination of Khalid very hard, and then there was that terrible situation with his younger brother being held hostage. That would have been a strain on anyone's nerves. It certainly was on mine, so I can only guess how dreadful it must have been for Farooq.''

Michael's face was wiped clean of expression, a sure sign that he was hanging on to his self-control by a thread thinner than gossamer. ''Mrs. Hullman, you mentioned something about Farooq coming to pick up a package he'd left with you? What did that package look like exactly?''

Phyllis shrugged. ''Just your standard express package. FedEx, I believe it was. Farooq sent it to me from Germany, along with a note asking me to keep it for him until he had a chance to collect it in person.''

''Do you remember when the package was delivered here, Mom?''

''Yes, because it came the day after I got home from my cruise. That would be January 6.''

Michael and Verity exchanged shocked glances. ''Tell me that Farooq didn't send my mother the guidance system for Saddam Hussein's nuclear missiles,'' Verity said.

''He can't have done something so criminally irresponsible,'' Michael said. ''The software was in a box that was rigged to detonate if anyone tried to pry open the lock without using the proper key. He isn't reckless enough—vicious enough—to mail something so hazardous to an elderly lady he has every reason to like and respect.''

Phyllis flashed them a look of mild puzzlement. ''Are you suggesting that the package Farooq mailed to me might be dangerous?''

''It's possible,'' Michael acknowledged. ''But, thankfully, nothing bad happened while the package was in your possession. Although it's frustrating to know that Farooq's already visited here and collected the package. Very frustrating, in fact."

"But Farooq hasn't collected the package," Phyllis said. "That's the whole point. He's left it here for you and Verity. When I told him the two of you were getting married, he asked me to give you the package as a wedding present."

Verity stared at her mother, dumbstruck. Michael, by contrast, muttered a string of highly explicit curses in Kashmiri before stopping abruptly on the appalled realization that Verity's mother quite probably understood every word he'd said.

If Phyllis did understand, she decided to make it easier for everyone by pretending ignorance. "I put Farooq's package on the coffee table, so I wouldn't forget to give it to you. You can see it for yourselves."

Verity and Michael ran into the living room. Sure enough, an oversize padded envelope rested neatly on the coffee table.

"Do you think it's safe to touch?" Verity asked.

"I don't know." Michael knelt to take a closer look as Phyllis followed them into the living room. "Let's hope Farooq dismantled the explosives now that Andrew Breitman is behind bars."

"Oh, for heaven's sake!" Phyllis exclaimed. "Of course it's not rigged to explode." She grabbed the package from the table and showed them that the end of the envelope wasn't even sealed. "Heavens to Betsy, there's nothing very exciting inside here, I assure you. Farooq tells me it's a really fancy piece of computer software that's worth quite a lot of money, and a file of papers you need for some legal case you've both been working on." She held out the envelope. "Here, look for yourselves."

Verity removed a thick folder of documents from the envelope. Then she upended the envelope over Michael's cupped hands and shook until a small data disc in a transparent, sealed case fell into his grasp.

"It's got my initials scratched on the case. My God, I think we're looking at the guidance software for Saddam's nuclear missiles." Michael gave a quick, incredulous laugh.

"What's funny?" Verity asked.

Michael shook his head. "We've had governments and villains on three continents searching for this," he said. "And all the time it was here, in your mother's house, protected by nothing more than a padded mailing envelope."

"Right before he died, I think Khalid tried to tell me that my mother had the software," Verity said. "I asked him where Farooq was hiding, and he responded with some comments about my mother's gardens and azaleas. I shouldn't have been so quick to jump to the conclusion that he was rambling. As for the key Khalid gave me...I wonder what it opens?"

"Probably nothing of significance," Michael said. "Giving you that with such fanfare was simply a ploy to throw Andrew off balance." He gestured to the file she was holding. "What's inside there?" he asked.

Verity rifled through the pages inside the folder, handing them to Michael as she spoke. "Bank statements from various money-laundering havens in the Caribbean, photographs with attached negatives of Andrew Breitman in the company of various men and scantily clad women, along with a sheet that identifies those men as arms dealers and other dubious international traders Andrew definitely shouldn't have been meeting. Plus a five-page, single-spaced statement from Farooq detailing every arms deal he ever participated in. That statement is signed and notarized, by the way.'' She looked up, her forehead wrinkled with worry. "What in the world are we going to do with this, Michael?''

"I'm going to call Collin Krenz," he said. "Collin can send in the Marines, summon the FBI, come down here in person to pick it up or do all three of the above. As for me, I'm not available. I'm getting married.''

Verity smiled. "Me, too.''

Michael took her into his arms. "Yeah," he said softly. "You, too.''

USA *Today* Bestselling Author

GINNA GRAY

THE WITNESS

In the blink of an eye, the life of renowned concert pianist Lauren Brownly changed forever. She witnessed a grisly murder, and discovered a devastating truth: *Her career had been financed by the mob.* Now Lauren's testimony against crime boss Carlo Giovessi could finally bring him down.

Forced to trust FBI agent Wolf Rawlings, she is put into protective custody. With mob hitmen hot on their trail, Lauren and Wolf are desperately fighting for survival....

Available September 2001 wherever paperbacks are sold!

MIRA®

Visit us at www.mirabooks.com

MGG832

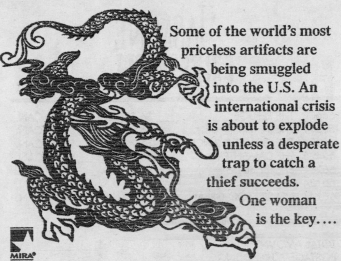

JASMINE CRESSWELL

66608	THE REFUGE	___ $6.50 U.S.	___ $7.99 CAN.
66511	THE INHERITANCE	___ $5.99 U.S.	___ $6.99 CAN.
66486	THE DISAPPEARANCE	___ $5.99 U.S.	___ $6.99 CAN.
66425	THE DAUGHTER	___ $5.99 U.S.	___ $6.99 CAN.
66261	SECRET SINS	___ $5.99 U.S.	___ $6.99 CAN.
66154	CHARADES	___ $5.50 U.S.	___ $6.50 CAN.
66147	NO SIN TOO GREAT	___ $5.99 U.S.	___ $6.99 CAN.

(limited quantities available)

TOTAL AMOUNT	$_____
POSTAGE & HANDLING	$_____
($1.00 for one book; 50¢ for each additional)	
APPLICABLE TAXES*	$_____
<u>TOTAL PAYABLE</u>	$_____

(check or money order—please do not send cash)

To order, complete this form and send it, along with a check or money order for the total above, payable to MIRA Books®, to: **In the U.S.:** 3010 Walden Avenue, P.O. Box 9077, Buffalo, NY 14269-9077; **In Canada:** P.O. Box 636, Fort Erie, Ontario, L2A 5X3.

Name:_____

Address:_____ City:_____

State/Prov.:_____ Zip/Postal Code:_____

Account Number (if applicable):_____

075 CSAS

*New York residents remit applicable sales taxes.
 Canadian residents remit applicable GST and provincial taxes.

MIRA®

Visit us at www.mirabooks.com

MJC0901BL